This book is written in British English.

Copyright © 2021 by Jan Foster

Published by So Simple Published Media
First edition April 2021

Cover Design
© J. L. Wilson Designs | https://jlwilsondesigns.com

Paperback ISBN-13: 978-1-9163408-5-5
E-Book ISBN-13: 978-1-9163408-4-8

www.escapeintoatale.com

THE NATURAE SERIES
DISRUPTING DESTINY

By Jan Foster

THE NATURAE SERIES

1427AD – SOUTH WEST ENGLAND

The growing pains were excruciating. Tearing his skin, continually stretching as new cells formed, split and formed again. In his conscious moments his body railed against the constraints of the cocoon, ripples of agony searing through his gangly limbs, straining for release yet finding none. He had no concept of how long he had endured the pain, only that it was ever present, peaking until he could bear it no more.

Gradually, he became more lucid as the pain diminished. In those brief moments, he was aware of light filtering through the thin membrane, and a shadow hovering over it. This time, consciousness arrived and with it, a realisation that the agony had gone. His nails unclenched from his palms, leaving bloody half-moons. Working his hands up past his naked chest to his face, his fingers sought instinctively to remove the source of the suffocation. The shadow darkened, and he heard it say a muffled, "My love..."

The yearning to join the voice, to be free, drove his panic. A guttural sound came from his throat as he clawed frantically at the suffocating veil. With a squelch, his nails snagged a hole and he pulled, straining with his entire being to enlarge it. Taking a huge gasp of breath, he realised that tender hands were smoothing limp membrane away from his face.

"Open your eyes," she said, that gentle yet somehow familiar voice again, as her touch wiped mucus from his nostrils. The panic subsided in him and, for a moment, he was aware only of his heart thumping uncomfortably in his chest, beginning to slow as the breaths came easier. He forced open his eyelids, turning his head in her direction. Focus blurred before clearing, then began to blink from the light streaming through the window behind the shape.

Part of him expected the pain to return when he moved his limbs, yet instead the joints felt lubricated, smooth. Stretching out, he became aware again of the cool, wet membrane, now slipping from his naked body. Feeling it with his toes and hands, it suddenly revolted him. He instinctively jerked away from it, falling towards her.

His knee hit the earthen floor hard as he fell, and the jolt sent a quick wave of pain through his leg. To his surprise, it wasn't the same kind of agony as he had so recently endured - quite dull by comparison. A pale hand clasped his arm, supporting him as he straightened to look up at her properly.

"My love..." she repeated, and his eyes finally came into focus on her mouth. Small white teeth peeked through smiling red lips, framed by long silver-blonde hair. He knew her... he knew that voice and he recognised her smell. Lavender, witch-hazel and fir - all mingled to provide a scent that was uniquely hers. His arm reached up to touch her face, still not daring to speak, and in one smooth movement, he stood to his full height, instinctively yearning to be nearer. As he breathed in, her arms joined his and they clasped each other. Their eyes locked together, searching for confirmation that their very souls were still intact.

From the edge of his vision, he glimpsed iridescent wings unfurling from behind her. He was mesmerised by the light from the window aperture which shone through them like the finest of stained glass, illuminating and shimmering. He felt his shoulder blades quiver and, turning his head, saw his own newly formed appendages rise up, silvery translucent grey yet with the radiance of hers catching the sunshine. In wonder, she reached out and stroked the edges of his wings; it tickled as rain falling on cold skin.

His senses exploded at her touch and the immediate surroundings rushed at him, overwhelming him. Almost involuntarily, his toes scrunched away from the vibrations of the worms wriggling through the earth beneath his bare feet. The distant call of a lone seagull circling high above briefly deafened, piercing his ears to the point of painful before fading as it glided away. His heart pounded as the volume of the next noise washed over him. As his gaze darted to the window, he frowned, before his drowsy mind identified the ominous rustling sounds - fir trees creaking in the breeze accompanied by the crackle of pine cones flexing to share their seed.

He turned back to her, wide-eyed and seeking reassurance. His newly sharp focus met a gentle, knowing smile and his grip tightened. Opening his mouth to try to speak, all he could taste was the burnt ashes emitting the last of their woody tang, chalky and spent as they lay in the hearth. Instead, he gulped sour air with a tinge of iron lingering on its edges. He swallowed to clear the mustiness from his throat, hoping the other smells and sounds would stop their assault as well.

Drawing in a deep breath, feeling his chest expand without the anticipated stab of pain, he recalled - he'd needed something, anything, to take away the pain from the injury.

The blood. Running his tongue around his mouth with the lingering iron taste, he remembered the blood. But not just his own. Mingling, warm and salty, rich, red. He had absorbed the long history of her Lifeforce, and she his - a much shorter, human life. He jerked away from her gaze; something akin to shame caused him to study the ground beneath him as he searched his foggy mind for clarification.

Her blood held the only promise she could make him at the time, and neither of them had understood the consequences. But, he would have done whatever it took to stay with her.

Then, the change had begun. Numbing his senses as she had bundled him tightly, suffocatingly. Somehow, she must have known he needed to be wrapped - she hadn't mentioned in their frantic discussion before they shared blood, he was sure. He looked up at her in horror, reeling from the invasion of the memory. Stepping back, his face formed the question before he could speak it.

"I didn't know..." she tailed off, her hand clasping his arm with a wobble in her voice. "I... I'm sorry. I'm sorry for the pain. I've never done this before," she said. "The wings are... unexpected. I thought it would be as it is for animals, you'd just heal. But you were in so much distress, I felt I needed to cocoon you, like a pupae. When I saw the lumps form, I hoped the wrapping would make it easier."

She blinked, but her eyes still pleaded for understanding. Forgiveness even.

Drawing a ragged breath, he took a moment to reply. Should he tell her that it had been unbearable? That he had changed his mind? Was that the truth, or just a remnant of the hurt talking? A childish plea to return to his former self?

He contemplated how best to respond to her unspoken request, searching the depths of her pale eyes as he tried to calm his breathing. The familiarity of her shapes, her colours and scent reassured him. And with that comfort, he remembered he had been enthralled by her. That, from the minute he had unclothed her and revealed the truth of her, there had been no other thought in his mind but to join her. The knot in his ribcage eased as clarity returned. How could he ever have thought to pull away from her when all he wanted to do was be with her? And, if possible, be more like her? Love itself had infused their ribbons of blood, binding their destiny together, for what would now be an eternal lifetime.

He felt a waft of cooler air soothe his neck, rhythmical as a heartbeat. His lips lifted and he felt a rush of unexpected giddiness as he acknowledged her unintended gift. His own wings, beating without effort, as if they had always been there.

He had chosen this. Chosen of his own human free will. He knew what had been done could never be undone.

"No longer Tarl, the smithy's son," he whispered as he stroked her pale face. "Change is upon me." He pulled her closer and searched her luminous blue eyes in wonder and forgiveness.

She knew then that she had truly changed her own destiny; the only future she now had was with him by her side. "And I, I relinquish Aioffe... She was alone, and now is not," she said, with conviction and hope in her voice.

He could never know what it had cost to change her intended fate, for him and for herself. She had no intention of telling anyone that 'duty and obedience' were no longer a part of her destiny. Those chains of responsibility fell silently from her shoulders as she took his hand, whispering, "Together, we can be truly free." She tilted her head to one side, eyes flaring as she absorbed the noises outside. "But, we need to go now - before we are discovered!"

CHAPTER 1 - SEPTEMBER 1534

Tendrils of smoke filled the young man's sensitive nostrils with the lingering scent of waxy paper, apples, sea salt and lichen-covered bark, evoking happier memories of the last five years. Tasting the essence of their temporary home as if that would commit it to the past only, he had to subdue the cough tightening his throat. No matter how many times they ran, the thought of starting over again sat on his heart, heavy and full of dread and sorrow. He swallowed down the bitterness, resolving to look to the future. He tried looking up at the clear skies, but the canopy of stars through the array of amber leaves blurred as his eyes welled. Shaking his long blond fringe away, he jabbed at the embers. Bright sparks gracefully leapt into the air and twinkled before vanishing with a quiet pop.

The snap of a branch behind him made him spin around, but his face quickly lifted into a smile as he saw her. Pale in the moonlight, her skin always glowed clearest at night, lighting the shadows with its luminescent tone. She smiled gently at him and held out a slim hand. "Ready?" She said softly.

"Soon," he answered, taking her chilled fingers in his and leading her to the warm log at the fires' edge. In the still, dark forest where they were most comfortable, they sat companionably, slowly pushing in their paper identities nearer the glowing core. The moment of sadness he felt earlier lifted in her company; she was, and always would be, his partner in their long journey to survive. Together they would carve out another future, in another town. It never got any easier, no matter how many times they resettled.

He replayed memories through his minds' eye - the lowered gazes from the once welcoming shop-keepers, a lull in conversation amongst the previously courteous ladies after church when they approached. Then, inevitably, the anger. Always under a veil of suspicion, the striking young couple were ultimately people with no verifiable roots who never truly fitted in.

Often, it started innocently enough with the women noticing a peculiarity about the newcomers - even after years of living in the community. Talking, gossiping about why they weren't quite 'right'. Then the menfolk joined their wives, voicing their anger, their sense of injustice. Before long, something would happen which wasn't 'usual', and, having nothing more than guesswork and gossip to interpret, sometimes the mob mentality would begin. Despite their efforts to lie low, the couple would find themselves hounded out of town, if they missed the warning signs and delayed.

Here, the apples had tasted so juicy, the surroundings so beautiful, they had almost left it too late to move away. Life here had been unexpectedly rich and varied, with its frequent visits from travelling performers and community rituals celebrated with gusto and wine. A temperate southern climate made it harder to resist the temptation to feed from them, especially her - she was trickier to keep sated. The people in this seaside township were generally so happy and full of Lifeforce, it was hard to leave. Some he had counted as friends. Stranger still to have no time to say goodbye or make their excuses for leaving.

The sunlight was just starting to pick through the forests when he heard the voices, faintly at first, then

12

growing closer. Then, the crash of dogs bounding through the drying undergrowth. Picking their way nearer to their hideout, he knew they would have discovered their empty rented house by now and come looking for them in the nearby copse. Maybe even the bodies of the animals they feasted on, desiccated and hastily buried in the dead of night, had been found.

He rubbed her shoulders in his lap, gently whispering, "It's time, my love, we need to go. They are close." She opened her eyes and sat up quickly, blinking in the pinkish light of dawn, her ears suddenly picking up on the sounds as they got closer. The dying embers of the fire would give their location away, and she hurried to pick up the heavy leather sacks she had brought with her earlier.

Without warning, a large, shaggy-looking dog bounded into the clearing. Pulling up and planting its feet wide, it paused to glare at them, judging as it sniffed. Then, it lifted its head and started barking loudly. The clipped yaps ensured that other canines arrived, circling them and noisily declaring their hunting success. Salivating jaws anticipated the reward awaiting them from the men not far behind.

The hounds didn't advance on them, instinct warning them they were not top of the food chain in this instance. But they wouldn't betray their masters and back away. Dark pairs of eyes fixed on the couple, unblinking. Hunter versus hunter. Beast versus beast.

The fae were trapped. He stepped towards one, making to shoo it away, but the dog growled, digging in with its haunches and baring yellowed teeth in a snarl. Fetid breath puffed in the crisp dawn light, surrounding them with a foul-stenched net.

"We will be seen if we leave from here," she

murmured, barely audible to most ears over the noise of the barks and snarls. She hurriedly fixed straps behind her, the bag altering her slim silhouette, making her look strangely unbalanced with a protruding pot-belly where it hung.

"Probably, but it's a risk I think we need to take," he said. "I'm willing if you are?" Despite his long cloak, now draped over his chest, he also appeared cumbersome with his front-strapped sack on.

"Over 'ere!" Shouts, sounding close, followed by dull snapping branches as boots crashed their path through the undergrowth.

She nodded and pulled the bonnet from her head to free her hair. Shimmering wings unfurled, the morning light bouncing off them as it streamed through the tree leaves. "Straight up!" he said as he bent his knees to lift off, his darker wings already freed and waving slowly.

They shot up through the canopy and into the bright sunlight. Shrinking below, the fields were dotted with sheep and horses, mottled green and brown hedgerows marking their boundaries. Small thatched dwellings laid low to the ground, their stone chimneys spouting thin wisps of smoke as early morning fires were stoked. Higher they flew, out of the range of the voices shouting, cussing as the enraged and frightened humans found the still-warm ashes of the fire. Higher, to where the birds circled, swirling in formation around them.

Looking up through the trees, one of the men saw their odd-shaped silhouettes, out of reach of arrows, disappearing into the clouds. Shaking his head, the notion that he had witnessed something not of his world was forced from his mind. It did no good to stir up further talk of the devil amongst them. A man would only have to spend yet more time in the confessional and at prayer if he had seen anything sinister, after all. Best not to mention it.

*****

"Who shall you be today, my love?" she called over the clouds. "I like the name Joshua!" He smiled and shook his head, grinning at her. "You like Joshua because you liked the boy, not because you like the name, I think."

"He had the sweetest tasting Lifeforce I have had in a long time," she said, remembering, "but I nearly got carried away. I caused this relocation, and for that, I'm sorry."

"You are insatiable, in more ways than one," he called back, moving closer to grasp her hand mid-air. They slowed, joined hands, then fluttered to face each other. In the brilliant sunlight, they gazed at each other, searching, studying and reconnecting. Together they hovered, hands clasped around the bulky sacks filled with their only belongings, two halves of a lumpy, bejewelled butterfly. In the unfiltered light, high above the clouds, their love glowed through in its intensity. It would be absurd to think that they had ever blended in - no human would have mistaken them for mortals were they to glimpse them now. Fair skin, ash-white hair almost translucent as the sunshine poured through it, and wings rippled with rainbow tones, fluttering as they lingered in the moment.

"I can't promise more boys like him," he said, looking at her lips as he leaned in for a kiss. "And we must try to blend in more next town, and not risk losing control with a human, however much we become lost in their energy. We can survive without them, you know!" He reproached, but still with love in his tone. "We could have stayed longer if only we had been more careful. I think the lad will recover with some rest. The young usually do, then attribute their lack of get up and go to overdoing it, or some sort of malady."

She smiled and nodded, but nevertheless felt remorseful. Her need for sustenance from the unseen joy humans emitted was compulsive, necessary even. The Lifeforce fae-kind gained from its root source in blood was enough for him, but satisfying her needs was more dangerous and required crowds of people. Keeping control of herself during these times was always a challenge. A moment or two longer in her thrall, and it would have been too late for that poor boy. She sometimes forgot herself in those heady inhalations, but had so far never broken her own rule of not killing a child in the heat of the inhale. But youth, they were so free, so deliciously innocent. Their Lifeforce had no filter and its purity was sublime.

"I just want to build a home with you, where we can live in peace. I don't think that's too much to ask?" Joshua's begging broke through her guilt-laden reminiscing.

She pulled back from the embrace and stroked his face, feeling the boyish stubble along his jawline. "I know, I wish for that also," she said wistfully. "Maybe this next time..."

"You always say that..."

"I know."

"Never satisfied," he teased.

He flapped his dark wings and spun her around and around. She leaned her head back and relaxed, allowing him to take the lead in a dizzying spin. They both laughed at the release of the exhilarating action. As he slowed, he lowered his face to embrace her again.

"My head!" she said, breaking off the kiss. "It's still spinny... if this is what death feels like, I could die right now, happy. It's like a little death."

"Believe me, this is not what dying feels like," he said, nuzzling her ear. "I could remind you what a 'little death' feels like if you want though?"

Her grin broadened, "You'll have to catch me first!" She darted upwards, playing. Like dancing dragonflies, they dashed around the skies, giggling and whirling.

"I won't lose you again, minx!" He caught her slender ankle, "I will follow you, find you, hound you down like we are hunted now, even if there were an arrow still jutting from my side!" He paused, hovering up to look her fully in the face earnestly.

Stroking away loose strands of hair from his cheeks, she whispered, "Never, I'll never truly run from you. Nothing will ever part us." They embraced again, and he gave her bottom a squeeze through her skirts. Squealing in mock outrage, she pushed away from him and dashed off. He followed, of course, and they continued their journey north together.

*****

They slowed after a few hours and dipped down through the cloud blanket, to where it was raining and grey. Flying lower, yet still out of sight, they scanned the ground with hawk-like eyesight for a group of houses - a town, not just a village. The occasional straight Roman road cut gash-like through the landscape. He pointed northeast, and together they gracefully swung around and headed for a small wooded area they noticed, close to a sizable cluster of dwellings. Rough tracks weaving their brown trails around the countryside meandered through fields less enclosed by hedges than they had been in the south. Through the drizzle, the patchwork of leaves turning golden amber enticed them for the cover it could afford.

They landed by the side of the woods and pushed aside undergrowth to enter the forest. Hidden by branches, the couple dropped their packs and loosened their garments, secreting their wings close to skin. Helping each other, they straightened their attire, pushed hair back into caps and tucked smock edges neatly into jerkin and kirtle. A last check before hoisting their belongings onto their backs, a brief kiss for luck, and their windy and unusual travel method was obscured.

Returning to the muddy track, they picked their way through the puddles left by carts and carriages, and headed towards a cluster of buildings ahead.

"How about Annabella? For me. Mistress Annabella Meadows," she said, as they approached an inn nestled on the crossroads of the road into town.

"I'm flattered you remember my little treats," he said, glancing down and smiling at her. "And a fitting way to honour her charms. I plan to demonstrate how stimulating I found her Lifeforce, just as soon as we find our next abode." Giggling, they pushed open the faded oak door and entered, hoping to buy a room for the night where they could rest. It was getting dark, and experience had taught them it was best to view a new possible home in daylight. The smell of damp leather and stale ale assaulted their noses as they crossed the threshold, but there was comfort in the humanity within and a warm hearth.

CHAPTER 2 - A FRESH START

A sunnier day dawned, and a steady stream of carts, horses and other folk heading to market trundled down the track to town. A few traders staying at the inn the night before had already set off at first light to set out their stalls, woken by the inn's cockerel. Not needing breakfast, Joshua and Annabella had snuggled back down in their straw bed and enjoyed each other before packing their bags once more.

Vacating their temporary lodgings, the young couple walked at a steady pace the few miles towards the town. Although they pasted smiles on their faces to all who passed them, anxiety was buried under their woollen capes and only acknowledged by the firm grasp of each other's hands.

The initial hurdle they faced was that it was unusual for people to uproot and arrive to live somewhere else, unknown by anyone. Communities, especially in rural areas, were small and close-knit, built upon a shared history and a long set understanding of where they sat in the economic and social scale of things. It was an unexpected - and welcome - happenstance to discover they had arrived in time for market day. The crowds ensured their presence in a new town would be less noticeable amongst all the other visiting traders. Joshua and Annabella were all too aware of their luck as they circumvented puddles and jumped over to the side ditches to allow carts to pass.

However, even their fortunate timing couldn't dispel

their nerves entirely. Each time they resettled, there followed a period of adjustment, a careful note taken of reactions to their arrival and continuous assessment made about their reception by the community. More than once, they had encountered hostility and suspicion from the very start and had swiftly fled overnight to find somewhere more suited to their needs.

It boded well that they had just spent a surprisingly relaxed evening in the company of travelling merchants and a few locals in the inn last night. Although the bawdy shanties sung as the night wore on were unknown to them, the tone and tales contained within were comfortingly familiar. They had both participated energetically in the applause, and the crowd noisily appreciated their contribution. Constantly the couple remained alert, at pains to not proffer any opinions in the heated discussions which followed as the ale flowed.

As it had been in their last town, undercurrents of religious tensions were running high in the area surrounding Beesworth. The growing reform movement was on the verge of becoming dominant, with King Henry only recently imposing himself as the Head of the Church of England. Newly emboldened Protestants passionately advocated their simpler faith as being the truest path to spiritual enlightenment, after so many years skulking in the shadows. Yet most people still clung to their centuries-old Catholic religion, distressed at the fabric of their beliefs and rituals being torn away by royal decree. The impact of Henry's proclamation was the source of much consternation, with blame firmly placed on his new companion, Anne Boleyn.

Rather than become lured into the debate, Joshua and Annabella had retired to their room at the back of the inn.

They had long ago learned that to get involved invited elaboration about their own beliefs. They followed the rules decreed at the time, and would attend the local church as required. To do otherwise would attract suspicion, even if the strands of religion were currently evolving. For many decades, conversations about theology with each other had decades been avoided. It was the one aspect of their union where each held very different viewpoints.

The muddy track widened as Joshua and Annabella approached the township, giving way to a hodgepodge of buildings. On the outskirts, the houses were traditionally constructed with cruck frame timbers in their distinctive V shape lined the road. Where space permitted, or to replace ruins, recently built dwellings with a striking black and white half-timbered design began to appear.

As they walked deeper into the township, where side roads started to peel away, two or even three-storey buildings came into view. Occasionally, fully stone-built houses broke up the monochrome, and the rooflines varied wildly in height. The road grew firmer underfoot as they reached flagstones and cobbles of the main thoroughfares. Strips of common land interrupted the clusters of buildings; muck and mud pervading into the township as livestock rotated around fields.

Joshua relaxed his grip a little on Annabella's hand as they joined the throngs of people heading towards the centre of town, or waddling home with baskets and bundles. Despite Beesworth being further north than they had visited in the last century, it was similar to many other towns they had lived in. In the morning sunlight, the stark stripes of black and white walls brightened the narrow streets, even those with jetties overhanging perilously above.

They rounded the corner of a single storey parish church, and faced the large market square before them. Shops and craftsmen seemed to go out of their way to raise the volume of noise with their sales calls and crafting demonstrations, adding energy to the general hubbub of the market. Business was brisk, but the town would likely be quieter and more sedate in following days.

"Looks promising?" Joshua said to Annabella as they picked their course through stalls and small herds of sheep. "It looked about the right size from above," she replied, her eyes keenly taking in the surroundings and the crowds as they thronged about the green. "And it seems busy enough today..." She tailed off, pausing to look at some delicately woven 'madder red' cloth at a stall. The woollen fabric was smooth to touch and had barely any of the bobbles of imperfectly spun threads so often found in local markets.

"Tis a pretty piece," the stallholder offered. "Would make some lovely sleeves for Christmas! From Norwich, this 'ere is. They do make a good red." Her smile revealed browned teeth, like a dark scar sitting in her fat, ruddy face, with wisps of greying hair poking out from her small frilly cap fashioned from a bright green cloth. The overall effect of hat and rounded face on top of a rotund figure reminded Annabella of a fading strawberry. Inwardly she felt a pang of relief - the unfortunate effects of aging would not show for many centuries, especially not her bloodline.

"Perhaps later," Annabella said, her fingers feeling the texture once more before moving on. She would be in need of supplies soon so didn't want to appear unfriendly, but the other cheaper fabrics the merchant was offering were slightly grubby and smelt of damp from their journey. A seamstress by trade, Annabella usually preferred to buy from shops which took better care of their stock. There was a lot to be said for the new fashions in fabric which travelling merchants offered, if clients were conscious of keeping up with the trend-setting classes.

Walking away from the market, Joshua and Annabella wandered down the widest street leading from the common land at the centre of the townstead. Delicious smells of fresh-baked bread and pies wafted out, countering the more unpleasant scent of excrement in the drains down the sides of the cobbled road. The shops they passed had open windows to attract custom as well as to air the spaces after the wet weather. Many had no glass in the aperture at all, only greased blinds which were drawn up to let in the light or dropped to offer scant protection from the elements.

Joshua and Annabella drank in the more pleasant smells the streets offered, and smiled at each other, optimistic for the next well-practised step in creating a new life. So far, the townsfolk had appeared friendly and polite, even if it was purely a sales gambit for the benefit of strangers.

It didn't take long to find the Guildhall, proudly boasting its large overhang into the street with ornately carved and painted heraldry symbols running the length of the eaves. Inside, Joshua made enquiries to an ageing clerk at the main table in the Grand Hall vestibule about any glazed, vacant shops with lodgings above or behind. As a silversmith, security was essential to Joshua, and window panes also suggested both affluence and respectability.

Shuffling rolls of paper, the grey-haired officer sized the couple up before disappearing into a side room. He emerged with a faded scroll detailing the town map. Using a candle for extra light, he then proceeded to study it, muttering to himself as his gnarled fingers ran along the street lines, as if mentally ticking through a list of the town's inhabitants.

Finally, he looked up and pointed to the options. Offered the choice of two which were immediately available, they chose the one which had been vacant slightly longer and was less central. The map detailed the landlord to whom their rent would have to be paid with clear boundary lines. The clerk shuffled amongst some papers before confirming that the shop they selected was within their budget and the glazing was reported to be in good order.

Joshua took out his leather purse and made sure to create a satisfying clink as he rummaged. The clerk's eyes began to glint at the prospect. Pretending to consult with Annabella about the rent, which was not the most extortionate they had encountered, but still not the cheapest, a few coins then passed hands and the clerk agreed to a few days grace for their papers. Joshua could always forge more references once they had some privacy - many years of travelling had equipped them with sufficient resources to recall names of now-dead 'patrons' to authenticate their stories.

Desperate to settle as soon as possible, Joshua proffered a few extra shillings to the clerk to consider giving them a key today. They promised faithfully to sign the lease papers later that week when they had been formally drawn up. Annabella fluttered her eyelashes and pleaded extreme exhaustion, so the agent took pity on them.

The decision for the clerk was simple - they appeared

to have readily available coin, looked presentable and honest, and frankly, he wanted the long-vacant shop let so he could claim his kickback. It was a risk worth taking. Few people turned up at his desk this well presented, and he prided himself on his instincts. Christmas was coming soon, and he had mouths to feed. The clerk hastily drew up a receipt for a deposit which he felt would suffice, suitably absolving himself of the blame should their verbal agreement fall down. The couple were confident, having glanced at the general state of the dwellings they had passed, that the abode would be at least habitable. And so the deal was struck.

*****

Annabella and Joshua found their new home at the end of a side street, close to the Guildhall and just a little further away from the market square than most people would probably have wanted for passing trade. However, its location was ideal for them, affording easy access out of the town and into the countryside so they could come and go with minimal chance of being observed.

The shop itself was, as to be expected from a long-vacant building, dank and dark. The rushes on the floor dealt up clouds of foul, damp smelling fug as they pushed open the door. "No matter," Annabella said carefully, casting her eyes around the dim shop floor, also their front room.

"We've been in worse," Joshua muttered under his breath as he closed the door behind them.

Walking over to the counter, he swept aside the discarded papers strewn across the top and peered behind to assess what other detritus was left hidden there. A

25

skinny brown rat darted out, running along the edge of the darkened room, its eyes catching the little light from the dusty windows. Annabella quickly dipped down and grabbed its tail as it ran past her, then grasped it by the neck. "Snack?" She said to Joshua in a sing-song voice.

"Maybe later?" He smiled as he rose off the counter. She shrugged, wrinkling her nose as the ratty taste would do little more than quench her thirst. First she inhaled deeply, her mouth close to its pointy teeth, then delicately bit into its neck and sucked. Throwing the dried husk into the fireplace, she wiped a pale hand across her lips, her eyes sparkling once more.

The upstairs was in equal disarray, its previous tenants having vacated in haste, leaving dislodged dust balls, odd socks and bits of kitchenware clearly dropped or left out of hasty packing. In the oak-panelled main bedroom overlooking the street, a wooden sided bed filled with old and mouldy straw awaited them, along with a large battered chest in which they could keep their belongings and clothes. A smaller second room overlooking the south-facing garden was lighter, and could be used to house Annabella's sewing.

They began by lighting fires and flinging open the windows to air the dampness out from the shop floor, before unpacking their scant possessions. Later, they would lay fresh rushes on top of the old, musty ones - it was considered healthier not to disturb them and release goodness knows what into their accommodation.

Finally, having wrenched free the swollen-shut back door, they investigated their outside space. The yard was half the size of the house, smelt of rotting fallen leaves and was clearly neglected. In the far corner they found remnants of a kitchen herb garden, shaded too much by the ramshackle fence. Annabella leant over the desiccated stubs and breathed over them.

After a few seconds, the brown plants began to straighten, the stems turned green as new energy flushed through them and the dead leaves dropped to make way for fresh growth. Over surprisingly little time, Annabella would transform the tiny yard to a blooming, scented haven, from which they could readily supply their abode with fresh-smelling plants to help keep at bay the inevitable odours of human life and ward off unwanted humours.

Returning inside, the couple changed their clothes and stretched their wings briefly before opening the bedroom blind for airing. This was a well-practised routine which brought them pleasure. A fresh start, no suspicions around them yet, and the chance to breathe freely again, for a while at least.

It was late morning by the time Joshua and Annabella stepped out of their shop door, now wiped clean of dust and cobwebs. With new hairstyles mimicking those of their fellow townsfolk, they set out towards town on the muddy cobbles, looking every inch a happy young couple ready to make their way in the world.

Arriving at the marketplace, today less frantic with activity, they made their way around the shops in the square. Buying just a token item or two from each establishment afforded them not only the opportunity to introduce themselves politely but also to assess the competition and likely customers they could expect. Where possible, they requested the goods they purchased be delivered. They could then welcome, at the very least, the delivery boys, if not the actual tradespeople to their own premises, and make a good first impression.

Leaving Joshua discussing grades of silver ore with the blacksmith the next street over, Annabella returned home to begin preparations. She filled the bashed-up old kettle left behind by the previous tenants and placed it on the hearth to warm. She had brought flour and other dried goods back with her and set to baking small pastries to offer.

As she worked, she hummed a little Fae ditty to herself, taking a moment to reconnect with that part of her history which must always remain hidden. In her rare time alone, the tune reminded her of home, of Naturae. Somehow though, today, the song also prompted thoughts of her unwelcome duty, of ties that had been cut. She stopped singing, kneading the dough with renewed fervour. That world was estranged, so remote, so claustrophobic. Here, at least she was free to do what she liked, be who she wanted - within reason. She stretched out the dough, pulling at it with strong, slim hands, then smoothed away the bumps and shaped it once more to rise.

Annabella clapped, then rubbed off the excess flour - especially from the silver ring which Joshua had given her. Rinsing her hands, the circle returned to its polished state, and she smiled as she twisted it into place on her fingers. In this human realm, she wasn't alone. Looking at the sweet-smelling roses which Joshua had bought for her earlier reminded her that she would never again be lonely. One person had chosen to make her the centre of his life. On arriving in each location, a new bunch would adorn their house. They had a little game, she and he, of how long she could keep the blooms fresh. Over the past century, she had never yet picked up a petal.

She looked around at the smartened, clean room, with

the warm scent of baking and light streaming in through the windows. Her heart gladdened. Although generally happy wherever she was with her love, she sometimes wondered if she didn't also enjoy the challenge of a change as well. She tried so hard to be content in these human towns. To fit in and settle. But they both acknowledged that she liked to travel, to seek out all that the world had to offer. This particular house suited her well - in the distance she could see that the road outside led to an open landscape with many pockets of woodland. She could barely wait to explore the area and find out what secrets it held, but would have to rein in this urge until they were properly established in the town.

By the early afternoon, the couple had laid out the stock they had managed to bring with them - garments neatly pressed and displayed, and silver trinkets softly glinting on the shop counter by the flickering firelight. Candles placed on corner shelves, ready to brighten the room once darkness fell. It wasn't long before deliveries began arriving - handed over in person by nosey neighbours and fellow shop-keepers eager to assess the new arrivals. They warmly welcomed each with the offer of a drink and delicate savouries, to be nibbled whilst a not-so-subtle interrogation took place.

The patchwork of lies about who they were and where they came from had evolved over the decades, but remained in essence the same. Minor modifications or embellishments added according to the area and the ever changing times. It was a story designed to elicit both sympathy and admiration for their fortitude and luck. Both orphaned at a young age, no family to speak of but met each other through apprenticing in London. Following the sad demise of their aging masters, they married and decided to make their way into the wider world to trade and put down roots. On their travels, they had heard how lovely and welcoming this town was, and so had chosen to see if the rumours were true. And of course, they had excellent references from their sadly now deceased patrons.

Almost always, their story passed muster. Some people even claimed knowledge or kinship with the aforementioned but long, long dead patrons which the couple mentioned. It was always a source of amazement to Annabella that individuals would use any opportunity to claim the slightest social leverage with such distant relations, even those hundreds of miles away.

One of the most frequent questions related to London: why had they moved away from the bustling capital, where the King was rumoured to appear amongst his people? Joshua always gave the same reason for leaving - rents too high, cost of food too much, streets too dirty, and they longed for wider open spaces in which to walk and breathe cleaner air. Oh yes, a rural community was far more appealing to a young couple starting out in the world. And of the King - no, they had never seen him, he was cloistered away in his palaces hunting in his own grounds, or on a Progress around the country, and wasn't it sad he so rarely visited this corner of his realm?

Annabella usually held her tongue and left Joshua to talk during these introductions. This appeared as if she was a good, dutiful wife who let her husband lead, but in reality it was by prior agreement with Joshua. Her own views on royalty were too hard to swallow for most folk on a first meeting. Some might have said treasonous. She was a nervous liar as well, too prone to gabbling whereas Joshua had learned their fabrications like a travelling player would lines.

In most areas, their tale was enough to satisfy. It provoked a local pride in their community and played to underlying suspicions that the Monarch was aloof, uncaring about the common man. This seemed especially true in current times, as King Henry was moving towards enforcing a change in religion upon his subjects, which appeased only some elements of society. In the less populous, rural areas of the country, Protestantism was viewed as a dangerous threat to their familiar religious way of life.

Joshua and Annabella knew, having longer lifespans, that these civil disruptions would likely pass and change again. Whilst they lived alongside humans through the challenges which each transition of monarch heralded, the social and economic structure on a local level was largely the same as it had been for many centuries. They had learned that in order to stay hidden, it was easier to not express opinions yet live by the letter of the law and religious dictates. The irony was, not being mortal themselves, Joshua, and especially Annabella, were more widely versed in scripture than the majority of the clergy.

*****

Tired after a long day of charming people, Joshua sat down on the recently vacated stool by the hearth and picked at the buttery crumbs remaining on the attractive platter which they always managed to escape with. Annabella began to wash the cups and tidy away, moving swiftly around the room as if she had energy to burn. He ventured to break the silence. "I'd say the plate, not to mention its delicious contents, was as much of a success as usual."

The piece was unlike anything most folks had ever seen, often the subject of a passing compliment. It featured an eye-catching and intricately woven pattern of swirls, with holes in between the weaving and golden edging. Highly polished silver proclaimed its value, but it also held an otherworldly quality. Frequently, Joshua was asked if he was the maker of such artistry and he was forced to answer that no, it was his wife's family heirloom, no-one knew its provenance. "The ladies always covet it, and the gentlemen always weigh up its value," Annabella would say afterwards.

However, as a conversation starter, the plate enabled Joshua to subtly bring out his own showpieces. Delicate jewellery - embellished and engraved tankards and tiny keepsake boxes which were his speciality. He tried hard to keep up with the modern trends in design, feeling that influence grounded them in the present times more, layering their disguise and avoiding questions about their eternally youthful age. He was always conscious, perhaps more than Annabella, that they must be at pains to blend in smoothly and quickly to a new town. He sometimes felt that she was a little too risky in trying to set themselves apart, above the crowds, with their work in order to be a success. Whilst beautiful, her clothing designs leaned towards eye-catching flamboyancy. Only occasionally had they found a local who wanted to purchase 'court fashion' finery in the less extravagant towns they settled in.

Annabella poured them both a too-stewed cup of the honeyed drink she had prepared and sank down beside him. "I feel as if we are making a good start," she carried on, relaxing at last, "and they seem welcoming enough to newcomers at least."

"Aye," he nodded, "although, their accent is hard to follow sometimes."

"We will adapt," she said. It had taken decades of living in the south of England for his original Gaelic twang to fade, whilst she almost intuitively could understand and fall into the regional dialects. "'Tis further north than we have been for a long while, and will come back to us in time no doubt."

"I heard nought to cause concern so far," she remarked, in case he had overheard anything to alarm them which she had missed whilst engaged in other conversations.

"Yet." Joshua remained cautious. "No-one sounded too sorry to see the back of the Thomas's here before us. A rough sort, apparently, gone back to York for family reasons. We should take care to distance ourselves from any knowledge of them."

Annabella rolled her eyes. He was always more on edge in the first few weeks. The more sociable of the pair, he maintained it was more to do with making sure they would be a welcome addition to a community. It would take him building a rapport with local tradespeople over a few drinks in the inns of the town before he would relax into his surroundings. For herself, she was quite content to remain at a distance from the locals, whilst maintaining a facade of openness. She was the cool assessor of the pair, able to read peoples' true intentions before he could.

"The blacksmith and his wife, the Tunns, seemed very welcoming. Although goodness knows with four children and another on the way, it must be hard for them to make a living from just his forge," Annabella said.

"Aye, especially with the coinage due to change yet again, probably worth even less soon."

"These are indeed troublesome times," Annabella replied sagely. "But they will come around again, they always do."

"I think she had some money come to her from family," Joshua said. "Although why would she have settled for a 'smith if she could have had more? It's a tough existence, no doubt."

"Maybe she didn't have a choice - perhaps there was a child on the way? Or maybe she loved him."

"I'd like to think it was the last one." He sighed, reaching to stroke her arm. "But I suspect you are right with the first two guesses. Anyway, they seem pleasant people. We should try to make friends of them, given I will need to work closely with William if I'm to earn a living here."

"Margaret did look to be interested in the clothing here, although I think it out of her price range." Annabella was always torn when selling to common folk; frequently they simply couldn't afford entire new outfits which she loved to create. Often she ended up battling her conscience and discounting so heavily it barely covered the cost of the fabric - just because she longed to see people feeling better about themselves. Joshua was far more profitable in his endeavours and a harder haggler.

"I need to feed," Joshua said, rising from his chair.

"Shall we take a dusk-time walk then?"

"I think we should. I heard a little from Mistress Hooper, was it? Waxing about the mansion on the mound deep in the woodland. It sounds promising to have gentry almost on the doorstep. Maybe we should have sight of it before we go a-bed?"

Annabella smiled, "I'll fetch the cloaks."

They loosened their wings from beneath their clothing

and fastened long woollen capes around their necks, draping the cloth so it entirely hid what was underneath. Holding hands again, they wandered down the muddy track away from the town towards freedom.

*****

Each time they entered woodland, it seemed to Joshua and Annabella like a homecoming, to long-lost family. Long tree shadows guarded the road which skirted the copse, but they were welcomed inside by giants, whispering and rustling in a light breeze. The discovery of a new forest, crisp at this season with fallen leaves in the fading sunlight, was a joy. Clacking, squawking noises of pheasants, woodcocks and the many other birds who called the trees home as they began their evening calls comforted the couple. The chatter swelled in volume as Joshua and Annabella turned off the main track and picked their way through the undergrowth.

They were hoping to find a natural clearing, in which to drop the veil of their cloaks and their identities and be free amongst the wildlife. Already, just breathing in the life surrounding them had energised both. They also needed the heady rush of a direct infusion of Lifeforce. Always quicker to spot movement, Annabella suddenly flew up through the trees and, with a rustle of her skirts, returned with a squirrel in her slim hands. Joshua smiled lovingly at her as she offered it to him first, and he supped delicately before passing it back to her to finish. They carried on through the woodland, using the dying sun as a guide. Eventually they stumbled across another track, rising gently up an incline.

"It may lead to the mound we want," Joshua said,

dropping the rabbit he had been finishing next to a large fallen tree, before climbing up it in one long stretch. He reached out a hand to assist Annabella up and over the log, causing her to smile. He was ever the gentleman, even though he knew she was perfectly capable of just fluttering over such obstacles. On the ground walking however, she admitted she was more prone than most to tripping. She reasoned that it was probably no bad thing he should constantly remind her to behave like a human by treating her as a lady. Whenever she fell, he was around to help pull her back up to her feet, pausing to smooth her hair from her face, plopping a kiss on her nose and telling her to take it one step at a time. It was never a chastisement, always a suggestion that implied she ought to slow down and think her actions through, both in walking and in life it seemed.

They came to the edge of the wooded track and looked up towards the summit of the mound. Bathed in the last rays of the sunlight, a mansion dominated the skyline. The hillside surrounding it had been cleared of all shrubbery and trees, leaving it boldly visible from all sides, like a bailey, only newer in construction. The rendering between the dark brown beams had faded to a greyish cream colour, lending the building a somewhat tired cast. The size of the long three-storey dwelling was perhaps what impressed Joshua the most, filling the space on top of the steeply rising hillock like the head of a pimple bursting up through swollen landscape.

The track continued to the base of the rise and they found themselves in a smaller cleared patch. A few posts for tying horses had been placed at the edge of a wider turning circle for carriages. Leading off from the clearing was a narrower, slightly overgrown footpath circling around to the other side of the hillock, for foot access to the house. They had approached the back of the residence, Joshua surmised. In the rapidly closing darkness, they would likely not be noticed, but should they be confronted, the pair lacked a reasonable explanation for their presence in such a remote spot, other than sheer nosiness.

Annabella glanced at the darkening sky and said with an air of defeat about her, "I suppose we shall have to wait until we are called upon to see the front of it."

"It's best we head home, yes," replied Joshua, "Soon be full dark my love, and whilst that isn't so much of an issue for us, we should not be spotted entering the town without some more obvious means to light our way. There would be questions."

They turned and began back down the track, taking the straighter route homeward. From a distance, they heard dogs barking a warning. Their presence hadn't gone unnoticed. Joshua tilted his head to look at the looming house and saw the tell-tale glow of a candle held close to a draped window. Walking was slower despite their quick pace, but flying was not an option.

CHAPTER 3 - THE FORGE

The autumn weeks slipped past them, and trade started to trickle in. Annabella was fast making a name for herself - her quick stitching and invisible seams won her much praise amongst the townsfolk. Joshua had been even luckier and was in receipt of a large commission for a dining set from a local landowner, who had heard tell of the biscuit plate. Not believing the heirloom tale, he was convinced that Joshua might actually be the craftsman, and ordered an anniversary themed collection of serving plates for his latest wife, the third Mistress Caldwell. The designs Joshua had drawn up overnight incorporated what he suspected the Master really wanted - bold gold-leaf edging embossed with a subtle pattern on lightweight, but functional platters.

The commission had arrived at the right time for Joshua; there was little he loved more than working alongside other tradesmen to get the perfect shape of silver, which he could then delicately embellish. This meant he could ingratiate himself with the local traders and craftsmen, which would build his reputation within the town. As he worked on the finishing touches back at their shop, polishing the silver and gold at the bench before decorating the tableware with his engraving burins, he chatted companionably with Annabella, catching each other up on the gossip.

The shop door opened with a whoosh of cold damp air, interrupting their cosy morning. William Tunn, the blacksmith, strode in dripping from the rain and deposited a sack of metal ore on the bench next to Joshua, grinning broadly at him.

"You won't find finer gold than in these rocks, boy!" William declared. "Come all the way from Wales. Comes out all rosy when yer polish it, they say."

Joshua opened the bag and picked out the pieces, holding them to the firelight to examine the seams running through. "These are worth a pretty penny, I'd say. How much did you get fleeced for this time?" He added wryly.

"Oh, never you mind that. Are you interested in the final product is what I want to know?"

"It depends how much you can get out of them," Joshua answered cagily. Negotiating on the basis of an unknown quantity of metal from a far flung supplier was always tricky.

"Share a meal with us tonight and we can discuss it?" William gestured towards Annabella, "I'm sure the wife would like to better know your Mistress here, and the brood always want to chatter away to new faces!"

"We'd be delighted to," Annabella said. She had warmed to Margaret the few times they had spoken and welcomed the opportunity for some time with a well placed gossip. Most especially, she wanted to know who was financially thriving, and might therefore need some clothing to showcase their success.

As it grew dark, Joshua and Annabella made their way carefully down the street, slippery underfoot after yet more rains. They turned past the forge which faced the road to the single-story stone dwelling behind. Annabella noticed just outside the doorway, miniature carved goblets and plates placed neatly on a low box. She smiled at the well-loved toys left out in the rain, picking up a cup to take in with her. Joshua leant across her, his lips tugged up at one side, and raised the ornate door knocker. The heavy blackened metal had likely been fashioned by William as it interwove the initials W and M. He paused though, rather than letting it fall, hearing raised voices through the thick planks.

"It's not just your soul in question here!" Margaret's voice carried the strain of her passionate beliefs.

"Tis the right thing, Marge, even now the King decrees it so..." William's deep voice countered, and they heard the loud thump of a fist slamming onto the table. The door was not so thick as to hide a gasp from Margaret.

"It isn't what the King wants. You know this William! It's all because of that goggle-eyed whore, Boleyn, and her foreign ways. Who is she to decree what we should do with our faith?"

"It isn't just her! Wife, you surely must see now that this false worship serves no-one. This kind of faith is not what the Good Lord wanted, and it's not what is said in the true Bible!"

"How can he deny the power of the Saints, who have so often helped us, saved us from harm?" Margaret was getting desperate, the pleading in her voice breaking with emotion. "Who will watch over our children when we are gone?" She broke down, sobbing, "I can't bear it. We will live in eternal damnation. How can they deny the miracles?"

"You have to give up your papist ways, wife, and stop harping on about what isn't true and right according to His holy words. If you could only know what I have read, if you could only hear what lies you have been fed for all these years, you'd see. It's not my soul which is in jeopardy here, but yours!"

Annabella glanced at Joshua; this wasn't the first time

they had heard such arguments between couples. Joshua, still holding the knocker aloft, looked down at the muddy rushes at the doorway. She frowned, why had she seen a flash of guilt in his eyes?

He sighed, wishing again that she would understand. Despite their not discussing it recently, he still struggled with his faith. Hearing others arguing about it made them both uncomfortable. After a century of living as a kind of creature not mentioned in the Bible, the question of his soul was something he desperately wanted to stop asking himself about, so confused was he. The shifting belief systems they were currently living through brought these thoughts to his mind frequently now, more than Annabella realised.

"It's not about what you can read, William Tunn! For even if I could, I know in my heart what is right. How can you deny the blessing that is the miracle of Eucharist, eh? You tell me how!" Margaret pleaded.

"It is but falseness, Margaret. Why can't you see? They led us all up a merry pathway for centuries! Oh, I long for the day when Tyndale's Bible will tell you the truth of it in our own language."

"You must not speak of that man! Promise me, husband, you must stay away from these traitors to the faith. I tell you, it will be the end of us if you keep pushing for change."

William roared back, "Wife! It will happen. It must! We must rid ourselves of these lies, for they damn us all! We must purge the church of all of its falsehoods. Why can you not see? To keep practising false idolatry is dangerous - you must stop it! To place your faith in some old bones that could be from anyone, and ignore the true pathway to Christ? I fear for you." There was real anger in

William's voice.

"Perhaps we should take a walk and arrive back in a while?" Joshua said under his breath.

"No," Annabella replied firmly. "They invited us. It is the time. We should interrupt before they fall out further."

Her hand covered his and with a gentle caress and an apologetic look, she pulled his hand off the knocker, letting it drop with a heavy thump. After a moment, the door swung open and Williams' enormous frame filled the low threshold, his face still cast with thunder. Annabella smiled gently up at him and proffered their neatly wrapped gift of home-distilled rose water. "Good evening, William," she chirped as if nothing was wrong. "I do hope we aren't too early?"

William's face relaxed, and he stood aside to let them in. Margaret hastily wiped her face with her sleeve and rose to welcome them inside the warm room. Annabella smiled a greeting and bobbed briefly. She then took one of Margaret's hands and squeezed it gently, before turning to the hearth at the far end of the room which backed onto the forge. In the corner, Annabella noticed the spinning wheel and carding brushes, and understood the piecemeal income this would provide for a growing family. Near the fireplace, the children rested on stools, their pale faces turned to look at the new people with interest. Their relief at the change of atmosphere was evident.

"Welcome! Have you met our brood yet?" Margaret asked thickly, gesturing towards them. Sniffing back the remnants of her tears, she straightened the light blue bonnet on her head and beckoned for them to stand. The family duly arranged themselves into a rough line as William pointed to each of them..

"Ned, Mary, Oliver and our youngest, Alice." Shy

42

faces peeped out from heavy fringes accompanied by a mixture of curtseys and slight bobs. They all shared the same mousy thin brown hair as their mother, rather than favouring the thick dark curly hair of William. "Trust me," William said jovially, "they aren't usually so quiet!"

Annabella widened her smile in greeting to them, before dipping into a deep curtsy before them. "How kind of you all to invite us to your lovely home, my dears, I hope you will excuse my muddy boots? I fear I tarried too long outside sipping your tea!" She held out the cup to the children with a wink. "For it is so tasty," she carried on, pretend-slurping noisily. The littlest one, Alice, giggled as Annabella quaffed then banged her chest with satisfaction. Eventually, Mary picked up the cue to play and made to offer her a refill from the kettle hanging over the hearth.

"Oh no," Annabella said, "I must leave some room for your Mother's delicious dinner, surely?"

"She's made the pottage with rosemary!" Alice piped up in a lispy voice, "I helped her strip it!"

"Well, I'm sure it will be doubly delicious. Thank you for taking such care to make it so," Annabella replied. "Is there anything I can do to help, Mistress Tunn?"

"Oh no, just keep them away from my feet whilst I get the bread out," Margaret replied. "It looks like you have some new admirers, who I am sure would love to ply you with endless cups of muddy refreshment."

Annabella laughed and turned back to the faces gazing up at her. Human children fascinated her, and she went to great pains to be accepted by them. This also endeared her to most women and mothers, although it did sometimes provoke uncomfortable questions about her childless state. Annabella arranged her skirts on a stool and held out her hands for another miniature cup. She caught Margaret's look of approval and winked.

The menfolk had turned to important matters of ale and rocks. They moved to the end of the long room, brightly lit with a line of candles with plates behind to capture the soot, and began examining the bag of gold streaked ore William had brought over earlier. Margaret, having recovered herself, set the table with wooden bowls and cups. Annabella and the children busied themselves arranging the stools and bench.

Calling the men over, Margaret poured them a small cup of weak but warmed ale. The youngsters stood ready by the pot to ferry the food as their guests took their places. Not expecting, or needing, much by way of nutrition of this sort, Joshua and Annabella ate only a small serving of the thin, tasty pottage. Everyone knew, after the poor harvest that year, that food costs had risen dramatically, and they understood the financial hardship it caused.

"How delicately flavoured. It must be the rosemary which makes all the difference," Annabella declared, wrinkling her nose and smiling at Alice. Joshua and Annabella politely declined second helpings and shared only one slice of the loaf. The family were clearly more in need of the filling meal than they were, so Joshua sneakily gave his half to Oliver, who sat next to him. The boy smiled up at him as Joshua whispered, "You must keep some meat on your bones, lad. I'm sure your father will have you working the fires tomorrow to get that gold out!"

Whilst the family were devouring their soup, the conversation between the women quickly turned into a gossipy introduction to the characters of the town; from Mistress Hooper, who could never keep a secret, but made the best-fragranced pomades to be had, to the unfortunate

Mr Bates, the undertaker, recently suffering from an ague which had caused him to slip and fall into the grave of the last poor soul buried in the churchyard over summer.

Annabella was intrigued to find out more about the local landowners. Lady Hanley of Hanley House (on top of the mound) rarely appeared in the town. Yet her presence in the area seemed to be closely felt, with people making assumptions in her absence as to whether something would please her, or cause her to show her displeasure. Rumour had it, she was afflicted with a temper which had led to the death of her husband many years before. Now she remained a glamourous but aloof widow, ever judgemental of the townsfolk's lives.

"She's generous with her money," Margaret said of her, "No questions, settles her dues promptly and without argument as long as it's of fair quality." Requests for supplies such as ingredients and a variety of household wares were reputedly ordered via short notes, delivered to the shops by a succession of small and quiet messenger boys, and collected by the same.

"They never tarry though," Margaret shook her head. "And they won't never speak ill of Mistress Hanley, although I never know if that's out of fear or respect," she wondered aloud, almost to herself.

Her aging steward, Mr Bray, was a larger and more visible part of the community and frequently the only representative of her estate in local proceedings. He was said to be average-looking in all things, blending unobtrusively into the crowds and always neatly dressed with a trimmed grey beard. Those who encountered him remarked that he was disinclined to gossip, even when seen in local drinking establishments. This, of course, meant that much gossip was made about him, as he was usually the sole voice of her Ladyship. His approval apparently voiced her approval. As such, Annabella reasoned that it could be of course entirely 'his' approval without 'her' knowledge of the matter at all. Annabella herself had not been introduced to him, although he had been pointed out to her last market day, so she should know upon whose orders he spoke.

Lady Hanley apparently rarely had visitors and only infrequently appeared at the local church, always dressed in new and dignified finery for special occasions, most notably around the Christmas Masses. Margaret clung to the belief that their local benefactor would somehow absolve them of having to relinquish their cherished rituals, so 'devout' was she herself.

"Some folks say, she won't stand for change to the services." Margaret's eyes flicked over to William, who glared back. Joshua kept his gaze at the table, whilst Annabella stood and began to pick up the plates. Annabella privately formed the opinion that the Lady Hanley couldn't really be considered devout if she so infrequently attended the Mass. She knew, from experience, the noble classes almost always followed the lead of the King, in appearance at least. Her Ladyship's intervention in the local religious activities seemed highly unlikely.

Sensing Margaret's comment might result in them being drawn into a debate which could become uncomfortable, she steered the discussion around to the children instead, asking politely if they were learning their letters?

"William tries with the boys, he does. Beautiful Latin he writes in, but I, alas, am useless with it," Margaret said, a little wistfully. "He learned everything he knows from the monks up at the Abbey. His parents were serving there, before he got apprenticed."

Both Annabella and Joshua looked at William with a new respect. It had taken years of surreptitious study to learn to read and write in both English and Latin; both now had beautiful handwriting which Joshua, in particular, used to forge their cover identities. Annabella patted Margaret's hand, and said consolingly, "There are other skills you teach your beautiful children. Don't fret. They are so bright and I'm sure do you both credit."

"Aye, but to read - and read well and wide - it is the path to knowledge and fortune," William said, grudgingly. "They need to make their way up in this world, or be left battering away like me until their bones can't wield a hammer."

Oliver spoke up, "Pa, I'll help you lift your hammer when you no longer can!" William smiled indulgently at the lad.

"You need to be stronger to lift a hammer than a quill!" Oliver carried on, flexing his arms and laughing at his brother Ned, who rolled his eyes. Older and quieter, William had previously mentioned to Joshua that he had high hopes for his first-born to follow a more scholarly path instead of being apprenticed to him in the forge. Joshua suspected what little money the family had spare went to sending Ned to learn his lessons at the Abbey in the hopes that he would make something more of his life than remain in this small town.

Annabella and Joshua shot a look at each other and knew this was a good moment to draw the pleasant evening to a close. Standing up and brushing himself down, Joshua said, "Tis late. We will take our leave of you now, dear friends. I look forward to seeing you on the 'morrow?"

"Thank you so much for sharing your meal and hearth with us," Annabella spoke directly towards the children. "The rosemary was just right!" She ruffled Alice and Oliver's hair with affection as she went to collect her cloak. After waving goodbye, Annabella and Joshua disappeared into the night. The forest was calling them and their empty bellies needed appropriate sustenance.

CHAPTER 4 – A STRANGE INTRODUCTION

The first Sunday morning in early December dawned crisp and frosty. Annabella snuggled into Joshua's arms and looked at the delicate shards of fingerlike-ice creeping up the windowpanes. The Lifeforce they had ingested the previous night still coursed warmly through her, strong and invigorating like the stag they had hunted. The infusion needed to last them both a good many weeks as Advent held stringent curfews and unusual nocturnal activity would be noticed. Joshua roused and dropped a kiss on her head. "To church is it, my love?"

Annabella buried her head into his chest and groaned. The legal requirement for them to attend weekly had lately become more of a chore. Whereas, in the decades before, religious fervour delivered a rush of Lifeforce, the current turmoil and confusion meant that truly passionate believers were in short supply. Although most humans still feared for their mortal soul, especially if they did not follow the letter of the law and worship at Church at least every Sunday, the upset caused by theological divisions diluted their once passionate entreaties to the Lord. This diminished the energy boost Annabella and Joshua gained by attending services, leaving them dissatisfied and hungry inside. Their expectations for today were low, which was why they had targeted such a large beast.

Exchanging the warmth of their sheets for the chill of the bedroom did little to lift their spirits. Joshua, already dithering about wearing his relatively new broadcloth gown to church, attempted to distract Annabella from her mission to pin her hair nicely by parading about the room in nothing but his hat. Although amused, she swatted his wandering hands away from pulling her back into bed, insisting that he needed to convey his craftsmanship status to all, especially as an important Mass was before them. He capitulated after she conceded a kiss, and they helped each other fasten laces and don their finest outfits ready for the day ahead.

They hurried the short distance to the main square, puffing clouds of breath into the still cold air. Upon joining the throng of worshippers clustered outside the Church of St Matthew, Joshua commented quietly, "You were correct, my love. Everyone seems to be wearing their best as well. But none are as beautiful as you are - especially without any attire." Despite herself, Annabella blushed.

"Time to test the town's devotion," Annabella muttered.

"Hush now," said Joshua, squeezing her hand as they walked through the porch and into the only slightly warmer building. "Let us keep an open mind and heart."

Although they had attended this church before, the season called for festive decoration. Additional candles, ivy, and other such greenery draped elegantly over the pulpit, rood screen and altar. The glinting chalice laid out in readiness for the sacrament indicated that the movement towards a simpler way of worship hadn't yet been enforced in this parish. Pots of whitewash hidden by the door suggested the daubing out of the colourful images of hope and salvation adorning the walls was imminent. Even the beautifully scripted verses painted in black to remind the congregation of their duties to God were under threat.

Annabella looked at the change and couldn't help but

smile at the vegetation surrounding them - bringing nature into a building reminded her a little of Naturae. Her usual view of the artwork during a dull sermon, which she had heard in roughly the same format for centuries, would be obscured but in a pleasant way. At least this church's surroundings were less focused on potential damnation and encouraged obedience.

As he took in the decoration, Joshua fought to quiet his mind. The ornate images around him used to bring serenity to his thoughts, but he had lost much of the blind faith of his childhood. Having undergone his transformation to fae, his belief system was now confused. How could he exist as a person with a soul to be saved, when what they were simply didn't feature at all in the Bible? Was he an abomination? He didn't feel like one, and didn't love like one. At times he missed the innocence of blind belief, of trusting that if he followed a set and God-fearing pattern to his life, he would be spared the perils of Hell.

Taking a pew towards the back of the Church, Joshua clapped a greeting on William's shoulder as they shuffled past the Tunn family seated in front of them. Margaret and William had recently been visitors to their own cosy home for a delightful and merry evening, leaving their children behind with Margaret's mother for a few hours' escape as the couples developed their friendship. Annabella warmly greeted Margaret and nodded to William, his cheeks ruddier than ever having come in from the cold.

Margaret leant over the pew and whispered with barely suppressed anticipation, "I expect her Ladyship will be in attendance today! She prefers to worship here to be with her people than travel all the way to the Abbey." Margaret paused, her eyes slid to William before she whispered, "I do wonder if she will intervene with the priest herself. I'm sure, and everyone says, she ought to make known her displeasure about the new services."

Annabella ignored the jibe and pressed Margaret instead with a polite enquiry about whether the season was likely the cause of Widow Bartlet's move from her usual seat opposite their pew? Margaret raised her eyebrows as her eyes slid to the rotund butcher at the end of the bench, sat a few feet along from the lady in question. Annabella's eyes sparkled, a new romance often meant extra indulgence on new clothes.

Although she pretended not to indulge in gossip, Annabella knew well enough that it was a necessary currency for keeping abreast of what was happening in the community. For purely selfish purposes, chitter-chatter was useful to divert suspicions about their arrival, or any unusual behaviour which the folk of a new town might notice. Gossip was, after all, a two-way street. Joshua, in particular, had a flair for 'accidentally' spilling a tasty titbit of hearsay to draw attention away from their nocturnal peculiarities whilst chatting at local drinking establishments. Such news would likely filter to wives and mothers by the next morning. Deflection was protection, as far as Joshua and Annabella were concerned.

Margaret kept glancing around but most especially at the entrance. For her friend's benefit, Annabella formed a look of excitement on her face, then turned her head also, as if that would cue the entrance of the much-feted Lady herself. Seeing no-one of consequence, Annabella sat down on the hard benches and arranged her green woollen cloak around her. The room quietened as the priest began to walk up to the pulpit, followed by the incense bearer. The choir took out their music sheets, but the doors creaked once more.

The congregation's heads whipped around to glare at the late arrival, expecting them to be shamefaced, creeping in just as the service was about to begin. They instantly forgave the distraction as soon as they saw the dark jacket of Mr Bray holding the heavy door open for his mistress, the Lady Hanley.

Attired in a deep red coat with fine golden embroidery embellishing the sleeves, and a black hat with a red tinted feather protruding stylishly from the side, her Ladyship cut a slim, dashing figure. Pausing briefly to sweep a clear gaze across the packed hall, she confidently crossed the threshold and glided between the pews. Already admiring her taste, Annabella examined her as best she could through lowered eyelids. A modern dress style belied the faint crows-feet disappearing into wisps of raven hair.

There was no mistaking the presence of the woman. She commanded the congregation's attention absolutely as she progressed regally forward. Those still daring to look at her were unlikely to achieve eye contact, and even less likely to receive a welcome smile from her haughty face. Unintentionally, Annabella's flickering eyes met the old woman's as she passed their pew. The cool look lingered upon her for somewhat longer than she felt entirely comfortable with.

The atmosphere in the church seemed to electrify with her arrival. The elderly priest, sensing the charge in the room, began the welcome liturgy to establish focus once more towards worship. Annabella twitched in her seat, even more unable to concentrate than usual. Her feeling of unease didn't dissipate as the service continued. She mouthed along at the appropriate times, but her eyes kept being drawn to the front pew. Her view of the Lady was hampered by William's large back, so she wriggled whenever standing to see if she could position herself better. Joshua raised his eyebrow whenever she fidgeted, but she couldn't help it; she was keen to leave as soon as was practical.

As the service drew to a close, they waited in their pews as was polite when gentry were in attendance. Lady Hanley took her time returning up the aisle, her smooth glide punctuated subtly by pauses to acknowledge the local citizens doffing their caps and curtsying to her as she passed. She slowed as she approached their bench, pale eyes flicking curiously over them.

William quickly leant over the pew, gesturing wildly with his arm and with enthusiasm called out, "Your Ladyship! May I introduce our new arrivals to the town? Joshua and Annabella Meadows - famed far and wide for their silverworking and stitching!" He beamed at his own cleverness.

Annabella bent her head and dipped into a deep curtsy in an effort to repair the damage William's impropriety and enthusiasm might have done to their introduction. The movement did nothing to subdue the tightness of anxiety in her stomach.

Joshua straightened himself and doffed his brown cap with a flourish towards the matriarch. In contrast to Annabella, he always leaned towards seizing opportunities when they presented themselves. In business at least, he was the more confident of the pair. Now, riding on the coat-tails of a successful and well-appreciated commission, he was on the lookout for further work.

"Your Ladyship, we have recently taken the tenancy in your vacant shop on Wood Street," Joshua said. He turned on his smile to charm, as Annabella called it. "We look forward to providing the town with the finest silverwork and the most beautiful dresses to be found hereabouts."

Lady Hanley's gaze narrowed as she appraised them. She nodded slowly, lingering her cool eyes on Annabella, before moving onwards.

Annabella breathed out as the sensation of being clinically examined passed. As soon as was polite, she took Joshua's hand and marched home with him in silence. The unease in her stomach remained until they closed the front door behind them.

*****

It was somehow a slight surprise the next morning when a small, pale-looking messenger boy appeared at the shop and requested Annabella to attend Hanley House. The stomach-knot returned as soon as the words tripped from his mouth. The order was to measure up her Ladyship for a new winter dress later that very day. Annabella gave the boy a hunk of warmed bread and dripping to nibble on whilst she wrote a suitably effusive note promising to visit. Proclaiming himself to be called 'Arry, like the King', the lad provided no further information about the request, just that he was to wait until a reply was given then bring it straight back. He was clearly hoping for more than a snack but sensing monetary favours were not forthcoming, he accepted a second piece of bread for the journey with a cheeky grin.

Joshua was working at the Tunn forge, and not due back until much later that day. Their shop had been busier than usual that morning, with piecework repairs coming in and going out in readiness for the festive season. Annabella, uneasy that she couldn't discuss the request immediately with him, decided to close up the shop, then walk via the forge before heading to Hanley House. Gathering her cloak around her and packing a small bag with some dressmaking essentials, she set out.

The smells of food and forging intensified as Annabella drew closer to the main square. Chilly air and lack of wind meant the aromas of daily life travelled further, it seemed to her. She could never quite get used to the unwashed human smells of a town, although the horse droppings and other animal faeces didn't bother her. They were natural scents which most humans tried hard to blanket their noses from with pomades and perfumes.

Cheer filled the air all across the square. Cold red-nosed faces smiled and nodded greetings as neighbours went about their business. As she approached the forge, Annabella could taste the charcoal smoke in her mouth, her heightened senses picking out the oaky tang. Joshua was working a large piece of silver on an anvil, hammering it down to flatten it out. Blond hair, dank with sweat and smoke but still brighter than most, made him stand out in the darkened recesses of the room. Annabella had always liked watching his strong arms handling the heavy tools, the view of his muscles clenching as he wielded the weighty hammer so precisely upon the anvil. It reminded her of the first time she had seen him in his father's smithy, some hundred or more years before.

Such was the noise from the bellows and the banging from both Joshua and William, she had to wave and flap her cloak to make her presence known. She didn't like to get too close to the fires, fearful of them spitting ash. Joshua looked up and slid his hammer down on the ground.

"Why hello there, my lady wife." He beamed at her,

"Errands to run?" He approached and placed a light kiss on her cold nose. Oliver paused the bellows so they could converse easier, and he could take a breather.

"I've been called up to Hanley House, to measure up for a dress for her Ladyship," Annabella said, her tight face betraying the mix of emotions she felt. The previous night, Joshua had rubbished her earlier sense of unease about Lady Hanley's probing gaze, pointing out instead the opportunity she presented. Annabella held his eyes whilst he considered his response to this announcement.

"Do you want me to come with you?" He eventually asked.

"Do you have time to?" She didn't want to beg, and really, she thought to herself, she ought to attend alone. Joshua was probably right - this was probably no more than newcomer nosiness.

He looked down at the piece he was working on, then shrugged.

"I'd rather not have this get hardened, if truth be told. But if you want me to come, I will." He glanced at the flat disc he held, chewing on his lip with regret. To let the metal get too cold whilst being worked meant it would have to be melted down and started again; a waste of a morning's work. Annabella knew this.

Determined to quell her own uneasiness, she said lightly, "I'm sure I can manage on my own, 'tis only a measuring. I just thought you might like to see what the fuss is all about."

"There will be other fittings," Joshua said, a grateful smile spreading across his face. "I'll gladly join you for some company then." They shared a brief hug before Joshua picked up his hammer and nodded to the boy to begin leading the donkey around the fire again.

*****

In the daylight and dry weather, the walk through the woods to the mound was quicker than Annabella remembered. Feeling calmed by the fauna around her, she had almost convinced herself that her nervousness was unwarranted, and that this was simply a business transaction from a highly thought of new client. Reaching the clearing at the bottom of the rise, she noticed a beautiful grey horse tethered with a finely stitched saddle and embossed reins. Such a fine beast could only belong to someone with wealth; Annabella wondered if it was her Ladyship's mount. She continued onwards to the narrow curving pathway and began the steep ascent. The path was well maintained and, in parts, flat stones had been laid to create steps. Young - well, only five centuries old - and fit, Annabella was still slightly labouring for breath when she circled to the top.

Catching her breath at the end of the track where a small patio lay, the view across the countryside almost caused her to lose it again. A deep frost still glinted on the lower fields despite the midday sun already past its peak. From this vantage point, the flatter landscape rippled a patchwork blanket of silver, green and brown. Usually, flying high and mostly at night, a vista such as this was not afforded her, so she took a moment to appreciate the peaceful rural scene. Beesworth itself seemed closer, her eyesight enabling her to even make out people as they walked through the streets.

As she had kept her head down to watch her step climbing the steep hillock, she hadn't fully appreciated the looming bulk of the mansion until she dragged her eyes around to it. The house up close was one of the largest single dwellings she had ever seen. Its footprint was unusual - a tall yet narrow building, almost as if it were a terrace of houses perched atop the mount, encompassing the slim summit. It could have easily been mistaken for a long barn, were it not for the peaked apexes of the windows and doors symmetrically adorning their way along the length of the building. It reminded her of a monastic church, as well as, disconcertingly, Naturae's High Hall.

Annabella thought it must be a windswept spot as there surely could be no inner courtyard for protection, unlike the many substantial houses or manors she had visited previously. Most grand houses functioned with a central space which provided a measure of protection from the elements as well. Some, having been extended with extra wings tacked on hither and thither, ended up looking distinctly unbalanced. But not Hanley House. It had deliberately been built large enough in the first place to accommodate whatever family and their supporting retinue of servants could require.

Making her way past plain leaded glass windows edged with roses climbing seductively around the apertures, she counted the windows up. The house was a full four stone stories tall. Each room must also enjoy high ceilings, she realised, which would be costly to heat. As she reached a doorway, she realised it was the front door, and paused for a minute to consider which entrance she should be using. Commonly, trades and delivery folk would use the back door, but she hadn't seen one on her approach to the building. She carried on past the heavy oak double doors, admiring the elaborate carvings on them as she went.

Resisting the temptation to peer in through the windows as she passed, Annabella instead looked at the view, imagining herself surveying that vista every morning - what a feeling of peace it would give, and one of mastery of the world. She shuddered slightly at that thought, having no desire to rule over anyone or anything.

Reaching the furthest edge of the building, past a newly built chimney stack on the end gable, she turned the corner and followed a narrow track around the side then rear of the house. The edges of the hillock dropped sharply away from the path which was barely wide enough for one person to teeter along. Peering over, she could see steep steps cut into the grass, leading down to a small and neat stable yard on the fringes of the woodland.

Finally she reached the back door, which was much smaller, plain and as unremarkable as the front doors were remarkable. Annabella raised her hand to knock but it swung open and a welcome blast of heat enveloped her.

Standing in the doorway was Lady Hanley herself, looking regal in a richly embroidered emerald bodice and yellowy-green skirt trimmed with fur. Her black hair was almost completely hidden by a white linen house bonnet. Annabella sank into a deep curtsey again and stayed down until she was acknowledged.

"Thank you for attending so swiftly, my dear," Lady Hanley said, her voice low and modulated. "Please come in and warm yourself."

Annabella stepped over the threshold as the Lady stepped backwards, watching her all the while. The large kitchen was indeed cosy and deliciously fragranced. Rich undertones of spices and herbs mingled with the woody smell of the fire and pottage cooking over the hearth. Annabella waited next to the large empty table in the centre of the room, and gradually lifted her head to meet the old woman's pale watchful eyes.

"My thanks and gratitude for inviting me to attend on you, my Lady," Annabella said, her voice clear yet guarded in tone. "I understand you are interested in a new gown?"

"Yes," Lady Hanley replied, turning into a doorway out of the kitchen. "The light is better at this time of day towards the end of the house. We will adjourn there so you may show me some samples. Assuming you have some with you?" She turned and looked at Annabella piercingly, challenging her to have arrived properly equipped.

Thankful that she had thought to pack some fabrics with her, Annabella nodded and patted her bag. "You may leave your cloak here," Lady Hanley motioned towards a tall hat stand adjacent to the doorway. Annabella's would be the only cloak hanging.

As they walked down a dim, candle-lit passageway into a wider central corridor with lighter panelled woods, Annabella sensed a faintly ominous presence about the house. No natural daylight penetrated the hall; all the doors were firmly closed on either side. But, aside from the steady footsteps of her Ladyship leading the way, the mansion was utterly silent. Annabella's sensitive ears even picked out the rustling of the grass outside. The absence of any other noise made her heart race. They were completely alone, most peculiar for such a large establishment.

Reaching the furthest door, Annabella realised this was the room which she had approached as she had climbed the hill. Lady Hanley watched as Annabella took in the light and airy space before her. A warm fire crackled at the end of the chamber, framed by dual aspect windows which allowed the sunlight to stream in. Facing the fireplace were two enormous and comfortable looking high-backed chairs, upholstered in what once had been a rich red silk with golden braid edging. In the centre of the room, a small table was set adjacent to a high desk, its matching chair tucked neatly underneath. Rather unusually, the furniture was fashioned from lighter coloured wood, rather than the heavy dark wood traditionally favoured for a study. Six low-burnt candles rising along the side of the slanted desktop told of late evenings spent writing or studying.

An entire wall housed floor to ceiling bookcases filled with tomes, the top shelves crammed with scrolls of paper. In between the casings, Annabella could make out wallpaper, faintly inscribed with swirls in misty green. Their shapes were strangely familiar to her, although she could not place them without closer, more obvious, examination. More shocking still, the walls did not, as custom dictated in these times, contain Biblical verses or illustrations, to remind the occupants of their duty to God above all else.

"You are surprised by my decor, I think?" Lady Hanley broke the silence with a quiet intervention.

"No, my Lady," Annabella replied. "Tis only that it is such a large room, with a fine aspect." This was the first of the many lies she would tell that day.

Annabella and Lady Hanley settled upon fabrics relatively easily, as the old lady was quick to reach decisions and had clearly a design for the embellishments in mind. As she took out her measuring parchment, Lady Hanley initiated a thinly-veiled interrogation.

Annabella thought she managed to navigate the questions successfully, at first. Lady Hanley questioned her unusual name ('My mother was taken with a fancy for all things Italian, on account of her former Mistress being from Europe'); her former employment and apprenticeship ('My mother was a seamstress for many a Lord in the South, and I learnt from other seamstresses who had worked in the Court, before relocating to the country'); and her childless status ('My Lady, we have only recently been wed and are keen to make a livelihood and home for ourselves before a family may come along').

Lady Hanley remained silent as each lie tripped from Annabella's lips.

Catching the woman's eye, Annabella realised that her every movement was being studied intently. It was unnerving, so Annabella fell silent and tried to signal her unwillingness to continue chit-chat by neatly inscribing measurement notes on the narrow reel of paper at the desk.

Bending down with her right hand on the woman's waist to reach the measuring parchment to the floor, she felt a light touch on her back from her Ladyship, more of a sweep, just below her shoulder blades. The bump of her wings, Annabella knew, was barely visible beneath her blousy smock, but still, it was a curiously intimate action. Stiffening momentarily, she drew herself upright. With a guarded face, she turned to the older woman, who appeared completely unabashed. Lady Hanley merely raised the corners of her mouth, twitching a smile but there was a strange darkness in her eyes.

A look that said it wasn't an accidental brush.

An expression that spoke volumes of knowing exactly what she had touched underneath the simple garments of a seamstress.

CHAPTER 5 - DISCOVERY

"You didn't see her face!" Annabella said firmly to Joshua, her fists clenched as she paced before their fireside. She wore a simple white night shift, having just bathed, yet her temper was rising. Through the thin fabric the outline of her risen wings was obvious, tension causing them to stand proud of her back.

"There's no reason for alarm," he replied calmly. "I'm sure it wasn't deliberate. How could she know?"

"She knows."

"Even if she did *know,* what do you suppose she would do about it?"

"I don't know!" Annabella cried out, "I just don't know!"

"We - you - have done nothing wrong. We are what we are," Joshua said, crossing the small room in two strides. "She might just leave us alone." He tried gently guiding her arm to sit down. This argument had been going around and around between them for several days, and he was tired of it.

"Do you want us to move now? When we are just getting settled?" Joshua offered again. It would probably be the first time they had left a town without being hounded out of it, and Yuletide was a bad season to appear in a new place. She knew this, but he felt obliged to repeatedly offer his support. Despite her worrying, the discovery of another creature in their midst was not something he perceived as a threat. In fact, to him it was more a curiosity. An opportunity.

Annabella acceded and sat down, staring into the flames, contemplating their options. The wind gusting cold and wet outside made them both feel more inclined to stay put in their cosy shop. Joshua knelt as he took her hand and leant forward to stroke the white-blond hair from her face. It had a tendency to drift upwards when she got agitated, and would soon be dry from the heat of the fire.

Joshua caressed her concerns away. "I can't see her gossiping in town about us. I also can't imagine her telling all her many visitors about the strange bumps she may or may not have felt on your back. I say," he finished softly, "we stay put, and keep our ears open for anything untoward."

Annabella turned her back to him, offering him her clothed back and wings to stroke as if she needed comforting, childlike once her tantrum passed. She felt tears prick at the back of her eyes and blinked them away. The gratitude she felt at having him so close to her, so well able to keep her calm and grounded, sometimes overwhelmed her. She knew she would be lost without him, and these moments of intimacy they shared.

"Let us carry on with the Christmas festivities, which I know you like," he whispered in her ear before dropping a kiss on her neck. "And, we can see if she does anything to show her hand in the next few months before we make a decision."

"At least the dress is nearly done," Annabella said with a sigh. "I'll have to go back for a fitting shortly. Next week probably, as she wants it finished before Christmas Eve Mass."

"I'll come with you," Joshua said, reaching his arms around her to encircle her with an embrace. "Nothing will happen, I promise, whilst I am there."

She snuggled back into him and rested her head on his shoulders. Any plan was better than no plan.

*****

Hazy dawn light peeked over the hills on Wednesday of the next week, marking just two weeks until Christmas. Joshua and Annabella trudged their way up the track to Hanley House, both silent with apprehension and concentration. Having rained all night, the going was slower and the slippery climb seemed steeper. Whilst walking around to the back door, Annabella peeped through the windows as she passed them. Room after room, she noticed the empty faded grandeur of the furnishings lurking in each dim space. It implied the lady of the house most likely spent the majority of her time in the library-study in which she had been measured. Annabella still caught no sight of servants. At least she wouldn't be alone, she thought, glancing up at Joshua and exchanging a smile.

Once more, the back door opened just as they reached it. Lady Hanley gestured for them to enter. "My husband, Joshua, came with me to ensure I did not fall in the mud and spoil your Ladyship's dress!" tinkled Annabella, a little too brightly. She curtsied, then pulled off the knapsack he wore. He doffed his cap and bowed respectfully at Lady Hanley. His smile didn't reach his eyes and her face remained stony. They stepped inside the kitchen and put the bulky bags on the floor to take off their capes and hats.

"What a striking couple you make," Lady Hanley said as they both removed their outer attire and hung it neatly. "I should use your hair to shine the way at night! What a shame to hide its brightness under a cap."

Annabella froze and her eyes flicked up to meet

Joshua's in concern. Joshua tried to make light of the comment, saying, "Your Ladyship is too kind. My wife's fair hair indeed lit up my life when I first saw it!" Annabella forced her face to relax then, with a loving look at him, she gathered herself along with the bags they had brought.

"I have no need of you cluttering my fitting," Lady Hanley dismissed him. "You can warm yourself by the kitchen fire if you wish, whilst we conclude our business in the Library." Joshua, expecting as much, moved toward the stool adjacent to the fireplace. He paused, then said, "Would you like me to carry the bags through though, my Lady?"

"I'm sure that won't be necessary," her Ladyship replied. "I would imagine, having sewed it, Mistress Meadows is perfectly capable of carrying it a short distance!" The way she said Annabella's name made Joshua's heart sink a little. Perhaps Annabella had been right. But how much could she know about their lifestyle and assumed identities?

Put in his place and his curiosity curtailed, Joshua sat down on the stool, turning his hat around in his hands. His mouth tightened as he watched their retreat but he was grateful for the time alone to process the implications.

After a last resigned glance at him, Annabella followed Lady Hanley to the room at the end of the corridor once more. On the desk in the library, a large bound book with thick velum pages rested, unopened. Annabella only noticed it because on the cover ornate golden swirls adorned the leather, and it had no title on the spine as most books did. Lady Hanley saw her interest in it and took her arm, guiding her closer to the window to begin the fitting. In the corner, changing screens had been

67

placed in readiness, presumably brought down from a bedroom recently as they had not been there the last time. The room was warm from the low fire and the only light filtered in through the windows. It was a cloudy day outside, so the brightness of the furnishings seemed even more faded in the slight gloom.

Annabella had begun to pull the wrapped fabric from her bag to distract herself, when Lady Hanley turned her back to her with a slight clearing of her throat. "Oh! I'm sorry, Your Ladyship, of course!"

Annabella began to tug at the laces on the bodice of Lady Hanley's dress. Once loosened, Lady Hanley stepped behind the screens in the corner to remove her skirts, then the kirtle, bodice and sleeves.

Annabella hastened to arrange the beautiful gown skirt she had stitched ready for Lady Hanley to step into when she thought she became aware of another presence in the room. Turning around and checking, she saw no-one, although she was certain she smelt something lingering, or someone. The only noise was the rustle of Lady Hanley dropping her stiff attire to the floor behind the panels. Annabella sniffed, trying to place the familiar scent which had appeared.

Lady Hanley stepped out from behind the screens and approached. Even dressed in just a smock, demi-bum roll and corset, she had a presence. A forceful dignity. To Annabella, it wasn't the cool superiority which unnerved her. It was the unacknowledged fear that the old woman knew what she was. Her Ladyship's face fell short of haughty, but she was definitely using her hawk-like gaze to examine Annabella, no matter how much she tried to avoid meeting her eyes.

Looking down at the skirts, Annabella ventured to

move the conversation into neutral territory as soon as possible. "I hope that the decorations around the waist and edging are satisfying to your Ladyship?"

"They seem neatly done, I must say."

"And the sleeves match the kirtle, as well as the gown," Annabella continued, hoping to elicit further approval as she pulled the skirts over the woman's head.

"They will look very fine, for many outfits," Lady Hanley said casually. She reached over to pick up the embroidered sleeves from the arm of the chair where Annabella had draped them. Annabella drew the ribbons of the kirtle skirt tight around her waist and reached for the gown to go over it. The folds of the fabric fell as gracefully as a waterfall over the bum roll with a rustle to the floor.

Lady Hanley looked down at the dress with a look of mild approval on her stern set face. "You've done a good job," she said, somewhat begrudgingly. Keeping her head down, Annabella carefully adjusted the stiffer fabric at the front then moved behind to begin lacing, pulling tightly to draw the edges in smoothly around her Ladyship's slim physique.

As Annabella pulled the ribbon systematically through the eyeholes, she realised the old lady was barely breathing. She paused, "Is this too tight your Ladyship?"

"No."

Annabella continued, her nimble hands working up the corsetry. She hesitated again at the top of the stays... for there, the gap between the shoulder blades seemed wider.

Like hers were.

A chilled silence sat heavily about the room. Even the crackling warmth of the fire seemed to vanish. How had she missed this when doing the measuring? Annabella's mind whirled. Then she cursed herself inwardly, as she realised it was her own fear of discovery, and its implications, which had caused her to overlook the obvious about her client.

"They were cut," Lady Hanley finally said, still motionless. "Many centuries ago."

Annabella looked down at her feet to hide the shocked look from her face. A myriad of queries tumbled around her mind, jostling for priority. Experience suggested her best course of action was to stay silent, not open her mouth at all. The tingle of fear that swept through her kept her frozen, as prey would be to a hunter's appearance. More than just being cornered, she was also terrified questions would spill out and the trap would be sprung.

Lady Hanley turned and took Annabella's hands in her own. Through her long eyelashes, Annabella looked up at the old woman. She tried her hardest not to let her own face betray any of the emotions or questions swirling. She failed spectacularly under the piercing gaze of those darkened eyes, which examined her steadily.

"I know," Lady Hanley said flatly and without emotion. "I know who you are."

Annabella rushed from the room. There was nothing else she could think of to do but escape. Run. Flee.

She tore down the corridor and tumbled into the kitchen. By the fireside, Joshua had already jumped to his feet. Although he reached out, even his long strides were unable to prevent her fall.

"Go!" Annabella blurted out. The edge of panic in her voice alarmed Joshua. Ignoring his enquiring eyebrows, Annabella scrambled up, wrenched open the door, and dashed out without saying another word. Bewildered for just a moment, Joshua peered up the passage, half expecting to see Lady Hanley in pursuit. The absence of footsteps did nothing to quell his racing heart. He grabbed their cloaks and followed Annabella, not even pulling the door shut behind him.

As he loped down the hillside, he glanced back at the house and saw the outline of Lady Hanley at the window. He could sense she was following their every move as they spiralled down and out of sight, into the woods. Joshua sighed. Their bags would be packed again tonight he feared.

CHAPTER 6 - JUST ANOTHER CHRISTMAS

When he finally caught up with Annabella in a clearing in the woods, she was near fully undressed. Her instinct to flee had almost totally overridden her sensibilities, he surmised, for it was broad daylight and a not especially secluded area from which to launch themselves into the air.

"What's happened?" He said, panting slightly from the exertion of running to catch up with her despite his relative fitness.

"She knows!"

"We've barely got here, how can she know?"

"Because she is..." Annabella paused and corrected herself, "*was* Fae."

Joshua rubbed his forehead. Even though he had spent the time in Hanley House's kitchen wondering about the implications of Annabella being discovered as fae, it was somehow still shocking to find another. In over a century, across the country they had lived in, they had never encountered any other fae. The odd witch, definitely a few daemons and a vampire once or twice, but never a fae to his knowledge. Creatures smelt different to mortals, more intense somehow, when you got up close to them.

"Well," he reasoned, "then she is one of us, surely?" He couldn't understand Annabella's reaction. He rationalised that there must be others like them, somewhere in the world, but Annabella had always avoided discussing where. He had long since given up pressing for more details. She got very defensive and insisted that they must stand alone, live their own life, not for or with anyone else.

Annabella's shoulders sagged and she paused her frantic de-robing to look at him in desperation. "You don't understand, she is Outcast too. She knows... me."

"Then we should try to find out what she knows?" He couldn't help but feel a little frustrated. Annabella was the only fae he knew or had ever known. He was keen to discover out more about his 'new' race. How were they made? What did they look like? Annabella was so vague about it all, as if it was not important. But to him, it was. On the occasion of his re-birth, he remembered in the confusion of it that she had been surprised. But how else were fae created?

"No, there's something about her I just don't trust," Annabella said, calmer and more decisive now. "There'd be a reason she is Outcast."

"How do you know she is?"

"Her wings. They were shorn off."

Joshua winced. Having painfully grown them, he was most conscious of his wings. It was what set them apart from other beings; that and their incredibly long life. He felt an ache in his shoulder blades at the very thought of these precious body parts being dismembered.

All of a rush, his dismay spilled out. "How? How can a fae do that? Was it another fae who cut them off?" Then, after a breath, "Why?"

Annabella turned away from him and began to adjust her clothing again, making ready to fly. He caught her arm and pulled her back around to face him.

He pleaded, "It doesn't matter, we shouldn't have to leave. What can she do?"

"It *does* matter! You don't understand!" Annabella

drew up to her full haughty height in defiance. She jerked away from his grasp and stomped across the clearing. Her wings extended as she turned to look at him coldly.

"There is so much you don't know, and that may be my fault. I wanted to protect you. If you love me, you have to accept this is the way it *must* be."

Annabella paused, waiting for him to respond with something other than open-jawed shock. Although she fully expected him to fall in line with her, inside the nagging guilt about her secret rose to gnaw at her again. She pushed it away and kept her stern face pasted on. But, the longer they stared at each other, the more her little voice of doubt that he would not comply with her wishes crept in.

Joshua looked steadily at her, considering his options. A male dominant society suggested he ought to demand obedience from his woman, but they had never worked that way as a couple. Every fae part of him screamed that this was his soulmate and they should be together. That, no matter what, he should support her. His logical mind told him that there was no reason to fear this time. They had such little information to work with, except Annabella's instincts.

And yet, her instincts were usually spot on.

So, he should go too.

Except... except he didn't want to.

"If we are going, let us at very least go home and get our things." His heart pounding, Joshua hoped that if he was calm and reasonable, she would see the benefit of his suggestion.

"They don't matter! None of it matters! We need to leave now!" Annabella insisted. But at the same time, her wings were dropping slowly.

Joshua held out his hand to fill the awkward silence between them. "We could be gone by nightfall," he said. "If you really want to. There is little she can do in broad daylight anyway." He watched as her eyes darted over the belongings on the ground; they had come to the Hall with little more than her seamstress bag, and left without even that. There were items which, no matter how hastily they left, they always managed to take with them: tools, clothes and the like. "Let us at least gather the means for us to make a living again?" He picked up the clothes and walked over to her, as one might a frightened bird, approaching with caution for she still could rise into flight.

Annabella looked up at him, the fight draining from her face as she accepted the wisdom of his suggestion. As she calmed down and rearranged her clothing, Joshua watched her lips clench and unclench as she inwardly tried to convince herself that perhaps this was a more sensible course of action after all.

Overhead, a kestrel lazily circled, its eyes keenly observing the pair as they embraced before moving off.

*****

They picked their way silently through the forest to stay hidden until they reached the edge, then diverted through a field to reach the track into the town. As they approached their little home, Annabella sagged against him, exhaustion overtaking her as the remnants of the adrenaline rush left her. Inside, and safe at last, Joshua half carried her to the stool by the fireside and set the kettle on to make her a warm drink. He knew what she really needed was some Lifeforce, but he didn't wish to leave her to hunt in case she somehow rallied and started packing.

He locked the door and pulled down the blinds against unwanted observers; business could wait.

"Do you still want to take off?" He ventured quietly after she had sullenly stared into the flames for a while, her cup untouched yet warming her hands. "I can pack if you like?"

Annabella closed her eyes and bowed her head. Her shoulders began to heave as the tears came. "I hate this," she mumbled. "The constant running."

"I know," Joshua said, covering her pale hands with his. "But this is the price of freedom, you said."

"It is, and yet I know you long to be still, to belong somewhere."

Joshua looked away. It was true, his human part yearned to fit once more, but his love for her drove him to live this lifestyle which she insisted was necessary.

"I fail you," she whispered, her head so low he could hardly make her words out, even with his enhanced hearing.

"Never!" Joshua said fiercely and pulled her close to him. "I chose you, and I chose to live like you do!"

"I can't belong," Annabella wailed.

He didn't have an answer for that, so he just held her tight until the shaking from tears and emotion ceased.

As the light outside turned dusky, Annabella roused herself from the comforting arms of her lover and looked up at him, stroking the line of his chin as though to familiarise herself again with his face. He pinched her slightly upturned nose in response and they giggled like teenagers.

"So Mistress Meadows," Joshua said lightly, "what's

next then? Are we fleeing the 'fae who can't fly', or are we going to wait it out a while?"

Annabella paused and considered. On the one hand, everything she had learned from living in hiding for the last century or more screamed Run! Danger! But this was not a situation they had encountered before. Not a human who discovered their secret, but one of their own kind. It raised a new issue for her in particular, opening afresh the wound which she had sealed off for too long.

Somewhat calmer now, she realised that she also wanted some answers. She didn't recognise the old lady, but that didn't mean much in itself - how could she be expected to know every fae from a hundred years ago? Recall every face which she had blocked from her mind? Not every fae lived in Naturae after all.

More importantly, there was Joshua to think of. He brushed her cheeks with his long fingers as if reading that her mind had turned to consideration of him. She gazed into his eyes, churning with indecision. There was no-one she trusted more, but still she worried about his reaction. Was it time to tell him? Or could she keep his innocence a while more? That he had questions about their race, her homeland, her background, she knew, but to reveal even some of what fae-kind were risked everything they had. Even just a small amount of information would doubtless lead to more questions, and the whole sorry mess might unravel. Her confession would assuredly change their relationship. It had to. But how much longer could she protect him from the darkness of the destiny she escaped? Was it fair?

Deciding with a heavy heart, she said, "Until we know more... maybe I was too hasty. We should stay until we understand the truth of it."

"That would mean we need to ask her, surely?" Joshua said.

Annabella rolled her neck and began to rub the tension away. After a moment, she said, "I just need time to think." She glanced up at him, "About what might have happened to her. Why she was Outcast like that."

Joshua nodded and took over massaging her shoulders. "I would like to stay," he said. "I think it is wiser to find out what we can. If you are right, we will always have the advantage of flight if we need to hurry away at speed. Perhaps after some sustenance, then sleep, we can figure out how to find the answers we need?"

Annabella recognised this temporary reprieve from what she knew he must be desperate to know. In truth, she was feeling drained and needed Lifeforce after the height of recent emotions. "Let me wash my face? We can head out after the sun has dipped? I think better unbound."

"After full darkness has fallen would be safer," Joshua said. "It is Advent still. But we will find something small to tide us over until the Fayre, I'm sure."

Annabella cuddled back into his chest. She had completely forgotten about the festivities ahead. Maybe staying was the right decision.

CHAPTER 7 - AN UNFESTIVE FAYRE

Joshua managed to avoid bringing up the recent revelation for almost three days. During the daytimes, both kept busy apart, working alongside their friends and neighbours to decorate and prepare for the annual Yuletide celebration. During the long curfewed evenings, they awkwardly focused on their own business projects in near silence. He missed their easy rapport; although they were both trying to care for each other with thoughtful gestures such as unexpected purchases of flowers, or a neatly pressed nightshirt laid out on the bed, the lack of a truthful discussion began to weigh heavy between them. It wasn't often that they argued, let alone avoided talking about concerns, but on this occasion, each had different reasons for the avoidance.

During the work days, each tried in their own ways to enquire about the history of Lady Hanley. Annabella's information gathering had been less than successful; the ladies were more inclined to gossip about the fashions her Ladyship favoured and ask her questions about Hanley House instead. Trying to hide her discomfort, she was forced to keep her own replies brief and elusive. This meant the women, in turn, didn't offer up much knowledge either. Few had visited the mansion, and that was what they all really wanted to know about; the gossips had nothing solid to reveal about its occupant.

That afternoon, the couple were changing clothes in silence, ready to attend the Yuletide Fayre. Joshua, determined to set a time frame on their impasse, remarked almost casually, "Maybe after the festivities, we can share what we have heard about the Lady Hanley?"

Annabella stiffened as she adjusted her cloak fastening. "I'm not sure I have much to tell," she said lightly.

Joshua had little choice but to let it lie for now. He busied himself pulling on his boots, yanking the laces as tight as his lips were pressed. He was miserable.

"Hurry up," she said, her voice impatient. She passed him his cloak and helped him fasten it, then took his hand and squeezed as if to apologise for her snappiness. Despite himself, Joshua softened. They had been looking forward to enjoying the ambiance of the celebration and he wasn't surprised at all that she was keen to get going. The energy they hoped to draw from humans was a different kind of fulfilment from the Lifeforce they required to survive, but equally alluring and intoxicating to them. In order to drink it in, they needed to be in the midst of throngs of emotionally charged people.

The air outside was crisp and still yet released the scent of warmed spiced ale and spit-turned meat. Annabella and Joshua hurried towards the sounds of music and laughter which carried along the roads, inviting one and all to join the festivities. Passing open-fronted shop windows purveying a brisk trade in pies and bunches of wintery smelling herbs, Joshua raised an arm in greeting to William as they went by the forge. A small crowd of men stood around laughing as they supped the warm ale William was selling from a large cauldron next to his fire.

Joshua and Annabella paused to see what was so funny, but they quickly realised it was just the japes of one man impersonating another, fueled by an early start on the brew. Joshua passed some pennies to William in return for a fill-up of their cups, which they had tied to their waists on slim cords. Joshua politely nodded thanks, before they set off up the road again towards the clamour of crowds in the square.

On the green, the small stage which Joshua had helped construct earlier in the day was now home to a rag-tag band of player-musicians. They traversed the country frequently, bringing with them ditties and news from afar. In return for a meal and a warm bed at the inn, they sometimes played of an evening before moving on the next day. This particular band was apparently a regular feature at the Yuletide festival and had been in residence for a week, preparing some play-scenes as well as warming up the crowd for their big performance that afternoon. They would be financially rewarded by the Abbey as long as they also included enough hymns and religious messages alongside the entertainment.

Annabella drew Joshua closer to the stage, but lurked in the crowd so that she could study them. The band turned out to have nine players, ranging from teenagers to the inevitable patriarch of the group in his mid-fifties. At this point in the festivities, they were wearing no stage make up. This was important to the couple - to ascertain if they had seen them before or not. Travelling players had amazing memories, and if they happened to have appeared at festivals in other parts of the country where Joshua and Annabella had also been, there was a risk of them being recognised.

"I think the blond boy is familiar," Annabella said, after a few minutes of discreet observation.

"No," Joshua said with conviction. "He's similar to the player in Aylesbury you are thinking of, but younger. He can't be the same person."

Annabella looked down as a small chilly hand filled hers, and a green knitted capped head appeared by her elbow. "Alice! How lovely to see you!" She smiled down at the child who had snuck up through the crowd.

"Mama said you would be here, lis'ning to them play," the girl lisped back, little pearly teeth a stark white against her red cheeks and nose.

Annabella and Joshua looked around and spotted Margaret in the crowd, waving to them. Joshua lifted his still steaming cup to her and gestured down towards Alice as if to say, 'she's here and all is well.' The band finished the song to a smattering of good-natured applause, then launched into a jollier tune. All about the crowds started bobbing and swaying along, break-away groups of people danced in pairs or fours, clapping their hands and stamping their feet in time to the well-known melody.

Annabella and Joshua breathed in the atmosphere of the celebrations as they spun in a circle, laughing as they 'flew' Alice with their arms. Drawing the energy from the surrounding crowd, this was a much-needed injection of the vitality of humankind. They moved, like addicts, within the masses, drunk on life itself, dancing with strangers and mingling with neighbours alike.

During a break, a few rousing songs later, Joshua realised Annabella and Alice weren't next to him any longer. He looked around at the throng of people, most now panting from exertion or moving away to purchase more refreshments. He stood on his tiptoes to see over their heads, looking for Annabella's brown bonnet. The crowd was thinning, and he quelled his initial panic at her disappearance by telling himself she was probably just talking to a neighbour on the fringes of the green.

He picked his way past clusters of laughing people

slapping their shoulders in mirth, already merry with ale and dance. Family groups played at stalls offering small food prizes for downing apples from spikes with catapults, children darting in and out of legs and skirts. Reaching the road to the side of the square, he pushed through the throngs, brushing against them and knocking pomade boxes, releasing spicy scents of nutmeg and cloves in his wake. His progress down the main street was further impeded by a large gathering of wassailers, preparing to spread the seasons' good cheer by offering blessings to households later that evening, whether they were welcome or not. Tall crowns of pheasants' feathers perched on their heads, affording them extra height. Problematically for Joshua, their costumes obscured the view ahead.

He couldn't see her. Covered in a neutral brown cape and bonnet so typical of women in town, he had to almost pause to look in everyone's faces to check it wasn't Annabella. He took a deep, calming breath and carried on searching, moving along the row of shops and houses.

He pulled up short when a man blocked his way. Mr Bray. Joshua looked wildly around him to see if Lady Hanley was also in attendance. He could see no sign of her, but his heart began to race regardless. As he made to dodge past the dark-coated obstruction, Joshua realised Mr Bray was studying him with his head slightly tilted and eyes narrowed.

"Have yer lost something, Master Meadows?"

Joshua noted the tone of concern in his voice; it did nothing to quell his rising panic. But then, from a passageway close by, a scream pierced the air. The sound carried like a dagger to him, cutting through the babble of the crowd. It turned into a wail and Joshua spun around to the direction it originated. Fear tightened his throat. He rushed towards the alley, Mr Bray followed.

A middle-aged woman Joshua didn't recognise crouched over a knobbly bundle in the muddy passage. Her wails continued as her hands shook, hovering over the air above the form in horror, not touching it. Approaching slowly, Joshua briefly closed his eyes in thanks - the lump was far too small to be Annabella. Relief turned to shock as he looked closer.

Beneath a torn and tatty dress, the skin had been pulled so taut over the body it was practically desiccated. A skeleton, its bones barely covered. The tiny head was pale, so pale. Joshua recognised the hair and the small nose, upturned even in death. His heart almost broke at the thought of the pain this would cause. Poor little Alice.

Mr Bray gently pulled the wailing woman up and away from the body and passed her to others who were hovering, crowding the passageway. He looked down over Joshua crouching over Alice, his eyes darting about the damaged body. Joshua looked up at him, not sure what expression he expected to see, but he had to know. Mr Bray's cool brown eyes shifted to meet Joshua's, now filling with tears.

"Well, this is a pretty pickle, eh?" Mr Bray said calmly, no tangible emotion in his voice which Joshua could discern. No accusation at least, he noted mentally with some relief. Joshua knew only two kinds of creatures which could leave bodies like this, drained of all life. And there were only three fae in this town, as far as he knew. Was Mr Bray aware of his Mistress's secret?

From the entrance to the passageway, shouts could be heard as people raised the alarm. Joshua was now trapped. Pinned with a corpse and a man of respectable repute, there was no possibility he could leave without it looking like the actions of a guilty party.

He spun around on his heels, searching the ground. Half buried in the mud, he spotted the fallen green cap Alice had been wearing. An imprint of a boot had pushed it down into the sludge, trapping it in situ. The size and shape of it suggested the owner was a male, but a quick glance at his own and Mr Bray's feet confirmed it was too slim to be their own.

Joshua slowly stood up, his eyes still searching in the dimming light for anything else. Mr Bray, understanding what he was doing, also started to look around the passageway. "Stand back," Bray ordered the approaching people, and he held out his hand in warning. Joshua walked further down the mud, looking where he placed his foot before stepping along the sides of the alley, as he scanned the stone walls.

Only a few strides later, he spotted a slender tuft of brown wool. The colour was the same as Annabella's cape, snagged on a roughened corner of the wall. Carefully, he plucked it off and raised it to his nose. The scent of his lover was faint but discernible to his heightened senses.

She had been here. With Alice. He raised his nose again, smelling the air, the walls, the mud. There was more, something else he couldn't quite place - iron from the few droplets of Alice's blood on the ground was almost overwhelming it.

Joshua was aware that Mr Bray was appraising him as he stood, absorbing tainted air as he tried to place the strange yet oddly familiar scent.

"I ask again, Mr Meadows, have yer lost something?" Mr Bray's tone had turned chilling.

Reaching out with his mind, Joshua could still sense Annabella was close, but where? He also felt a tinge of panic about the faint connection. Tainted with fear somehow. Without realising he had said it, Joshua breathed "Annabella," before turning, running down the passage.

*****

Bursting through their shop door, Joshua called out hoarsely, "Annabella! Annabella!" He rushed up the wooden stairs with no thought for the bangs his feet made against the wood. He had run through the back streets and managed to avoid the crowds, who were probably by now in uproar as word of the discovery spread. Time was not on his side, Mr Bray would surely have raised the alarm about Annabella being missing. Back at the passage, the look in the man's eyes confirmed he had suspicions. Like an idiot, by running he had endorsed them. He was furious with himself, and Annabella. Before long, it was highly likely an angry mob would be banging on their door and they must be prepared to flee.

"Annabella!" He shouted again; she was nowhere to be seen inside their bedroom either. He flung open the chest and started grabbing at clothes, papers and the plate to push into one of their bags. Downstairs, he grabbed his rolls of tools and the little travel bag Annabella used for threads and fastenings, stuffing it all together into their largest leather sack. Slinging it over his shoulders, he ran out of the door and pulled it tight behind him, if only to slow the mob down slightly when they inevitably descended. Glancing down the street, he was relieved to see it still empty of people. Word of their complicity in murder must not have gotten out yet. He jogged towards the woods, his mind whirling with desperate questions and worries.

His pace slowed as he reached the edge of the forest. A drizzle had started, and the mud was thickening, pulling on his boots. As he walked, he kept sniffing the air like a dog. He hadn't fully formed a plan except he had an inkling - if she wasn't at home, Annabella might have come out of town to connect with nature and ground herself after the meal she had just had. He could barely make out her scent but, he thought as he grew closer to her, it would grow stronger, guide him.

Despite his anger, there was no question in his mind that he would follow her, find her and leave with her. But killing a child? Very rarely did they completely drain a human. Only in extreme circumstances, under threat and being pursued, had they resorted to it before. What threat could the child have been?

Perhaps he hadn't realised the connection which Annabella had made with Alice? Fully draining wasn't at all necessary, and it shocked him that Annabella could have lost so much control. In truth, he was also hurt - he too had taken a shine to little Alice, to all the Tunn family. His wife had been even more foolish - unlike her - to so prominently display her mistake.

They had no choice now but to leave. He was resigned to it, but he wished he had had more time to prepare themselves as usual for a clear departure. Wished he had more time to consider their options, how best to depart. But the unravelling of events this afternoon had been too hasty, forcing a decision before they had discussed likely outcomes.

As he stomped, mulling the situation in his mind, the more he realised how out of character leaving the exposed body had been. How peculiar. Burying the corpses was second nature to them - almost ritualistic. Unless she had been disturbed, just as she was sated?

He reached the clearing they often frequented to stretch their wings. The sunlight had almost gone now and the last stretches of the light were filtering through the evergreens, casting deep shadows through the drizzle. There was no-one else there.

"Annabella!" Joshua called out. He tensed, listening for a reply. To his left, birds squawked and then, with a sudden flapping noise, chattered angrily in the air as the flock moved up and away from their roosting tree. He spun around; the avians sounded disturbed, and by more than his shout.

Joshua dropped the sack to the ground and hurriedly took off his jacket and shirt to free his wings. Listening carefully as he worked, he kept his wings lowered, packing his coat and putting on his cape so he could fly if necessary. Movement was more restricted by lugging bags, but he reminded himself he wasn't hunting a prey that wanted to run, but Annabella - who he hoped would be pleased to see him.

His sensitive ears picked up a rustle in the distance, hunter's instinct already on high alert. Although it could be a deer or hog, he fancied it sounded larger, so he followed that direction. He carefully tracked through the forest, only being quiet so that he could be more aware of his surroundings and pinpoint her location better.

It was slow progress and, as he slipped past dripping trees, he wondered if he should perhaps double back and find a pathway rather than be guided by the direction of the noises he was certain he heard ahead. A definite crack of a branch close by reassured him that he was getting nearer to his quarry.

Then, muffled sounds. Annabella's pitch! His nose immediately picked up her aura, and he frowned, identifying a sour tinge to her unique smell. He froze, eyes shooting through the dim spaces between the trees as he listened. He tried again with his mind to reach her, but there was something blocking it now, entirely. There was that other unfamiliar scent also, much stronger than Annabella's. His heart quickened and then sped up even more when he heard the awful sound of fabric ripping. Joshua gave up on stealth and started running, dodging between the thick trunks of trees as he pushed his way through the fauna to reach her.

As much as he tried to hurry, his ears were filled with the increasingly desperate noises made by Annabella competing with the noise of branches and undergrowth snapping as he pushed his path through. Panic began to set in and his breath grew ragged. He didn't want to call out as he realised Annabella was not alone. How had the townsfolk had found her before he had?

He was close now, the acidic scent of fear overwhelming. He could hear Annabella clearly grunting and trying to struggle against something. More fabric being torn.... Joshua pushed himself in between two large conifers obscuring his view and burst out into another clearing.

Annabella was pinned to her knees, held down by two larger fae with brown wings already primed for flight. Her hands were bound tightly behind her as the fae wrestled her elbows away from her back, tearing the fastenings of her dress and smock to pull out her wings. His beautiful, brave lover was wriggling, arching her back in pain, trying to stop her captors from pulling at the delicate limbs. She turned her head and locked her vivid blue eyes desperately with Joshua as he appeared. A tight gag covered the lower half of her face - he could only just see her eyes, wild and desperate through her hair, tangled and floating around her head.

Without hesitation, Joshua charged. He had barely taken a few steps when he was intercepted by a body blow, throwing him to the mossy woodland floor. Of a singular intention to reach his love, Joshua had not noticed anyone else when he had come crashing through the trees. But this airborne fae then landed hard on his chest, pushing him further into the soft earth and pinning him down.

Joshua's ribcage audibly cracked at the sudden weight and pressure, all air pushed from his lungs. Wings squashed into the earth - a sharp stabbing pain in the right one flashed the thought to him that it was likely broken.

Joshua's head snapped around to glare at his assailant - a finely balanced pale face with a long nose and clear blue eyes much like Annabella's victoriously smirked back. A silver arm-guard, engraved and shining, smashed at the side of Joshua's face. Slowly returning his head to look at him after the glancing blow, Joshua realised that the fae's skin glowed - the glow of a recent meal. The fae's mouth twisted into a sneering smile. Joshua tipped his head back, trying desperately to pull air into himself. The sneer widened and fingers clenched around his exposed throat. The pressure tightened just below his ears.

Despite Joshua's predicament, his arrival spurred Annabella into renewed resistance. She managed to shake off one aggressor and tried to fling her body towards Joshua's. The distance was too great to reach him. With a muffled howl of frustration, she kicked out at the other assailant still holding her elbow. The fae clung onto her arm despite doubling over in pain from her kick.

He pushed her back down onto the ground. Annabella's face crumpled, staring at Joshua in horror, held down by the fae's knee. The blond-haired fae sitting on top of Joshua drew out a dagger from his shin-guard and held it to Joshua's throat. He leaned in to apply maximum pressure to the vulnerable flesh. Narrowed dark eyes challenged Annabella, daring her to try to resist again under the threat of Joshua's life.

The fae who had lost his hold on Annabella scrambled to his feet. His boots slipped on the moss as he rose - his foot kicking Joshua hard in the head. Joshua's ear screamed in pain. His eyes felt like they would pop from their sockets as the pressure built behind them following the blow. But that was the least of his concerns.

Desperately clinging to consciousness, Joshua tried once again to raise his head, but the knife against his neck had slashed deep when the kick occurred. Warm blood started to trickle down his collar. With every rapid heartbeat, he could feel more pulsing out. A cool hand released his throat but moved to his jaw, pinning his skull to the cold ground, keeping the slash wound open.

Through the descending haze, he kept reaching for Annabella but his hands were trapped by the calf-length boots of the captor astride his chest. The battle for air faded in significance, as his mind realised the wound on his neck was more dangerous. A seductive darkness called to him, telling him to close his eyes. With his exposed ear, he could still make out Annabella's muffled cries, but he could barely make out the forms of the bodies wrestling with her.

A surge of desperation pushed him to keep fighting. With every muscle screaming, he urged his limbs to twist away, escape the force pinning him down. On his face, felt the wind of wings beating, applying pressure onto his chest, resisting all his puny attempts to free himself. Joshua's body rebelled, refusing to try anymore. He could feel his extremities no more.

Then, all he could think about was the dripping - the warm blood from his neck an unwelcome contrast to the encroaching chill sweeping up, deep inside his body.

A delicate clink of metal broke his reverie, and Annabella cried out again - was it his name? A gust blew over his exposed skin, as if that was where all his senses started and ended. Joshua thought he heard the buzzing flutter of wings. His eyes widened, focusing as best he could on three hazy figures rising out of the clearing as one clump. Annabella's calls began to fade as darkness replaced the loss of his light. He barely noticed when the pressure lifted from his chest, as he sank into the quiet embrace of the void.

CHAPTER 8 – HOMECOMING

Annabella's fingers flexed. She felt earthy dust rake in her fingernails. Her eyes flew open, and she understood her face was pressed against the dirt. The dank smell from the ground clogged in her throat as she gulped, but there was no avoiding breathing in. In the absolute darkness, even her enhanced eyesight couldn't make out much of the space she occupied. She stretched her legs, hearing the whisper of fine, strong metal ropes pulling along through the floor-bolts as she tried to manoeuvre herself into a position where she could sit. Her hands were still bound at the wrist, aching from the strain. As consciousness and her senses returned to her, she realised her whole body ached.

The smell told her where she was. Home. Naturae. Only there could you find that peculiar tang of peaty decay. Worse yet, she knew precisely where at home she was.

In the Beneath.

Where the impure were kept. Where they would never be found nor see sunlight again. Where they died.

Oh! And Joshua!

A sob escaped her lips as she remembered how he had tracked her, fought for her, and then been left. Dead.

Was he? She reached out with her mind for him. Nothing. A void.

She'd smelt his blood, seen how much of it had pumped out - no-one could survive that loss. Battered, held down and then slashed by her own brother Lyrus. She knew he would have finished the job. Killed without thought for who he was, like an animal he'd hunted. Although Lyrus must have known he was significant to her, ultimately it hadn't mattered.

The guttural moan emanating from her broken heart filled the chamber and echoed back at her as if to further enhance her sorrow. She had never known such paralysing pain as swamped her entire body now; her heart burning; she collapsed onto the earth in agony. Her mind's eye played images of his dreadful death - his body broken and abused, and then the wrench of being pulled away, leaving him alone there.

She yearned to join him in dying, for surely that would be better than this unbearable pain. Annabella began wailing and thrashing against the chains that bound her legs and hands, pulling to vent the inner agony as well as testing how far they would stretch. Her wings were now tied together, clamped at the top ridge with a cuff. Every movement she made with them sent shock waves rippling down her spine and around her chest. She wriggled and pulled ever more violently until she passed out, dropping to the floor as her mind tried to reprieve her by shutting down.

*****

When she woke again, Annabella was in a wooden chair, her body bound tightly to the frame. Through her closed eyelids she sensed she was out of the Beneath, somewhere lighter. Yet she kept her eyes firmly shut, unwilling to let anyone see her pain. Childlike - if she couldn't see them, they couldn't see her. As her waking thought had been of Joshua, before she even realised she was making the noise, she moaned again. Tears spilled unbidden from her eyes and she sobbed quietly.

"Pitiful," a familiar voice spat. "That you should waste your precious tears."

Annabella didn't look up. There was no need to visually confirm who she knew was speaking.

"Should I put you back Beneath until you have regained some measure of control over yourself, child?"

The sobs just wouldn't stop coming. Her chest began to ache from heaving against the bindings.

"Take her back down," the imperious voice commanded. "I will see no more of her today. Maybe by tomorrow, she will be reasonable."

Annabella felt smooth, cool hands under her arms, lifting her chair and all. She squeezed her eyes tightly shut, refusing to follow the ornate and familiar surroundings as they carried her down again. She would rather be alone in the cold confines of the Beneath with her sorrows. Rather be anywhere but where she was. Naturae was no longer her home. Joshua had been. And now he was gone. In that moment, she again wished there would be no more tomorrows to face without him.

They set her down, back in the cell, and loosened the bindings holding her down. The light chains fell with a soft whisper to the dust, sending particles of the peaty floor up to her nostrils. Annabella heard the dull click of the lock closing and then silence. The chill of the deep, dark earth seeped into her bones. She sat stock still, her head bowed, a tangle of hair falling over her face. Her mind became numb as her yearning for a release from her own body overtook her. One abiding thought crystallised.

The realisation that one's own death meant freedom from this earthly pain dawned. It nagged at her, refusing to be dispelled by the shaking of her head. With no-one to condole with her, no-one to tell her to force nonsense from her mind, the weed-like thought took root.

Nudging her consciousness into considering the possibilities, memories of Joshua intruded. Unwelcome, stained by her agonising loss. And insistent in the darkness.

She remembered when they had first truly met - having already run away as lovers and his turning. After some weeks of living in hiding, exploring his new form and its needs and limitations, Joshua had broken down, unable to align his new condition with his expectations for after life. That she had no 'faith', no belief system at all to speak of, was something of an anathema to him. She had almost lost him over it. Her failure to understand what he was going through almost cost her their partnership.

She recalled the early days after his conversion to Fae, how he would sit penitently like she was now, head bowed. But, he was in prayer, a habit he lost many decades ago. At the time, he said he was praying for their mortal souls, for forgiveness for their sins. He had wanted to go to a church, make confession to a priest. He knew that what he would be confessing to was unbelievable. He would be considered a liar.

Although he wouldn't have been lying, their very existence as different beings was ignored in every holy word. He thought that no priest could have been convinced he was telling the truth without literally exposing his new body as well as the fears in his heart. The realisation that he could never expose what he now was to anyone, not even in the sanctuary of a confessional, was the root of his despair. Humans, it seemed, were built to share.

Except, there were some priests who might have understood. Some were eternal beings themselves. She knew enough of Fae history to understand what the vampires had done after the Blood Wars. How they had shaped the new Christian religion and tailored it to their own needs. How Joshua's own, deep-rooted faith, was in fact, shaped by soulless beings who craved blood as much as faekind craved Lifeforce.

However, she had never told Joshua the truth about his branch of faith. Not even in his darkest moments, for fear it would send him into a deeper spiral of woe. She herself had wrestled with her conscience on this, longing to help heal him, yet aware that the reality could cause him irreparable damage. There were no right answers.

Frowning to herself, questioning why her mind seemed determined to make her think about that period, she reached for more of her memories. For countless days, he had sat like she was now, bowed in a chair, unmoving. The conflicts Joshua felt, his fears for their eternal damnation in the event of their death, were very real to him. The daily rituals of a practising Catholic, which she didn't see the need for, were a routine. She hadn't realised the significance of them for him when she first suggested their escape. During this dark time, she came to understand just how different Fae and human were in their daily lives.

At the time, they had argued, cried together, and failed to reach a mutually satisfactory conclusion over what the future held for them. Joshua had questioned if she even had a soul to be concerned about, and that worry remained with her for some years. The question resurfaced now, clutching the warm wooden sides of the chair as if grasping something solid would reveal the invisible. As soon as he had asked of her soul, in the heat of an argument, he had answered himself immediately with 'Of course you must have, because how can one love without a soul?' She had no answer to it, even now. With no-one to provide them with explanations, inevitably, they stopped discussing it.

It took years of her occasionally altering their routine for him to realise that there was no difference if he did or didn't follow the rules of his faith on that given day. And, gradually, he had seemed to stop thinking about the consequences of what they did in this life affecting their 'after' life. Even though the Bible hinted at immortality on another plane of existence, decades when their own bodies didn't age eased his acceptance of this aspect of being fae.

In turn, she had realised that in order to pass for human, there were some necessary routines. Grounding them in the current faith like a costume to wear. So, she learnt to don the mantle of a faithful and God-fearing wife, to facilitate their existence. But, it was just a costume, cloaking who they really were.

Focusing on the present, on survival, was their salvation as a couple. Talk of their future was relegated to the next day, the next week even, with no sense of it ever ending. They became comfortable with their habit of fleeing danger, under threat of discovery. No matter how hard it was to be caught in the cycle of starting over, they began to believe in each other, rather than something intangible like a god. They didn't let each other down; there was always another place, another opportunity, as long as they were together.

One night, under a full moon, sated by a midsummer's feast, they had pledged themselves to one another for eternity. Without having planned the emotional exchange, they promised to live in the moment always. This 'wedding' (as they later called it, to give it legitimacy and name the event) signalled the end of Joshua's belief in the church's teachings. And, she realised, the beginning of her belief. Her faith in him, and them. Annabella smiled at the memory of that night. It warmed her in the chill of the Beneath - that such a promise had led to so much happiness. At the time.

But now, her faith had been torn away from her, ripping the soul Joshua said she had away with him. His death helped her understand the depths of his pain as he had questioned over and over what happens after life, now he that was Fae. At the time, she simply hadn't understood. If you have no faith, you lose nothing when it's gone. But this, this feeling of emptiness inside, this was the absence of faith and it was terrible. So terrible she couldn't bear it. And certainly not for eternity.

She wanted to die. She yearned to be free, not just of this prison, but of her own pain and loss. Her heart broke again every time she thought of the strength Joshua must have had when facing this very concern. Her body responded to her mind's need to shrink into itself and become small.

Annabella felt herself falling, unbalanced as she contracted her limbs around her. She allowed herself to tip from the chair, then land with a dull thump on the earth. She curled into a ball and squeezed her eyes shut.

Strangely comforted that her mind had provided her with the solution to the pain, it now turned to practicalities. The notion of dying was something she simply hadn't given much thought to. Fae lived eternally, unless their life was cut short by someone killing them. It was almost impossible to kill oneself. The lust for Lifeforce became all-consuming, uncontrollable. The need to sustain one's body was a primal instinct; the urge to feed grew to a point where it was violent, overwhelming, and she had never really tried to resist it.

But now, she could see the courage it would take to fight that instinct. And that was what she wanted to do. Joshua's old faith inspired her - fasting, suppressing that compulsion to survive, would bring her closer to him, to death. And maybe, with it, the release from this terrible pain.

The decision came as a relief.

Screwing her eyes up, Annabella realised that they were finally dry. She refused to let herself worry about what happened after that. It didn't matter, only that this pain ceased. All her life she hadn't seriously considered what there was after life. Heaven, Hell, Purgatory - these were church constructs to keep people obeying the rules, and to her mind they were meaningless. She had seen enough death in her life, watched enough lifeless corpses of animals, to see that there was nothing after life. Once the spirit is gone, only a husk remains.

Of course, she had never actually seen a fae die, but she assumed it would be the same as for any other animal or human. Fragments of a life lived which would eventually rot into the earth which sustained the body, to give life once more to another. This was the cycle of nature and evidenced all around her.

A husk is what she decided to become. In the darkness, she smiled to herself.

CHAPTER 9 - A GILDED CAGE

Joshua became aware of being dragged, half carried, but he was so cold he could not define his whereabouts. There were two men hauling him - he could smell their sweaty exertion. The scent of blood alluringly close distracted from the rain pelting down on the backs of his legs as they tugged him through the woods. Each breath he took was painful, so he had to breathe shallowly when he was cognisant. He kept fading in and out of consciousness, groaning as he came to. Pain from his chest and his head made his vision swim and he would quickly lapse into unconsciousness again.

Manhandled into surroundings which were blessedly warmer, he roused a little more, and opened his eyes. The room started to fade around him, but not before he recognised that he was looking at somewhat familiar kitchen table legs. He snapped himself back into awareness and tried to raise his head. The movement caused a stabbing pain in his neck to suddenly increase, but his vision blurred before he could see detail. He passed out again.

*****

"We will have to get his wet clothes off before we take him upstairs," Lady Hanley said, standing next to the kitchen table before she moved to close the door behind them. Mr Bray nodded towards the scissors hanging on a nail by the fireside, too out of breath to speak. Lady

Hanley bustled about the trio and tried to help by pulling his shirt fully loose from his trousers.

"Lean him on me," the monk said, his voice low and melodious. He then rearranged his clasp so he was holding Joshua in an upright embrace, hands linked together around the dead weight of his torso.

Lady Hanley took the scissors, snipped the fastening of the sodden cloak around Joshua's neck. Carefully, she peeled its heaviness from his back. Her mouth dropped as she exposed the huge wings underneath. The right one was kinked at a horrible angle, tattered beneath the blood and mud smeared on the lace-like panes.

The monk's mouth tightened as their eyes met. "Puts a different complexion on the matter, doesn't it?"

Mr Bray stood back, shock and scepticism conflicting across his drawn face. Turning away as if he could not bear to witness any more of the peculiar sight, he escaped to the hearth to prepare a jug of warming water. The monk heaved Joshua up from his chest so Lady Hanley could cut away the front of his shirt.

Joshua moaned as the movement pushed together his broken ribs and sternum. The swelling was already discoloured with an enormous hematoma spread across Joshua's broad torso. His neck wound they left bandaged with the strip of black cassock Maister Jeffries had used for now. The rag was dripping with blood seepage and would need delicate but firm pressure on it to stop.

Lady Hanley stepped back to appraise the damage. "Take him upstairs," she said, beckoning Mr Bray. "I'll bring warm water to wash away the blood, then we can see what could be done to help. Maister Jeffries?"

"I am already doubtful as to what I can treat," the monk responded, "but I will, of course, try." Joshua blacked out again.

*****

The smell of yarrow and sage hit his nostrils, comforting yet strange to him, and overwhelming. Joshua wrinkled his nose and tried to move his head away. "Calm now," he heard in a soft voice, and warm hands touched his cool skin. "Do not try to move." His eyes flew open in shock. Taking a moment to adjust to the dimness, gradually he focused enough to confirm his suspicions: Lady Hanley sat beside him.

Swivelling his eyes to take in as much as he could without moving, he realised he must be in Hanley House. Nowhere else locally would have such an ornate chamber. The bed canopy was a sumptuous red, its curtains tied back on the side but otherwise draped down to create a cosy enclosure about his bedding. The air smelled stale, cloying in his throat with the mixture of herbs, illness and smoke from an unseen fireplace.

"Water?" He croaked, but his voice sounded alien and thick. Lady Hanley guessed his meaning, picked up a carved cup and dribbled a little into his parched mouth. The liquid was tepid, bitter. Willowbark, his taste buds identified. It's been many, many years since I've needed that, he thought. More alert now, he realised the yarrow smell was emanating from an enormous thick poultice covering his entire rib cage. The warmth of it comforted, yet the weight of it meant he was still labouring to breathe.

"What you need is blood," Lady Hanley said. "Now you are awake, I will get fresh brought to you."

Joshua made to nod, but the slightest movement of his neck shot pains through him like stabbing knives. He realised his head was banging on one side, so he drew up his arm to rub it. Even in the low light, he could see his bare biceps were darkened with bruises. It ached to move, as if his limbs were weighted with lead to pin him in the sheets.

He tried to speak again, but Lady Hanley had left.

*****

The next time he awoke, he was not sure of how much time had passed, but the room was lighter. Tentatively, he sought to move his head. His neck sent searing warnings advising against it, but the urge to try overrode the physical protestations. Bearing down with his hands, he tried to push himself up the bed. A stabbing refusal from his biceps prevented him from holding his own weight. He collapsed back onto the pillow, panting shallowly.

The door opened and Mr Bray came in, his lips pinched together as he looked at the bed. He walked briskly to the bedside table and picked up the cup there to give to Joshua.

Joshua tried to meet his eyes in thanks, not even attempting to speak for he knew it would hurt until he had lubricated his throat. Avoiding his gaze, the old steward grunted something to himself, before turning stiffly on his heel and leaving again.

Joshua sipped - the liquid was even more bitter now that it was cold, but he knew willowbark would alleviate some of his agony. He slowly drained the cup. As his mind cleared, fragments of the events which had led to him being here rushed their way in.

As if being hit afresh in his chest with a crushing blow, he remembered Annabella, pinned down, reaching for him. The pain in his heart intensified as, to his disgust, he couldn't remember anything after that. His own aches told him that he was severely injured, but had she been?

What had happened to her?

He bit back a sob. The pain of not knowing what had transpired was tearing him apart, and his heart beat faster as he tried to quell a rising panic about her fate. With his mind he attempted to reach out, somehow touch hers for reassurance.

Nothing. Their connection seemed severed. A wall of loneliness hit him again in his rib cage - the pain of it made him blink and he moaned. The noise reminded him of the sound the stag had made as it died in their arms not days earlier. He could barely gasp a breath as his thoughts turned too quickly to the dreadful likelihood that she was gone. Taken from him. And very possibly dead. Unbidden tears rolled hot down his face. His hands found their way to clasp each other at his breast, as if binding them in prayer could help.

He lay there, the wetness of his tears soaking into the bedding and his fingers almost breaking his knuckles as they clenched so hard together. His foremost mind grew strangely blank as he tried to force his breath in and out of his broken chest.

He realised then that he was mentally praying to a deity he no longer thought he believed in, but there was no-one else to salve this deep anguish. His mouth began to form the lamentations of prayer, begging in a language of ritual to a god he had forsaken. Not pleading for his soul, however, but for Annabella's. Staring up at the red canopy, Joshua mumbled a liturgy as if his life depended on it.

The door opened once more, interrupting his whispered fervour. Lady Hanley approached and gazed down at him. He continued whispering, although the pace slowed as he reached the end of the Latin verse. His eyes slid up to meet hers as his lips mouthed the closing words.

Her face took on a kindly countenance as she heard the verses he was muttering under his breath. "Look, Maister Jeffries," she said victoriously as he stopped murmuring. "There is the proof I needed."

From behind her shoulder, a bald man wearing a black Benedictine habit peered at him. From his neck swung a large wooden cross upon a beaded necklace. His wrinkles and the swift manner of visually examining Joshua as he lay spoke of years of experience. Eyes which sparkled with intelligence met Joshua's and the monk offered a thin smile. Joshua felt both comforted and confused at his presence. Recognisable by smell - this was the other man who had helped bring him here, however long ago that had been.

"Now," Lady Hanley continued, her tone efficient, "I'm confident you will feel much better after a meal."

She bustled back to the doorway and returned to the bedside holding up a cage, simply fashioned from black iron. Joshua's heart quickened as he smelt its contents before being able to make out the form hidden inside the straw lining the base. Lady Hanley placed the cage on the bed and unclasped a little lid at the top. As she reached in and grasped the neck of the rabbit to pull out, its legs gave a slight flick in acknowledgement of the change in its surroundings. Swiftly, Lady Hanley brought her other hand up to hold its limbs still as she passed it towards Joshua. Holding the nape of its neck to his mouth, she nodded encouragingly.

Joshua raised his eyes to meet hers. Although the smell of the animal was undeniably alluring and his craving was almost too much to bear, how could he *feed* in front of her? In front of the monk? He was confused. Whilst he suspected the monk might have seen his wings, and even if Annabella had been correct about Lady Hanley being fae, it seemed improper to drain a live beast before them. Why was Lady Hanley deliberately exposing their fae nature to the monk?

Keeping his gaze, Lady Hanley pushed the rabbit closer to his lips again, and murmured, "Go on.... or do I need to puncture for you?"

Joshua lowered his eyes and, with as much control as he could muster, bit into the nape. He tried hard to drink slowly, neatly, but the rush of energy from its fresh blood consumed him. He sucked thirstily with ever-larger gulps. It took but moments, it seemed, for the rabbit's skin to shrivel, the bones crushed with the sudden pressure of his suck. All that remained was a crumpled ball of fur, tiny claws sticking out of the empty sack.

Lady Hanley removed the furball and replaced it in the cage, before drawing out another from the straw sanctuary. Slightly wild-eyed with the rush of Lifeforce he had ingested, Joshua lurched forwards, raising his hand to grab the second creature before it even had a chance to fear its fate. Caring less now about the messy sight he must be, the brown fur of the next rabbit was soon mottled with droplets of blood as he tore into its flesh. He drank deeply again, slowing to savour the last moments of liquid before allowing his head to back onto the pillows.

His heart thudded almost painfully in his chest, but he could already feel the easing within his limbs. He closed his eyes. The exaltation of the Lifeforce continued to course around him, tempered with shame and sorrow. Joshua's face crumpled as he squeezed his eyelids tightly shut in a vain attempt to stop the tears from flowing again.

"You must rest further," Lady Hanley said as she turned to leave.

Jeffries sniffed the air close to Joshua, before turning to Lady Hanley. "I will need to change the poultice." Joshua had the disconcerting feeling that the monk was almost tasting something - his face looked distracted, nervous even. Jeffries turned towards the door and muttered to Lady Hanley as if Joshua were not even present, "He will still be in pain. Lifeforce cannot heal broken bones, only time can do that."

Nor can it heal a broken heart, thought Joshua, and now there is all the time in the world to feel its ever-present torment. He turned over in the bed. His chest screamed in objection but he couldn't bear to keep his face upturned for all to see as he sobbed into the pillow.

*****

Lady Hanley brought him many more rabbits in the days that followed. Each time she came, and as he grew stronger, he tried to press her for answers to the many questions he had. In response, she told him to rest, explaining he needed to heal, and avoiding his requests for information of any sort. Her manner was always courteous, and he was very aware he was a guest who was wholly dependent on her kind nature. Joshua struggled to overcome his innate respect for his superiors, so kept his questions polite, but his frustration grew.

Lying awake for longer periods, his ears picked up little by way of noise about the House. He began to form the opinion that there was only himself, Mr Bray and Lady Hanley in residence. No servants appeared to light the fire, it just seemed to be constantly warm in the room. He had only a passing concept of time of day, for the room remained a barely fluctuating dim. Occasionally, Mr Bray would silently appear, ignoring all conversation Joshua might attempt, to presumably report whether he was still alive or not, awake or fitfully asleep.

He managed, after what he surmised could only have been a few days of recuperation, to haul himself to upright without his head spinning too much. His first action was definitively human in nature, and there was no small amount of relief in using the chamber pot next to the bed. The exertion of standing and breathing - with the thick poultice Lady Hanley insisted he kept on underneath tight bandages - made moving difficult. For a moment, he was tempted to collapse back into the warm sheets. But, he reasoned to himself, there was nothing the matter with his legs now - he should use them.

Leaning first against the bed frame, he lurched himself towards the doorway. From there he could appraise the room, which had been hidden by the drapes surrounding his bed until now. There were no pictures or decorations, just warm, ochre yellow walls, with a light oak panelling rising halfway up. Joshua found himself impressed by the simple elegance of the design. The window was firmly shut against the cold, only one inner shutter partially ajar, letting in a thin stream of sunlight to slice through the dim.

He turned to the door, expecting to be able to swing it open easily and as silently as it had opened for his hostess, but to his horror, there was no handle. Where a latch should have been there was only tiny screw-holes. With his fingers, he tried to pull the edges of the wood, but the gap was too narrow, flush to the frame. Then he tried - pinching at the sides of the panels and hooking his fingernails under the beading, to drag it open, but to no avail. The door stayed firmly shut.

Joshua walked carefully over the faded woven rug at the foot of the bed, the floorboard creaking slightly with his weight, and made to examine the shutters and window. The vista was breathtaking, but he gave it no more than a passing glance before examining the metalwork on the frame. Although hinged, and with delicate latches holding the leaded window fast, he could see on the outside there was a brace at the bottom of the sill - preventing the window from opening more than a few fingers wide.

It was a prison. A beautiful, well-appointed prison.

*****

In the darkness of dawn, Joshua reached his decision. Dressed only in a borrowed nightshirt, Joshua knew he wasn't in the most practical of clothing for his plan to work, but he could find no alternatives. His original clothes had not been returned. He positioned himself leaning against the wall near the doorframe, ready to carry out his next move. Waiting, listening for any sounds within the house other than his own breathing. As much as he could, he rolled his shoulder blades to loosen the tight bandages strapping down his wings. There were no utensils with which to cut them and free himself further, but in his mind he had a plan. Like a caged wild bird, he focussed only on one thing - escape.

He heard a slight creak of floorboards in the hallway outside, then silence. Joshua unconsciously held his breath, tensed for the tussle ahead. The pause seemed to go on forever - why were they not coming in? A chink of pottery, then the door silently swung open.

Joshua waited until the figure was halfway into the

room before he shoved it towards the bed and made to rush out of the doorway. He did not stop to look at the damage he inflicted - the crash of plates and splash of liquid told him the person was probably headed towards the floor as well. He immediately barrelled into Lady Hanley, stepping out of the gloom of the hallway.

"Stop!" She commanded, in that firm, imperious voice. "There is no need to flee. You are quite safe here."

He had made it half a stride out of the bedroom, but the exertion of raising his arms to push the entering figure was actually more painful, and had taken far more energy, than he had anticipated. Annoyed - mostly with himself - Joshua panted out, "It's not my safety I'm worried about! Why am I being kept a prisoner?"

Lady Hanley stared at him for a second before she spoke. "Then let's talk about what you are worried about. I expect you have many questions. As have I."

A reasonable response was not what Joshua had expected. Blinded by his grief, he had convinced himself that he would get no answers from her Ladyship, given she had avoided talking to him at all. The urge to run from danger was so innate, so exactly what Annabella would have done, he had become consumed by thoughts of freedom. He had decided his best and only option was to flee Hanley House and find out what he could about where she had been taken afterwards.

Frozen in the hallway, half of his mind screamed at him to push past her Ladyship, make haste with his plan and escape. The other half, ruled by the pain in his chest, refused to send the 'run' signal to the rest of his body.

The monk appeared by his side, his cassock darker with liquid now wasted on the floor. With a cross look on his gaunt face, he said, not without sarcasm, "Perhaps you

111

have time for me to examine your wounds before you go? Or is all of our care to be undone?" Maister Jeffries pursed his lips and shot a glance at Lady Hanley, silently sharing their scolding of the unwilling patient.

Joshua looked down in shame. Maybe he had been too hasty in this. Ungrateful even. If his room was indeed a prison, he had not so much as asked to leave. Although he wasn't sure why he had been placed in confinement, nothing about their actions towards him had actually shown malice or ill-treatment, he realised. In fact, they had almost certainly saved his life.

He mumbled an apology under his breath, not wishing to look up for fear they would see the disappointment and frustration which had sprung wet into his eyes. Feeling somewhat like a naughty child, he turned and sloped back into the bedroom and sat down on the bed. Breathing shallowly, for the pain was great, Joshua then submitted to the gentle hands pulling off his nightshirt. Lady Hanley moved into the room, observing as the sticky bandages were carefully unwound.

"I will need more warmed water," Maister Jeffries instructed Lady Hanley, breaking her trance. She nodded. "Mr Bray!" She called, looking to the doorway rather than meeting Joshua's eyes. After a few moments, there was a heavy clump of footsteps and Mr Bray appeared, his face a mask of neutrality. He took in the mess on the floor and Joshua's discomfort. Bray's thin lips curled up as if he had been expecting misbehaviour.

"Yer'll need more water 'fer it then?" His tone was sardonic.

"Yes, and then I think we will take refreshments in the library whilst this is cleared up," Lady Hanley said. She turned to the coverlet and began to pile the soiled bandages on to the tray. Mr Bray hesitated in the doorway, balefully staring at the wounds being exposed. Avoiding Joshua's eyes, the servant winced and recoiled when he saw the bloody crusting on his wings. Not knowing how badly they were injured, Joshua took this to mean the appendages behind him were in very bad shape.

Maister Jeffries continued wiping the dried poultice from Joshua's chest using the bandages he had just removed. "I will have to bind you again," he said slowly, his fingers beginning a painful examination of each of his ribs. Joshua realised this was the first time the monk had addressed him directly. "You will be more comfortable talking when strapped up."

"What of the poultice?" Lady Hanley asked. "Should we fetch more?"

In command now, Maister Jeffries nodded. "Mr Bray, the brown jar to the side of the hearth - perhaps you would be so kind as to bring it up." The servant, his lips pressed together then left without hesitation.

As Jeffries moved to wipe the foul-smelling mix from Joshua's back now, his deep voice dispassionately said, "Almost every bone in your chest was broken. They are still disconnected from the spine. The poultice and your own..." he paused, "healing ability, will help bring the swelling down so they can get into their rightful place. You must not twist your chest though. This morning's exertions have already moved the ribs out of position again."

Joshua could well believe it, for still every breath in was like fire pouring into his abdomen. He could feel that his rib cage was out of alignment, especially without the bandages to give it support. "My wings?" There was little point in beating around the bush with their existence.

"The right one is probably broken in several places and badly torn. The left, however, looks less damaged." Maister Jeffries didn't mince his words as he delivered the bad news.

"Will they heal?" Joshua asked, with an ache in his voice.

"That I do not know," the monk replied, not unkindly. "I am somewhat lacking in experience of these matters."

Lady Hanley laid a cool hand on Joshua's shoulder. "You could not be in more capable hands. Maister Jeffries is as skilled as it is possible to be outside of Naturae in healing fae."

"Naturae?" Joshua asked, confused.

"The Fae Queendom, of course?" She frowned.

Joshua looked at them, bewildered. Yet his hunger for knowledge restored his strength.

"There is much I would ask you both?" He put his hands down on the side of the bed, attempting to rise.

Maister Jeffries quickly placed his hand on Joshua's arm, preventing him. "Not yet," he said firmly, as Mr Bray reappeared bearing a jug and the poultice jar.

CHAPTER 10 -
UNTANGLING THE TRUTH

Maister Jeffries had bidden Joshua to hold his arms out so he could bind the chest once more after re-applying the smelly poultice. It stuck, claggy, to his wings as they were carefully positioned by Lady Hanley in readiness for the bandages. The whole experience had been very painful, even with Lady Hanley supporting one arm and with the other clinging onto the bed curtains as the monk focused on winding the linens around and round, encasing his torso entirely. The tight binding, however, gave him some relief once tied. Although he could not draw a deep breath, Joshua found he could pull in shallow breaths with more ease as the warmth of the herbs penetrated his skin.

They staggered their way as a threesome down the dark panelled hallway. Leaning more on Maister Jeffries for support, Joshua carefully descended the stairs. When the pain from breathing and moving got too much and made his head swim, he would pause to gather himself, before focusing once again on putting one foot in front of another to plod along the corridor. Lady Hanley extricated herself from Joshua to open the door at the end of the passage.

Annabella had previously described the room they entered, but she was perhaps more accustomed to lavish surroundings than Joshua. The sheer number of books was astounding to him, lining almost an entire wall. Some bookcases held bound tomes of vellum - he could smell their acidic tang and even identify the beasts from which they were made. Other shelves housed tightly wound scrolls, neat tags dangling from the wooden pole ends with handwritten titles on.

A crackling fireplace at the far end cheerfully invited them to share its warmth. On a low table close by, two jugs of warmed liquid sent tantalising spirals of scent into the air. Wine and willow bark tea - Joshua's spirits roused at the prospect of some pain relief. His senses were in danger of being overloaded at the change of scenery.

Behind one of the wing-backed chairs facing the fire, the little cage had been placed. A rabbit snoozed in the straw, its tail all that was visible. Joshua was struck by how thoughtfully they were accommodating his recovery. By simply leaving his chamber, the house became less of a prison, and he desperately wanted to just sink into his cosy surroundings and be at ease. But he could not relax, nor let his guard down. Years of running had taught him so.

Maister Jeffries supported Joshua's arm as he gingerly sat down in the nearest chair. Oh, but it was comfortable! Lady Hanley pushed a feather filled cushion behind him as he leaned back into the nestling embrace with a grimace. Jeffries pulled over the high-backed wooden chair from the desk and shook his arms free of tension before sitting. As if assisting Joshua had been no labour at all, the mistress of the house perched on the edge of the easy armchair.

"Joshua," Lady Hanley began, "I would ask about your creation." She studied his face for a reaction as he stared into the fireplace.

The flames reminded him of the last time he and Annabella had sat so comfortably together in their little shop, the night before the fayre. Then Joshua realised he wasn't even entirely certain how long ago that had been, and the sorrow in his heart threatened to rise within him.

Trying to keep his voice steady, Joshua said, "I would know about what happened to my wife."

Lady Hanley looked down at her hands. Realising they were empty, she stood once more to pour him the willow bark tea. Joshua let the silence hang.

Maister Jeffries chuckled, breaking the sudden ominous threat hanging in the room. "I too would like to know, both of these things and more!"

"How are you here?" asked Joshua, realising that the monk's continued presence in a private house was against usual protocol. Surely he was supposed to be at the Abbey?

"Maister Jeffries has been of great assistance to you," Lady Hanley snapped. "You are in debt to him, for his skills have doubtless saved your life."

"For that, I am most grateful," Joshua said. He could ill afford to be rude and alienate his 'hosts' if he wanted answers. "It's just...." he trailed off, not quite knowing how to phrase his question so it wouldn't appear offensive.

Jeffries met his eyes with apparent honesty as Joshua studied the old man's face. The flicker of the fire cast orange tones onto the temples of his shining bald skull, giving the illusion that his skin was alive and moving. Joshua noticed the monk's nostrils flared slightly as he breathed in - a little like when he and Annabella drank in Lifeforce. Yet he felt there was something blocking the monk's persona, guarding the essence of him so that it was unknowable.

"You are wondering how I come to be here? To treat your kind perhaps?" Maister Jeffries spoke softly.

Joshua nodded, reluctant to share his own story without a better understanding of the company he was keeping.

117

Lady Hanley interrupted the monk before he could elaborate. "But I would have some answers from young Meadows here first, before he tires."

"I can tell you what I know," Joshua said, turning away from Jeffries' gaze. "Although clearly, that's not much."

"What do you know of your creation?" Lady Hanley repeated.

Joshua chewed on his lip in the silence which followed, understanding now the weak bargaining position he was in. He would need to share before he would get answers to his questions. He had nothing to lose at this point, for they both knew who he was, just not how he was. Joshua pushed aside his irritation at being so dependent on them and took a deep breath.

"A long time ago, many, many years past, I fell in love. With a girl. Her name then was..." He stopped, wavering about how much of this he should reveal, how far back he should go. Then he remembered that Annabella had insisted that Lady Hanley knew who she was, so he decided. He said a name he hadn't spoken aloud for decades, "Aioffe."

Lady Hanley's eyes danced with victory, but her smug smile didn't reassure Joshua.

"We have known many other names since then. She was different, and I knew that from the earliest times we spent with each other." Joshua leant his head backward into the chair as memories of that first, that only, love flooded back to him.

"You cried out that name," Jeffries mused, "in your fever. Eeefa, like Eva - I wondered what you were saying. Keep going..."

"Aioffe thought we could never be together, not truly

together as we wanted to be. She told me that her life was not her own, how she longed to be free. I encouraged her, as she seemed so happy with me. Eventually, we decided to leave. No - *needed* to leave.

"I couldn't continue to keep her existence a secret to my family, yet there was no future for us where we were. We both knew she was too different for them to accept. There would be too many questions. I only wanted to be with her and it was clear that if we wished to build a life together, then we had to go. I wanted it more than anything. I had come to be of a mind that there was no point to a life without her in it."

Joshua looked up at them and was reassured to see that the Maister held a kindly countenance to his face. Lady Hanley seemed thoughtful. As he paused, her eyes narrowed, and she raised an eyebrow when she caught his gaze. Taking as deep a breath as he could, he carried on.

"We ran away. Travelled as far as we could. They were hunting her, the Fae, so we never stayed long in one place. I slowed her down, I knew. We also had to hide from people, humans like I was. Then, I became injured, one night after we were discovered hiding in a barn, by the farmer. The arrow he shot me with as we ran pierced my ribcage. I was close to death. Aioffe rescued me, but... I had to change to survive."

Lady Hanley lent forward, staring hard at him. "Change how?"

He took a sip of his willow bark tea. "She told me there was a way. And I came to understand that the price to be with my beautiful Aioffe, forever, was to not stay as myself. I understood that the only way to have an eternal life with her was to become Fae. Live... like her."

Joshua looked again at his confidants, his heart

clamoured in his chest in the hope of acceptance. Her Ladyship was gazing into the fire, deep in thought. Jeffries silently urged him to carry on his tale with a shooing motion of his hands. Joshua looked into the flames himself, then taking a deep breath, he said, "And so she made me."

Lady Hanley did not shock easily; instead, there turned a look of hope on her face as he spoke. Joshua had expected revulsion, and turning his head, he saw Jeffries looking strangely at him, curiosity in his eyes.

"But how?" Lady Hanley frowned, then glared at him. Once again, Joshua felt very young and ill-educated on faekind.

"I drank from her," Joshua replied. He hoped that the simplicity of his answer would make it obvious that he would prefer to avoid going into the details of the intimate ritual which had passed between him and his lover.

"That can't be all," Lady Hanley insisted. "That is how vampires are made, not fae."

"Vampires must be distantly related to fae," Jeffries argued. "It makes sense that they should create in the same way."

"But they don't," said Lady Hanley, "and they haven't for centuries. No one has."

Joshua turned away, his pain-addled mind attempting to process her revelation.

"Where were you when the change happened?" Lady Hanley pressed.

"A village, I think. We travelled for days to get there." His mind was still distracted by his own rarity.

"How did you get her out of Naturae?" Lady Hanley urged, leaning forward.

"I don't know where Naturae is," Joshua said honestly.

"I lived in a small fishing village called Burwick at the bottom of the Orkney Islands. We took a boat to Scotland and walked from there."

"But I don't understand how you met her then?" Lady Hanley started getting agitated and stood to pace before the hearth.

"She would visit for our markets," he said simply, innocently. "She had hurt her ankle the first time we crossed paths, so I helped her into the village."

He smiled at the memory of their initial encounter at the roadside. He hadn't known until much later that the stormy weather had caused her to land awkwardly as a tree fell in the wind. He still recalled the forest-like smell of her hair as he ended up carrying her back to his father's forge so she could rest and get dry. His family had gone to the harbour where the market was, but he loved to walk in the rain.

Those first few hours together seemed a lifetime ago. They were completely alone in the cosy room behind his family's forge with the rain battering outside. From that moment on, the seeds of their love were sown as he cared for her through her pain. She had breathed his Lifeforce in deeply then, and he willingly gave it to the golden-haired girl. She was like no-one he had ever known, then or since.

"Over the years, she and I would arrange to meet whilst the markets were on. She was afraid the villagers would somehow be frightened of her, but she loved to watch them with me. Just us, sat together on the hillside. She would tell me what was happening, ask of what people were talking about. Of course, we were too far away for me to see, so she had to describe them for me. It was a game we played. Then, at the close of the day, she would leave with promises to return when she could, as long as I would swear not to follow her. I never saw where she came from, and she always left in darkness." Joshua sighed, the pain of parting from her then was nothing compared to that which he felt now. He fell silent, staring once again into the flames.

"I don't understand how you came to know she was Fae?" Maister Jeffries probed. Joshua raised his eyebrow in a look that clearly indicated their relationship had gone beyond the boundaries of clothing.

"Then why did you not run from what you surely must have known was danger?" Lady Hanley sounded incredulous. "You must indeed be a rare man not to have feared her strangeness."

Joshua sighed. "I didn't care." He looked at Lady Hanley, with tears in his eyes once more but no shame. "All I knew or cared about was making her happy. To be with her when she was content, laughing, you know... happy? It was truly the most magical... thing I had ever, *have* ever, felt." The lump in his throat rose up and he felt like he might suffocate. Joshua clenched his fists and clamped his mouth shut. He had already given away too much of himself, he did not want to let them spoil his memories of Aioffe.

"Why do you talk of her as if she were dead?" Lady Hanley said.

"Because I can feel her no longer!" He burst out. "They took her! Those fae hurt her, then... then I don't know what happened. Why did they take her from me?"

The anger in his voice, and the sense of bewilderment affected them all. Lady Hanley looked down at her hands, colour flushed to her cheeks. Maister Jeffries' eyes slid over to her, "What do you know of this Mary?"

122

Lady Hanley's composure stiffened and she stopped pacing the floor. Jeffries frowned, "Mary, I fear you are somehow more involved in this than merely caring for the boy."

Silently she moved towards the windows and gazed out. Joshua carefully stood up too, his movements surprisingly fluid. He wanted to go and shake it out of her, but something in her stance told him that she was poised like a bird about to take flight. To intimidate her now would possibly mean he had told all he had to tell with no recompense.

"I beg you, your Ladyship," Joshua said in a stilted manner, "if you know something, anything about what happened to her, you must tell me." After a moment, when it seemed as if his plea had fallen on deaf ears and he feared their unspoken bargain to share would be broken, Lady Hanley's shoulders slumped as she turned towards him. There were tears too in her eyes, melting the icy gaze she usually wore.

"I fear I have misread the situation, Joshua." Her words were calm, but there was a regret underneath them. "I have, perhaps, been a foolish old woman."

Maister Jeffries approached and touched her arm. The intimacy of the gesture struck Joshua as peculiar, hinting at a history between them which was more than that of a healer and patron. Jeffries propelled her towards the chairs, leaving Joshua standing.

Joshua's head started banging with pain from being upright, clouding his judgement. He reached up to rub the bandage to his throat and remembered that he owed his life to this strange woman and unusually knowledgeable monk. He forced himself to be patient and let the Lady speak, but he was not fully in control of his anger by a long way. He should have known there was nothing altruistic about him being brought here.

"Joshua," she began falteringly, "when I met you, I did not know you for what you are." She considered her next words. "I was more intrigued by Annabella, or Aioffe as I also knew her. Or rather, knew of her."

Joshua felt like his heart skipped a beat. Annabella had not been mistaken, she was Fae. Lady Hanley continued, looking down in her lap as if confessing. "It was I who informed her family of where she was."

"That was not for you to say!" Joshua, unable to contain his frustration, shouted at her. "You know nothing of our lives! You should have asked her if that was what she wanted!"

"You are correct," Lady Hanley said, her lips tight. She didn't often admit to being in the wrong. "I should have spoken to you both first. I can see that now."

Joshua turned away from them both, his eyes darting around the window as his mind once again shifted to thoughts of escape.

"At least tell us why then, Mary." Jeffries frowned, "You owe the boy that."

Lady Hanley avoided looking at Joshua, who was gripping the sides of the armchair as much for support as in tension. "I recognised her," she said.

"What of it?" Joshua spat out, disgusted at the old lady's interference. Lady Hanley looked a little taken aback at the venom in his voice.

"I felt they should know she was safe and well..." Lady Hanley ventured.

Joshua breathed out, although it was painful to fully empty his lungs, trying to control his temper. Patience...

He forced himself to ask, "Why did they take her?"

124

"I didn't know they would." Lady Hanley said, "I thought they would be happy to know she was still alive. I expected they would send someone to take me for questioning. That would have been more... usual."

"Why? What gave you the right?" Joshua raised his voice again - the injustice of the situation railed against his better judgement. He glowered at her. All those decades of running, and one of their own kind had betrayed them. He couldn't believe he had been so foolish, deeply regretting his assurances to Annabella.

Lady Hanley recovered herself and her voice turned to its more usual imperious tone. "I'll tell you, but you need to understand the circumstances, before you judge me."

Joshua waited, still poised to strike but it was clear that her Ladyship would demand the right to speak in her own house, supported by Maister Jeffries. The human part of him felt a little ashamed that he was even considering attacking a member of a higher social class than he.

"I knew of Aioffe's disappearance over a century ago. I saw the devastation her absence caused. Her mother, she was inconsolable. She was already weakened by..." Lady Hanley paused to find the right words to explain. "She was torn apart by the betrayal, and she took it out on us. On all of the Fae." She extended a shaking hand to pick up the cup of wine which had been warming on the table. Delicately, she took a sip before continuing in a steadier voice.

"The court was in uproar. No trace of Aioffe could be found. It was as if she had just disappeared. Up and left with no means of tracing her. Her mother was furious at first, searching far and wide to bring in anyone who had known her. They brought anybody who even knew of our kind back, and tortured them for information. She was so sure that someone would know where Aioffe had gone. But no-one did. Most never left again." Lady Hanley shuddered.

Joshua nodded to himself, "We told no-one when we left, took nothing save for a small bag of clothes and a few bowls, plates, that sort of thing. She said it was for the best."

Lady Hanley turned to the window, her face vacant as she remembered. "As the years passed, her mother became more and more bitter. She considered that there was a huge conspiracy to keep her apart from her daughter, that we were all against her. Before long, just the mention of her name was an act of treason. All pictures of her were taken down, but those of us with long lives don't forget. Without Aioffe, we had no hope either of change.

"Some felt this was the natural way - that the decline of the Fae was inevitable. We had been slowly dying out for years. Some thought the Queen herself had killed Aioffe, an attempt to somehow elongate her own rule. Others thought she was taken, to be the salvation of faekind somewhere else. We were divided as never before, living in fear. But no-one could challenge the Queen's authority, it was just not possible."

"The Queen?" Joshua was taken aback. He felt as if someone had plunged a dagger into his heart yet again.

"Aioffe is the next, the only, heir to the Queendom of Naturae. Or did she not mention that to you?"

CHAPTER 11 – WHAT LIES BENEATH

"She's refusing to eat," Uffer, the First Lord of Anaxis said, with some compassion.

"Then she must be *made* to!" Queen Lana snapped, pausing in her pacing about the map on the High Hall floor. "I will not tolerate this foolish behaviour. She will eventually feed, we all do. She's just not desperate enough yet. I shouldn't have to remind you that you have one job, just one prisoner to control. Do not make me regret placing you in the position."

Uffer knew her threat was not an idle one. Queen Lana had a volatile nature, a fierce temper, and Uffer understood how precarious his current position was. His rise to his current posting was, he thought, largely due to the successive failure of his predecessors to obtain information about Aioffe's disappearance from her friends and contacts. He himself had been a low-born soldier, barely eking an existence in the court riding on his vine's reputation. Having survived the Great Search, despite coming back with actually very little information, he elevated through the ranks by virtue of being alive and returned. Many had set out on the Great Search and not come home.

"My Queen," he tried again, although his voice wavered as usual in her presence. "Perhaps if you were to talk to her? She might respond to your requests in person?"

"I have no wish to speak to her. She must come before me. She must beg for forgiveness for what she has done."

The Queen drew herself up to her full height. Frail though she was, her tall, rake thin figure was still intimidating. "I will not allow such insolence in a child." Her huge wings rose up behind her back, framing her silhouette. Sunlight bounced off the iridescent green panes onto the floor like a thousand spotlights.

Uffer dipped his body in a bow and backed away towards the doors. He dreaded returning to the Beneath, even though it was where his duties lay. The return of Aioffe was perhaps the biggest upset the court had ever known. It was also the brightest hope his people had had for many a century.

Having made his way down the darkened passages, circling lower and lower through the roots of the trees above, Uffer pondered his options as he approached the cell where the Princess was held. His stubby brown wings fluttered furiously to propel him over the muddy floor, sometimes scraping the sides of the passages. His nostrils fought to become increasingly numb to the dank smells which grew stronger as he descended.

Uffer felt he had very few options but to try and cosset the girl into reality. Not that she would like it. The Fae Court was far from what it once had been. She clearly couldn't be set free again - that was out of the question and would mean his life was almost certain to be cut short. He couldn't torture her - he could not believe it would serve any purpose, nor was it his style. Whatever information she might reveal about where she had been was irrelevant, as she was back now.

She must be made to see that there was no other option but to submit to the Queen's demands and prepare to take her place on the throne.

He sighed, frustrated by his own lack of progress. Yet,

he could not see how the pathetic, sobbing being currently in his care could be 'made' to eat. Feeding was a necessity, how was she resisting for so long? Nothing seemed to work, no amount of threats or being placed in Her Majesty's sight. She remained stubbornly unresponsive, uncooperative.

The idea came to him, as he considered how far the poor girl had fallen, that his only hope was to try a measure of kindness towards her. So far, she had not communicated anything yet he knew he had to reach her. If she responded to a gentler approach, he could report progress. He might, in turn, survive when the time came. 'And it can't come soon enough' - the thought just popped into his head and he pushed it away quickly. He wasn't sure which 'Time' he was looking forward to. He only knew something had to change, and quickly.

Uffer thought back to the few moments in his life when he had been shown kindness, how that had made him feel. Only before the Sadness came had he felt sympathy, generosity, kinship even. And that hadn't been with a fae at all, but a human, one who had seen him as something more than just a guard. So perhaps giving something of himself, showing himself as more than a soldier-fae, would trigger a reprieve for his lost Princess from her own misery?

Reaching the Principle Cell, he took out the keys clanking on a ring fastened to his belt, and dropped them round and round, feeling the teeth until he came to the right one. He hoped the chink of the keys would provide some measure of notice to his prisoner, so he wouldn't have to rouse her. He felt uncomfortable even touching her.

Uffer's key turned noisily in the lock and a chink of

129

dim light widened across the floor. He bent over her as she lay motionless facing the earthen walls. Aioffe's glazed eyes stared ahead into the darkness. Even though a part of her surely heard the soft movement of wings behind her, she didn't move.

"Are you awake?" His voice seemed very quiet, even to him. "Princess, let me help?" Annabella's eyelids closed, shutting him out. Uffer shook her shoulder, but Annabella remained listless.

"My name is Uffer," he said, "and I can see you are in great distress, my Lady." He grew increasingly concerned at the lack of response. Surely she could hear the kindly tone in his gruff voice? "I will return shortly with sustenance. There's not much to be had. I believe you would benefit from it."

There was no reaction from the figure on the floor, but Uffer felt sure she could hear him and was not asleep. "Her Majesty only wishes to see you returned to her," he tried to convince her, as much as himself. "She bears no ill will and would only like to be reunited with her child."

The lie tripped from his tongue before he could stop it. He knew full well that although the Queen did not wish for her daughter to die, there had been no indication over the past century that she sought a loving reunion with the Princess. Moreover, the Queen's primary concern was that her daughter should dutifully toe the line and continue to rule when the time came for her own demise. She appeared to have every intention of trying to mould Aioffe into a likeness of her own cruel self, by any means possible.

Annabella curled herself together, groaning. At least she was alive, thought Uffer as he closed the doors. He hadn't completely failed to reach her.

CHAPTER 12 -
APPEARANCES CAN BE
DECEPTIVE

The warmth of the fire did little to relieve the chill coursing through his bones. Joshua held his reeling head in his hands. His reverie was interrupted by a brisk knock to the Library door. Mr Bray walked in and advanced towards the group by the fireside. "It is the hour. We must depart for Christmas Mass," he announced in clipped tones, ignoring the tension in the room. "Your Ladyship? The horses are prepared."

Joshua glanced up - the shock at the servant's intrusion into his frantic attempts to jigsaw together his new knowledge evident on his face. Mr Bray glanced at his open jaw then looked straight ahead, every inch the servant rising above the unusual gathering in front of him.

Lady Hanley gathered her skirts and stood. She placed a hand on Joshua's shoulder, "We will talk further after you have had some rest."

Maister Jeffries then also rose, drained his cup of wine and set it back down on the table. "I should return to the Abbey," his low voice said evenly, as if this were a perfectly normal closure of a conversation happening between friends. "I will accompany you to Church however, Mary, whilst our guest here recovers himself. There is a matter I would discuss with you in private."

Mr Bray looked deflated. "Am I to remain here alone then?" He asked curtly, "With him?"

"Mr Meadows will need assistance to his room, yes, Mr Bray." Lady Hanley straightened her bodice. "And he will likely require the rabbit."

"Very well," Mr Bray capitulated, although his lips tightened. He begrudgingly bent down to help Joshua stand, and together they followed Lady Hanley and Maister Jeffries from the cosy room.

The journey back up the stairs was just as painful as the descent had been, perhaps even more so now the weight of recent revelations bore down on Joshua. He tried not to lean too much on Mr Bray - the older gentleman was clearly not accustomed to carrying heavy objects and flushed red in the face from the exertion. The servant's wiry physique was maintained by constant exercise, rather than hauling dead weights.

Reaching the yellow-hued bedroom once more, Joshua sank down on the bed gratefully. It pained his chest to lift his legs up to the covers, but he managed with only a faint groan escaping. His bare feet, he noticed, were cold since leaving the warmth of the fireside and walking through the chilly hallways of the house.

"Might I have some bed-socks, please?" Joshua requested of Mr Bray, as he turned to leave the room.

Mr Bray frowned, not expecting this perfectly ordinary request, then grunted, "I will fetch some." He straightened his back as he closed the door tight behind himself.

Alone, Joshua was finally able to mentally sift through the implications of the conversation in the library. He marvelled at how, in just a short space of time, he now knew so much more of the Fae. Of Aioffe. More than he had discovered in over a century about her home, Naturae. Their relationship had moved from gentle questions about her life, which she deflected in the early stages of their knowing each other, to a firm refusal to discuss anything about it as they planned their escape. Joshua, dazzled and in awe of her very presence in his life, had been reluctant to challenge her, to persist with pushing for answers.

But he had known there was more, had sensed her dread at returning every time they parted. Lying in his lonely bed in the forge, he had often wondered what she was so afraid of, yet compelled to return to. She would tell him that he didn't understand - her life was not terrible, or uncomfortable, it was merely different, and not how she wanted it to be. Each time she parted from him, his world, it only reinforced her desire to leave her home forever, she had said.

And meeting him, falling in love with a human - he had thought that was the reason for her being Outcast. It was a word she had only infrequently used, without explaining what that really was or meant. It had only recently reared up in their conversations around Lady Hanley. When he first heard it, Aioffe reassured him that being Outcast didn't matter, that they were destined to be together. Even though it was an irreversible decision, he knew it was one they both made.

His natural guilt at being the cause of her banishment was no longer a burden he should carry, Joshua realised. By falling in love with him, she would not be alone when she escaped. Their love had emboldened her to leave with him. Caught up in their passion, they had chosen to forsake all others. For them, that had also meant forsaking all family obligations, so that they might be free together.

He hadn't realised that the list of what she was abandoning included duty. A throne. A Queendom. Would he have encouraged her if he had known, he wondered?

Shaking his head to drive the confusing thoughts, Joshua stood up, wincing as he then shuffled to the window. Outside, the countryside was grey with drizzle, low clouds blocking the sunlight from drying the wet fields below. The weight of what Aioffe had run away from in choosing to be with him slipped into a sense of horror. She had given up her Queendom, her birthright. For him, a lowly blacksmith. And not once had she expressed regret. He couldn't imagine King Henry doing such a thing, or any royal person in fact. Most monarchs, it seemed to him, wanted absolute power, and nothing and no-one would keep them from it.

As if the sun had come out in his mind, he suddenly understood why she had kept them moving away from areas where passions ran high over the battles between the houses of York and Lancaster. The question of who should be king, and king after that, loomed over their human lives as it must have loomed over hers before they eloped. They had darted around small villages to the south, skirted on the edges of larger towns like Norwich and hidden themselves, avoiding all discourse where people could take sides for one family or the other. The relative peace following the ascent of King Henry the VII, and then VIII, had enabled them of late to settle for longer in towns.

As his mind turned in circles, trying to resolve his feelings now there was a different complexion on them, Mr Bray returned. Barely opening the door, the servant shoved the rabbit cage in, threw the socks on the bed and grumbled, "Merry Christmas." The door pulled closed and his footsteps banged away down the corridor.

Joshua ate the rabbit and felt much restored. His heart still ached with loneliness, sadness, but he felt more like himself than he had in days. Were it not for the tightness in his chest and inability to walk more than a few paces without the room spinning, he would have considered himself recovered. The Lifeforce had given him optimism where before there had been only negative emotions. The bunny must have lived a happy life before, he thought wryly as he leant down to put the husk in the fireplace.

Moving easier now, he banged on the door and shouted for Mr Bray. Joshua braced himself against the doorway and listened for noise in the corridor. Eventually, after banging and calling a few times again, footsteps approached. This time Joshua stood away as the door opened, and a pointed nose peered cautiously around, ready to slam the door shut should an ambush happen again. Joshua smiled and said, "Mr Bray, I have no quarrel with you. Please enter at peace."

The old man hesitated, stood partially in the doorframe, keeping his hand on the latch outside as if braced for trouble. "What do y'want?" Mr Bray's brusk voice held no fear, nor acknowledgement of his servitude. It verged on rudeness.

"Only to ask for some clothes? And water, and a tooth cloth and soot? For my teeth," Joshua said.

"Yer feeling better then, I see. Pretending you are a human again, now are we?" Mr Bray said. The large glass of port he had just downed began to take effect.

"Something like that, yes," Joshua smiled. Smelling the alcohol on the man's breath, he joked, "I could even see myself having a sneaky festive tipple before long." Their eyes met and Joshua fancied he saw the servant's shoulders relax a little.

Mr Bray retreated, still taking care to lock the door behind him. Minutes later, he returned with washing materials as well as frayed - but clean - breeches, shirt, a jerkin and jacket. Joshua wondered whose they were, but guessed at Bray's own items of clothing.

135

"No boots," he barked. "Ladyship said, no boots. Not that yer need 'em," Mr Bray muttered under his breath.

Joshua frowned, then ventured an apology, by way of trying to rebuild some trust between them. "I am sorry I have put you out so much, and I apologise about you missing the Christmas Mass on my behalf."

Mr Bray nodded his acceptance. Joshua continued, for he felt he owed the man something more. "I would also like to thank you, for I do recall you brought me here. I think I would not be alive today without your efforts."

"I tracked you to the forest, thought yer were dead," Mr Bray said, then brushed a fleck of wool from his sleeve.

"I'm certain if you had left me there, I would have been."

"T'is well then, that I found yer." He drew himself up slightly, his pride in saving a life evident now it had been acknowledged.

Joshua, sensing an opportunity, asked for more. "And Maister Jeffries, how did he come to be in the forest also?"

"Kestrel. Her Ladyship sent one to the Abbey when I sent a boy back with the message about what happen'd in the town. She thought you might need some calming and suggested we look to the woods." Mr Bray made to leave the room, but Joshua reached out to touch his sleeve.

"I owe you both a debt I can never repay, Mr Bray. Her Ladyship too. Did you see what happened? To Annabella?"

"No, I only found you by following a scream of your name. Then I saw the figures in the sky. She weren't making it easy for 'em." Mr Bray said. The recollection cast a shadow of pain across Bray's face. No woman deserved such treatment, whether they had wings or not.

"You saw them?" Joshua asked, "Which direction did they go?" A glimmer of hope entered his heart.

"I had only just reached you, barely could make out anything." Bray shook his head, and started for the door.

Joshua's heart slumped again. By saving Joshua's life, Mr Bray had lost any clues about where to look for Annabella.

Pausing before he left, Bray muttered by way of consolation, "Following those... things weren't exactly on my mind at the time. Too busy hollerin' for help, I could see yer bleedin' an' pale-like. Besides, I'm not exactly 'equipped' to follow where only birds ought to be."

Mr Bray glanced back at the man sitting on the bed. He was so young looking. It almost tore at his heart to see a fine lad so battered. Had he any idea what he had got himself involved with, Bray wondered? In all his years of serving Her Ladyship and her former husband, he had seen some strange things. That this ordinary-looking lad had wings was bad enough, confusing enough. Losing one's wife, not that Bray had ever had one, must be hard as well. The whole situation didn't sit comfortably with him, not at all.

Mr Bray grunted, "Sorry," and left. He had no intention of getting further embroiled in it than he already was. It was not his place to either, Bray reminded himself. These strange goings-on were not of his concern. He double checked the latch on the door was closed tight before heading down the passage. There was a Christmas lunch to prepare and prayers to say - best to focus on his proper job. Deeply ashamed to miss Mass, he hoped Lady Hanley had made an excellent excuse on his behalf. He worried the congregation would ask awkward questions the next time he visited town. Questions he would find

137

himself struggling to answer. A lifetime of honest and respected service, and he had now he was reduced to fetching and carrying for a fugitive. A peculiar, unnatural one at that. He clamped his lips together as he stomped away. Her Ladyship owed him more than one glass of port for this, he reckoned.

*****

Joshua felt almost normal by the time he finished pulling clothes on, though they fitted a little tightly around his biceps. They were serviceable - plain and functional, although the seams were not a patch on the fine stitching Annabella ensured he usually wore. He was unable to button the jerkin about his chest. The pain of dressing aside, he smiled, remembering how Annabella would embroider a tiny heart inside his clothing, a private reminder. It seemed appropriate to him that these clothes did not boast such an embellishment, as if its absence would propel his own heart to meet the challenge of seeking hers for their reunion.

His sense of optimism restored, he nurtured the glimmer of hope that Annabella was alive. Given what he now knew of her past, he convinced himself that the fae wanted his lover to return home, to face the Queen perhaps? If they had intended to kill her then those soldiers could have easily done so, but they took her instead. He still needed to know more about Naturae, and where it was, so that he could make all possible haste to get there and find her.

As he rested on his pillows, pondering the limited travel options for when he could make his escape, the door downstairs slammed so hard it reverberated up to his sensitive ears. He started to pull himself upright, ready to face the next step of moving.

"You will put us all in jeopardy!" Lady Hanley's cross voice floated upwards soon after. Joshua strained to listen for an answer but caught nothing. "Well, I don't know what you expect me to do about it!" Lady Hanley fumed. A thump of steps followed, ascending the wooden stairs like a drumbeat. His doorway flung open, and she entered, her face furious and flushed.

"As if I don't have enough to deal with, with *you* hiding out here too!" Her flashing eyes took in the fact that Joshua was clothed, standing now, and looking at her calmly.

"At least you are dressed," she snapped. "I hope this means you are ready to give me some answers before I decide what is to be done about all of this!"

The venom in her voice surprised Joshua - gone was the conciliatory, caring tone of the woman who had nursed him for the last few days. Here before him was the temper he had heard tell of in Beesworth. The one which, if rumours were true, had killed off her husband with its ferocity. Joshua almost laughed, for in part the passion in her voice reminded him of Annabella's child-like tantrums. This he could manage, he thought.

Joshua turned on the charm. "Your Ladyship, the act of getting dressed has made me realise the full extent of the tender care and ministrations you have given me. I would most humbly thank you, from the bottom of my worthless heart." He hoped his flowery protestations would serve to break the spell of the temper. Lady Hanley turned and studied him, surprised by his sudden eloquence.

Taking a deep breath, as much as his bindings would

allow, Joshua continued. "Although I am but your unworthy patient, indeed, I am your servant and filled with only gratitude for all that you have done for me. I would be honoured to answer all and any questions you might have in which I could, perchance, assist in your quest for knowledge of my situation."

The words just kept spilling from his lips as his head bowed in supplication, as Joshua brought to bear his years of observing the upper classes and their speech mannerisms.

"I would beg your forgiveness for my ill-begotten state of mind, and indeed, health. For I owe you such a great burden of debt for my treatment, it is but the least I can do as I have no other means of recompense for your efforts in restoring my lowly self."

He wondered if it was worth attempting a bow at this point, but, looking up through his blond eyelashes, he saw a panel of faces gazing at him with a variety of expressions upon them.

Lady Hanley had a small smirk on her mouth; it twitched up and her eyes betrayed a sense of amusement at him. Open-mouthed Mr Bray had joined her and was staring at him, more aghast than anything. Maister Jeffries was half in and half out of the doorway, a look of puzzlement adorning his face.

The tableau of people froze for a heartbeat, before Lady Hanley broke the silence with an audible intake of breath. "I think there is much we should discuss, Master Meadows. Including how it is that merely putting on clothes entitles you to speak as a courtier!"

The customary haughty look returned to her face, accompanied by a raised eyebrow. The tension in the room lifted somewhat. "We will adjourn to the Library."

Lady Hanley swept out of the room, passing her cloak to Mr Bray as she went. Maister Jeffries twitched a smile, the glint in his eyes as he looked at Joshua spoke of admiration for how he had disarmed their cross patch hostess.

*****

Downstairs once more, the trio warmed themselves by the flickering fireplace in silence. The room was not adorned with any festive decorations - Christmas might well be happening elsewhere, but there was no hint of it at Hanley House, bar the elaborate attire of Lady Hanley.

"The Mass went well?" Joshua broke the quiet.

Lady Hanley answered, remnants of frustration in her voice. "As well as could be expected when the town is in mourning for the loss of a young soul."

"T'was not I!" Joshua blurted out. How could he have forgotten the discovery of poor Alice? "Please, your Ladyship, you have to know that I would never..."

Lady Hanley turned to look Joshua full in the face. "I realise what you are," she said as if pointing out the obvious, "but I don't believe you would do that." Joshua looked down, knowing he had come close at other times in his life. She glanced towards the door before continuing. "Besides, Mr Bray told me he had witnessed you beforehand. He said you were as shocked as he."

Joshua felt humbled. As grumpy as the man had been earlier with him, he appreciated that Mr Bray had spoken up for his honour, not to mention his swift actions in bringing him here for recuperation.

"Of course, he lost you shortly afterwards, but at least had the presence of mind to tell me who he thought you were looking for. Although, being unaware of your wife's nature, he sought to get to the bottom of where she had gone, in case she also was killed. A most diligent man." Lady Hanley paused.

"I instructed him by return of kestrel to follow you instead. At the time, I thought you merely her consort, and therefore, her loss was likely to make you talk more."

Her gaze was steady as she appraised Joshua. "Your arrival here was not a coincidence, Master Meadows. I had to be sure you would not repeat anything which she might have told you about me."

"Perhaps," Joshua said gently, "you could elaborate upon your situation...?"

Maister Jeffries had remained silent through the conversation. Now, he leaned forward and poked the fire. "What is in the past should remain there, Mary. Although, I'm pleased your intentions towards the boy appear to have changed," he said carefully. "Now that we know the full extent of his partnership with the young Fae-Queen."

Joshua felt the absence of Annabella rise again in his chest, threatening his composure during this most strange of conversations. His lover would have been less reticent to push home the question, but he was acutely aware of his powerless position and the caution required to get the answers he wanted.

"And what are your intentions, my Lady?" Joshua asked.

"I confess, I am uncertain at this point," she replied lightly.

"I must find Annabella." Joshua couldn't keep the note of pleading from his voice.

"Aioffe," corrected Lady Hanley. "Annabella does not exist. You should call her by her given name."

Joshua gritted his teeth, it was not for her to instruct him on how he thought of his wife. It suited him to call her by the name they had chosen together, not the name which she had left behind. "She was torn from me, I have to go. The longer I wait, the more danger she could be in! Anything left behind of her will disappear."

"Leaving here is not wise," Maister Jeffries said. "Lady Hanley and I have discussed this matter, and we feel it best if you remain here."

"For now," Lady Hanley confirmed.

Joshua wanted to stand up and shout, but his present weakness prevented him so he banged his fist on the chair arm instead. "I cannot!" The pain reverberated around his ribs and for a moment he struggled to breathe.

"But you must," Lady Hanley kept her voice calm, not abashed or threatened by him in any way.

"I am not your prisoner. I have done nothing wrong!" Joshua could feel the passion rising up in his voice, perhaps too much for present company.

Maister Jeffries leaned over and placed a restraining hand on his shoulder. "My lad, you are in no fit state to be going anywhere."

"And where would you go anyway?" Lady Hanley added, somewhat harshly. "You can hardly go back to Beesworth. The entire town is convinced that your wife is somehow involved with the child's death, either taken by her killers or fled the scene!"

Pointing out of the window, she cautioned, "They have already had the dogs out to pick up the scent. Mr Bray has been down to try to head them away from my lands, but I fear it will only be a matter of time before they come knocking."

Joshua knew too well what that meant. In the absence

143

of anything tangible evidence-wise, it would not be long before the rumours about his disappearance made it look as if he had a part in it all.

"Once the Yule restrictions are lifted, little will distract them from their hunt for the killer," Jeffries said to fill the silence that followed.

"It is a worthy cause," Joshua said hollowly. "But they are mistaken if they think we - Annabella or I - had any part in the harm." He felt defeated, for he had no desire to start again somewhere else without his wife. Had no desire to do anything but find her. Despondency started to take grip, as he acknowledged to himself that his current state of health prevented him from doing much to better the situation. Worse still, he had absolutely no idea where to even begin looking.

Mr Bray entered the room bearing a tray of cups, a steaming jug and a plate of marzipan delicacies. He hesitated as everyone turned to look at him, then set the tray down. "Thank you, Bray," Lady Hanley said politely.

"Will *he* be partaking of the goose?" Mr Bray's eyes slid towards Joshua.

"My guests will join us, yes." Lady Hanley spoke with a wave of her hand in dismissal.

Jeffries stood up quickly. "Many thanks, Your Ladyship, but I fear I should take my leave rather than dally with you all. As you know, there is a matter there I should attend to."

"Rubbish! You too can't very well go back to the Abbey right now, can you? Having accompanied me so publically to the Church in Beesworth as if I were some frailty who needed cosseting, when instead it is you who needs my help." Lady Hanley snapped, throwing her hands in the air. "It appears I am the host of waifs and misfits this Christmas!"

"I apologise for the inconvenience I have caused," Maister Jeffries said.

"You should retrieve what you need from the Abbey, before it is too late." Lady Hanley reconsidered. "You will go after dinner when the chances of you entering unseen are better. The monks will be lolling about with wine by then, I am sure."

Joshua looked at Maister Jeffries with interest. He knew little of routines at the Abbey, but surely the monk would already have been missed at this most holy of times?

Jeffries dithered, but Lady Hanley quickly commanded him, "Do not involve the boy in your affairs!"

"My Lady, the matter stays between us, and us alone. I shall return to the Abbey with all due haste after dinner, however, and leave in the morning."

"People saw us at the Church together, so they will look here first when your absence is noticed." Lady Hanley warned.

"My Lady, I am but a lowly infirmarian. There are some one hundred and twenty monks residing in the Abbey. Brothers who will cover my absence for some days during the festivities before I am missed."

Lady Hanley snorted whilst looking unconvinced.

"Is the matter settled then, your Ladyship?" Mr Bray said. "The Maister and Master Matthews, both for *our* Christmas repast?"

"Quite settled," she replied. Mr Bray marched to the door, muttering under his breath as he left.

"Is your work at the Abbey how you came to be versed in healing, Maister Jeffries?" Joshua said, keen to understand how the monk fitted into the picture, and attempting to diffuse the tension.

Lady Hanley made no effort at subtlety or looking about to check Bray had gone. There was a vengeful relish in her voice as she casually said, "Maister Jeffries is more than a skilled healer. He is a witch."

Joshua said, "In a monastery?" His experience of witches was limited, and, given what he himself was, he gave little weight to commonly held human superstitions about them consorting with the Devil. It seemed that anyone could find themselves falling foul of such accusations, these days they were only sometimes proved. A true witch, he supposed, might come in all guises.

Maister Jeffries' pursed his lips tightly and glowered at Lady Hanley. "I would remind you, Mary, that witches are able to sense liars, and guard many secrets. You would do well to remember who has kept your secrets these past years."

"Pah! We are apparently past secrets now," Lady Hanley dismissed the monk's outrage, as only one of superiority could have with a wave of her hand towards Joshua. "The world is far more confusing than you could ever credit it for. There have been enough lies told. I am sick of it."

"What lies do you think there have been, your Ladyship?" Joshua spoke up - for he had been utterly truthful in what he had said, if not elaborate. He noticed Jeffries squirming about in his seat after her outburst also, and he didn't think it was because he had been exposed as a witch.

Lady Hanley leaned forward, her shrewd eyes glittering in the firelight. "Lies about what is happening. Covering up who we really are. Lies about what we are, and worst of all, lies about what we've done," she accused.

She glared at them both for a moment, then glanced away. Joshua realised she was also referring to herself. "What else have you done?" he asked, quite reasonably.

There was a moment when, as he studied her face, Joshua could see the conflict within her. Regret at her accusation of lies, perhaps? It had been a poor attempt to move the conversation away from herself. The flash of remorse he thought he'd seen bothered him. Was it maybe weighing on her also?

"I have told you everything you have asked," he said, "but you haven't answered any of my questions. What have you lied about?" He knew he was on the right track when she broke his gaze again, her mouth tightening as she looked away. "If you are so sick of lies, start with the truth, no matter how painful. I would rather hear it from your own lips."

Maister Jeffries glowered at her, his dark eyes cautioning her. Lady Hanley fidgeted with her skirts, laying them neatly about her in the seat as she considered her words. Joshua waited, aware of his heart thumping. Not from fear of challenging a member of a higher social class than he, but he was very aware at that moment of his own vulnerability. There was every chance that she would close off the conversation and deny him any more information which could be useful to him.

"I haven't lied," she said, then glanced at Jeffries. "But I have not told the whole truth, I admit." Before she spoke again, she moistened her lips, and carefully phrased her position. "I didn't inform the Fae court of Aioffe's location out of the goodness of my heart. I..." She looked down at her hands, then slightly shook her head as if arguing with herself.

The two men let her wrestle with her conscience in

silence. "I wanted to be taken home!" she said.

"But I thought you were happy here?" Maister Jeffries said kindly. "Even after Lord Hanley left us?"

Lady Hanley turned her face so they wouldn't see the tears spilling onto her cheeks. Pursing her mouth, she tried to keep the tremor from her voice. "I was. And yet, I wasn't. I am tired of this existence on rabbits and occasional infusions of religious fervour. I am tired of hiding."

She signed, and her head drooped. Once she started, it was hard to stop. "I am aging and I do not want the questions. The suspicions about why I do not age as quickly as humans. Yet I cannot bear to uproot it all, leave this place, and start again like you and Aioffe."

"I don't understand," Joshua said. "You have everything you need here, even a servant who, forgive me, seems to know all about your needs and supplies them?"

"I'm afraid, lad, that for Mary, it's not quite the same as the freedom you and your 'Aioffe' enjoy." Maister Jeffries answered for her, shaking his head.

"I have no wings now," she sighed.

Although this was no revelation, Joshua had began to feel sorry for the old woman. His momentary sympathy didn't last as Lady Hanley confessed more.

"When I realised who 'Annabella' was, my only thought was that she would be my route back. Back home, wings or no wings. After the Great Search, I thought I knew the way things were done. People were brought in, taken Beneath, and eventually, they said all they could about Aioffe - even if it was lies and false leads. Some were set free, others were not. I expected my information was enough to get me released, perhaps even reinstated, even if I was Outcast before. It was solid, much-needed

148

news which I would have willingly given. But they came and found her themselves. I was so sure they would take me back to Naturae for questioning first."

"You thought you could sell Aioffe's whereabouts?" Jeffries looked at Lady Hanley incredulously.

"I can't believe how selfish you have been!" Joshua exploded.

"I know, and I have apologised," Lady Hanley said through gritted teeth. Even though in the wrong, she didn't like being challenged, especially by a mere tradesman.

"I don't think you were in your right mind, Mary," Jeffries shook his head in disbelief. "From what you told me when we first met, the Queen is unforgiving of traitors. I find it incredible to think that you would act so rashly."

"I wasn't thinking clearly at the time, I admit." Lady Hanley took to her feet quickly, glaring at Jeffries. "Because *someone* was pestering me about a stupid, heretical book!"

The monk had the grace to look abashed at this accusation. Lady Hanley continued glaring at him, her nostrils flaring as she breathed in and out.

"I think you underestimated her. The Queen. Badly," said Maister Jeffries, trying to draw the argument back around to Lady Hanley's confession again.

Joshua had a more pressing question. "Have you told them about me?"

Lady Hanley paused a moment then said, "No."

"Why?"

She turned the full force of her glare to Joshua. "At the time, I had no idea that you were anything but a human plaything. A companion."

Lady Hanley paused, her eyes sliding back to Jeffries before she muttered, "I realise now I need to consider my options more... completely. Before I can decide what to do next."

Joshua exhaled. His chest hurt as he fully emptied it of air. The room was warm and he was sweating slightly from the exertions of the conversation. Maister Jeffries remained leaning forward, elbows resting on the chair arms and his fingers laced in front of him. In the silence which followed, he began to tap his index fingers together, as though in thought, whilst staring resolutely into the flames before him. Lady Hanley sat once more and glanced at the clock in a vain attempt at avoiding any further questions.

"Am I correct in thinking then," Joshua mulled the question half in his mind as his mouth formed the words slowly, "that my existence is a problem? Or is it something which is of... value? Is that the right word?"

"Not of value in itself," Maister Jeffries said. "More that you are fae at all is of greater interest."

Joshua frowned. "How do you mean?"

"Fae can only be created from royal blood," Lady Hanley explained. "We are all made from blessings by the Queen herself. Fae are not born, we are grown as pupae and blessed into being. The Queen is mother to us all."

"But, I was human?" Joshua was even more perplexed now.

"Exactly," said Lady Hanley. "And you are the only fae to be 'made' certainly in my living memory, which is over a thousand years. The Princess must be more powerful than anyone ever imagined her being."

At the window, a pigeon rapped its beak on the thick glass, causing all the library inhabitants to jump. Lady Hanley walked over to let it in; the blast of the chilly air a sudden contrast to the stifling heat of the room. She untied a note from its leg and, after reading it, passed it to Jeffries. "It would seem your matter has become more pressing after all. The Commissioners have arrived," she grumbled.

Jeffries' face screwed up as he read the tiny writing. Crumpling the message, he then tossed it into the flames. Standing up, he seemed distracted as he straightened his robes. "If I may beg your leave. I will make haste to the Abbey and return as soon as I can."

Joshua tried to stand, wincing as he levered himself up using the arms of the chair. "Is there anything I can do to help?" Joshua panted through gritted teeth. The confessional atmosphere of the afternoon led him to feel he should at least offer.

"Of course not!" Lady Hanley snapped. "This is not of your concern. You may take my horse, Jeffries. She is fitter than that old nag you ride. I will come and instruct the boy to saddle it up myself now, whilst you gather your cloak." Practically pushing the monk from the room, they left Joshua on his own by the fireside.

In their absence, and rather than sit and relax, Joshua wondered whether there would be a map on the bookshelves. It had been years since he had last seen one, but even one detailing Lady Hanley's lands would be of use in determining where he was in relation to other parts of the country. Anything to give him a sense of direction for when he did make his escape. Annabella usually guided them flying, intuitively and from using the sun for bearing. With a pang, he yet again mourned her absence, wishing he had asked her about how she did it at the time. Given it could be dark when he escaped, the sun would be of no use to him.

Walking past the desk, he glanced at the open book on

the surface. It appeared to be a diary, in the middle of being written. At the top of the cream page, copperplate writing started with '20 December 1535', clearly that weeks' annotations. On the left of the dated page there ran lists of household accounts, jobs to do and wages to be paid. He noticed an entry for the butcher for the goose, as well as a little smudged symbol next to an entry for Meadows, presumably the dress which Annabella had been making for Lady Hanley. The same swirl prefaced a note written at the bottom of the ledger. The writing was tiny, so he picked up the leather-bound notebook and held it up to the candles on the side of the desk to see better.

The script was like nothing he had ever seen before. He could recognise English, Latin, even the odd bit of Greek and French, but the letter formation made no sense to him. This looked more like squiggles and dots. There was a beauty to it though, almost a pattern of waves with loops and splashes. At the end of markings there was a distinctively English question mark, firmly inked.

He turned his attention to the right of the page, similarly covered with the lyrical markings It reminded him of handwritten written sheet music. He presumed that the writing was Fae in origin, but never having seen Annabella write it, he obviously couldn't read it. Joshua turned to the shelves, scanning for other books or a map which might be of interest. Painfully bending down to the bottom shelf, he saw two orderly lines of ledgers identical to the one in his hands. Flicking through one at random, it seemed to cover a year of weekly entries, dated and annotated like the diary on the desk. He quickly counted the booklets - there must have been over fifty, and a full shelf above it, probably another fifty or so. That gave him the idea that Lady Hanley had been here almost as long as

152

he had been a fae. How had she kept up the pretence? Why had she aged, but he and Annabella had not? But then, he supposed, if she was really over a thousand years old, who was to say what he would look like in nine more centuries. But Annabella, she was far older than he supposed, he realised.

"I didn't take you for a sneak," the Lady herself said, as she caught him in the act of replacing the ledger on the shelves. Joshua jumped, he had been so absorbed in his search he missed the tell-tale footsteps approaching. Ashamed of himself, he said, "I'm sorry, your Ladyship, I meant no harm."

"Your curiosity is to be expected," she said, although with a note of hurt in her voice. "I had assumed you would have shown me the basics of common decency before you went poking around my house without asking."

"My Lady," he said, standing slowly and approaching her. "I have wronged you once more, and I beg your forgiveness. I am at a loss as to what to do next. I know so little, it is hard for me to make sense of what I have learnt this day. I ask you, please do not judge me harshly."

Lady Hanley again looked disarmed by the charm in his voice. "I can only hope you will keep your traphole shut about anything you saw in my diaries? Or heard this evening." She challenged him to defy her superiority with a haughty look.

"Of course, your Ladyship! I remain but your humble servant!"

Lady Hanley nodded. Between them, they both knew how much their lives depended on secrecy in this new and uneasy alliance.

"In that case, we shall dine whilst we await the return of Maister Jeffries, and then you must rest." Lady Hanley

153

closed the conversation, before more questions could be asked and tempers riled.

Their eyes met, and behind her lashes, Joshua could see the wheels spinning still. She had misjudged Joshua before when they first met, and even with the knowledge now of what he was, and where he had come from, there was still a level of mistrust between them which he did not know how to surmount. Why did he get the impression that she thought she held sway over him still though? It puzzled him as he walked after her from the room.

CHAPTER 13 - DRESSED TO IMPRESS ?

Annabella felt the fractionally colder air brush over her wings. Instinctively, she turned groggily to see its source. Through half-open eyes, bleary with exhaustion, she distinguished several figures approaching. The room brightened as they placed their candles on the floor around the walls. Pulling herself upright as much as the silken chains would allow, her wings fluttered against the mud, shivering. Annabella drew her knees to her chest and rocked herself into a little ball. Her movement had acknowledged their intrusion and she immediately regretted even responding to it. It told them she was alert, conscious, when really her head was barely able to keep a thought in it she was so tired and cold. Now, she tried to shut them out and ignore them.

Her posture caused the new arrivals some concern; if touched, would she lash out like the feral beast they were worried she might have become? Uffer had his doubts, but he was more concerned for his prisoner's mental state of mind. It had already been over a week since she had come into his care, so to speak, been his responsibility. Each day he had failed to even get her to acknowledge him, let alone speak. He approached, his arms outstretched with a dish on it. The smell of the salty fish assaulted Annabella's nostrils, intuitively she recoiled further in horror.

"It's as much as we can offer right now," Uffer said encouragingly and pushed the plate forward. "You must eat, my Lady."

Annabella's glance flickered between her knees over

the dead fish. It had been days since she last ate, yet its grey staring eyes echoed her lifeless existence. She had absolutely no desire to touch his offering, no matter how well-intended its presentation to her was. The smell of it alone reminded her too much of her previous miserable entrapment here in this Queendom.

Another fae, a woman she vaguely recognised in the dim light, approached cautiously. "If Your Highness would like," she began in a wavering voice, "we could help you bathe and dress before you dine?" The woman crouched down to her level, tilting her head and offering a gentle smile.

Unmoving, Annabella ignored her.

"The Queen has requested your attendance, your Highness," Uffer said. "There will be others at Court also. Surely you would prefer to present a..." He tailed off, struggling for the right motivational word, "more appropriate presence?"

Uffer clearly considered that she gave a hoot about her *presentation*. Annabella almost smiled at the banality. What her mother or the Court thought could not be further from her cares.

Gentle hands began to stroke her bowed head and the smell of dead fish receded slightly as Uffer backed off. Annabella didn't flinch, but neither did she pull away. Physical contact with another turned out to actually be quite soothing.

The awkward silence in the room was broken by the sounds of a large object being dragged in, followed by pouring. Through her knees, Annabella watched as a procession of worker fae entered, emptying jugs of steaming water into the tub and leaving again. The stroking on her hair kept a steady pace, smoothing her ratty tresses.

When the water-bearers had all left, Uffer said softly but with a firmness reminiscent of Joshua, "Your Highness, we do not have long before the Queen requires your presence. You have nothing to fear from Elizae." He gestured towards the woman beside Annabella, the one stroking her hair still. "She is here to help you." He turned, pulling the door shut behind him and turning the key.

The older fae shot a look of concern at this measure, but having submitted to her caresses, hoped that the princess was calmer. The poor child was more akin to a wounded animal.

Elizae straightened, walked over to test the water, then turned to the sorry ball of Annabella on the ground. "Come now," she said, "Let us get you out of these tatters." Her strong hands pulled at Annabella, gently at first, then more insistently to try to pull her upright.

Annabella resisted - not only was she weak, but she had no intention of playing along with what was obviously her mother's wishes.

"My Lady!" Elizae insisted, pulling on her arm. Annabella let her pull but kept her weight centred on the floor. The wrench in her shoulder was actually a slight relief from the pain stabbing continually at her heart. After a few more tugs, Elizae gave up and dropped the arm. She banged on the door and almost immediately the scraping of the key sounded and Uffer reappeared.

"Not co-operating," Elizae spat out, her annoyance a harsh contrast to her earlier soothing tones.

Uffer strode over to Annabella, huffing through his nostrils and lips pinched together. Hauling her up by her armpits from behind, Annabella's wings began to beat furiously, bashing around his head. Her body hung,

157

remaining limp, a dead weight in his arms. With an audible heave, he hoisted her over to the tub and held her dangling over it.

Annabella had her eyes tightly shut but she could feel the air moving around as he used his wings to balance himself as he bent over. The water was warm on Annabella's bare toes, then calves. He lowered her down, fully clothed, into the tub. Annabella forced herself to relax and let her legs crumble into the wetness rather than bear any weight.

Instinctively her arms straightened as her torso entered, so she wouldn't completely submerge in the embracing warmth. Her head wrestled with itself - the conscious part of her wanted to force herself to fall forwards, sink deeper, entirely, and allow her mouth to breathe in the water. Put an end to it all. Subliminally though, her body was resisting this directive from her mind, holding her half in, half out of the deadly invitation. On all fours, Annabella froze.

Whilst locked in this battle within herself, Uffer stood back and held her wings firmly together. This pinned her in the tub most effectively. Elizae began scooping water over her head. The warm rivulets ran down Annabella's cheeks and towards her mouth. Annabella spat. The peat and bogs from the landscape above left their mark in the water's smell and dank, sour taste, as well as turning it a slightly brackish colour. She began to keen, writhing to escape the taint of the place she hated. The sound, even to her own ears, was forlorn and desperate.

Thoroughly damp, Elizae yanked and tugged to unlace the wriggling bodice. She pulled off Annabella's outer clothes until she was in only her shift, discarding the garments in a heap on the muddy floor beside the tub as if

158

they were no more than wrappings. Annabella sobbed, wobbling on her limbs like a newborn animal taking its first steps. As the steam rose up from the clothing, releasing the familiar scent of home, of Joshua, her wails grew louder.

Having never particularly understood the commonly held human belief that bathing invited into the body bad humours, Annabella reconsidered. She tried to breathe in, to hold the essences of the fuggy air, to retain that semblance of who she was. Arching her back as much as Uffer's grip would allow, she recoiled against the dark water invading her skin, marking her with this location. But the sense of where she had come from began to drip away.

To Uffer and Elizae the smells were both alien and unwelcome - the essences of humankind long forgotten or never known. Annabella's lamentations made a difficult situation almost unbearable, but they ploughed on with the tricky task. Elizae took a scoop of coarse sand-soap and firmly began to lather Annabella through her shift. Rhythmic motions intended to calm as well as cleanse.

Annabella's muscles tensed, fighting both the entrapment of Uffer bearing down on her wings to keep her in the tub and resisting the brisk invasion of her body by Elizae. Her keening cry started to sound ragged and filled the room as she endured the fastest wash down Elizae felt she could get away with.

Elizae progressed to dousing her with the warm water again. With every rinse, Annabella mourned. Eventually her tears slowed their hot insistence, the urge to lash out dissipated. A part of her blinkered mind acknowledging that the woman was only trying to help, to do her job as bidden. Her body relaxed a little, realising that the ordeal was close to ending.

"Better now?" Elizae said, her tone gentle once more. Annabella shook her head, refusing to meet the woman's eyes. She whimpered, more to herself than to elicit sympathy from Uffer and Elizae. The vulnerability of her position right now, as the water cooled her skin and pinned her shift to her slender frame, was not lost on any of them. Annabella felt a jerk, firm but insistent, on the top of her wing-join where Uffer had been holding them. It forced her to sit upright in the tub yet she lolled her head down still towards her chest.

Uffer's hands moved to under her arms again and he heaved her up. This time Annabella allowed her legs to bear the weight. The fight was over and there was little point in resisting further. The chilled air of the cell hit her wet shift and the shivering started, only subsiding as she submitted to the woman patting her down with a rough towel as Uffer held her firmly in place.

Elizae then put her hands under Annabella's arms, gripping her whilst Uffer fetched something from near the doorway. He returned and swiftly fitted a clamp over the top of her wings, tightening it with a key so that they were held proud of her body but unable to move. He then bent down and unlocked the chains from her legs. A freedom of sorts beckoned. Not the kind of freedom she wanted though.

Uffer left the cell whilst Elizae stripped the sodden undergown from Annabella, then clothed her as she would a child who had given up the fight. Annabella allowed her limbs to be placed into a fresh, but still peat-scented undershirt which tied at the back. Then Elizae manhandled her into a loose shift dress, again, fastened to account for wings behind. Taking a fine bone comb, Elizae tugged at

160

her tangled wet hair, pulling it straight.

When she had finished, Elizae stood back to admire her handiwork, saying, "Well that looks almost like you." The simple tailored dress clung to Annabella's narrow frame, its deep jade green striking against her near-white skin and long blonde hair. The fabric was woven with a silver thread, so delicate it shimmered in the candlelight. However, the slumped posture and downcast face belied the sad truth; a fine dress does not fix a broken princess.

Annabella kept her face neutral, considering her options whilst the ministrations were being made. It did feel better to be in clean, comfortable clothes once more, she admitted to herself, but it didn't change anything. She was a prisoner, an Outcast, and no amount of pretty garments and kind words could change the ache in her heart and the despair in her head.

It was plain that Uffer and Elizae intended for her to go before her mother, but she could not imagine what purpose this would serve? Was she to be paraded like a trophy before the court? Or a jester, to be poked at and made fun of? Would she ever be free again? Could she...?

Annabella's legs buckled and started to sink to the ground. Her head whirled with anxiety about what was ahead of her. Elizae caught her arm before she could collapse. "Now then, this isn't the end of the world, my Lady." How could she possibly know that, Annabella thought? Elizae took her arm and began to drag Annabella towards the doorway where Uffer was awaiting.

He looked her up and down and swallowed hard. In the flickering light of the candle he held, the slim figure before him seemed more familiar, yet there was a quality about her which did not fit his expectations. The fragile pale face which looked up at him was so different in cast

161

from the Princess Aioffe he had watched from afar those many years ago. It looked softer, less angular. And weary.

Annabella met his eyes, and she saw the sadness and resignation she felt reflected back. They both knew she wasn't ready for the onslaught that awaited her.

"I will escort you to the Hall, your Highness, but there I must leave you." His voice was low and conciliatory. Then his kindly tone returned to a formal footing, "I apologise for the wing-clamps, but I am under orders."

Annabella nodded in understanding. She bore him no ill-will, and he had made it very clear that he would carry out all instructions to the letter, regardless of how they were achieved. Sighing with resignation, she determined that it would be better to discover her fate directly from the source. With dread pulling heavily upon her every fibre, she forced herself to step out of the cell.

Emerging from the tunnels which lead to the Beneath, Annabella glanced around, absorbing the familiar walkways through the tall trees ahead of her. Worn, dried-up steps of light grey wood stretching upwards into the treetops. Once they had been edged with greenery, but now the side ropes were frayed and tatty. The network of walkways were obviously not much used except by bound prisoners or fae who were no longer able to fly. Annabella was shocked despite herself at the decay into which they had fallen since she had last flown over them. Come to think of it, she had never actually walked on them. Perhaps they had always been so poorly maintained, so pale?

Annabella's head swam, for she hadn't eaten for days and now the exertion of the steady climb made her pant for breath slightly. Behind her, Uffer plodded dully upwards even though his wings were free and he could have flown;

he was on his guard in case she should try to escape. Annabella began to use the rough guide ropes to help pull herself up the increasingly steep slope as the steps neared the balcony level. Her bare toes had to grip the wooden planks to maintain her footing as the walkway moved slightly in the breeze. It was colder up here; the cells under the deep roots of the trees now seemed welcomingly warm by comparison to the bitter exposure outside.

As she stepped onto the balcony platform, she realised that she could see the vista stretching further than ever before. The mists held by ancient magic which shielded the treetop palace had receded, faded to the edges of the forest. There was still a wall of low cloud in the distance, where spindly evergreen trees could be seen on the outskirts of the island. This realisation was frightening, for the mists kept their Queendom hidden from casual observers.

Turning to survey the view from her high vantage point, the full extent of the decay was horribly apparent. Once green and lush trees were now brown and bleak as far as she could see. The pale carved wooden structures forming the palace which had once shimmered in the sunlight looked dull and grey. Outlying buildings perched on branches, vacant.

"My Lady," Uffer interrupted her reverie; his arm pointed at the vast arched doorway into the main hall. Annabella drew herself up and took in a deep breath. Her cold feet seemed to act independently of her mind and turned towards the doors. Falling in line behind the First Lord of Anaxis, Annabella felt the crunch of dried up, unswept leaves littering the platform and the sorrow of the decline in Naturae chilled her soul.

Entering the archway into the outer atrium, with its

high vaulted ceiling, the doors to the inner palace swung open as they approached. Flanked by two guard fae, Annabella and Uffer entered the dimly lit vestibule. Uffer's boots made a tapping sound as he walked past the trunk in the centre and across towards the white entrance to the High Hall. He pushed open the double doors. Even the silver inlaid swirls on the exterior had tarnished to a dull grey, Annabella noticed, as she passed through.

Her eyes remained downcast and she focused on following Uffer's brown boots to navigate the room. From the corner of her eyes however she could see the many other boots - white, bracken, lichen green, pointed, painted - of the court in attendance. Silence fell as the pair made their way through the crowds, parting to let them through. Annabella could feel their eyes though, studying her, assessing. Then the whispers, swelling like a wave as she shuffled past.

"Is it really her?"

"Should she be here like that?"

"Oh! Poor child..."

"She has come home!"

"There will be a change now, it's certain."

Try as she might, Annabella couldn't shut out their voices; some carrying the weight of hope and expectation, some clearly disbelieving what they saw in front of them. All were judging.

As they approached the dais, Uffer moved away to the side. Annabella lifted her head in a gesture of defiance, borne of centuries of behaving according to her royal status. Whilst she dreaded facing her mother again, her pride would not allow the court to see her weakness.

Prisoner though she might still be, she was Aioffe, Princess of Naturae.

Stood alone as the crowds had shrunk away from her, a voice inside her screamed to run at that moment. She resisted the urge, knowing also that it was futile to try to escape. Instead, she stopped walking, bracing herself, on the wooden floor map before the dais. Right on the north-east of England. For courage.

Narrowing her vision, Aioffe looked up at her mother and met her gaze. Clear blue eyes clashed against dark brooding ones, linking the small space between them as lightning jumps from sky to tree. Queen Lana straightened, her enormous green wings rising shimmering up behind her. The twisted white throne she was sat upon creaked as she lifted from it, hovering above Aioffe. The subjugation began.

Looking over Aioffe's head now, Queen Lana addressed the courtiers in a thin yet unwavering voice. "See - she has returned to us!" Her arm had swept wide then pointed suddenly down for emphasis at Aioffe, as if the crowd were somehow unaware of the girl standing before them. "But do not be deceived!"

Aioffe couldn't take her eyes off her mother's slim form, her wings fluttering gracefully to hold court above her. She had aged considerably, Aioffe thought, with no sense of emotion towards the Queen.

"She is not to be trusted!" Her mother screeched, her familiar voice piercing as if it would cut her to shreds. "If we are not *vigilant*, she will be the doom of all of you, of all of us."

Aioffe looked around in confusion. The bewildered eyes of the assembled fae focused back on her. They were still judging her, she realised, watchful and wary now after the Queen's proclamation. Aioffe opened her mouth as if to speak, but she didn't know what she could say to counter this accusation. She wasn't to be trusted, that much was true; the very instant she could leave Naturae again, she would. Even if she wasn't breathing, she would leave somehow. The Queen's doom-laden hyperbole though, that was new.

The accusations continued to pour from Lana's twisted mouth. "Who knows what she has told of our ways? And to whom?"

The silence of the assembly was broken by murmurs and renewed whispers. In response, the Queen flew higher until she was several feet above the crowd, waiting until the noise died down. The only one permitted to fly within the building, Queen Lana had long ago learned how to use the height advantage to bend the court to her will. Aioffe closed her eyes. There was little point in trying to reason with her mother when she was in full-on theatrics.

"She will remain here, *in constant view*, when the court is assembled, but return to The Beneath. She will live there, as the Outcast she also is."

Fluttering down to land gracefully on the dais, Queen Lana leaned forward to thrust her gaunt face towards Aioffe's. "She will learn to do her duties," she spat in a quieter, but no less forceful voice.

Aioffe looked once more at the floor, inflaming her mother with defiance was futile. At least she knew what to expect now. And, in truth, it was a far lesser punishment than she had expected for what she had done. She thought about Lady Hanley, with her docked wings and felt momentarily grateful. But Aioffe also knew, given the chance, she would rebel again. Her mother was right about that. Having not said a word, Aioffe turned and walked slowly out of the hall. The weight of disappointed expectations from the crowd followed her, and her heart sank even more than she thought was possible.

CHAPTER 14 - TRAPPED

Joshua was having trouble sleeping. The Christmas evening meal had passed with a false air of celebration and a sprinkling of politics. It had felt like a deliberate attempt by Lady Hanley to steer clear of any discussions which might provoke further loaded questions from Joshua. Mr Bray, rather unusually Joshua thought, had joined them at the table and had put away a fair amount of wine as he gorged himself on the thin goose he had cooked for them all.

Mr Bray had broken the stiff silence with talk of a town close by, where land rights were being questioned as other landlords made attempts to move in on long-held common-land grazing rights and oust tenants in the process. It was a subject which Joshua was able to partly contribute towards, having seen it in other parts of the country. The disputes often ended up in the Courts of Augmentation, held in cities, so he had scant knowledge of what transpired in the legal proceedings before a decision was forced and families were evicted from their historic lands. Their subsequent spiral into poverty led to the increase in beggars on streets, or they turned to peddling tatty wares or worse, thieving, to feed themselves.

Maister Jeffries did not make an appearance, and despite Mr Bray grumbling about missing Mass, all discussion about religion was firmly quashed by Lady Hanley, expressing she 'had no desire to blow air on an already smouldering fire.' Bray had lifted his glass to that, before mumbling something rude about how women should not be able to exert such influence over a king. He had avoided direct conversation with Joshua all evening, preferring to take the opportunity of a mealtime with his Mistress as a way of showcasing his knowledge on local and legal matters. Bray was careful to defer to her superior position, but Joshua sensed a desire for the servant to demonstrate his prowess and assert his importance, as if he were of equal status to Lady Hanley.

Neither Joshua nor Lady Hanley had eaten much, just enough to be polite. Bray however, tucked into the festive boiled pig's head, shred pie and wine with relish. He put away more than Joshua would have expected for such a trim man. The weather outside was cold and the large, dark-wooded and unadorned dining hall, obviously infrequently used, hadn't quite warmed up either.

The conversation at table then took an unpleasant turn, as Mr Bray started bemoaning the recent influx of travelling people, peddling their wares at the market and leaving behind them a trail of crime and theft. 'Heathens, the lot of them,' Mr Bray had labelled the gypsies. Joshua wondered if he attributed Alice's death to them, but he couldn't be certain that Bray was so easily blinded to the strange circumstances of the body, and not merely finding a scapegoat which was more conveniently explained away.

Tired after a long, emotional day, Joshua had made his excuses to retire as soon as the last course of sweetmeats had been brought in and offered around by a then slightly lurching Bray. Tucked up in the warmth of his bed, eventually his mind gave up trying to make sense of everything, and his eyelids started to droop.

As he was sinking finally into a deeper sleep, his ears caught the sounds of boots outside in the corridor, the leather squeaking on the floorboards. Jeffries, Joshua thought to himself, I'm glad he made it back.

Then there was a creak as his doorway opened, and shuffling feet quickened their pace, harder and faster as they approached the bed. His eyes flew open in the darkness. Joshua tried to sit up, but his chest stabbed with crippling pain at the sudden movement. An arm quickly reached over his head to grab the neighbouring pillow. With a speed his bleary mind could hardly keep up with, the feather stuffed gag was slapped down over his face and weight applied.

As the pressure on the pillow suffocated him, he couldn't even sense any smell to help identify whom it might be assailing him. Had his attacker from the woods found him? Come back to finish what he started? Somehow this manner of murder felt too subtle for that. And that meant he had a chance...

Lashing out with his legs, core muscles screaming with the effort, Joshua brought his hands up to try to knock the assailant's arms away from their grim task. Then he felt the weight of their body begin to press down on his face, adding a torso to the firm pressure on his head. Joshua kicked out again, wrenching his legs off the bed, his heel knocking the piss pot underneath it with a loud clank. A muffled deep guttural laugh came from his attacker, as he kept piling his weight onto the pillow, ignoring the writhing torso beneath.

Joshua, now starved of oxygen, continued lashing with his legs, kicking the boards of the bedframe to try to get enough movement so that he could throw the man off. His strong arms rained down blows to the body of his assailant, but still it resisted, continuing to press down on the pillow.

Suddenly the pressure lifted, and Joshua heard the dull thud of a body landing on the floorboards.

170

"How dare you!" Lady Hanley's voice rang muffled through the feathers, then she lifted the pillow from Joshua's head. Joshua gasped in the muggy air, his lungs' craving overriding the increased pain in his chest from the sudden expansion of his ribcage. His eyes slid to the left in time to see Lady Hanley deliver a well-placed kick to Mr Bray's rib cage. That manic laugh erupted again.

"In my house!" She scolded down at him.

Mr Bray's guttural noise was turning hysterical now. "He's not natur'l!" Mr Bray's words were barely discernible through the laughter which had now consumed him like a drunken madman.

"Have you learned nothing, you narrow-minded dalcop? You forget your place." Lady Hanley said haughtily.

The laughter ceased suddenly, and Mr Bray's voice turned cold, his hatred apparent as he spat out, "He has no place being here, not like your Lord Hanley. T'aint right or natur'l. He'll bring us all down!"

"*He* is no different to *I*," Lady Hanleys voice matched Brays in iciness. "And *we* are different to Lord Hanley!"

"Aye, he was a wrong'un too!" Bray snorted, "and that were bad enough!"

"How dare you talk of my husband in that way! After all these years of service, you ungrateful sorner!"

With a surprising amount of speed and fuelled by wine and ire, Bray turned his body and lurched himself off the floor. His face turned puce with renewed anger. He clenched his fists, dripping with urine. He rushed at Lady Hanley, his arms outstretched to shove her. "Garrrh" - the noise of the attack was as brief as the few steps he had to take to gain momentum. Bray's hands landed squarely on her breasts, shoving her hard onto Joshua's chest. Joshua's nose rebelled against the stench of wine and adrenaline briefly before the air was forced from his lungs once more.

Rebounding quickly, Bray spun on his heels and ran out of the room. Lady Hanley had fallen awkwardly, painfully, on Joshua, but immediately she recovered and rolled off his body as soon as Bray's hands left her chest. She staggered over to the doorway and fell against the wooden panel, slamming it shut.

"Oh, rats!" She panted in the silence that followed as they gathered their breath. She rolled her eyes, realising that she had just locked them both in.

Despite the pain in his chest, after a few seconds Joshua couldn't help but chuckle. The absurdity of the situation hit Lady Hanley after a moment as well. The tension in the room dissipated as they both chuckled to themselves. Then, glancing at her, Joshua felt a kinship with the older fae. "Thank you, once again," he said as their laughter died down.

She raised a hand and waved it away as if her saving his life had been nothing. Joshua looked again at his saviour. Despite the exertion she had the same luminescent skin Aioffe had, especially as she was dressed only in a long white nightshirt, her greying hair long around her shoulders. Without the coif, her loose hair alone took years off her age. He could appreciate the armour which her fashionable clothing had provided in the battle to blend in with humankind that their kind faced.

"I mean it, your Ladyship, I owe you my life once again," Joshua said earnestly, the full impact of what had just happened hitting him.

"I'm sorry I didn't arrive sooner," Lady Hanley said. Joshua leaned carefully over to the nightstand and righted the candle which had fallen over in the kerfuffle. She crouched to look around the damp floor for the matches.

"What was he thinking?" Joshua mused aloud. He had underestimated the man, clearly, and Lady Hanley's obvious physical strength.

"In his own way, he was trying to protect me."

"How am I a threat to you? I can barely walk!"

"But you will recover," Lady Hanley said, calmer now. "Bray has limits, like any man does, and your difference is just too much risk for him, I think." Finding the matches finally, she lit the candle. The tallow scent and low flame was more for comfort and propriety, both had no actual need for it with their fae eyesight.

"There must be something more behind his attack, your Ladyship," Joshua said. "This was about more than me being 'different'."

Lady Hanley sat on the bed, next to Joshua but not so close as would be improper. "My late husband..." she trailed off, unwilling to spill more secrets to the stranger, no matter how they were connected. She sighed, for in truth her reluctance to tell was more about denying the facts to herself than it was about wanting to keep the knowledge from him.

"Please?" Joshua encouraged. This fragile trust he sensed between them would be pushed he knew, but he needed to utilise his advantage whilst she was clearly on the cusp of shedding light on the matter for him.

Lady Hanley sighed again. "How I wish it was as easy as that," she said, with sorrow in her voice. "Over the years, Bray has become more than a faithful servant. He has kept our secrets, gone about our business, and protected me from the harsher judgements of the world."

"I can see he has served you diligently and as a dedicated servant would," Joshua said, "but that still doesn't give him the right to try and kill me to protect you."

"I know," she sighed. "I know. But there was a time, some years after I... arrived here, that I had need of his protection. It was so long ago now though, I had hoped he would have forgotten, moved on."

"Was it your wings? Did someone hurt you?"

"No, no, the wings were almost the least of it in the end."

"Then why? Why does he feel he, above all others, should be the defender of this household?"

Lady Hanley stood up; she needed to pace. "As the Great Search was going on, I was sent out to try and find Princess Aioffe as well. My family-line had a long history of spycraft, I was trained in duplicity. I still had to maintain a court presence, but would travel the continent then report back on my findings about activities of the other creatures in the nearby realms. When Aioffe disappeared, all spies were re-deployed within Naturae's realm to search for any sign of her."

"I met Lord Hanley when he was travelling to negotiate with James of Scotland at Inverness, on behalf of the English King, Henry V. I was tired, I had been flying a long time, and I desperately needed sustenance. I was resting at an inn when he came in, so full of energy and light..." She was momentarily lost in the memory.

"Please go on," Joshua interrupted her silence.

"It was inevitable," she smiled. "We were drawn to each other, as if our creature blood had magnets within." Then Lady Hanley looked away, almost girlishly embarrassed to admit, "I didn't try to resist him too much, I confess. We travelled north, heading back towards Naturae so I could appear at court as planned, then leave for good, without arousing suspicion."

Joshua felt that strange sense of kinship surge again, with added sympathy. He knew what it was like to be in love, knew the power of its allure and how nothing else seemed to matter.

"I'm surprised you went back, if it was as bad as you say there. You must have known you would displease the Queen if you returned without any information?" Joshua asked.

"Oh, I realised, but Captain Lyrus knew where I was searching. They would have come to find me if I hadn't returned. I determined the best thing to do was pretend everything was as normal and just report in, then leave again. Also, I was careless, leaving traces which I should have hidden. I was passionately in love, and it made me stupid. Of course, Lord Hanley couldn't fly, so that slowed us down."

"I thought you said he was a creature too?" Joshua was surprised.

"Daemon, a halfling they are called sometimes. Not fae." The matter-of-factness with which she spoke belied the uncomfortable truth that such mixings were very strictly forbidden.

"Oh..." Again, Joshua felt at a disadvantage - Annabella had completely failed to inform him of much about the shadowy world they inhabited.

"Anyway, eventually we arrived near to Naturae, and I left Lord Hanley, Michael, in the town to rest and flew home. Sadly, I had already been missed. I was late and Lyrus was waiting for me."

Joshua had to know, "Who's he?"

"The Queen's son - Aioffe's vine-brother - one of many Lana had turned into expert torturers. He is as royal as you could get without being a female. And as twisted, like his mother. Anyway, as my family returned, each of them had been questioned, but then, I was late. I tried to say I had been waylaid by weather - I didn't know my brothers had already talked of how lovely the climate was for the time of year. My excuse just didn't stand up to scrutiny."

Lady Hanley continued pacing, her bare feet almost soundless in the quiet chamber.

"Did they hurt you then?" Joshua asked, although one part of him was afraid of the answer.

"No, I was put in the Beneath - it's the Naturae gaol. A terrible, dark place." She shuddered, but realising that more detail might upset Joshua, she resumed her tale. "As far as they knew at that point, I was just late and hadn't any information to tell about Aioffe, so I was guilty of a bad job. Not quite enough grounds for punishment, but close."

"Then, what happened to your wings?" Joshua said, confused.

"After a time - I'm not sure how long, but Michael said later he'd waited for me at least a month, they let me out to see my family. I was so broken by then I confessed to my brother what had occurred, that I intended to leave. There was an Ambassador he said, a well-respected family on the continent who could help us if we went there. My brother helped me, gave me the courage to carry on with my plan. But it didn't work....."

Her voice wobbled as the emotion returned afresh. Lady Hanley stopped and bent over, clutching her hand to her stomach as if she had been dealt a body blow. Joshua stood up from the bed and approached her. He reached out to touch her arms as a gesture of comfort, but she swatted them away angrily, cross with herself for the moment of weakness.

She swallowed hard, and carried on. "I flew back that night to where I had left Michael, but I was followed. They didn't trust anyone. And once they saw who I was meeting, they made a judgement on me, on us. I think they suspected we would leave England, and Naturae's dominion as soon as possible, escape abroad. So they entered our room at the inn and overwhelmed us. Michael was knocked about, when they threw him off me. He was injured very badly. Then, they pinned me down to the floor, and cut off my wings so I could never return."

Joshua winced. The mere thought of it sent shivers through him. "But Lord Hanley? He survived as well?"

"After a fashion," Lady Hanley said sadly. "They drained most of his Lifeforce from him. We were both near death."

"We remained holed up in that awful place, tried to lick our wounds, so to speak. We dared not seek help, of course, even though we were close to the Abbey at Inverness. The Dominicans lived there at the time. One of the monks - so young then - saw my love trying to catch something alive in the marshes for me. In his poor state, Michael was flailing about and crying, apparently."

"Jeffries?" It began to fall into place for Joshua.

"Himself, yes," Lady Hanley nodded. "He'd been sent to live at the Abbey, expelled by his own family for his odd abilities with animals and plants. I think he knew, even then, that he was a witch. Jeffries, just then only training to be a healer, brought Michael back to the inn and Michael begged him to examine me. We were clearly acting so oddly - shifty he called it - he felt obliged to help us."

"He does seem the kindly sort."

"Kind, yes. Talented, no doubt, but he's got his own dilemmas to westle with," Lady Hanley warned, defensive of her friend but under no illusion either about the conflicts within the monk.

"Although Michael had recovered from his injuries with rest and food, I was not faring so well. Jeffries helped treat my wounds. I don't know what he did, but where they had cut off my wings in haste, they had left ragged bits which weren't healing. I think my humours were out of balance. I couldn't even take myself to feed, although the craving was so bad I was a danger to everyone. Michael tried to bring me live animals, even offered me himself, I couldn't bring myself to hurt him more than he had been already."

"Eventually, Jeffries and Michael took me to the Abbey, to hear the Matins there. I think they thought it would be my last rites, and both were at a loss as to what else to do to lift my humours. The singing though...it did something to me, uplifted my soul I suppose."

"The other Lifeforce," Joshua agreed. "It's not the same as Lifeforce from the blood, it's a different sustenance." He knew well the energy that congregated humans celebrating could have. The promise of it alone had kept Annabella and he staying in Beesworth when they should have left. And she wouldn't have been taken from him, he thought sadly. A wave of desperate loneliness swept over him again and he ached deep within.

Lost in his thoughts, Joshua stared at the flickering candle, trying to push away the creeping panic he began to feel. What if they had cut Annabella's beautiful wings? Would they do that to a princess?

"Whatever it was, I felt nourished, and started to eat

178

voraciously to recover properly." Lady Hanley said, disturbing his reverie.

"Would they cut Annabella?" Joshua blurted out. Lady Hanley turned her head and looked away from him.

"I cannot say," she replied quietly. "Since I left, I had to sever all contact with that place. Until now. I do not know what she would be returning to."

"I must go. Find her." Joshua stood up, casting his eyes around for the borrowed clothing. "I cannot leave her there."

"Yes," she finally agreed, sighing. "It is not safe for you here either."

They looked at the door, both wondering about how to escape the situation they found themselves in.

"Jeffries!" Joshua said, a brightness in his voice as the idea came to him. "Surely he will return soon?"

"Or Bray sleeps it off and realises what he's done in the morning." Lady Hanley didn't sound worried. She patted the bed and Joshua shrugged. For all his desperation, the prison of the room could not be escaped at that moment. They sat there in silence for a while, staring at the door. To Joshua, it almost felt companionable.

"So," Joshua said conversationally, "you didn't finish about Mr Bray?"

Mary perked up. There was actually something cathartic, she realised, about confessing her story after all these years.

"We were able to travel out of Scotland and made our way down to England. My Lord had lodgings in London, so we lived there for a while. I found it too hard to survive on just church-going alone - I needed to be close to woodland. Eventually, we moved to make our base here when Lord Hanley was gifted these lands by the King.

Michael built this house so that I might have the privacy I wanted to meet my needs, yet still have a public face. He designed it all himself, you know, except the Library. That was my room."

"So Mr Bray started work for you then did he?"

"Yes, he was but a young lad at the time. We didn't want many servants, but he was the only survivor of the plague and had no-one else and nowhere else to go. We took him in, and he has been with us ever since."

"He knows your secret though?"

"About what happened to my wings, no, but he has seen the stumps. And the feeding, I think it's more he sees a 'pattern of behaviour' which he keeps quiet about. He's a smart man, likes his position and won't do anything to jeopardise that, I'm sure."

"Well he did!" Joshua said forcefully. "He risked everything when he tried to kill me!"

"Did he though?" Lady Hanley's cool manner returned as she protected her servant. "No-one bar Jeffries and Bray know you are here. No-one would miss you," she added, cruelly.

Joshua knew she was right. He nodded, staring at his hands, the thought that he had lost everything he held dear ran through his mind. He felt momentarily envious of her, she had managed to survive amongst humans with a home of her own and keep her secrets. He had failed spectacularly each time he and Annabella had tried.

"Mr Bray was there for me, when Lord Hanley wasn't." She paused, glancing at Joshua warily, then looked away. He might as well know the full extent to which Mr Bray would protect her. "Michael, like so many daemons, became unhinged towards the close of his life. He would rant and rail at the slightest thing - from the weather to the food on the table."

She looked around the room wistfully. "In the end, we had to keep him here, for all of our safety."

Joshua studied her from the corners of his eyes. The choices she had been forced to make in order to survive showed as the furrows on her face deepened. She seemed to age once more in front of him with the memory.

Looking down at her hands, she confessed her final woe: "More than once, Mr Bray had to interrupt a violent... situation between us. He saw the damage that Michael himself, in a passionate rage, had done to me. He knew of my shame. He shielded me from others who might have seen it also, nursed my wounds and looked after my business whilst I recovered. He even fed me when I couldn't walk. I suppose it's a form of love. I cannot cast him out after all he has done for me."

Joshua nodded slowly, humbled. He hadn't realised the extent of the relationship between servant and Mistress, how deeply they relied on one another. "Surely," he ventured after a while, "if he knew what we were, he would think I wouldn't hurt you?"

"He knew you were different, but he is afraid of things which are 'different'. Lord Hanley was perfectly normal, until he wasn't. Mr Bray has come to view everything which is peculiar as a threat to our 'normal'. He's not good with change. Although, that said, he does have a remarkable ability to rise to the occasion when needed."

This much Joshua couldn't disagree with; the man's level-headedness in a crisis or strange situation spoke volumes of his intelligence and experience. It was a shame Mr Bray was so threatened by his presence in the house, but at least Joshua could understand why now. That didn't mean he liked the attempt on his life, however.

Joshua wondered how attempted murder would sit on Mr Bray's conscience when he sobered up. After all those years spent reconciling his appetites with his own mortal soul, he almost felt sorry for the man. Their faith took a dim view on killing another, and Mr Bray seemed a passionate and God-fearing believer.

Joshua sat next to Mary on the bed. The room needed the slivers of the dawn light to warm it, for the fire had gone out. A easier silence fell as they both sat in contemplation and awaited rescue. Joshua somehow felt comforted by her presence, despite all her cruel remarks and endangering Annabella. He hoped that come morning the Lady would stick to her word, and let him leave with the dawn.

CHAPTER 15 - ROYAL REALITY CHECK

Annabella, as she thought of herself in the darkness and solitude of the cell, soon became exhausted by the routine she numbly followed. She felt as if she was losing herself, a gradual erosion of the person she had been when free and living life with Joshua. She curled herself up into a ball and replayed memories of times together in an effort to maintain that link with the person she had once been. It was painful, but part of her couldn't give up on the hope that someday that woman would emerge once again.

She missed Joshua with an ache that had become a familiar constant companion in her chest, but little by little, it was becoming more bearable. It was as if by replaying the memories of their love, she kept him alive. A safe place she could retreat into with him when needed.

Aioffe, however, submitted to the daily dousing by Elizae, was compliant with the walk each morning to the High Hall, and trudged 'home' each afternoon to collapse on the muddy floor in a heap.

The exhaustion came from the constant scrutiny she faced every day as she sat on the stool, now placed on the step below the throne for her to sit on. Aioffe endured the arrivals of Fae Ambassadors and courtiers who were announced to the Court. Paying homage to her mother, the endless parade dispersing as soon as they had been acknowledged with a bleak nod from the Queen, to whisper about 'the situation' in small groups. She had no interest in finding out anything about them as they lurked on the edges of the High Hall, shooting glances at her then murmuring between themselves. Aioffe kept her face neutral at all times in public, her emotions firmly in check as she dutifully observed the daily rituals of court life.

Her exhaustion also stemmed from hunger. The lands around the Palace were so deprived of Lifeforce, over-harvested over the past century, they offered little by way of sustenance. As a result, almost all of the Court was forced to exist on meagre rations of fish. Although caught daily by the workers who ventured out each dawn, by the time they returned with the catch, the fish were dead. Whilst fae can survive on the blood and last remnants of the Lifeforce contained within, most courtiers were starving. The workers, able to feed on the fishy Lifeforce fresh from the seas they hunted in, stayed stronger than the increasingly frail and old-looking courtiers. Even the Ambassadors ended up staying for lack of energy to leave, always present rather than appearing and disappearing as they once had through their liaison function. Naturae was more isolated than it had ever seemed before.

Annabella lost count of the days, for they blended into one seamless round of boredom. Alone in her bare cell, she began to dream of escape once more. For little other reason, it seemed at the time, than to be able to feed properly again. To nourish her soul as well as her stomach. Uffer brought her daily fish which she ignored, yet it took one awful incident for her to realise that she needed to ingest them. But, only enough to sustain herself for when an opportunity for freedom presented itself.

That morning, Queen Lana had (as usual) barely acknowledged her presence, but someone else did. Newly arrived from Europe, Ambassador Spenser had journeyed through England to visit Naturae. He was unlike any of the other courtiers, even those who had visited from abroad, dressed with a panache she identified as human handiwork of the best quality.

Her interest in him was further piqued when, having taken her hand to kiss it, he gave her cool fingers a little squeeze upon release. This most human of actions, the subtle flirtation of a more-intimate-than-required touch, jolted her into meeting his eyes. Within them, she saw sparks of humour, intelligence and warmth. She smelt that he had fed properly. His skin had that recognisable glow about him which suggested not only a recent ingestion of Lifeforce had happened. Her nose wrinkled as she struggled to identify another particular scent he carried about himself. It took but a moment to realise it was sex. He had had actual relations! Very recently, too.

She brushed her loose hair from her shoulders and met his gaze with increasing interest. Her heart thudded slightly within her chest. Not from attraction, but hope.

"It is good to see you, Princess," said Ambassador Spenser. "My people will be most reassured to learn of your return."

The Ambassador had released her hand by then, so she turned to the Queen and said lightly, "I would speak with Ambassador Spenser of his people, your Majesty, so that I might learn more of our family abroad."

The Queen sat upright in her throne and considered. Having heard absolutely nothing from her daughter since her return, not even an acknowledgement as her mother, it aggrieved her that a stranger should prompt her to speak. And a foreigner at that. On the one hand, this could be an indication that Aioffe had capitulated and wanted to honour her duties, finally. On the other, she didn't trust her.

"You may remain here to discuss matters," the Queen

decided. If she could listen in to their discussion, then perhaps she could gauge more about Aioffe's intentions. Bowing his head in acknowledgement, the Ambassador turned and pulled a nearby chair up the stairs, arranging it so he faced them both on the dais. His wings tucked behind him neatly into the gap in the middle of the seat back and he lent forward, as if to speak in confidence with Aioffe.

"My Lady, it brings my heart joy to see you restored here, to your rightful place beside your mother." Ambassador Spenser spoke so formally to her, yet Aioffe sensed from his tone he would have preferred a more casual or private conversation. Studying his face, she remembered that she had seen him before, but only a few times before she fled. He had never shown the slightest familiarity with her, she was certain.

"I would know how your people have fared this last century, my Lord Ambassador?" Aioffe inquired.

"They too have suffered, like here, of the decline in the worship Lifeforce, but we have lands which are plentiful in other ways, your Highness," he told her. "We remain quite a transient populus."

Aioffe recalled that the Fae in Europe were more tribal than here and frequently moved the location of their courts in order that they may stay undetected. Fortunately, Europe was largely covered in forest, so it was much easier to hide without the ancient - now receding - mists they required here in the Islands of Orkney.

"You must indeed thrive, and it would seem you are able to gather sufficient Lifeforce to travel the distance here?" Aioffe said casually, although his eyes told her he knew the unsaid query behind her question.

"How and where he gets his Lifeforce is something we

186

are all interested in." The Queen said dismissively, but she was all ears nonetheless.

Looking directly at the Queen, Ambassador Spenser said accusingly, "It is simple, your Majesty. We are careful, yet we do circulate within the human population."

Lana sniffed, then sneered, "That is your want I suppose, but it can only lead to trouble." She looked pointedly at Aioffe, "As my daughter here will attest to."

Aioffe shot a glance at the Ambassador, then turned her head away slightly from them both.

Spenser studied Aioffe. From her expression, it appeared that she did not agree with her mother. Indeed, he had already surmised that she had spent significant time probably living amongst the humans. Possibly on the mainland, if not even in his territories. He had heard of a search throughout the English Isles after her reported disappearance, but could she have survived there all alone after all?

And yet, here she was, returned to Naturae and by her mother's side. Was it possible she had not come home of her own volition? He straightened and casually looked behind her head, to her shoulder blades. There was the usual lump from wings but hers were covered by a fine cloak.

Aioffe twisted fractionally, sensing he was looking to see if her wings were still there. She rustled them a little as she adjusted her dress, making sure to try and illustrate that under the fabric they were restricted, but nevertheless, wholly there. She smiled, saying, "Your Grace, it would please me greatly if you would tell me more about what is happening in England, as I believe you have recently travelled through?"

"I would be delighted to, your Highness. As you are

no doubt aware, our human's religious beliefs are gaining popularity within your lands as well. Perhaps..." he tailed off as, from across the Hall, a loud thud interrupted them.

The court rustled as everyone looked over at the far corner where the noise had originated. Aioffe's mouth dropped. She glanced back at Spenser, equally shocked with raised eyebrows. Then back to the sight of a worker fae hovering over an elderly courtier. Dead on the floor.

The Queen rose from her throne in one graceful movement and flew over. "Get rid of it at once!" she commanded imperiously. Another worker hurried over to the gathering and began to pull the courtier. Aioffe swallowed and blinked; even the dead-carriers in England showed more respect. The worker fae were literally dragging the body across the floor in some kind of sprawling spectacle! Legs splayed, his clothing caught on the edges of the wooden floorboards as they tugged at the corpse. There was a dreadful ripping sound as the loose embroidered top snagged and tore, causing the first fae worker to have to turn the saggy torso to free it. His face wrinkled in disgust.

Aioffe rose from her stool, crying out, "This is a disgrace!" Courtiers and workers turned away from the sorry scene, towards her instead. Vacant stares dropped onto their faces to hide their shock at her intervention. "Show some respect and carry him out," she continued. Her mother looked at her with amusement.

"He does not deserve respect," the Queen spat. "If he chooses not to avail himself of the supplied foodstuffs, then he is the only one to blame for his weakness!"

Aioffe and Spenser looked at each other, aghast. From the corner of her eye, she noticed the worker fae had smirks upon their faces. Her eyes narrowed, hoping she had been mistaken. A cruel kind of sneer, definitely. Had they been providing sustenance to the courtier? Why did she have the sense they were happy about the death? Was it as simple as one less mouth to feed? The questions swirled around Aioffe's head and she stared at the floor in front of her, blinking.

A quiet voice intruded, as the Ambassador muttered darkly, "This is not the only place where this happens." He stood up and took her hand once more. He bowed, saying gallantly, "I will try to ensure they treat him properly, my Lady." He let her hand drop and strode over to the door, following the worker fae who had resumed tugging the body out.

Aioffe snatched a glance at her mother, wondering what she would do if she followed them out? The Queen cooly met her eyes and her thin lips tightened into a snarl. The warning was enough to make Aioffe reconsider, and she dropped her head again. Now was not the time to create more waves in what was already a stormy situation.

CHAPTER 16 - JOURNEY

The door latch clicked, causing Joshua to jerk awake. He had dozed off, leant against the bedpost. By the window, Lady Hanley also turned and made her way over to Jeffries, standing in the now open aperture. Joshua smiled in relief as he took in the welcome sight of the tall robed figure. "I imagine your first task for Bray will be returning the latch to the door," Jeffries remarked wryly as he entered.

"Thank you for returning with such haste," Lady Hanley said somewhat sarcastically. "We could have done with your presence last night."

"I had a visit from a slightly smelly but very repentant Mr Bray not an hour ago," Jeffries explained. "He is waiting for penance for his misdeeds downstairs. I'm not entirely sure what transpired, but certainly he wasn't keen to come up himself."

Joshua smirked, "As well he shouldn't be!"

Jeffries looked him over with curiosity, "Too much wine again?"

"He has crossed the line," Lady Hanley said, "and behaved most rashly."

"Rashly?" Joshua burst out, glaring at her in astonishment. "Trying to suffocate me is 'rash'?"

"Well, perhaps a little more than rash," she clarified. Jeffries' face fell, knitting his grey eyebrows together with concern.

"We need to discuss plans to move on from this," she continued, all business and ignoring Jeffries who had advanced to examine Joshua. "For all that I am willing to harbour you for your safety here, I will not have my own servant be driven to such deeds through their own discomfort at the situation."

"I can't trust him," Joshua said, "and I want to leave. I don't exactly feel safe here now, and I must find my wife."

"But..." Jeffries paused, unlacing the top of Joshua's nightshirt and frowning at the slipped bandages. He dropped the fabric, saying, "You are not well enough. You should rest."

"I cannot," Joshua replied simply, "I need to leave here."

"There will not be a repeat of last night," Lady Hanley said defensively. "I am certain of that. I shall expect you both forthwith in the kitchen."

She swept past the monk and turned towards her chambers down the corridor to get ready for the day. Jeffries gently pushed Joshua back flat onto the bed without saying anything further. His lips were clamped together as if he was holding his tongue, but the anger at the newly realised threat to his patient rose off him in waves.

"I'll help you dress, then we will sort this sorry mess out," Jeffries said after a few minutes of poking and feeling at Joshua's rib cage. "I take it you can walk with less pain now?"

Jeffries and Joshua made their way down the staircase. In truth, Joshua felt well enough to have just used the bannister for support, but the monk held his arm firmly as if he would not be swayed in his care for his patient. They walked down the darkened corridor towards the kitchen. Although Joshua was not afraid to face Bray in the light of the morning after, he was somewhat hesitant about what would happen. His mind was resolved to make the best of the situation and hasten with getting out of the strange house. After that, he wasn't sure of his plan.

The fire was being tended by Mr Bray as they entered, sparks shooting up as he dropped a large log onto the embers. Hearing their approach, the guilty servant stood tall as if unrepentant, his fists clenched at the bottom of straight arms. His face belied his defiant stance however, and Joshua could read the conflict within.

Lady Hanley, now dressed in a deep red gown with a white trim to the overskirt, bustled in behind Joshua and Maister Jeffries. The effect was festive but did little to lift the tension. Although red was a common colour, the fine cut of the cloth suggested the required reminder that she was in charge of this household. Outside, gentle snowflakes had begun to fall and a thin layer had built up on the windowsill.

Striding to the head of the table, she pointed for Mr Bray to sit down. "It seems to me," she began, as Jeffries eased Joshua onto a stool, "we need to make urgent arrangements for travel." Her eyes narrowed as she stared hard at her servant.

Mr Bray looked startled, banishment wasn't what he was expecting as chastisement. "But..." he began to bluster, "I have served your Ladyship all these past years..."

"You will not be travelling, Mr Bray," she snapped, "although your actions of last night beggar belief." Her cold eyes flashed in annoyance. "You will, however, recompense Mr Meadows for the insult you have shown him by your misdeeds, by making due haste to prepare for his leaving with care and attention. Quickly and without complaint. One can only hope that he sees fit to excuse your miserable existence once he is well again. I will not speak for a guest in this household, but I believe he would be infinitely stronger and more subtle, were he to seek revenge for your ill-thought out threats to his person!"

Joshua couldn't help but smile. He hoped this meant he would have his freedom, and considered it very unlikely he would return to Beesworth, let alone Hanley House. Her warning had Mr Bray shooting a baleful look at Joshua, no apology in his eyes. There remained little doubt in Joshua's mind that, given the chance and enough liquid courage, Mr Bray would continue to protect his Mistress and household from interlopers.

"Maister Jeffries?" She turned the glare of her attention, somewhat haughtily, to the monk. "Do I take it you have retrieved the item which has caused you so much consternation of late?"

Jeffries shifted in his seat, and a flush rose on his face. He nodded briefly and patted the slim satchel held across his body by a broad strap. Joshua looked at the monk in surprise. What relevance did that have to his own, hoped for departure?

"Then we are almost set." Lady Hanley placed her hands on the table and lent forward towards the assembled group. "This entire affair shall not be discussed with anyone outside of this room," she ordered. "What has happened of late - the death of that poor child, the disappearance of the strangers, the activities which sadly transpired last night, the 'book'.... There will be no mention of it. Anywhere. The boys have ears, we cannot risk them overhearing something. It is fortunate that they keep to the stables and do not enter this house. The town will whisper, rumours will abound- we cannot blame them for seeking justice. But Bray and I will say nothing. The gossip will die down, as it always does."

She looked at Bray for his confirmation, to which he

nodded and studied the floor intently. "You will deny all knowledge of the Meadows and their whereabouts, Mr Bray. And you will not frequent a tavern in the town again. I cannot trust your loose tongue. Do not think I am unaware of your affection for my port, but you will refrain from any opportunity to forget yourself outside of this household. Or you will also have to leave."

Bray's chin was so low, it rested on his chest from the chastisement. A flush also rose above his neckline.

"You two," she indicated to Joshua and Jeffries, "will leave here immediately and travel North."

Jeffries looked at Joshua, who had already paled from sitting upright. For a moment, he feared Lady Hanley's instructions would be to silence him and order a return to the Abbey, when he had already determined his route away. But his mind spun to the practicalities of journeying with an invalid. "Your Ladyship, the boy is not well enough to travel."

"He has to, as do you. You will accompany him to ensure his well-being." Lady Hanley had realised that this course of action removed both the objects of worry from her household, and she wanted now to ensure they reached their goals so they didn't return. Her eyes shared the same forcefulness as her statement.

"I will supply my horses to take you as far as the nearest river port, whereupon you will charter a boat to ferry you northwards. Joshua cannot ride far, and you cannot...fly."

Mr Bray snorted, "Neither can the creature!" Joshua's lips tightened. Prejudice had overtaken repentant Bray once more.

"That is correct," Lady Hanley said, but she warned him. "That will not always be the case, Mr Bray. And I remind you to mind your place in this household, lest I decide to cast you out for your behaviour to my person last night as well! You will be gifting Master Meadows your new frieze coat." She sniffed and glared at the servant, who looked put out at his much-prized new clothing being ruthlessly donated on his behalf.

"You are very kind, your Ladyship," Joshua said, "I would find travel by horse exceedingly difficult it is true. A boat is the answer, and I thank you for suggesting it."

Maister Jeffries looked at Lady Hanley, sensing he too ought to placate the woman and endorse her plan. Instead, ever practical, he pointed out, "Mary, we do not have the money for a boat!"

"I will supply you with adequate funds," Lady Hanley said simply. She wasn't sure how much it would cost to charter a boat, but it was worth it to remove her problems.

Her plan was born out of the realisation, through the haze of the dawn light, that her only realistic course of action was to try to lie low. Rid herself of the contentious bodies in her house, whilst continuing hiding, and forget about returning to Naturae altogether. She wanted nothing more to do with the issues which Joshua's presence had brought. As she had dressed in her clothes that morning, she had contemplated that his existence would upset the Fae world so much, it was not a safe harbour for her either. Far better to live out her days in peace and security here amongst humankind.

Another part of her was cross with herself; selfishly motivated actions in betraying Aioffe had caused repercussions she hadn't considered. Could never have considered. And now, the only solution was to get rid of the potentially larger problem posed by her husband. Sending him on his way towards her might be akin to

195

sending a lamb to the slaughter, but at least she could stay away from the fallout.

Pushing Joshua off on his quest as quickly as she could also afforded more time to organise relocating herself. At least for a while, until the possible hunt for her was concluded. She doubted Aioffe could keep quiet about her exiled existence for long, and she would not expect her to leave out mention of Joshua, or even herself.

What to do with Bray was another issue - she supposed he should stay here and run things in her absence, but would he stand up to the torture which no doubt awaited him should they find him? Mary very much doubted it. No, he would have to come along too. Or be... disposed of. For all her loyalty to her servant, how could she ever trust him again after he had attacked her?

*****

Dressing with haste in Lord Hanley's old clothes, which Bray had dragged down from the attics, Joshua felt invigorated. Admittedly, he also felt like a new, richer man in the borrowed brocade short-length gown he was wearing and tan doublet and hose. He had to accept help from the stoney-faced servant to pull on his 'new' frieze coat, which would certainly shield him from inclement weather at sea, as well as the ride. They had parted without saying a further word.

Standing outside waiting for the stable boy to strap his recently retrieved bag to the back of the saddle, Joshua realised he hadn't been out of the house for over a week now.

"Tis at least a fine morning for it," Maister Jeffries announced as he joined Joshua in the yard at the bottom of the hill. A scant layer of snow rested on frozen ground but had at least stopped drifting down for now. "What are we waiting for?" he said, gesturing towards the house. "She won't be coming down to say any goodbyes, you know."

Joshua looked up at the house looming over them. He thought he could make out a figure at the window, but it could equally have been a trick of the light. Anxious to get moving, he was surprised to find he felt a pang of sadness at leaving. Whilst it hadn't been a welcome respite, Lady Hanley had been a gracious hostess and he was somewhat trepidatious about what lay ahead for him.

Although he had impressed upon her Ladyship his earnest thanks earlier, she had seemed distracted, almost dismissive. Whilst packing a sack with her husband's old clothes in for him, Joshua had tried to ask where Naturae was, but Lady Hanley curtly pointed out that she had too much to do here, covering up his tracks, to draw him a map. The vulnerability and companionship he had glimpsed during the night was entirely cloaked once more, and her shortness this morning made him now question if he had ever even sensed it.

Her abrupt and nervous manner also betrayed a fear about the consequences of him searching for Annabella, but being too desperate to leave, he didn't press her about it. Without his love, he felt lost. Unable to think clearly or trust his own emotions, he doubted he was reading other's intentions correctly either. But he knew, the only solution was to find her. Even the slightest chance that she might still be alive was worth chasing. He looked to the sky briefly, and resolved to place his misguided trust in the Lord instead, to guide him as he went. Joshua had nothing else left to lean on.

Stepping onto the mounting block and stretching his

leg over the pale mare which a lad brought forward for him, Joshua raised a hand to the window and nodded. It never hurt to be polite when taking one's leave, even if it was under slight duress. Jeffries mounted with surprising ease for a man of his advanced years, and pulled his mount in front of Joshua's. The monk faced resolutely forwards rather than looking back, before kicking his horse onwards down the track.

They progressed at a steady pace, Joshua behind Jeffries' lead as they wound their way down the hill further and began making their way through the forest. Joshua breathed in the fresh pine scent and smiled to himself, remembering happier times hunting amongst the trees. The caw-caw of birds heralded their passage but Joshua felt little fear of discovery. Their chances of being seen were slim, for it was barely two hours after dawn and the day following Christmas festivities. Many would be slow to rise today having gorged themselves in the mid-winter feasting.

Jeffries swivelled in his saddle as they reached flatter ground. "Can we pick up the pace some? We need to make the river by nightfall," he said. Nodding, as his ribs were already hurting from the gentle lumber of his horse's walk, Joshua replied by nudging his mare's flank. Riding wasn't comfortable, but at least he felt more in control of his muscles as they flexed and clenched to rise and fall with the trot. The biggest relief was, however painful, to be breathing in cool air and moving towards his destination.

CHAPTER 17 – INVISIBLE

The next day, Aioffe had a new purpose to her steps towards the High Hall. Even Elizae had commented upon her renewed energy, attributing it to the meal left for her. How her skin was more of a 'usual' colour, although Aioffe could see in the shined steel mirror Elizae presented her with that morning, it was still far from the luminescence of old. The dead fish had been revolting, but, as she now realised, in the absence of anything else, eating it was a necessity.

"Uffer," she said to him as soon as he entered the cell, "might it be possible for me to collect my meals with you? So they arrive fresher?"

Uffer, taken aback by actually being addressed for once, could only stumble over his response. "Your Highness, that would not be.... suitable. The Queen would not like it."

For all of his bluster, he could see no reason why the Princess shouldn't be allowed to have more freedom, especially now that she was more compliant with attending Court daily with no issues. As he watched her face fall, he said, "I will ask if it is possible though?"

He hoped dangling the offer would be enough to keep her behaving nicely, as a Princess ought. The Queen's warning, about not trusting her, still rang in his ears, so he carried on with his escort duties as diligently as before. He had no intention of asking the Queen, but it couldn't hurt to give her a little optimism, a small hope for a change to her circumstance, could it?

Once in the High Hall, Aioffe looked around, searching for the interesting Ambassador Spenser. He was not visible, and her heart sank. Had he already gone back to Europe? To feed back that she was returned? Slumping with disappointment, she stared dully at the courtiers streaming in then standing in clustered, gossiping groups.

After what seemed like hours of not a lot happening, the Queen broke the tedium. She reached up the hand which had been smoothing her skirt and straightened her already straight crown. Then, turning her head just a fraction as if the crown would slip if she moved too fast, she said, "I am pleased to see you are looking a little better today." Lana glanced down at Aioffe on her small stool on the step to be sure she had her attention.

Aioffe glanced up at her mother, then bowed her head, acknowledging the rare compliment. There was something in her tone which suggested she would be more approachable this time. "I am well. Thank you, your Majesty." Her loose hair fell over her face and she reached up to tuck it behind her ear, before turning back, observing the crowds hopefully. After a brief pause, Lana put her hand lightly on Aioffe's shoulder. Aioffe turned to face her fully in response to this surprising invitation. She couldn't remember the last time her mother had touched her.

Without looking at her, the Queen said, "What happened yesterday...it is not uncommon. However, the foolish man chose - poorly - to refuse his right to the food which is provided." She drew herself upright and drew in a long breath. "I suppose he thought it would show 'great strength of character.' Being able to resist feeding for that long." Her lips pursed, then she looked up, into the high white rafters of the Hall. "He was of little consequence anyway, and his stand against Our Throne simply means one less mouth to feed."

Aioffe gasped. "But why would he starve himself to

protest against the throne?"

The Queen waved her arm across the breadth of the room as she said, "Because they are all here at our pleasure, don't you see?"

Aioffe didn't. The confusion turned into a frown on her face. The courtiers were as much of a part of the Court as the Queen was. It was the way it had always been.

"Without us, they would not feed at all!" Queen Lana sneered.

Aioffe looked around the room, seeing the structure of the upper levels of Fae society with fresh eyes. The Queen made and controlled the soldiers and worker fae, who protected and serviced the needs of ancients in Court - the Nobles, Ambassadors and the Queen. The model of serfdom, a hierarchy of who owned or worked the land, was as familiar to her from the human world as it was in the Fae. In Naturae, the difference being that Fae Nobles were unable to hand their lands and influence down to their offspring, as not only did they live near eternal lives, but they had no children, only vine siblings. When first exposed to the complex arguments about inheritance caused by human definitions of land ownership, Aioffe remembered thinking how much simpler the Fae world was. Until a Noble died.

That an ancient should choose to end their life was unthinkable to Aioffe. It served no purpose. "Who will oversee his lands now?" she asked, curious about what impact the death would have on court life. The Nobles had for hundreds of years been more ceremonial than anything else, their presence at Court a ritual left over from the times when their lands had needed representation and their offerings contributed to the whole. However, as humans had increased in population and found alternative ways to worship or nurture the land, the Fae Nobles found it increasingly difficult to live in secrecy, and had more or less permanently moved to Naturae.

"They revert to me. I could not possibly endow more land on any of the Nobles. They fail miserably to bring us any benefit from what they do have," the Queen said. "Which is why it serves no purpose as a protest. There is no consequence." Her lips pulled together in a tight smile, before the Queen blinked and resumed her stony gaze ahead.

If this was intended to reassure her, Aioffe thought, it failed. She saw it clearly now. Court life was a trap. Being dependent upon their host for all things, tied to an inflexible hierarchy. Cursed with an eternal existence and unable to perform any other function - in what other way could one end a fairly dull life?

Aioffe looked closer at the groups of Nobles. Their grey pallor reminded her of her own weakened state. Her mother, she realised, perpetuated this prison, although why she couldn't understand. Overfeeding from the land, even from the nearby depleted human populace, meant that the trap constantly tightened. The lack of Lifeforce suggested most were now too weak to return to their own lands. The journey itself would take too much of a toll on their energy levels. Why hadn't they gone before it got to this state? What was there to stay for?

Looking around at the ornate hall, with its silvered edging and carved wooden walls displaying their proud heritage, nostalgia and sadness swept over her. Soon, their race would doubtless be consigned to history as well. There was an inevitability about it. Perhaps her mother was right to keep them gathered here, to gain some solace in the company of their own kind in these, their last days.

And yet, something inside her still rebelled. She knew, from her own experiences, that there was another way. There was food - however unpalatable. There was hope. Her own experience of living amongst the poor and starving in the human world was proof. Other ways to satiate one's appetite for Lifeforce were available.

But the cost was exposure. All she, and all fae, had ever known was hiding. One or two fae, as she knew well, could live alongside humans. It was dangerous, but it could be done. But many fae? They would inevitably be hunted down for their differences, identified by their peculiarities, as witches were across the country. And fae were far more obvious...

*****

Tired after a long day of waiting in silence next to her mother, who had refused further discussion and retreated into her own thoughts, Aioffe trudged to the Beneath. Uffer, diligent as always, walked beside her. As they made their way down the balcony steps, she saw two workers hovering, watching her. As she made eye contact with them, they pulled back their lips into a little pointed teeth smile of somewhat cruel superiority, before fluttering away with their stubby brown wings through the forest. Aioffe was left feeling bewildered by their attitude. Frustrated also, because - with her wings clamped - she could not follow to challenge them on it.

"They should not be so bold," Uffer muttered.

"Why were they looking at me like that? Is it because I may not fly?" Aioffe didn't really expect him to answer.

Uffer paused, frowning. Since her request earlier, he had been wrestling with an innate desire to be honest, and his role as keeper. He could not help but want to protect her, yet to shield her from the truth was at odds with her intended purpose in Naturae. He had seen enough in his short lifetime to know that with knowledge comes responsibility. And wasn't she supposed to be learning her duties? Deciding, he said, "It's not your 'containment' which causes them to feel like that. It is because they *think* they are stronger than many at court now."

"I do not understand why the courtiers don't simply do as the workers do, and feed themselves?" Aioffe said. "It is really a simple matter of finding an animal and eating it as it's dying. What's so difficult about that?"

Uffer snorted, she really had no idea. "Your Highness, with respect, the workers are a different class, endowed with skills to hunt and born to serve."

"You weren't always titled, were you? I don't recall ever seeing you in a high rank before I left, and you have somehow managed it. Do you hunt to feed yourself or have you gotten so noble now, that you depend entirely upon the workers also?"

Uffer was a little affronted, but she asked a valid - if naïve - question. He said stiffly, "One does not lose the skills with which one is born, merely adds to them. Who do you think has been providing you with the food you were refusing?"

"Well, there you are then! Why can't the Nobles add to their skills and learn how to hunt?"

"Their wings, your Highness, are not able to hover. Or dive." Aioffe remembered, Noble wings were almost ornamental. Small like worker wings, but fragile, translucent and thin. Even when they travelled from their lands to and from Naturae, it took many weeks as they had to stop frequently.

Uffer explained, "They are too weak to hunt, even if there were land animals here now. Nobles do not get the same kind of sustenance from animals the way that we workers do. Their Lifeforce needs are, I understand, different. The food they are provided with keeps them alive, though. Their needs are met."

"Their needs are clearly not being met!" Aioffe found she was clenching her fists, upon which she forced herself to relax. Her frustration was not with Uffer and she could ill afford to upset him. "I still cannot understand why they don't adapt somehow?"

"I don't believe they can, your Highness," Uffer said, shunning meeting her eyes.

Aioffe noticed he had drawn his height up fully and his wings were outstretched as if ready to fly. There was a pride in his background, she could see it now. For all his correctness and willingness to please in order to move on, he had crossed the century-old boundaries and survived.

"May I speak with the workers? I would like to see more of what they do?"

Uffer looked at her, his forehead wrinkles forming deep furrows as he raised his eyebrows. The shock of her request, the change of tack, pulled him up short, and they stopped descending the rope bridges. "But why, your Highness? These are not royal matters? It would be unseemly."

"I wish to know what is happening across the whole of Naturae." Aioffe almost mimicked her mother's imperious tone, pulling herself up to her full height to look more forcefully into his eyes. "After all, it will be my Queendom someday."

"I would need to speak to the Queen..." He turned and carried on down the steps. Uffer's dismissal did nothing to salve his deep unease about her suggestion. He was fairly certain the answer would be 'no'. Even suggesting it would probably have negative, maybe deadly, repercussions. He frowned, pondering the potential outcomes in his mind.

Aioffe touched his arm, softening a little towards the man as she sensed his fear. "If you prefer, it could be our secret? No-one would have to know and I promise, I won't make any trouble for you."

Uffer searched her clear eyes, felt the truth in them, and the trust she was bestowing upon him. She really was a child, with no idea what consequences her actions could have. He turned away, her intense and pleading gaze too much for him. Gruffly he said, "I'll think about it," and took her arm to push her onwards, downwards again.

"I would far rather hunt for myself too, you know. Of course, now I am aware that it is you who brings me the fish, I'll take more care to eat them. But I do wish I could help you with your burden." Aioffe chattered as her bare feet reached the bottom of the steps.

"That will NOT be possible," Uffer retorted with another of his snorts. "It is far too dangerous for one such as yourself to travel to the feeding grounds. I am under direct orders to ensure you cannot use your wings. So unless you have learnt how to float or swim, your Highness, it is out of the question! I know you asked me this morning to speak to the Queen about it, but I haven't. I..... I'm not even sure I would ask her. In fact, I won't. It's just not possible."

Aioffe had to smile a little at this outburst. He hadn't even questioned that she would be able to hunt for herself, only that it wasn't currently permissible. She knew then that she could persuade him. Sooner or later, he would come around to her way of thinking.

It took a few days of careful and subtle flattery before Uffer changed his mind. Aioffe knew he hadn't gone to the Queen with her request, because there had been absolutely no change in her mother's attitude towards her. Aioffe wondered if, through showing an interest in the Queendom, her mother might bend a little. But, if anything, the Queen appeared colder than usual, perhaps regretting their discussion about the dead Noble.

In between complimenting Uffer on his fine fish, and even trying to strike up a conversation with an equally wary Elizae, Aioffe tried to observe the worker fae around her. Although there had been no other 'incidents' either in the Court or outside of it, the workers began to fascinate her. Before she had escaped, fires, cleaning, laundering, just 'happened'. In her naivety she had taken it for granted, barely noticing who or what made the palace function as if it was something magical and unquestionable. But having lived in the human world, as ordinary humans did, she had to learn quickly how to do these household chores. She found it extraordinary how they were making the meagre resources available last, with tired and out-dated equipment.

Alone in her cell, Aioffe passed the time recalling the early days of her life with Joshua - how clumsy she had been with cooking and cleaning. Baking was a skill which particularly eluded her for decades. The number of breads she had burnt, biscuits broken, and pans upended as she forgot to pick them up with a cloth padding! Thankfully, they hadn't needed to rely on her cooking skills to survive, or Joshua, when human, would surely have died from starvation, or indigestion.

She smiled to herself in the darkness. How lucky she had been to fall in love with a man who could straddle so many roles within a household! He was enviously described - by those few who saw the extent of his assistance - as 'rare', because he could turn his hand to all manner of women's work. Although, they were unaware it was because she herself was so useless and unaccustomed to labour. It was also a blessing that they had such few possessions - she was uncommonly untidy. Many centuries of invisible people cleaning up after her meant, in the human world, she was always slightly shocked by the mess when entering their bedroom, yet somehow she had never acquired the habit of picking up her own clothing once discarded.

Now aware of their presence, and having an understanding of their labours, she couldn't stop noticing the worker fae. Everywhere she looked, she saw them. In their drab leather tunics and little to differentiate themselves from one another, she realised that they had mastered the art of silently coming and going around the Palace and surrounding forest over millennia. Short brown wings fluttered as they lurked in doorways, waiting unacknowledged, to serve or clear. Yet she noticed the exteriors of the Palace were now unkempt, wondering if it was because so few courtiers or the Queen ventured outside?

As she was escorted to and from her cell, Aioffe wondered what they were whispering about in about the dark corners. Sometimes they fell silent as she and Uffer approached, ducking their heads down subserviently, but then shooting glances or sniggers at their receding backs. She found their behaviour quite unnerving. Their faces were so similar; the only differences between them were of age, and even that was hard to discern in the gloomy shadows in which they kept themselves. That they aged at all was alien to her. It somehow made them more human. She knew she too matured, but it was at such a different rate from humans or worker fae who lived at most a few centuries, she would probably be killed before dying a natural death.

No-one of her line had ever actually died from old age, she knew. But then, time catches up with everyone eventually, she supposed. She estimated her mother was well past a millennium, probably several centuries more. Although haggard now from rationed Lifeforce, the Queen would still rule for hundreds of years yet, unless something brought about her death sooner.

She also found herself studying Uffer on their journeys. He had more muscle than some of the other worker fae, and he took more pride in his appearance than most. His tunic was clearly newer and cleaner, and he wore his sash of command to differentiate himself from the other workers and guards, now more visible once she started to look out for them.

Uffer, meanwhile, had been wondering how he could manage to comply with his charge's request yet still maintain his trusted position with the Queen. He knew he could in no way bare-faced lie to her, nor could he dare to ask her permission. Without an appropriate reason for Aioffe to be away from the High Hall or the Beneath with its guarded entrances, he was left with little choice but to be underhand. Something he wasn't very good at. With growing surprise at himself, now, more than ever, it was important for her Highness to see the realities of the Queendom she would one day inherit. She was different, not as... Royal, as one might have expected after all.

Uffer returned to Aioffe's cell that evening, to find Aioffe pacing. "Here," he said, thrusting a stained but serviceable tunic at her. "Put this on." She turned and a smile spread over her face. She managed to stop herself from running over to him for a hug of gratitude. He had come through! Instead, she took the rough fabric with a nod of understanding and retreated to the far end of the gloom to change. Uffer waited outside the door and kept an eye out for guards patrolling the tunnels.

At the edge of her cell, Aioffe saw the little seed she had found on her clothes and planted a few nights ago, had started to make a tiny shoot. Its pale, wavering translucency reminded her that she too felt lost and alone in the darkness. Without light, the plant was doomed, just like the rest of them. But somehow the very fact that she could still breathe life into something that was dormant felt almost as hopeful as a candle in the night for comfort. She took its presence to be a good sign - she was not entirely dead inside herself, despite the heaviness of mourning in her heart.

When she pulled the heavy door open and peered out, Uffer inhaled sharply, realising the flaw in his hasty plan. Her hair, lightly golden and shimmery, would instantly give her away. Seeing where his eyes were looking and understanding the dilemma crumpling his face, Aioffe thought fast. She rubbed her hands on the walls of the tunnel, then tried to pat the dry mud into her mane. Uffer shook his head and did a kind of smile to himself as they both realised the light dust would just shake off her hair.

"Don't laugh!" Aioffe said, a mischievous grin threatening about her mouth.

"We aren't at all grubby, you know," Uffer said. His

forehead attempted a frown, but his lips twitched into a smile. For a moment, Aioffe had wondered if she had somehow offended him by implying workers were dirty. He reached down to the gourd hanging from his belt and poured some into the packed soil.

Aioffe bent down and mixed the dust into more of a paste, then began to apply it to her hair. "I've no idea how I'll explain this away to Elizae tomorrow," she joked, working the sludge through the strands.

"It will dry and you can brush it out, I'm sure." Uffer poured a little more water into the earth. When she thought she had covered up, she smoothed her hair back and wound it into a bun at the nape of her neck before looking up at him for approval. Lifting the candle up to see better, Uffer pointed at a smudge on her cheek, left by a strand of hair. She knew he couldn't be so bold as to touch her, so she took his gourd and washed her hands off, then wiped her face as she dried them on her tunic.

"I can't let your wings free," Uffer said, regret in his voice.

"I understand." Aioffe did, however much it pained her. No amount of mud make-up would hide their size, even clamped down. She had already dressed with the appendages under her tunic. Dropping her shoulders into a stoop and dipping her head, she hoped she would pass for a worker. Perhaps one whose wings had been docked for disobedience.

"You must keep your head down at all times, and don't say a word! Keep to the shadows." Uffer instructed as they walked. His heart was already pounding. Her neat teeth and fine-featured face, in fact, almost everything about her physique, would betray her, were anyone to look close enough. His only hope of success lay in trusting her to stay

211

out of sight.

Aioffe looked at him, her clear eyes sparkling with anticipation. His face fell. "This isn't going to work!" Uffer said, frowning properly now. Even covered in mud, she looked too different, too extraordinary.

"It will!" Aioffe touched his arm and gently pushed him down the tunnel. Sighing, Uffer had a feeling of impending doom, but there was little chance of changing her mind and returning now.

Led by the flickering flame, Uffer and his charge padded along in silence. Reaching a junction just before where they would normally have emerged at the foot of the great tree they were under, Uffer turned and took Aioffe through another dark passageway. To her shame, she had never even noticed this tunnel existed before. Onwards they trudged, and the smells changed as they progressed. The dankness of the Beneath smelt overwhelmingly of peat, but here, after what seemed like hours of walking, there was the lingering smell of the sea, of salt and reeds and sand.

Aioffe breathed it in through her delicate nostrils, and, although it wasn't a fresh scent, she relished the difference to her accommodations. It reminded her of happier times in beach-fronted towns. They must near the surface - her ears picked up distant murmuring, people chatting in low voices carrying on the faint breeze. Then suddenly she felt the freshness of air on her face. Rounding a bend in the passage, she saw ahead a zig-zag of rough-cut stairs in the earth.

It was beyond dusk as they emerged from the ground. She could hardly make out where she was going as the light of the candle cast little brilliance through the thick mist. She knew they were still in the forested area by the touch of the dead trees, their twigs reaching out to scrape her arms as they silently navigated a thin pathway. Before she escaped, Aioffe had loved watching the shimmering mist, ideally from up high. Here, inside the fog, it was cold and wet on her face. She could taste its salty magic on her lips, and felt a new appreciation of the heavy camouflage which enveloped them and their lands.

Uffer quickly reached back and held her arm in warning as a fae flitted a little too close to them. They both froze. Letting his breath out, he blew out the candle quietly. Once the flutter of wings receded, he took her elbow to help guide her better as he picked his way through the paths which he knew so well, but were utterly new to his charge. Their progress was slow, but, he thought, safer. The murmuring voices grew louder as they drew closer to the source.

As it was dark on their approach, Aioffe recognised they had arrived behind a cluster of low den-dwellings. Underlying smells of habitation wafted towards her and she wrinkled her nose. Ahead, a glow of firelight and sparks lifted, illuminating a space within the trees and hovels. She could make out shadowy figures hovering, flitting around the clearing. Uffer pulled her down, hidden beside one of the wooden lean-to structures. A barking of laughter, not of joy but with an edge of nastiness about it, spread through the group. Aioffe realised that the fae were holding some kind of meeting, not a social gathering.

"Our time will come!" A confident voice then shouted clearly over the noise. There followed a loud double clap of hands, then many responded with a deeper slap-thump type of noise. Aioffe tugged on Uffer's sleeve, a silent question on her face.

He leant across and whispered, "I should not take you

closer, your Highness!"

"No, I understand. But what are they doing?" There was both curiosity and fascination in her voice.

"It is... I will explain later." He really didn't want to get into it now, it was too risky. Curiosity overcame Aioffe, as she pushed away from their hiding place. He tried to catch her arm, but she was too swift. She tiptoed around the structure, edging closer to the gathering. No-one noticed her in the gloom as she dropped to a crouch by a woodpile. She felt Uffer's warm body next to her as he silently crept to join her.

They watched and listened but the conversation had quietened. After a while, Aioffe glanced at Uffer, his brows were tense with a frown and his lips tight. She laid a hand on his arm, as if to inspire trust in her. She had no intention of exposing them, but her heart raced with exhilaration from their subterfuge.

The workers dispersed into smaller groups, keeping their discussion low. Even from her closer vantage point, Aioffe struggled to distinguish specific voices from their fervent debate. Through the lingering mist, Aioffe could not discern facial expressions, but she heard the hatred in the tone of their whispering. A tone of subjugation, borne of misery and tiredness, and increasing bitterness and contempt. She recognised it from a century of living amongst it herself. Leaning in, she accidentally dislodged a log. A face swivelled in their direction as it landed with a thud on the ground. Aioffe glanced at Uffer with wide, apologetic eyes.

Sighing as he realised the predicament they were now in, Uffer shook his head and stood up. To Aioffe's surprise, he began to walk towards the group. "May I bring someone to you?" He said, in a quiet voice to one of them, who turned at his approach.

"Aye," came a deep reply. "If you are quick."

Aioffe took this to mean she should appear, so she stepped out as if she hadn't been lurking behind a pile of logs at all, and followed Uffer as they trooped into the dwelling.

The entrance archway was fashioned out of low interlocking branches, blackened with rot from the mist which permanently surrounded the settlement. As the group ducked through into the room, Aioffe kept her head down as Uffer had instructed. Her eyes watered as they acclimatised to the slight increase in light within the dwelling and the smell. There was no fire to warm the inside, instead, at the centre of the near-circular space, the trunk of a long dead but still upright tree. In tiny, sooty recesses in the wood, shells of all sizes lit the column, moss wick candles burning fish oils. Eventually drifting upwards and out through the twigs which made up the walls, the smog bathed the room with a thick, fishy fug. The atmosphere stung and she blinked rapidly, wrinkling her nose against the stench.

Uffer walked to the lit up trunk, and was soon joined by two workers, both similar in appearance. Aioffe wondered what had Uffer differentiated about this pair from all the others. She waited by the entrance, keeping her head down. From under her eyelashes, she noticed movement around the sides of the room, bundles of resting forms disturbed by their arrival.

"I have a woman with me," Uffer began, gesturing towards her. "She is a prisoner, but has nearly served her time. She now seeks to relocate from the other settlement to this one."

"What did she do?" The fractionally taller of the fae

215

piped up.

"She accidentally tore one of her master's coats," Uffer improvised. "She's had her wings cut and is banished from serving, but she still has use, I'm sure."

"An' there ain't many more of us to replace her!" The other fae said, bitterness evident in his voice. "Who does his high and mightlyness think is going to fix his clothes now, then? I bet they haven't even noticed she's gone! Until they need something else fixing or fetching." A few fae around the edges of the room laughed.

"There's plenty of room in the women's quarters, I'm sure. It's not like the bed spaces are being filled once vacant," the first fae said flatly. "As for work... well, you'd have to speak to Thania about that. Why can't she go back to the other settlement though?"

Uffer thought quickly, "Umm.. she..."

"I just want a fresh start," Aioffe mumbled, approaching the group. She almost let her eyes drift up, before Uffer jumped in. "Yes," he said. "She needs to stay away from the trouble, keep her head down."

The group sniggered. "There's no escaping the *trouble* here either!" The second fae's dark eyes roamed over Aioffe with a sneer on his face and he leaned towards her. "Are you sure you aren't the trouble as well? *Accidentally* tore a coat...." He sniggered cruelly.

A reedy female voice enquired from behind, "What about her loyalties? Are you with us... or hanging on the fringes?" Moving in front of her lowered vision, the woman's tattered robe and her lined face told the tale of age and hardship. Aioffe didn't quite know how to respond. Her heart was already racing, and she began to feel trapped as more workers seemed to appear from the shadowy edges. She smelt a tinge of fear, but it was her own.

"I'm sure you will find her suitably aligned with your views," Uffer said, trying to reassure Aioffe with his eyes.

"Suitably aligned!" mocked the second fae, "Look at you, with your fancy wordings!"

Uffer bristled. The female fae shuffled over to the entrance, guarding it with a twisted grimace.

"Whose side will *you* be on when Our Time Comes, eh?" The fae began strutting and sneering as he goaded Uffer.

"I didn't come to start a fight," Uffer protested, "I just wanted..."

"You just wanted to what?"

"I just wanted to find a place for this... woman... to go to after she finishes her time in the Beneath."

"Oh, he 'just wanted to find a place' eh?" The second fae snarled, "Has he forgotten where he came from, eh? Something special is she, she can't go back to where she came from? Where *you* come from?"

Aioffe became very conscious of her heart thumping rapidly as the fae goaded Uffer. She was surprised by their reaction to what was an act of kindness on his behalf, were her story to be true at least. Uffer was doing well remaining calm whilst being poked at, better than she was. Her palms began to itch, and the urge to flee, push through the wall of branches to the outside, grew inside.

"Look," Uffer said, "I'm not asking for favours..."

"It's not a favour," the first fae said, studying Aioffe with his eyes narrowed. A firmness to his voice asserted his authority, his intention of reducing the tension which his comrade had stoked. "It's fine. Bring her to me when she has completed her required time with you."

There was an immediate shift in atmosphere, and

217

Aioffe dared to breathe again. The fae glanced around, satisfying himself that the potential for conflict had dissipated before turning to address Uffer. "But, make no mistake - the views from the other encampment are shared by most here as well, so she won't be escaping our plans."

"Yes! Our. Time. Is. Coming." The second fae curled his lip, then rose off the floor and clapped his hands twice. Aioffe's mouth dropped. Workers who had relaxed as the first fae agreed to Uffer's request, responded to the battle cry of the second fae by slapping their thighs. The cry for unity was brief, but effective.

Uffer nodded curtly to the first fae. Aioffe felt his light but firm touch on her shoulder, pushing her towards the archway. As they moved, she kept her head bowed, muttering, "Thank you."

From the corner of her eye, she saw the taller fae jutting his head forward. Her skin crawled as she picked up her pace, knowing he was examining her. He flew quickly across to the doorway as they approached, pushing aside the old woman as he blocked their exit.

Aioffe immediately ducked her head further. Or was that too obviously trying to dodge his gaze? The fae hovered, reaching out to tilt her chin up as they stopped almost mid step. The room fell silent and she could sense interest fall upon her once more. Aioffe watched his eyebrows knit as the leader searched her face. Her bright blue eyes, thin nose, full lips, and eventually, the matted mud-stained hair.

He knew. She tensed. Ready to run, but held his gaze for a heartbeat.

"My name is Thane," he said, then leant to her ear. So quietly that only she would hear, his deep voice threatened, "and I will see you in court, no doubt."

CHAPTER 18 - WHERRY WORRIES

By the time the sun had slipped low on the horizon, they had made sufficient progress for Jeffries to call a halt to their journey. They plodded into the courtyard at the Shire Inn, on the outskirts of a town close to the river Tyne, to rest for the night. The thatched single-storey building was busy with crowds of locals milling around to continue the festivities of the day before. Consequently, the mood in the bar area was loud and raucous.

Joshua found it too much to bear. He was frozen to the bone, although he wasn't complaining about getting off his horse at all, but his ribs pained with every breath he drew. The warmth of the fireplace was almost unwelcome in its contrast to the cold outside. An overwhelming odour of ale, unwashed people and over-cooked food made him feel nauseous.

They were too late to make enquiries in the town itself about wherries which might be headed northwards, so Jeffries secured them a place to rest - a shared room at the back of the building. They wasted no time retreating into the grubby sanctuary. The candle they had been supplied with by the young barmaid threw little light into the area, but Jeffries guarded its flickering brightness like treasure. The bedroom was warm but dark, and already had an occupant sleeping off his excesses in one of the floor beds. Although the smell of stale straw was off-putting, the chance of sleep was compelling to both travellers.

"Let me have a look at your bindings," Jeffries said, "before we rest?"

Joshua really wanted nothing more than to sink into the pallet and hope for a release from the pain of breathing, but he knew the monk meant well. Nodding, he began to strip off his coat and jerkin, unwilling to remove his warm hose or even boots. His outer clothing was tight and stiff from the wind, so Jeffries had to tug them over Joshua's large biceps. Joshua unbuttoned the close fitting doublet, pulled out his shirt and sank down to the bed with his back to the monk.

In the dim candlelight, Jeffries could see the neck wound had been weeping, its edges pulled apart from the exertion of riding at some point. The blood on the bindings had dried, and he decided that changing the bandages now would risk the deep cut re-opening. He lifted the shirt and felt the swollen rib cage underneath.

"I wish I could re-apply my poultice," Jeffries said under his breath. It simply wasn't going to be possible here - the chance of somebody seeing Joshua's wings was too great, no matter that the snores emanating from the bulk in the bed in the corner were deep and regular. There were five beds in total; any of the others could be occupied at any moment. He daren't even loosen the chest bandages, for surely exposing the skin in such a dirty place would invite bad humours into an already troubled area. Sighing, Jeffries patted Joshua on the shoulder and bade him to lie down and rest.

It seemed but moments before Joshua's wheezing joined the other body's snore, their noise adding to the undertones of celebrations from the front bar room. Jeffries said his prayers and laid down fully clothed on his bunk. He had slept on thinner mattresses than this, but rarely had his mind been as troubled as it was now. The chances of sleep were slim, he knew, but his body was tired after a day's riding. Maybe it would come given enough time.

As he tossed and turned, trying to get comfortable, he tried to plot their journey. The geographical permutations were of less worry. As long as they headed North, he was confident he could find where he needed to be, even if the person he hoped could help him at Tynemouth was no longer there. But would he be in time? That was the larger concern.

He considered his charge, wondering whether he would be up to an extended horse ride if necessary. He doubted Joshua's health could take the strain of riding fast though, which would slow them down significantly. He felt a duty towards his patient, of course, but he didn't know him well enough to trust him as yet with the importance, and urgency, of his task.

It had been a while since he had undertaken a protracted journey such as this, and it was unusual to have company to account for. Sometimes, travelling alone, he missed the monastic sanctuaries. The brotherhood of his fellow monks had been a slight comfort to ease his innate loneliness. But these last few weeks, swarms of King's Commissioners taking stock of all Catholic holdings were forcing him into action. Before long, he sensed he would need to shed this monkish disguise, step out into the light, and face the consequences. Lying in this uncomfortable bed, considering the events which led to him being here he acknowledged destiny was about to force him to travel a different path.

Last night, when he heard that the King's Commissioners had arrived to assess his own Abbey, there had been no time to plan; he had to act. He absolutely did not believe the placations and false reassurances of his

Prior that this was only the equivalent of a stock take. Any fool could see the 'stock take' would soon become a 'take' once that reckless warmonger Henry and his crony Cromwell realised the amount of gold the Church possessed. He had long been disgusted by how far the faithful had fallen in expanding their bellies on the taxes of the poor. The vast network of monastic institutions, Dominican or otherwise, were now little better than peddlers, promising a slip of paper which guaranteed a comfortable afterlife.

Jeffries tried to move his sense of identity to a point of acceptance, rejection of his sense of self as a monk even. He would never return to Beesworth or its Abbey again. The Abbey had for a long while been a prison from which he yearned to escape. He just hadn't known how to until the circles of fate had spun around and Lady Hanley, dear Mary, had provided him with the means and the excuse to leave. The opportunity to further their cause and embrace his new purpose, had fallen into his lap with the arrival, only days before, of a most precious parcel and task. He glanced at it, lying just there, on him. With him. A lowly monk.

A witch.

A spy.

A double-crosser.

A non-believer.

A heretic. A traitor.

He shook his head to dismiss these titles which would have inevitably been bestowed upon him had he not escaped. Waiting for the dawn and about to make the boldest move to change the course of a country that he could ever have envisaged.

But before he could reach that point, that openness, he

had a task to do. This monkish cover (as he now saw it) was necessary to open the doors to achieve it. He turned and gazed out of the window, where distant stars had appeared. He got up and walked to the aperture, trying to identify familiar shapes and patterns in the sky. It comforted him that the skies and stars stayed in a constant cycle. How many others, of all creeds and abilities, had watched the same nightly transitions, wondering about their place on this earth and the next?

His experiences with other creatures had persuaded him to acknowledge that there were other facets to faith. These alternative viewpoints should perhaps be given more credit than the doctrine of the established Church. Although the monastic life was all the structure he had ever known, he had grown up knowing he was different. His travels and encounters had complimented years of training in the more traditional human healing arts. Along the way, he had encountered many other witches, and vampires - hiding their peculiarities in plain sight within the walls of the only houses of learning. There were even other kinds of humans - a hybrid of peoples, it seemed, which some creatures called daemons. They feared them more because they didn't fit entirely into the mould of one species or another, didn't follow the conventions of any, each of them entirely unique. Lady Hanley's husband had been such a man, capable of causing the most chaos of any being he had encountered.

He glanced back at Joshua, wondering about the depth of his faith. Unlike Mary, hearing Joshua's fervent prayers in the Latin tongue was not a surprise to him. In his experience, creatures such as they leaned on the familiarity of ritual as a way of denying their own peculiarities. Indeed, the Catholic Church had gone to great lengths to incorporate many older rites in its efforts to encompass all. Except for the Fae ways - the Church paid scant attention to those. Therefore, surely such a being ought to be more questioning, as he himself was, about the religious doctrine of the Catholic church. Jeffries turned back to the sky, his lips pressed together, deciding. He could not risk discussing religion or his task with the lad. Mary had an unnerving ability to sense half-truths; perhaps it was a quality of the fae which Joshua also possessed?

But it would have been pleasant to share in his secret wonder and joy at the book, with someone at least. He then considered his network of others, who share his dissatisfaction, the many others emboldened by the Protestant movement from Europe. Supporters who had encouraged the evolution of his own beliefs, after much soul-searching. He was not as alone as he feared when he first asked himself these questions. He knew religious change was unstoppable now, and he welcomed it.

Sending yet another silent prayer for strength, gratitude for his divine intervention and wishes for an answer to his purely practical issues up to his Lord, Jeffries fell asleep clutching his satchel to his chest whilst awaiting a response.

*****

The next morning dawned crisp and breezy, which encouraged the travellers. They paid a few of Lady Hanley's groats for a warm bowl of oats each and a gently spiced ale to help set them up for the day. Joshua and Jeffries, although tired, were keen to make progress so their horses were saddled and loaded without delay. Having struggled to arise from his low bed with his aches, as he settled himself painfully back into the saddle, Joshua looked forward to the gentle sail down-river.

The overnight frost had hardened the muddy tracks leading to the small town, so the going under foot and hoof was easier than the day before. They heard the docks before they came into view around the river bend. Seagulls and terns swirled over the early morning fish haul, calling as they circled, awaiting a dropped meal. A few carts waited by wooden jetties, ready to ferry the loads into the countryside for markets and refill the local shops. Although it was still the advent period, many simply couldn't afford not to ply their trades for the whole twelve days. An illegal yet brisk trade occurred along the sides of the road on approach, with opportunistic peddlers waving their wares at wives and servants hurrying to replenish supplies after the dip in business from Christmas.

Jeffries had to help Joshua dismount - his swollen rib cage meant he found it painful to bend at the waist, even the amble down from the Inn had caused a flare in the inflammation. "I'm glad we don't plan to ride much today," he panted as he leant on the monk for support.

"We must find a larger wherry or perhaps a shout to enable us to take the horses." Jeffries looked over at the assortment of boats clustered around the jetties. Most were small fishing craft, their mid-mast sails bobbing gently on the calm river. "I'd rather not have to leave them," he added.

"They would fetch a good penny though," Joshua said. At that moment, he would prefer to crawl to the ends of the world than have to haul himself back onto the mare.

They led the horses through the throngs of people and carts, scanning the harbour for a suitable vessel. "That one maybe?" Jeffries pointed at a low slung, wider-than-most boat, which had no canopy or seating, but looked sturdy enough to transport the animals.

Joshua glanced over. Although smaller than he expected, the empty craft had potential. He nodded, satisfied it would accommodate both his need to rest and Jeffries' preference for keeping the mares with them. "There's no-one there with it though?"

"I'll ask who the owner is." Jeffries made his way over to the neighbouring vessel where a girl was unloading, gutting and sorting a haul of fish into barrels.

Joshua hung a distance away, holding their horses as the monk approached. For the entire conversation, the lass stared down at the ground. Jeffries concluded his discussion by making the sign of the cross against her forehead, and she looked relieved as she turned back to her task.

"The boat owner has apparently gone to confront his wife about her cuckoldry," Jeffries said wryly as he returned to Joshua. "The astute lass thinks he will be in need of a trip away very soon, so that's perfect for us."

Joshua smiled, although the prospect of being stuck on a boat with a grumpy or angry boatman didn't exactly fill him with pleasure. "We shall wait here, I think," Jeffries carried on, "although it smells like a whore's arse." The stench of fish guts lingered despite the slight breeze. Joshua looked at the monk in surprise. Freed from the constraints of polite society, the man's colourful turn of phrase seemed at odds with the black habit he wore and the serene look on his face. He hoped Jeffries would continue to relax in his presence. Not only because humour would make the journey a little less dull, but also, he hoped the monk might enlighten him more with his experience of fae.

After what felt like an age, but in reality was probably barely more than an hour of waiting, a man in his middle years with a much widened girth trudged towards the boat, not noticing them as he stomped past. Joshua, sat on the jetty dangling his legs over and watching the activities in the port, then swung his limbs back up onto the wood with a slight groan. Leaning against a barrel as he read a small book, Jeffries grabbed his satchel and packed the notebook away before he approached.

"Good morrow to you, sir, I wonder if I might speak with you about your vessel?" Jeffries began. The boatman grunted in acknowledgement and started to uncoil the rope from the jetty. Jeffries took this to mean he would be open to further discussions and ploughed on. "My friend and I need to get to Tynemouth Priory. Can you take us, and our steeds?" The man looked up at the monk, assessing his honest-looking face, before raising an eyebrow.

"I wer' gamin' oot anyway," the boatman said gruffly. "I'm nah gan yem, tha's fer sure." He sniffed and ran the back of his grubby hand across his nose. "You's got monies, reet 'nuf?" He turned his weather-beaten face towards the well-dressed figure of Joshua, who now stood beside the monk. Rubbing his finger and thumb together, his mouth twisted into a lopsided, hopeful smile.

The light dawned on Joshua's confused face with the gesture. "You will be recompensed sufficiently, fear not." Joshua pulled a small pouch from his coat pockets. The boatman cast an eye over the pair and their pile of baggage and horses, before nodding. "Reet, A'll gan get some scran afore we set off, as A'm clammin'. Yous' can sort yourselves oot, then we gan?" He held out his hand for a deposit.

Chuckling under his breath, Joshua dropped two

shillings into the man's palm. Joshua had a suspicion he wouldn't see the man or their money again, but Jeffries purposefully blessed the boatman and smiled. Nodding curtly as he clinked the coins together, the sailor headed back across the harbour towards an ale house tucked just behind the frontage of the wharf houses.

"How long do I have to decipher that accent?" Joshua joked to Jeffries, loading their bags onto the boat. "With a reasonable wind we should be there by nightfall," the monk replied. He licked his finger and held it up. "Pray the breeze will be stronger once mid river."

The horses took a little persuasion to walk up the narrow gangplank on the slightly bobbing craft but eventually, both were secured to the fore-deck. Once aboard, there was no shelter to be had overhead as they waited. Their chosen vessel was designed to ferry cargo rather than passengers, so scant attention was given to personal or animal comforts.

Joshua, who had not been on a boat for some decades, was at first unsettled by the rocking movement of the tidal waters. He chose to sit hunched next to the horses, who had lain down against the side of the wherry, so he could try to gain some measure of warmth from their flanks.

Bored and restless, Jeffries determined he ought to haggle for supplies from nearby stalls, which would doubtless not offer the best value, but were at least convenient. He returned before Joshua could doze off. Bearing loosely bound bundles of slightly damp hay for the horses, he lugged a sack aboard, which he tucked under the benches at the rear of the long and wide wherry.

The hours before the boatman's return seemed to drag, and Joshua felt himself nodding off after stroking the horses' soft fur. A clang of metal nearby awoke him with a jolt. Stiffly, he pushed himself upright and peered over the sides of the boat to see Jeffries assisting the boatman onto the gangplank. "Ma cup!" The drunkard cried, his arm waving wildly towards where he had dropped his tankard on the cobbles at the harbour edge.

"I will retrieve it," Jeffries said soothingly, continuing to propel his rotund body up into the boat.

Heaving himself up to standing, Joshua shot a look of alarm at Jeffries. "Is this wise, Maister? The man can barely stand, let alone sail?"

"Ah'm jus' needin' ma sea legs, divvent worry lad!" The man's face turned from florid to slightly pale as he lurched his way towards the mast. Jeffries and Joshua watched sceptically as the boatman clung to the wood and breathed deeply for a minute. Suddenly, he rushed to the river side of the boat and noisily emptied his stomach of the ale he had so recently downed.

Turning back to his passengers, the boatman wiped his mouth again on his sleeve and shook his head. "Tae much feastin." A smile curled on his lips. He made his way over to a barrel fixed to the mast and opened the half hinged lid to scoop out some water. Using a small cup tied to the sides, the man rinsed his mouth then spat the remains overboard. "Reet," he said, good humour seemingly restored, "can ya' pull in the plank?"

Jeffries walked back down the gangplank and retrieved the metal flagon from the cobbles, then untied the ropes securing the craft. With what seemed to Joshua like a practised toss, he slung the cables on board and returned to the deck to haul in the gang. The boatman went to the rear of the barge and his grubby boots kicked a pile of rumpled and stained fabric tucked under the narrow seat. A small pink hand poked out and batted the offending leg away. The boatman leant down and pulled the waxy cloths from the bundle, revealing a slim, barely teenage boy nestled in the recess. "Gan away wi'ye," the sailor muttered, not unkindly.

Joshua watched in amusement as the lad unfurled himself from his nesting place and silently began to potter about the boat, rearranging lines and ropes to make ready the sail. Sporting a surly look upon his face, his gangly limbs spider-like as he climbed the mast to check the rigging. Once on deck again, he stole looks through veiled lashes at the passengers, presumably assessing them for how much trouble they would cause him, and whether they also might place a boot upon him. The boy seemed to give Jeffries an even wider berth than necessary, lowering his head further when in the monk's eye line and almost cowering.

The boatman retrieved a long pole from the sides of the boat and pushed off from the jetty. Passing the punt to the lad, he took position by the rudder and bade him punt the vessel into the current.

As the craft glided smoothly towards the centre of the wide waterway, the small crew unfurled the sail and hauled it up the mast. Joshua sat down on a bench at the front and looked out across the river. Jeffries joined him, silently watching as the wind tugged them closer to their destination. The sun now shone brightly overhead, replacing the travellers' concerns with a sense of optimism.

*****

The journey downriver took them past fields, irrigated by high tides and populated by small mud huts distantly visible from the water. During the days following Christmas to the end of Advent, no labouring was allowed except for the feeding of animals. Empty strips of land lay silent bar the rustling of patches of grass and reeds. In the stillness of the mudflats, flocks of lapwings and oyster catchers gracefully dipped their heads in the shallows, turned to face the gentle breeze whilst digesting their catch. The peace was only broken by gulls who clattered amongst themselves as they rested or fought with flapping violence over worms. Scant trees edged parts of the shore, spindly bare branches waving to them in the breeze. Few other vessels were out at this time of day and year, so their passage down river was barely disturbed by traffic. Joshua began to relax despite his misgivings about being on a boat. Progress was being made and that pleased him.

The helm had been given to the lad, who the boatman introduced to them as Thom, without bothering to announce himself or enquire after their names. This suited Joshua and Jeffries, for they preferred to remain anonymous. The river curved around Prudhoe Castle, the yellowed stones bathed in the sunlight as it stood proudly upon its hillock overlooking the landscape. A slight breeze plus the tidal flow picked up the boat's pace. Thom's master curled up in the boy's sleeping quarters under the back benches. His legs splayed across the deck next to the rudder and he had pulled a hat over his face to shield it from the sun whilst he dozed.

Jeffries shared out the bread and a flagon of wine he had stashed away in the sack. Thom remained surly-looking, even as he took a hunk of the loaf Jeffries offered and proceeded to demolish it. He shot nervous glances as the monk from underneath his lank hair as he chewed and steered. He looked more street urchin than sailor, Joshua

231

thought, in clothes which were too large for his slim frame. Jeffries settled down to read his little book again, but the lull of the boat's motion made his head nod and before long he too was napping in the afternoon sun.

Joshua let his mind wander as he watched the riverside go by. The ever present pressure to find his wife would pop to the forefront in these moments. An anxious knot clenched in his stomach as he followed the slow passage of the river - the worry they couldn't reach her in time. The thought that they wouldn't find her at all he pushed out of his head as soon as it entered it. There was no room for maybe, or possibly, only must and will. He felt sure destiny had brought them together, and he certainly intended to be by her side, wherever she was. And however she was.

He had a vague idea of the geography of where he was headed, having been born in the Orkneys himself, but that was over a century ago and much would have changed since. Although he knew from experience how far one might fly in a few hours, this still left a very wide scope for where Naturae could be. He was, he realised with some distress now he thought about it, wholly reliant upon Jeffries' knowledge for how to reach the Fae Queendom. The monk had never explicitly said he knew where it was. Joshua was pinning his hopes of finding his love on Lady Hanley having told Jeffries Naturae's location at some point, during their years of friendship. There was a distinct possibility that this had all been a ruse to get him away from Beesworth. What loyalty did Jeffries have to him, he wondered, to take him so far North? Or would he leave him as soon as he had fulfilled his own purposes?

Conscious that his heart had sped up to the point of painful, Joshua tried to breathe through the rising panic.

He considered shaking Jeffries awake to just ask that nagging question of 'Did he know exactly where the Fae lived'. He reasoned that he had not actually asked, in so direct a manner. Joshua glanced over at him, wantng to trust the man of God, and sensing that the monk had managed to reconcile his faith with his witch-ness and wanting to know how he had justified it in a theological sense. But, rather than initiate that much desired conversation, he was now wary, given their current circumstances. The risks of such discussions, giving away any information about their destination or talk of their differences and their religion, was too great. He kept silent instead and attempted to distract himself.

Joshua looked down the boat at Thom, who was concentrating on staying central in the river's current to maximise their speed. Grubby and slight though he was, his unhappiness dampened his Lifeforce significantly and Joshua felt no pull towards the lad. That would have been inconvenient, Joshua thought. There is little worse than feeling the desire to feed from someone in such a confined space and being unable to act. He was decidedly peckish; his last rabbit had been the day before yesterday. Human food would make no dent in his appetite.

Under the guise of stretching, he rolled his shoulders back and flexed his wings against the bindings. They felt less sore as time went on, but it still pained his chest when breathing or over-exertion. Even if he had the opportunity to hunt on land, he certainly wasn't yet in a fit state for it. But the thought of hunting made him look again at Thom, and a hunger then began to rise. The urge would only build, Joshua knew, no matter how much he attempted to quell it. With little else to think about, his bodily demand to heal meant the craving would become unbearable before long.

Joshua tried again to distract himself by picking up the small book lying in Jeffries' lap as he slept. Barely longer than his hand, the spine was thick yet unmarked with an imprint. The leather on the outside was of poor quality and much faded and scuffed. Opening it, Joshua expected to see some title of a religious writing or perhaps a picture depicting the contents, but the first few pages were ripped out. He flicked through the book and saw it was not in Latin at all, but English. He raised the little tome closer so he could better make out the tiny lettering within.

Each page had a heading such as '*On the discoverae of warts & pustulous boils*' or "*Traetment of Widows afflicted by Ague*'. Joshua realised it was a medical book - unsurprising given Jeffries had been ministering to him. What struck him as more unusual were the pages annotated with handwritten notes. On some sheets, the 'cures' were entirely crossed out and new recipes written instead in tiny but very neat copperplate. These additions did not suggest the use of any ingredients which Joshua was familiar with. Rather, one called for the 'laeying of hands at sundown,' another prescribed 'cat tongue used abrasively on the wounde.' Joshua glanced over at the monk's satchel - what had been in the poultices applied to him?

His pondering was interrupted by Jeffries stirring in his sleep. Hands reached down his cassock for the book which ought to be there. Upon discovering its absence, Jeffries quickly opened his eyes and turned to look at Joshua. Forcing a smile on his face, Joshua held out the book to Jeffries and remarked, "Not as interesting a read to me as it might be to some?"

"You presume too much, lad." Jeffries snatched it

from Joshua's hands. "You'd be better off keeping what you might have seen to yourself!"

"Is that the book which Lady Hanley was so concerned about?" Joshua leaned in and stared into the monk's eyes.

"That is not of your concern," Jeffries scowled back at him, but he reached for his satchel and covertly placed the notebook within. He turned aside from Joshua's raised eyebrows, and began to scour the landscape. The sun lay close to setting and the darkness of twilight beckoned. Jeffries stood up, needing a better fix on where they were. He scoured the flat landscape for clues. The river was widening, but he thought they still had not yet reached Newcastle itself.

"Will we make Tynemouth before dark?" Jeffries called out to Thom, who shrugged. Sighing, Jeffries made his way over to their captain and shook his shoulder to rouse him. "Wha?" the boatman said thickly. Blurry eyes met steely resolve.

"I am concerned we won't make Tynemouth by darkness," Jeffries snapped. "Should we stop before we get into Newcastle?"

The boatman sat up and rubbed his eyes, ran his fingers through his hair and unsteadily stood up to assess their location. "Naw," he said eventually, "Ah ken this river and we'll be owa by neet-fall a'Tynem'uth. Newcastle is nar, the lad tok us reet doon t'river. We jes' need ter dock before Prior's Rocks claims oos!" He finished dramatically and grinned.

Deciphering more from his doom-laden tone, Joshua looked over at Jeffries in alarm. Should the boat capsize he would surely die! He could barely raise his arms above his head, let alone swim. Joshua tried to conceal a shudder -

the sea was dangerous. Yet he was in no fit state to avoid travel on it.

Jeffries also had concerns. Making an unannounced entrance at Tynemouth Priory during the late evening would not guarantee them a room for the night, whatever story he spun. But, for his plan to work, he needed to visit.

He returned to the prow of the boat to watch with Joshua as they approached Newcastle. Before long, the dots of glowing firelight took the place of the setting sunlight and the wherry slipped through the town unobtrusively. The river widened as they passed houses and low jetties. Distant sounds of carousing could occasionally be heard, just snatches of songs caught on the wind. Jeffries pulled his cowl closer around his neck as the coldness of night bit in.

Approaching Tynemouth town, the wherry continued past the docks towards the edge of the long, wide harbour mouth, as if heading straight out to sea. The waters grew choppier as they approached where the current met the river-water. Taking charge of the rudder, the boatman grunted for Thom to pick up an oar and stand ready at the side of the wherry. Ahead, in the shadow of the walled Priory looming on the headland, Joshua could make out a small beach with a narrow jetty to the far end. But only just beyond that, large boulders jutted from the sea. Priors Rocks, he thought, and his heart thumped uncomfortably in his chest. Running too close to the treacherous cliff-face just beyond the landing jetty and they would be dashed against them.

Edging closer to the sea, the rise and fall of the dark waters caused the wide vessel to pitch and twist. Steering in the darkness was tricky. Jeffries started helping Joshua keep the now standing horses calm. The timbers creaked in protest against the incoming waves. Freezing water splashed over the prow as they dipped down a crest, soaking the horses and their feet. Salty water ran over the sides in increasing amounts onto the deck.

Thom was struggling to paddle his one oar to pull the boat through the waves, so Jeffries went to assist on the other side. As they tried to turn the craft towards the landing jetty before the headland, the wind gusted. The sail filled with air, pushing them side on, back up the Tyne.

Joshua stood helpless, holding the horses who began tossing their heads up in fear at the sudden change in direction. They were so close to land they could almost throw a rope onto the jetty, but there were no hands to catch it. Throwing into the rising wind would have taken a skill or luck no-one possessed. Joshua looked down into the dark waters. He certainly wouldn't fancy swimming through the unknown depths of the river mouth to haul them in.

Thom dropped his oar and dashed over to the sail to roll it up. Another gust of wind around the headland caught the heavy fabric, billowing it back out with a spray of water. This in turn yanked Thom's arm hard. The sail line suddenly tightened around his hand, causing him to release the other hand from the rope he was holding to pull the sail up.

Turning in horror from watching Thom struggle with the line around his arm, Joshua glimpsed a catastrophe about to occur. The boat was facing the wrong way to approach the turbulent waves!

The wherry rose against an incoming monstrous wave, lurching upwards at a precarious angle. Slipping backwards on the wet deck and crying out as he was caught up in the line, Thom landed sprawled on the wood. His arm looked unnaturally long as he screamed in pain over the wind.

Joshua let go of the horses and, grasping the edges of the boat, slid and stumbled his way towards the mast. Holding the edge of the bench, he hooked his foot under the lad's bottom as the craft dived down the other side of the wave.

Tyne battled tide, jerking them all with it's attack. Thom slid back up the deck. He squealed in pain as the pressure on his arm was released yet the angle from his shoulder down was very wrong.

Jeffries appeared next to the mast, his robes heavy with water, and worked to free Thom's hand from the now slack rope.

With barely comprehensible instructions shouted by the boatman, Joshua and Jeffries then tugged at the two ropes which Thom had been using to roll the sail up. Almost immediately the vessel seemed to calm. Leaving Thom prone on the wet wood, Joshua and Jeffries attempted to use the oars to help pull themselves inwards. The wind gusted harmlessly over the edges of the wherry as they moved away from the current but still, the waves battered, pushing them towards the jetty on a collision course.

"Best ter run 'er aground on't beach!" They heard the boatman call out, "I canna see the jetty to not bash into her!" With renewed determination and almost crying with pain for Joshua, the pair ploughed their oars into the water and paddled furiously. A few panting minutes later they felt the hull scrape on a gravelly shoreline and their blades barely scooped water - hitting the sand underneath instead.

The boatman ran to the side of the boat and jumped

overboard, stumbling in the foamy shallows, then dragged a rope from the prow. With a last burst of energy, he hauled the craft further onto the beachhead until it was more on land than sea. He then collapsed back, lying there on the wet, stony beach and caught his breath.

Joshua looked down at his hands in the moonlight. They stung as if he'd been burnt, but he knew once the redness faded they would be fine. He glanced across the deck, Jeffries was hunched over Thom. The boy had fallen quiet, emitting just the occasional moan as the monk gently felt around his shoulder.

"Should we take him to the Priory, Maister?" Joshua called over. Above the beachhead, the Priory walls loomed. Joshua deduced a building this size would have some kind of infirmary, and he had seen the flame-lights on the outcrop as they landed.

"It would be for the best," Jeffries advised, but, hearing this, his patient began quaking and flailing.

"No! No monks!" Thom cried out in obvious distress.

"They can help you..." Jeffries tried to interject whilst also holding the lad still so he didn't further damage his shoulder.

"He won' gan," the boatman called out from the shoreline. "Divvent mak' him gan."

"But why not?" Joshua said, "They have medicines there, he can rest?"

"He's afeared o'the monks 'cause they beat him afore," came the simple answer back.

"I will not hurt you, my lad," said Jeffries, attempting to reassure the shaking boy. "And neither will anyone else whilst you are in my care."

"No, no!" Thom wailed again.

Jeffries paused and looked closer at his frightened

face. He lent over further, until his head was almost intimate with the boy's. Joshua watched as Jeffries inhaled deeply and then blew into the boy's mouth, maintaining eye contact the whole while. His hands moved over the afflicted shoulder and arm as he steadily breathed into Thom's open lips. Joshua fancied he could see the breath glowing, and half expected Thom to writhe away from the intrusive face so close to his, but he didn't. Thom lay so stock still, he appeared entranced.

As the monk finished his long exhale, his hands moved down to Thom's arm and picked it up, manipulating it about into a straight position. Thom remained silent, his eyes gazing glassily upwards to the night sky. Even the waves around them seemed to quieten their rattling ascent on the shore. Joshua felt a note of peace and serenity glide over him, the like of which he had never experienced before in his life. The dark stillness of their situation less loaded with tension than it had been only minutes earlier.

After a moment, Thom's breath appeared to return to normal. Joshua looked over at the beachhead and realised that the boatman had, at some point during the treatment, approached the boat side. His rough face was inscrutable under the hat which had somehow remained perched upon his head.

Jeffries straightened and patted the boy gently on the chest. "Perhaps after all, there will be no need to visit the Priory, my lad."

The boatman looked momentarily confused, but his face turned to relief as Thom stirred and flexed his arm himself in wonder. "The shoulder was but dislocated," Jeffries said by way of explanation. "He'll be stiff after he rests, I'm sure, but fine after a few days."

"Thank ye," the boatman said gruffly, and he relaxed his tightened grip on the boat's side. "He's a good'un and I divvent ken what Ah'd dee w'oot him." He looked over at Thom as an indulgent father would a slightly misbehaving child, then said, "O'course, he won't be gettin' paid a'fer all the trouble yer took fer 'im.... but..." He turned to look at Joshua, "We did mak it 'ere b'neetfall." As his lips tugged up on one side, his hand flipped over and he beckoned with his fingers.

Joshua took out his purse and thrust some coins into the man's hand. "We appreciate the haste with which you transported us. Are you sure you won't come up to get some repast?"

"Nah," the boatman said. "We'll be reet 'nuf jus' here, divvent' worry. But yer can leave that flagon behind, fer warding off the chill?" A half-toothed grin accompanied his gesture towards the food sack. He leant in, then hauled the gangplank off the barge, onto the rocky beach. Behind him, a small flicker of a torchlight bobbed down the hill on which the Priory stood. They would soon have company, but would they be welcome, Jeffries wondered?

241

CHAPTER 19 – WHAT THE FUTURE HOLDS

Uffer held Aioffe's elbow, guiding her as they hurried away from the wooded settlement. Weaving at a jogging pace through pathways hidden in the mist, it was hard for Aioffe to keep up with the stronger fae. They both looked behind constantly, checking for patrolling soldiers, or if the aggressive fae had followed. It was not unlike the occasions when she and Joshua had fled, desperately seeking a space where they could unveil their wings and disappear into the skies above. But there would be no flying tonight. And no Joshua. Only Uffer, about whom she now felt conflicted, and nothing like as safe with. She swallowed back the hopelessness rising within her as they fled. To where, she did not know. And now was not the place or time to grieve her loss.

Uffer had gone the wrong way, he realised, as he neared the edge of the great trees beneath the Palace. Why had he taken this fork, and not returned the same way they exited? He mentally chastised himself, then blamed himself. Gritting his teeth as he yanked his princess along, he tried to shake off the mockery which that upstart Egbert had shown him. Not that he hadn't heard it before, but that wasn't the point. He'd put himself and Aioffe in danger by taking her there. He should have thought. Or resisted her better. He wasn't sure any more why he had assisted her. Stupid, that's what he'd been.

Uffer slowed his pace as they drew closer to the entrance to the Beneath. In the low light of the moon, shining through into the clearing, Aioffe could see the stomp of his feet echoed the cross look on his face. She tugged at his arm, ostensibly to catch her breath, but she felt she needed to say something to ease him, bring him back to her side.

"I'm sorry if I've caused upset," she began, "I realise how much you were trying to protect me, by not wanting me to see."

"See the truth?" Uffer spat out.

"The truth?"

"How we live?" Shame in his voice gave away how conflicted he was by his own rank and people.

Aioffe avoided his gaze for his sake by looking at the ground. "I didn't realise, that is all." Humbled, even saddened, that she had been so unobservant, so remiss, before.

"And now you know...do you wonder at why they are getting angry?" He almost growled, desperate for her to understand the implications.

Aioffe looked up at this funny, proud man with clear eyes. "I know that it is hard to live a life where you don't feel like you matter. I have lived that life too."

"I believe you may have." Uffer turned away, closing his eyes as his shoulders drooped. "I cannot stop what may come to pass, your Highness, but you should be aware of what is ahead. In all likelihood."

"Is it your belief too, Uffer, that their time is coming?"

Uffer then looked up at the base of the palace hiding high in the treetops. "I do not know what to think, your Highness." His words were chosen carefully before he dared to meet her steady gaze again. Those blue eyes of hers had a piercing quality. "Or when the time will come. But there is a rising before Naturae, although it may be futile. And you should know. As Princess, you should

243

know what's coming."

She knew about suppression. Knew of subjugation. Knew that the suppressed would rebel against their oppressors. It was a familiar battle the world over. The deadly consequences hadn't deterred Wat Tyler, a hundred and fifty years past, nor the priest John Ball. Even now, his rousing speeches were frequently misquoted across the breadth of England in taverns where unrest simmered against unfair landowners. The phrasing of the call to action by the worker fae was disturbingly similar, missing only the parts about casting off the yoke of bondage and recovering liberty.

She knew also of the chaos which followed such uprisings. But that was the human world, not her own. There, she could do nothing bar keep her head down, as she had done before, but here? What else was Uffer expecting her to do? An uprising of some sort was inevitable, human history proved that. Aioffe nodded slowly, acknowledging the burden he had placed on her, then sighed, and studied the ground. Lost for a moment with helplessness.

Her whole life she had avoided confrontation. Now, it appeared on the horizon to follow her like the fog rolls over the land from the seas. Impenetrable and impossible to navigate through. All one could do was wait it out and hope it cleared. But, her experience with journeys, and battles of all kinds, had taught her it was important to try to see the full landscape before the gloom descended, in order to swim through it unscathed.

Aioffe glanced up, noticing Uffer's lips were now pressed together, and his eyes were darting to the sides. "Is there more you should show me, Lord Anaxis?" Aioffe deliberately used his title in an effort to remind him that she valued him, if no-one else did. As she said it, she realised his rank was a complete fallacy. He could never be a true Noble and now, because of it, he could not return be considered merely a worker. He was stuck between worlds.

Uffer nodded, relief spread over his face, and he silently turned towards another track. There was no mist here in the centre of Naturae and he could easily pick the right course as they headed through the bases of the trees. Circling around giant supportive trunks, Uffer led her towards another part of the citadel. Forest here was usually lusher than at the main palace, but as they approached, Aioffe realised the towering columns were so dead there was even a build-up of cobwebs between the branches. The mist remained only as droplets on the cobwebs, dull with dust, waving geometric plates, floating in the sky.

It was deathly silent. Aioffe shivered. Without the eerie mistiness, the moon shone fully down through the thinned canopy, illuminating the extent of the decay. Uffer circled around the base of a massive grey tree trunk, and approached the hanging ladders which reached the treetop building above.

The climb was dangerous - the ropes so rotten that several times Uffer and Aioffe stepped on one, and it would immediately fray and unravel. Uffer decided it was safer for him to fly behind Aioffe as she ascended, in case she should fall. If a rung broke and she was unable to find a new foothold fast enough, without wings the drop could kill. Although no-one should be around in the dead of night, he was nervous about their discovery, distrusting of his own kin even. Being airborne also enabled him to keep watch over the palace and grounds.

Aioffe's arms ached by the time they reached the

landing platform outside the Pupaetory. She shook the tension out of them as she surveyed the long, prominent building in the treetops. Having flown over many cathedrals, she now recognised the similarity to this structure. Inside, the high ceilings echoed their soaring heights, a legacy of the Normans in England. But this was not a place for worship, its lofty dimensions had a practical purpose. Here, life itself was supposed to grow.

Vast wooden walls punctuated by stretches of narrow, tall windows to let in the nourishing light. All the way around the outside of the building ran a decked balcony. The balustrade had almost completely rotted away, and would provide no protection at all for young pupae, she realised sadly. Huge entrance doors were swollen shut and suffered from the same black rot which had pervaded the worker dwellings, although the carvings remained visible. With a quick glance at Uffer - still hovering above the balcony with a worried look on his face - she pushed hard on the doors with her shoulder and stepped inside.

The silence and stillness was unnatural. This should have been a place filled with noise and chatter. Even during the night, there ought to be people around to take care of the pupae. And yet, she sensed there was only one person in here, maybe the only for many years. She shivered in the darkness, goosebumps rose on her skin and she rubbed them as if that warmth would chase away the crawling. She had been so young the last time she had been in the ancient Pupaetory, probably some six centuries ago, she calculated. It hadn't been a happy place even then.

One of her many Nannies had brought her last, in an effort to illustrate how lucky, how privileged, she was. She recalled fluttering down this high-ceilinged walkway, which ran the length of several trees, through to the centre of the building. Beneath her, in the wide floor-space of the schooling area, she'd watched as they lifted the pupae onto blocks, then pushed off, over and over. Their wings were too small to fly with, so the pupae fell to the ground and cried. The nurse workers would simply place them back on the blocks to try again, as if the lesson was in how to bear pain, not how to fly.

Aioffe remembered sobbing in her chamber that night, her secret and foolish childhood hopes of finding a friend to play with dashed. That day, she realised those stunted forms were barely able to acknowledge her, let alone play flying games. Flying was something she had done before walking. She hadn't understood her larger wings and innate curiosity provided the impetus to explore and grow. Hadn't understood that these poorly developed pupae would never experience that joy. She did understand that she was different, not like them at all. For her, that realisation cut the deepest, the loneliest.

Off the hallway ran a series of rooms where the pupae slept and grew. As she walked past them now, Aioffe peeked in through cobwebbed windows to see row upon row of empty beds and cots. Neatly laid out yet covered in a veil of dust. She felt her heart sink further as she made her way down to the end chamber.

The door to this last room was smaller than even those for the dormitories. It hung ajar and she stooped to enter. The smell assaulted her first: a putrid stench of decomposing vegetation. Looking up, the glazed panes of the atrium were almost completely covered in cobwebs, glowing with a faint grey tinge as the moon battled to provide light for her to see. As she walked through the neat little pathways which separated the earthen beds, her bare feet slipped a little on the rotting cocoons underneath.

Aioffe stopped in the middle of the room, and spun slowly around, swallowing away the mouldy taste from the air. The only time she had visited the Pupaetion chamber before, on a rare visit with her mother, the vines had begun to wilt and she had thought it just the growing cycle, as a few were still green. Where before she had been unable to see the edges of the pupae chamber through the drooping leaves, now the rotten vines were silent, sinister ropes. Withered and brown, from ceiling to floor, they hung like bars of a cage. Aioffe felt as if she might suffocate. Her wings fluttered against the constraints as her subconscious need to escape grew.

She reached out to touch the nearest plant, to feel it and be grounded once more. In the palm of her hand the leaf lay, cold and fragile. Utterly dead. She pulled it off, near the stem, and felt into the hole it left... her delicate fingertip touched the warmth of the inner stalk. Not completely dead, but very, very close.

Kneeling down, she raked the soft and mushy composed earth aside to have a look at the roots. On this vine, they appeared very thin, undernourished and with a rubbery kind of spring to them. The plant would easily be toppled if pushed, and in no way could bear the weight of a growing cocoon. No wonder there was no more pupae here. Her mother had clearly not blessed for decades.

Grieving for the plants which had been abandoned and left to wither away, she then could not stop the tears which spilt out from her eyes. In the darkness, she sobbed for the end of her race.

Their time was not coming, it had gone.

Then she cried harder - heaving sobs - for all that was lost to her and could never be raised again. For Joshua. The sorrow poured out of her until the pain in her chest from sobbing meant she struggled to draw breath. And yet, she found she still couldn't stop the salty droplets cascading from her face, soaking the barren soil.

CHAPTER 20 - MATTERS AT THE MONASTERY

"Halt there!" An officious voice shouted out through the darkness, barely audible through the gusts of wind. Jeffries slung their bags over the horses' backs, and Joshua stayed close as they walked up the narrow cobbled causeway towards the torchlight.

"We mean no harm!" Jeffries called out. "I am Maister Jeffries, formerly of this Priory, and returned to visit." They waited whilst the guard approached.

Another figure arrived, also helmeted and with a sword drawn. "Who's he then?" the second soldier rasped out.

"Lord Hanley, accompanying me on a pilgrimage northward," Jeffries smoothly introduced as if the manner and timing of their arrival was of no import. "We have urgent need of your infirmary, as he was injured during our travels and I must dress his wounds. So lead on, and let us get out of this cold."

The guards exchanged glances, having appraised the sodden pair of travellers. The monk was unfamiliar, but they themselves were only recent posted to Tynemouth, and one black habit looked much like another in the dark. In unison, they peered over at the beached vessel, noticing the pair of sailors were already lashing a heavy cloth over the prow of the wherry for shelter. "Your boatmen will not be permitted in the castle walls," the second guard grunted.

"They will make their way off by morning, I am sure," Jeffries said. The guards turned and began clambering back up the steep hillock.

As they ascended the narrow pathway towards the Priory, tugging the horses behind them, Joshua felt a shiver of unease as they approached the looming shadow of the gatehouse. Nestled in the high walls, he could see through slits in the stones the welcome glow of firelight. Torch smoke drifted up from inside, signalling occupation, but with how many soldiers he wondered? Would he pass muster in his now bedraggled disguise?

The track then veered away from the gatehouse above, rounding the corner towards the cliff edge. In the distance, the moonlight highlighted the edges of a tall tower on the furthest reach of the peninsula, where a fire-created beacon cast a warning to sailors far out to sea that dangerous rocks lay close. Joshua sent a quick prayer of thanks that they had navigated the mouth of the river successfully; his relief growing the further away from the boat he walked.

As the pathway started to rise steeply and became narrower, the single file party slowed, concentrating on not losing their footing amongst the loose stones. Large boulders overgrown with moss disrupted the route upwards, causing the track to veer dangerously as it skirted the cliff edge.

Reaching the base of the wall, the guards led them inland a little to a small door, hidden in the fortifications adjacent to a round tower. No enemy, even if they survived climbing the tight, winding cliff pathway with defences raining down from above, would have been able to enter. The aperture was too low and narrow for a man in armour to go through. A lightly armoured soldier however, equipped with leather breastplates, was more than capable of squeezing through.

Opening the door, the first guard stepped into the darkness with the torch and paused, waiting for them to follow. Jeffries removed all of their sacks from the horses' backs, handed the reins to the guard who remained behind, and entered the tunnel, blocking almost all of the light with his tall body and bulky load.

Even with no bags to carry, Joshua had to stoop as he stepped over the ledge. At first, he stumbled a little in the gloom, feeling his way along the damp sides with cold hands. His eyes quickly adjusted through the short passage through the depth of the walls, before reaching another fortified door aperture.

"Watch the puddle," Jeffries warned, as Joshua's leg emerged from the doorway. Joshua paused and assessed the drop from the passageway. Already their escort had carried on ahead with the one and only source of light. He took as big a leap as he could, but still his wet boots felt the cold water.

Jeffries and Joshua hurried to catch the guard up as they crossed the large muddied inner area, and headed towards the Priory. As they splashed their way through the dark yard, several horses poked their heads over stable doors and nickered a warning at the intruders disturbing their evening.

Approaching another doorway across the courtyard, the guard banged for entry and waited. The wind picked up, swirling around the yard as it whistled over the crenels, then rain began to pelt down. Joshua started to shiver in his already soaked clothes.

"Compline," the older guard grunted, by way of explanation for the delay. Very faintly, the notes of harmonious voices carried in the breeze, worshipping in the church at the centre of the complex. "Might have to go and wait in the main Gatehouse," said the guard as they waited. By now, they had all started to feel the pinch of the night wind.

Sounds of a key turning brought welcome relief to the travellers, and the wooden door creaked open. A black hooded head with its face barely visible in the darkness poked through the aperture. "Visitors for you," the guard ventured, "said he was known here."

Jeffries spoke up confidently, "It's Maister Jeffries and my travelling companion - Lord Hanley - old friend. May we come in?"

The monk opened the door a little further, then peered out into the rain. Jeffries ducked his head forward, so that hooded figure could make out his face in the gloom. The cowl nodded then stood aside. They entered not the grand entrances which honoured daytime guests would have used, but the passageways linking the working areas of the Priory to the monk's cells. Dimly lit, the corridors lay silent and still. The monk motioned for them to follow, after he had closed and locked the door behind them. A feeling of exhaustion swept over Joshua as his senses took in the dank smells of habitation once more.

"Is Prior Blakeney still in Compline?" Jeffries enquired after the monk's retreating figure as he shuffled away. The hood paused and held his candle aloft to illustrate his nod, before setting off again up the corridor. "Then we will attend the Infirmary first. I know the way if you would like to return to your contemplations, Brother Edwin." The monk stopped and turned to look at Jeffries, holding the tallow candle closer to his face to study and confirm his intent. The monk's rheumy blue eyes ran over Joshua and once more, he nodded. Handing his candle to Jeffries, the monk shuffled off to his cell.

Jeffries led Joshua to the end of the passage, briefly walked outside again skirting the edges of the Prior's House, then across to a small courtyard close to the Gatehouse. They arrived at a narrow porch, then pushed open the heavy Infirmary door.

Joshua blinked as they entered the warm room, brightly lit with candles on head-height ledges running along the walls. Whitewashed and windowless, the room smelt strongly of herbs. Each side of the wide space featured comfortable looking beds, only one of which was occupied. The form groaned at the draught from the door, which ceased as Jeffries shut it behind him. Setting down the bags at the bottom of the furthest truckle bed, Jeffries gestured for Joshua to sit, which he gratefully did. The Maister then disappeared with the candle through another doorway at the far end of the ward. He returned with a cross look upon his face.

"I should have thought, it's kept locked," he said, running his hand over his bald head. "Brother Mort was always a stickler for keeping medicines safe. Not that that's a bad thing, just not ideal for our situation right now."

"I would be happy to rest here a while if you want to find him?" Joshua said, the tiredness evident in his voice as he lay back against the sheets. The straw underneath him was not fresh, but at least it wasn't moving. As he closed his eyes, the bed did seem to sway as the vestiges of the boat's movements played out their memory. He was actually feeling quite nauseous but, he reasoned to himself, he hadn't fed in a few days, so that probably didn't help.

Joshua's eyes sprang open as the entrance door latch rattled. A slim figure in blue servant's robes entered, her eyes widening as she took in the new patient. The jug in her hands wobbled on its plate, which she quickly steadied before stepping further into the room. "It's you!" she cried out. Her stare fixed on Joshua and she hurried over to them.

Taken aback, Joshua waited for Jeffries to respond. Priories were usually male domains, and rarely had he heard of women so close to monks' quarters, even if a convent was within the same grounds. Jeffries advanced to meet her in the middle of the room, examining her curiously. "I'm afraid we have arrived unannounced," he said. "I am Maister Jeffries, formerly Infirmarian at this Priory. And you are...?"

The woman bobbed in greeting, still gazing at Joshua as if he were a ghost. Almost absentmindedly, she said, "Nemis Claybourne."

"And how do you come to be here, Nemis Claybourne?" Jeffries asked gently, as he could see the pretty young woman was shocked, although he had no idea why. She looked pale and tired, the heavy dark circles under her eyes aged her. He thought her to be in her second decade at least. A patient maybe, he wondered, except she was wearing the robes of a servant. Female servants were not allowed to tend the predominantly male occupants here. A Priory Infirmary was frequently used to treat travellers and all manner of people who needed specialist medical attention, so perhaps she was in some way noble, with no other option for treatment? But then, why the robes and jug?

Nemis looked carefully at his black habit, damp and muddy from their travels, her bright blue eyes meeting his slightly hooded gaze. Her senses twitched, as did Jeffries', in mutual recognition of their own witch kind. The monk

255

was somehow familiar to her, but not as much as the boy sat on the bed. His young face was instantly recognisable, that often had he appeared in her visions.

"I have been given dispensation to assist in the Infirmary, Brother." Her words were careful, respectful. "I have some skill with herbs, however, I myself, am afflicted with an aegue, so I have need of being close to the Infirmary. The brothers have given me much support, so I do what I can in return."

"Perhaps I can help with your aegue," Jeffries offered. "I too have some skill with treating people.... afflicted. But I need now to treat Lord Hanley's wounds."

Nemis looked again at Joshua and made to tend to him at the bed also, but Jeffries stopped her with a gentle touch to her arm. "Is this fresh water?" He sniffed the jug.

"Yes," she replied, still not taking her eyes off Joshua. "I was about to refresh Brother Thomas."

"Are there any other patients here at the moment?"

"They made haste to attend Compline, the King's Commissioners are visiting and the Prior wanted full attendance at Mass."

Jeffries' heart sank a little; he had fled one group of these dreaded inspectors and sailed right into another net. "But I saw Brother Edwin? He let us in."

Nemis's voice grew more confident. "His vow of silence is chosen to contemplate the repercussions of the recent dictates from our King, for the Priory, Maister. Also he has taken to fasting, so is unreliable in the Mass. I'm told he cannot stand for long enough these days without falling to the ground."

Jeffries' mouth twitched - he knew well the pain of standing and singing the Mass when one's mind was elsewhere battling the temptations of hunger. Everyone

256

knew Brother Edwin had a voracious appetite outside of the regular periods of fasting, so this particular demon was likely to be a tough one to fight. Especially during this season of feasting.

Jeffries had warmed to the girl-witch, although something about her troubled him. It was not uncommon for their kind to find themselves hidden within religious houses - their oddities stood out less amongst all the other creatures who also hid in plain sight. But women witches tended to stay in the community, able to avoid detection through sympathetic social skills and more likely to pass off their activities as midwifery, cooking or just a 'female touch'.

He was also intrigued by her 'aegue'; witches generally enjoyed rude health and a suspiciously long life, yet she was clearly afflicted with something more unusual. He didn't understand either why she seemed to know Joshua. It was very possible that, with the much longer fae lifetime, they had crossed paths before. Joshua, though, had shown little recognition of the girl.

With a yawn announcing his intent, Joshua closed his eyes. Within moments his breathing had slowed into slumber. Jeffries was relieved. "I will have to bathe the wounds later, it seems. Myself," he added. Fewer questions would be raised if he could treat his charges' injuries in a more private chamber. While Joshua rested, he could have a look around whilst ostensibly gathering what he needed to prepare a poultice, Jeffries determined.

He also realised that Joshua, as Lord Hanley, could reasonably ask for their removal into one of the neighbouring cells reserved for 'special guests.' But, as the fae was resting peacefully here, he would have an opportunity to explain their presence to the Prior, without

257

the risk of Joshua giving anything away.

Nemis walked over to the bedside where the huddled Brother Thomas was shivering underneath the brown blankets. "His fevers again?" Jeffries asked, as he made his way to the doorway. Nemis nodded and began to pour water into a bowl by the side of the bed. "He also doesn't like the upset, I think. From the Commissioners. Their arrival seems to have set him off again." She set to sponging the sickly Brothers' temples.

"I shall return shortly," Jeffries said, deciding to trust her with his patient as well. "If Lord Hanley awakes, please let him know I will not be long."

*****

Jeffries circled the Courtyard then cut through the roofed cloister, his hood hanging over his head for protection. The elements were still raging overhead and it had begun to pour with rain. The cloister walkway provided little relief, its stone flagged floor dotted with muddy puddles which was barely any drier than crossing the sodden courtyard.

He remembered how truly uncomfortable life here had been, as the headland was buffeted by winds from every direction. Even the high fortifications and cloister didn't dampen their force. If anything, the howling of the winds made the monastery even more chilling, both of soul and body. This same chill penetrated his bones as he prepared to greet the Prior, who had unwittingly given him a welcome reprieve from this unhappy place many years ago. The sounds of voices faded as Jeffries reached the church and the Compline Mass came to a close.

He waited for a moment at the door of the massive

tower, receiving better shelter in the porch than he had been afforded in the cloisters. Within minutes, the oak-panelled door opened inwards and almost immediately the familiar smell of incense wafted out towards him. A procession of monks formed behind Prior Blakeney, ready to exit in unison. As they passed, the Prior glanced at Jeffries, his face forming into a scowl as he looked down his pointy nose and swept onward. Behind him followed two Commissioners, dressed in their long legal robes and rubbing their hands together against the cold. Meeting the eyes of all the monks who filed past him, Jeffries nodded greetings before joining the back of the processional.

In silence, the twenty-five or so black-robed figures processed steadily across the yard to the cloister, as if the winds and rain were not to be acknowledged. The Commissioners peeled off and ducked into the Prior's House as soon as they reached the edge of the columned square, leaving the line of monks to enter the same doorway which Jeffries and Joshua had entered earlier. The Prior continued around the cloister walkway, entering a set of double doors.

As the monks dispersed to their cells for the night, Jeffries followed the Prior into the Refectory. Picking up his pace, he walked through the long, high vaulted room, past tables now cleared of the evening's repast and wooden benches now pushed underneath. Servants had already prepared the decorations for the following day's feast for Holy Innocents Day, when a boy bishop would be elected and chaos would probably ensue. The Prior, ignoring Jeffries, continued walking towards the far door, intending to head for his private chapel in the grounds.

"Prior Blakeney!" Jeffries called, his lone voice echoed around the empty Refectory. This was ridiculous.

The man was deliberately snubbing him beyond the realms of common politeness.

The Prior turned at the doorway, "I did not expect to have to set eyes on your ugly face evermore," he growled. His curling lip revealed the enlarged incisor of a vampire. In the scant candlelight, his pale face seemed to glow with energy, fed by hatred for the monk before him.

"I have not come to cause trouble," Jeffries soothed, "although I fear you have enough of that with the King's Commissioners right now."

The Prior froze momentarily before smoothly releasing his shoulders to seemingly shrug the cares from them. "Then why have you returned?"

"I only come to ask for a night or two's rest, whilst I find a boat."

Blakeney looked sceptical.

Jeffries explained further, "I am travelling with Lord Hanley - presently resting in the Infirmary - on a pilgrimage north at his behest."

"Why is he in the Infirmary? And why appear so late at night like this?"

"He was injured on our voyage and his wounds need attention, which I am happy to provide, if I may beg your leave to use the medicines I know you have stocked in the Infirmary. We were delayed, and are both mightily tired from our travels." Jeffries allowed his body to sag a little, thereby physically making himself smaller and less of a threat to the powerful Prior.

"At least you have found yourself a patron. Is he an Anabaptist? Or some other 'new believer' like you?" The Prior frowned, torn as an idea occurred to him. Naturally change averse, he didn't like having strangers in his holy house. Yet, having been happy to be rid of the troublesome Jeffries, with his thinly veiled and vastly unpopular Lutheran questioning, perhaps now he could be useful. The surprise return of the eloquent Maister, surely now experienced in worse run establishments, could reassure the Commissioners that all was well in his own Priory.

"He is a Papist. Like yourself at heart, as we both know, Prior Blakeney." Jeffries studied the Prior with a shrewd expression. "I cannot imagine that for all these changes, you have surrendered and sworn allegiance as yet, to the King, the rightful Head of the Church."

Jeffries knew he was right - the Prior's face darkened in response to the accusation. He continued, "However, my Lord Hanley has desires to make a tour of the relics still to be seen in Scotland, where they continue to hold 'the true faith' dear." Jeffries was grateful he had thought of their cover story on the boat earlier. It made the lies slide so much smoother from his tongue. "And, I know these places well enough to guide him. After you cast me out, I spent months travelling the country, so I am familiar with where they can still be found. He might even wish to pay his respects to the Shrine of St Oswine whilst we are here - a small but significant contribution I've no doubt, but still..."

The Prior stroked his cassock. "That would be appropriate, Brother," he said, "That our revered relics should yet draw the attention of the nobility is always encouraging. Especially in these times."

Jeffries sensed he was winning the Prior around. "We will not be here but a few days, only long enough for me to talk to Master Kircaldy. I assume he is still here? He has a boat kept for his use in the harbour, if I recall?"

The Prior nodded slowly, his eyes narrowing as

considered for a moment. Then he made his own play. "I will require you to 'casually' meet the Commissioners, as a returning, and a 'visiting,' brother. In return for your board, and Lord Hanley's treatment, I would be grateful if you would ensure they are inclined to cut their visit short on the grounds that there is, and has never been, any impropriety here." His smile didn't reach his eyes. "Perhaps you could reassure them that if there are to be no charges of that nature, we will all be very happy to embrace whatever changes they write up in their Comperta which they request of us."

The Prior momentarily questioned to himself the wisdom of entrusting this mission to one of his former enemies, but better to make use of a quite obvious need for shelter than refuse his reasonable request. There was always a risk of him meeting the Commissioners at some other venue, outside his control, and he had been led to believe their report, the *Comperta*, would be drawn up shortly after their visit.

Jeffries was quick to snap up the deal on offer - and pushed for more. "If we might use the rooms to the side of the Infirmary, we will be out of your way. If Lord Hanley is well enough, we shall both join you for the celebrations tomorrow. I can mention it to the Commissioners early enough in the evening that they should remember my praise for your leadership."

He bore the vampire no ill will, although he assumed the Prior would think he might. It was unlikely the Commissioners would delve too deeply into his own background either, as he was merely a visitor like themselves. "I presume they are staying at your house, Prior Blakeney?" Jeffries speculated - this would explain why they were having this conversation in a potentially

262

public space.

"Indeed," purred the Prior. "They have made themselves most comfortable there. You may use the cells next to the Infirmary for a few days." Turning to leave, the vampire said, "Master Kircaldy will doubtless be availing himself of the seasonal ales in the town at this moment, before returning at some point, useless boy. He does maintain a vessel, but I doubt you can find any altruism enabling you to borrow it. Perhaps your Lord Hanley will be able to grease his palms with sufficient coin to enable your travels to continue?"

The Prior opened the doorway to the outside, then turned back to face Jeffries with his lips parted just enough for his incisors to be visible. "I hope to be bidding you farewell before the New Year."

*****

Joshua's head felt damp upon awakening, and for a moment, he wondered if he was still on that god-awful boat. When he opened his eyes, the girl in blue was hovering over him, dripping scented water onto his face. "You have come for me," she whispered. "I know what you are. I have seen it. And I know we have a destiny."

At this, Joshua's eyes flared in panic. He didn't like talk of destiny, especially from someone he didn't know or a priest. He shuffled up the bed on his elbows and stared at her. Her face was alien to him. Though he searched his memory, he truly had no idea who she was. He sort of knew that she had said her name to Jeffries when they met earlier, but he could not remember it.

"Please do not be alarmed." She tried to place a reassuring hand on his arm, which he shook off immediately. "I have seen. When I have episodes, I have seen us. That you are there gives me comfort. Where I must lead, however fearsome it may be, you are to follow."

Joshua felt his panic recede a little as he thought maybe she meant some form of vision, a prophecy perhaps? There was a strangeness about her. Even the smell of her was peculiar - pungent yet in a medicinal sort of way. Subtly inhaling, he recognised the same scent lurked around Jeffries. Was it particular to witches, or from being around too many herbs, he wondered?

"I don't remember your name...?" He stumbled out finally.

"I am Nemis. And you are Tarl," she encouraged, nodding her head and smiling.

"No-one has called me that for decades." Joshua's eyes widened. "Here, I am Lord Hanley, and that is how you should address me."

"As you wish," Nemis smiled. Joshua felt his frustration rising. Being enigmatic was one thing, but he felt quite vulnerable right now. The balance of who knew what kept widening.

"I don't understand how you know me?"

"Like I said, I have seen you, I have seen us. And we have far to travel. I will know the way when the time comes."

"The way to where? How do you come to be here then?" The questions tumbled out of his mouth before he could contain them. "Were you waiting for me? How did you know I would come?"

Nemis looked behind her, checking the form in the far bed. Their voices had prompted the sickly monk to start stirring, and he began to turn over in his pallet. "Not here, not now. But I will return and answer as many questions as I can. Soon." And before he could interject, she fled from the room.

*****

Jeffries and Joshua had a comfortable night, having moved into a nearby guest cell which was more comfortably furnished and afforded them greater privacy. Jeffries had banked the fire before they retired, so upon wakening the room was still quite warm, despite the continued lashing of the wind outside. Joshua slept the deepest slumber - his dressings changed, and a new poultice applied once Brother Mort had returned with a key to the medical supplies.

"I feel this need to make more haste northward," Joshua said, stretching out as he awoke to Jeffries pottering around the room, "but I honestly don't think I can face more sea travel in this wind."

The monk nodded as he poked the embers and threw another log on the fire. "I must attend Matins, then we will talk further of our plans. They involve a boat though. It's either sail, or a ten day cross country ride, and that is if the weather favours us."

Joshua grimaced, neither option appealed but a ship would be faster. "What shall I do here then?" Joshua asked, feeling a little useless, but at the same time, hoping the answer would be to rest and let the monk handle it.

"Nothing," Jeffries ordered, smiling as he turned to the younger man. "I will ask the servants on my way out to send in some food. You should eat whilst you can."

"They live like kings here! Would they have a nice live rabbit though, do you suppose?" Joshua was only partially joking. "Hardly the weather for hunting."

"There will be no red meat at this time, of course, and the rabbits will have been hung for a while," Jeffries said. "You shall have to make do with fish. It is possible there was a fresh catch delivered today. Even raw, it will sustain you in the ways which cooked food cannot."

Joshua blanched - raw fish was the absolute rock bottom of diets. He had hoped that at this time of celebratory abundance there might be some animals to be freshly slaughtered. "I'm not entirely sure how you will explain away the request for it uncooked though," Joshua mused. In a Priory, the kitchens were likely to be communal and well-populated, not very welcoming of visitors - otherwise he might have ventured there himself.

"Fresh fish skin is sometimes used in healing wounds," advised Jeffries. "I'll send Nemis. If, as you say, she knows what you are, then she might oblige. She should be able to procure something suitable without too many questions being asked."

Jeffries failed to mention that there was always fresh blood on hand through the common practice of bleeding which regularly took place at the Infirmary, ostensibly to re-balance the humours, but really it was used to sate the vampire's appetites. He knew Joshua had need of Lifeforce to heal quickly. From his experiences with Mary Hanley, he understood it to be a component of the blood, but garnered from living beasts, or as close to living as possible. He doubted very much the ethereal sort of Lifeforce would be in abundance at this miserable Priory.

Joshua settled back down in the bed, feeling safe and warm. Having escaped Hanley House, and endured two days of travel, he knew he ought to rest while he could in preparation for the next leg of the journey. Turning over to

266

face the wall, he tried to go back to sleep but thoughts of Annabella kept invading his mind. He tortured himself that he would be too late, she would be lost to him again.

Nemis's words came back to him, of destiny, and of their shared journey to take. Although he had relayed her conversation with him to Jeffries, the Monk had merely shrugged and enigmatically said she was welcome to come along for the voyage, and that he had more significant issues than an extra passenger. Yet still, Joshua felt uneasy about a shared destiny with someone other than his lover. Somehow it seemed wrong to be travelling with another woman. He hoped he would get more answers from her when she brought him food, but until then, he kept trying to push thoughts of her predictions from his mind so he could sleep.

CHAPTER 21 - FAELORE

Uffer flew around and around the balcony outside the Pupaetory. Watchful eyes checking the ground as he argued with himself about whether his risk had been worthwhile. When he saw the slim figure emerge, practically fainting with tiredness, he knew she realised the depth of the problem. Uffer helped her push the swollen doors closed, firmly shutting away the horrors within.

No new fae had exited the Pupaetory in over a half a century, perhaps more. The Queen no longer visited. As a building, it served only to remind people of their decline, so no-one visited it any more. Uffer had no inclination to see for himself, content that the rumours he had heard from now redundant nursemaids were sufficiently true to confirm what he, and surely all Fae, knew. As a race, they were facing a hopeless situation. He said nothing during the trek back down to the Beneath.

The fear of imminent extinction was driving the rebellious worker fae, Aioffe realised. In England, the threat to humans' mortal souls consumed their behaviour throughout their life, especially with the upheaval to their religion. Here, no such worries had ever existed about 'after life'. It was accepted that there was no existence after death. The more immediate fae concern was that there would be no further life.

No continuity of their way of life.

Of their race.

Which put a very different complexion on matters, she now understood. What does it matter if there is no future to work towards?

Why wouldn't you try and live right in the present, as lavishly and selfishly as you could? What is the worst consequence? Nothing. If there is no price to pay for taking what you want now, other than dying as you try...

If there is no consequence to your actions, if death really is the end of all things, then is no hope for the future. If that were the case, Aioffe wondered if she, too, might not want to take what she could, whilst she could.

Instead, she felt overwhelmed. Desolated. And frustrated.

And angry. The irrationality of her anger shocked her, but it also encouraged her. If she could still feel that passion, then she could act.

*****

Aioffe slept uneasily upon her exhausted return to her cell. Despite her interrupted sleep, she awoke with fresh ideas for her next steps. Before Elizae came in, she had combed the matted mud from her hair and was in the process of fashioning it into a suitably beguiling style when the older woman entered. "My, we must be feeling better," Elizae said. The warm pride in her voice suggested she claimed responsibility for the continued transformation of her charge.

"I would appreciate a different selection of gowns please," Aioffe asked, casting her eye over the drab shifts which Elizae clutched. "Something with more colour. And decoration," she added as an afterthought. Aioffe knew the value in appearances. Ornate clothing would help her feel more akin to the princess she was - and needed to be - to catch the eye of her target.

"As you wish, your Highness." Elizae bobbed and

retreated once more.

Uffer poked his head around the door. "All is well, your Highness?"

"Indeed, Lord Anaxis. Thank you." Aioffe didn't want to seem dismissive, but she did not wish to invite further discussion about the events of last night when Elizae could return at any moment.

Uffer said, "You are expected to appear in court shortly, however, I understand your brother wishes to see you in private as well. Today."

Aioffe frowned; she had pushed all thoughts of Lyrus to the back of her mind, and had no desire to meet him. In fact, she wasn't sure how she would react if she did see him, given he had killed Joshua. The pain in her heart stabbed again, reminding of her loss. It was all she could do to stop the hatred for him showing on her face. Whilst it might well have been her mother's command that she should be returned to Naturae, it was her own brother who had dragged her here. It was also Lyrus who ensured she had nothing to return to England for.

"In his chambers or the Guard's training room?" She said, wrestling to bring her feelings under control. At some point, she knew she would have to confront him. The question really was, would she be able to resist attacking him for what he'd done?

"I do not know. His page merely mentioned he was asking for you." Nothing on Uffer's face suggested good news, or bad, in his opinion.

"I see. Well, he will have to come and find me, won't he? Or you, as my Keeper." Aioffe turned back, finishing her hairstyle. She knew he was far more to her than just a Keeper now, but for appearances' sake, she did not feel it was safe to show as the complicit companions of last night. Elizae bustled in with a selection of colourful dresses, so Uffer left them to prepare.

Walking into the court, Aioffe did her customary sweep of the room and spotted her target immediately. Catching his eye as she made her way to the stool on the steps, Aioffe dipped her head to Spenser, who acknowledged her with an appreciative smile before finishing his conversation. Within moments, he arrived by the dais, bowing gracefully before the Queen. "Your Highness," he said, before reaching for Aioffe's hand.

"My Lady Princess?" His slight accent rolled her title from his tongue as a snake might slide through undergrowth. A subtle squeezing of her fingers, telling her he was as keen to speak to her as she was to him.

"Ambassador Spenser," Aioffe replied, smiling encouragement. "My thanks for greeting us."

The Queen looked over at her daughter. Why, Aioffe had positively purred at that Ambassador! What on earth did she think she was doing? The Queen sniffed and twisted back to surveying the court, although her ears remained tuned to their entire conversation. She supposed that any sort of interaction with the nobility would pay dividends at some point, although she wished it was with another. But, the court would see their future Queen talking to someone at least.

"May I say how that colour brings out the blue in your eyes, my Lady? It is truly lovely to see you restored. The Naturae court blossoms indeed with your presence." Spenser casually slipped into a well-practised flirtation. Despite herself, Aioffe felt the heat rising in her cheeks. How could he be so bold when her mother was sitting right next to her?

"I thank you, your Lordship. I hope you have time

now to tell me more of what is happening on the mainland?"

"Indeed, our conversation of last week was cut short, was it not, by that unfortunate incident."

"You said that in Europe, the Protestant movement was gathering steam. Have there been uprisings across England as well of late? Since the King's declaration?"

"Well, as you know, in England the momentum has been building, emboldened by the King's decree. Now Henry has sent out his Commissioners across the land to gather information from the Monasteries, I fear it will not be long before the people begin to feel the loss of their faith. My contacts in Scotland say they are watching the situation with great anxiety. There is a risk, even there, of the spread of Lutheran ideas."

His eyes narrowed, watching her reaction, before he continued. "Of course, others will be happy to see the changes, but whether the two sides will clash and rise against Henry, I could not say, your Highness."

Although not a believer herself, Aioffe understood the conflict which could arise from opposing viewpoints. She thought of the fervent believers - both Catholic and now Protestant - who subscribed so passionately to one view or another. She recalled too clearly the struggles which Joshua had overcome from his faith being challenged, or the passion in William Tunn's voice trying to persuade his wife to convert to his views.

Overall, knowing how the conflict was dividing families, she felt quite concerned for the humans of Europe and the realm which fell under Naturae's borders. Their conviction that their heavenly afterlife would be jeopardised if they failed to choose the correct way to worship led to near-violent confrontation amongst mortals.

To worry about the manner in which one practised one's beliefs, or what language they praised in seemed so petty to her now. Last night's discovery made their concerns pale in significance compared to the plight of the Fae.

She asked, "Have your family, and those in Europe, been able to satisfy their needs sufficiently through the disruptions?"

Spenser snorted lightly. "It's funny," he said, "the more threatened people are - that what they believe in is said to be a lie - the more fervently they seem to cling to their belief. This means they pray harder!"

"That was not always the case," Queen Lana muttered.

"But no-one threatened the humans here, did they?" Aioffe glanced at her mother. "These islands are a peaceful place, unchanged by time nor affected by our presence. There may come a time when these religious upheavals spread to here, but it will be a long time coming. I can't see how it would impact us, as there are barely any humans on the nearby lands."

"Your mother is correct, that was not always the case. Perhaps you recall your studies?" Ambassador Spenser's gaze flicked briefly to the Queen then back to Aioffe, trying to hide his unease about Aioffe's lack of historical knowledge.

The Queen turned away from the pair. It wasn't worth the time to explain to her daughter the long history of their lands. It had no relevance. Bored by their conversation, she shifted in her throne and stared glassily ahead. The sneer on her lips was the only indication of her disinterest in the wider affairs of her realm, although she could not deny there was a certain satisfaction in the human challenge to the vampire's grip on Catholicism.

"Please forgive me, Lord Ambassador, for I always

found the diversions of the outdoors more enticing than the study of lore when I was a pupae." A coquettish giggle escaped from Aioffe's mouth. Who is this girl, she thought as she heard herself? Spenser's warm smile in response made her feel like she was a player in some kind of theatrical endeavour. "I preferred to roam, rather than sit inside with papers." Her eyes darted between Spenser and the Queen, and she fluttered her wings, reminding him of the restrictions underneath her gown.

"Ah, then you will have seen the Circles of Faeth then?" Spenser leant forward conspiratorially. He checked the Queen - still resolutely ignoring them, but clearly she could hear.

"The stone circles to the south of Naturae?" Aioffe had visited the mainland several times to see the main ceremonial grounds of old, despite her mother's disparaging remarks about their defunct purpose. In truth, they part fascinated and part repulsed her with their desolation, however beautiful their aspect next to the great waters was. Frequent references to them in childhood songs had intrigued her, challenging her to seek them out once she was older and exploring.

"They are a reminder that belief is ever changing in facet. One faith would continue to prevail, but only for as long as people see the benefit in it." Spenser held Aioffe's gaze, as if he wanted her to understand a message behind his words. Aioffe stared back, unsure what he was trying to impart.

The Queen looked sharply at the Ambassador. She had never liked his family, merely tolerating him even now, and only because of their long history. She knew his cat-and-mouse power games. Her eyes narrowed and she pressed her lips together tightly. Was he accusing her of dereliction of duty? For centuries, no-one had dared to question, and now this European upstart was putting ideas into her daughter's head! This dangerous talk needed to be nipped in the bud immediately. "That will be all, Ambassador Spenser," she said, imperiously waving her hand to dismiss him.

With a last glance at Aioffe, he rose and bowed his goodbyes. Aioffe turned to her mother, more confused than ever. She knew from the look on the Queen's face that it was pointless to ask further questions. There was no alternative but to try to find out what Spencer meant for herself. Aioffe gritted her teeth and breathed out through her nose, utterly dissatisfied that she had failed once again to converse properly with him. Somehow, she needed to be able to talk to him without her mother hovering over her.

"Your Majesty," Aioffe said a few moments after Spenser returned to the throngs. A plan was beginning to form in her head. "I have been derelict in my studies, it would seem. Would it be possible for me to remedy this? It has been many years since I visited the Scriptaerie."

"It serves little purpose. It is only the present and the future which need concern you." The Queen jutted her chin out and continued staring ahead.

Aioffe pressed on. "I merely thought to try and understand what has gone before, so I might be better prepared for what may happen in the future."

The Queen glanced sideways down at Aioffe. Was she really softening, accepting, or was she being played like so often before? Lana studied her daughter's face, and started to wish that she felt more for her child, understood her more. But she couldn't. Her wilfulness was too much of a risk, too hard to rein in when given its head. Oh, but she

275

looked so like her father... she could hardly bear to look at her.

"I'm sure Uffer could accompany me?" Aioffe continued, gazing around the room as if this was a simple request for some time away. "The Scriptaerie is not far, and I could return quickly here, if you needed me. Your Majesty?"

The child would not give up, the Queen knew. She had always been relentless and unable to stay in one place and be still for long. This was partly why she was so frustrated with her offspring - too much of the wrong kind of blood in her. She supposed it was an improvement that Aioffe was even asking, rather than wilfully trying to escape. It was probably better to allow her a little freedom, let her think she was trusted. As long as she remained under constant guard and clamped, she couldn't get far anyway.

"Very well," the Queen sighed, as if it was a momentous concession. "Uffer will escort and remain with you." She beckoned Uffer and handed him a long key, retrieved from a wooden box sitting to the side of the throne. "The Princess may attend the Scriptaerie," Lana said, then muttered in a low voice, "I know you will keep a close eye on her." Uffer acknowledged her hardened eyes with a curt nod.

Aioffe tried her hardest to reduce the skip in her step as they made their way towards the exit, but no-one could fail to see her eyes dancing.

*****

The doors to the Scriptaerie had more recently been polished than other places in the palace, Aioffe noted. Gleaming silver inlaid swirls heralded the reverence

276

someone still had for the mysteries within. Uffer unlocked the door, then held it open for his ward to enter first. As he followed with the candle, the warm light cast a paltry glow but enough to reveal the rooms' unique dimensions. At floor level, the chamber started as a square, but as the walls rose they became cylindrical, forming a long tube. All the way up, lining the sides, shelves were crammed with concentric circles of scrolls.

Stepping onto a thick woven rug which echoed the swirls and circular walls by design, Aioffe briefly questioned her own youthful logic. Why, as a younger person, hadn't she wanted to spend more time in this cosy interior? Now that she saw it with more mature eyes, she felt excited instead of overwhelmed and trapped. Somehow, it had never occurred to her before that they were inside a vast, hollow tree. The ancients built the Palace incorporating the forest which provided their inherent structural support, but this room was the only place where the trunk was so wide, it was a chamber which you could enter.

In the centre, a large table featured carved legs which curved up to hold benches around the square surface. In itself, that one piece of furniture had always stood out - a square table ought not to be in a circular room, to her mind. Gazing upwards, the once lofty height of the room seemed smaller too, now that she had seen the soaring arches of Norman cathedrals. The ceiling was in complete darkness.

Uffer walked over to the candles nestled in the middle of the table, and began to light them. Gradually, their flickering brightness filled the space, although it didn't stretch to the top of the cylindrical chamber. He then flew slowly upwards as Aioffe watched from the ground, lighting tapers sticking out from the shelves. As he hovered, climbing around and around the tall room, Aioffe's mind whirled even though the warmth of the glow relaxed her. She breathed in the musty air, thickening with dislodged dust from Uffer's actions.

"I hardly know where to begin," Aioffe said, gazing up at the spiralled shelves, trying to identify some kind of markings which would guide her. A familiar childlike curiosity swept through her, tempered then by her centuries of experience cautioning about how much she still had to learn.

"I cannot help there, your Highness."

"Can you see if there are any scroll tags which mention the stone circles?" She called up.

"Your Highness," Uffer paused, "I cannot read..."

Of course, how thoughtless, Aioffe chastised herself. Only the Nobles and Royals would have been given such knowledge.

"Well, how can I find what I need then?" Aioffe sank down onto one of the benches and slipped her head into her hands. A tiny smile grew on her hidden lips. "Oh, it's hopeless, I shouldn't have bothered."

The dismay in her voice might prompt him to remove her bindings. It had been so long since she had been able to fly; the clamp not only caused her pain, but she knew in her heart she also desired freedom to let her mind process what she had learnt lately.

Uffer fluttered down and stood next to her, undecided. If the Queen was allowing her to go to other rooms within the palace, did this mean she ought to be freer to make use of them? The Queen hadn't explicitly said to him she was free, just to be watched. However, she had clearly given her permission for Aioffe to go into the Scriptaerie. A room in which wings were a necessity in order to make use of it.

This was a grey area, and he didn't know what he should do. The swirls on the tags hanging down from the rolled scrolls were more like patterns to him. The Queen must surely have known that he was next to useless with regard to researching here, or record keeping. So, therefore, she must have meant that his role was as guard only, and that Aioffe should be able to use the chamber as intended? It was a single-entrance room with a solid roof after all, and he didn't think she would be able to get past him were he to be guarding the door.

Deciding, Uffer took a small silver key from his pouch and lifted up Aioffe's cape. Within seconds, he had removed the clasp. With a sigh, Aioffe arched her back, stretching her wings. Uffer could not help but be transfixed by them, opening to their full, glorious extent. He had not realised how large they were until that moment, nearly twice the size of his, and so luminescent! As she flapped them gently, then gracefully lifted off, the candle-flames wavered, casting hazy coloured stains onto the surrounding walls.

A wide, relaxed smile spread across Aioffe's face. The full brilliance of it turned in appreciation to Uffer briefly, before her wings began to beat harder, propelling her towards the top of the chamber. Building up speed, she circled around and around the darkness of the top of the chamber. Spinning in decreasing circles until she seemed, to her spellbound observer, to be a blur of colour and wind. The tags dangling on threads from the rolled scripts around the shelves began to dance sideways in her draught. The dusty vortex she was creating almost pulled the breath from Uffer. He felt a moment of panic, of fear,

279

that she was out of control and would destroy everything around her.

But then she slowed, the spirals replaced by lazier flitting between the laden shelves. Her wings became more visible as they fluttered, darting her slim body around in the air, then hovering as a dragonfly would over a pond. With relief, as he had begun to feel slightly dizzy watching her, Uffer looked down. Grounding himself once more, with a few deep, heartbeat slowing breaths. After a few seconds, he saw her feet appearing as she landed in front of him. Her face flushed with exertion, but her eyes bright with anticipation.

She clutched a few, surprisingly wide scrolls, which she laid carefully on the surface. Her hands quivered as she fiddled with a knot holding the document together. Uffer's eyes widened as Aioffe then began unrolling the long parchment down half of the square table. It was hard to ignore the scent of wood and animal, released into the chamber as the document unravelled.

Aioffe bent over the table, studying the swirls. "I think I've found it." Aioffe sounded cautious, a little breathless still. "Would you like me to read it with you?" She turned and faced him, her hand pointed towards the markings. "As a Lord, you should try and learn a little of the written lore. If you would like, that is?"

Uffer felt strangely moved by the offer. Everything he'd learnt in his life had been from experience, Faelore was just not something he had ever needed before. He couldn't especially see that it would be needed now. His heart flopped over in his chest - her suggestion was an acceptance of his status, that he should have a knowledge of it. He also could appreciate that in order to advance, he ought to educate himself. Not that he'd ever imagined reading Faelore before, but now the opportunity was before him, he found himself tempted.

"This one," Aioffe said, picking up another scroll and pulling the leather fastening cords, "should be a record of.... yes.... the Stenness stones. The circles of Faeth. There are others nearby at Brodgar, larger ones but these were for the Late-Light. "

Uffer frowned, confused. Not least because all he saw when he looked down at the leather sheet was squiggles, line after line of them. Some, toward the top of the scroll, were indentations scratched on the surface. As the sheet unravelled along the length of the table, the swirling marks looked to be drawn on, reaching almost to the wooden end of the roll.

"See these?" Aioffe pointed at the markings on the top right, which were the faintest indentations. "They began recording the ceremonies here..." She tailed off as her fingers moved along what now became clearer to Uffer as a line of annotations. "Yet here," her hand stopped as the marks had just started to become inked in brown and changed in shape. "Something happened?"

"What?" Uffer asked. "Ceremonies for what?"

"Lifeforce," Aioffe muttered under her breath, concentrating instead on deciphering the markings. Even with all the candles, the yellowed glow they offered to read the faint scratchings by was barely sufficient. "Ceremony of Late-Light - unattended by Her Majesty. That's her, my mother's, symbol." Aioffe's slim finger traced a swirl that looked like a leaf with a small line coming out of it before continuing.

"In attendance was Lord Lyrus, Lord Philae of Egilsay, Lord Aegbel of Stronsay, yes yes, a list of Nobles.... then there's some numbers, see here?" She gestured towards some markings which stood out because they were straighter, not curved swirls. "That's Runish, and I think it means a date, but I'm not sure."

Uffer lent in. He'd noticed those kinds of marks before, carved into the stonework of some abandoned dwellings he'd flown over when hunting. "I've seen those, on the coast. They mark some human buildings, where the entrances are."

"Yes," Aioffe said, "you're right. The Norsemen left them. It was their way of writing language. Runish."

"So where the Norsemen lived, they wrote on their walls?"

Aioffe laughed, "Well, they wrote wherever they wanted. Carved it into stones, timbers, left their mark if you will."

"Then how did their writing come to be used amongst our Faelore?" Uffer said. A tingle of warning, a vague memory, began to creep into his mind.

"I don't know," Aioffe said. "Perhaps they somehow left their mark with us as well? Perhaps they knew of us? See.... here?" She indicated a place higher up the scroll. "They don't appear before this record at all. That's the older listings because there's the symbol for my Great-Mother. So these parts above must have been before the Sation Wars."

They both paused, examining the sheet further. Uffer started to differentiate the places where Runish was interspersed with the now more familiar swirls of Faelore. The Runish marks seemed to start towards the end of the script, so they clearly had been unimportant, or unknown, when the records began millennia ago.

"Here," Aioffe spoke softly, "it happens again. My mother wasn't present. She missed the ceremony the next time too. And then, there's a note that the *next* time, there were fewer followers..."

"Is this just for the one type of ceremony? The light one?" Uffer said, although he had no concept what other ceremonies there would have been for this outside his experience.

"Yes - there would be another script logging the other rituals at different times or places." Aioffe had only grabbed one of the several hundred scrolls which related to the ceremonial goings on.

Uffer looked up at the shelves again, "Would another scroll tell us more of the Norsemen?" he asked.

"Why? Are you interested in them?" Aioffe said as she kept examining the script in front of them. She smiled - Uffer's curiosity reminded her of Joshua, who had also held a fascination for tales of Vikings. Many times she had teased him about his blond good looks and muscles like a Northman warrior. His response was usually to gather her up in his arms and call her his wench, burying his head into her neck and promising to ravish her before he left for the seas. They both knew this was an absolute joke as he loathed boats, and neither would he leave her behind. If he could help it, of course...

"I suppose because I was so young at that time," Uffer said, turning away from her and moving towards the lower shelves so she wouldn't see his eyes. "My duties were almost entirely within Naturae. I was only really aware of their effect once their time had ended and past. Although I knew later of the trouble they caused in the rest of the realm, from others who accompanied the Nobles back to their lands. I lost kin to them, such was their violence. Suddenly, there were less of us. All because of the Norsemen, the giants from the North, they said. We

283

workers could never understand why they were so aggressive."

"That was only just before I was alive!" Aioffe exclaimed, studying Uffer. Holding himself slightly awkwardly, as if the confession made him uncomfortable. He appeared so much older than her but in reality was probably only a few decades maybe?

Uffer turned and smiled at her, with fondness, it seemed, yet his eyes remained guarded. "I was a young pupae when you were pupaeted, but I still remember the joy. Also the sadness."

"The sadness?"

Aioffe was surprised; no-one had spoken of being sad when she was young. But then, she realised, she had barely talked to anyone as a child. They had kept her cloistered in her rooms with only intermittent contact from nannies and waiting-fae whilst she was growing up. On the rare occasions she was allowed out, such as her trip to the Pupaetory, it was under heavy guard. She had no idea what was going on in the rest of the Palace, or Naturae, during that era.

Lana had made a duty visit on a semi-regular basis, but she could hardly look at her it seemed and spent as little time in her presence as possible. Aioffe always felt her visits were more out of obligation than a desire to bond with her child. She even had to address her as 'Queen' rather than mother - so emotionally removed. Quite unlike mothers Aioffe encountered in the human world. It had been a lonely childhood, devoid of connection with anyone. That other fae had been sad also was news to her, and she mourned that isolation once again.

"Tell me about the sadness," she said as Uffer looked

down. "I knew nothing of it. What happened?"

Uffer walked towards the doorway and ignored her question. He didn't have the answers she needed. It suddenly occurred to him that they had been away for quite some time.

"Please Uffer, I need to know!" Aioffe stood up and went over to him, turning his arm so he had to face her. His face had a guilty countenance and she wasn't sure why.

"It isn't my place to say."

"I don't understand. What caused it?"

"I believe this is a subject you would be better asking someone else about, your Highness. All I know is the rumours. The truth would need to come from some fae more qualified than I."

Aioffe was still confused, but she didn't want to make him more uncomfortable than he clearly already was. There was much more here to be learned, so she returned to the table again and dropped the subject. Perhaps her meeting with Lyrus would shed some light on the matter. She wasn't sure it was important besides. As her mother would advocate, it was in the past.

But this past, she felt as she opened up another scroll, was important. Not the more recent past of her childhood, but the circles. Why else would Spenser have mentioned them to her? Uffer joined her, brooding still, as she unrolled a shorter, although clearly much older scroll, judging from the dark edges. This one had been preserved with the softer surface on the outside, the shiny side of the leather inside carved so that the lines stood in starker relief to the darkened hide. Instead of the swirls of writing Uffer had been expecting, the lines formed shapes. A map.

"These are the designs!" Aioffe said excitedly. "The

sun moves here..." She traced the arc of a line which spanned the width of the scroll. "And concentrates the energy to here."

Uffer watched as she splayed her delicate hands to mirror the star-burst pattern in the centre of the squares forming the circle. Then, she moved her hands up, putting her wrists together, making a kind of pyramid with her fingertips positioned in some of the twelve square indentations. She looked up at him to check he understood. Uffer, however, was utterly confused.

Aioffe carried on, and looking down at the design once more, she traced the large pair of circles outside of the inner rings. "These, I've seen these before."

"At Stenness?" Uffer said. He'd never been that far before.

"Yes, they are the deep, deep surrounding."

"What for?"

"The people." Aioffe realised, "It's in the song?"

She began to hum a tune which was familiar to him but he couldn't quite place it. Seeing him still confused, she started to sing in a light, clear voice, rising up into the air.

In the darkness they came
To bring forth the light
Circles of light
Circles of life
Bring forth the winds
Breathe in the earth
Blessings will rise
In circles of light
In the deepness at night
Bring forth and surround
Blessings of light

Aioffe stopped. "The circles - they concentrated the Lifeforce." Without thinking about it, she rose several feet from the floor, turning mid-air as the realisation hit her.

"The less believers, the less Lifeforce. Can it be that simple?" The question was to herself, more than Uffer.

"But then why...." Tailing off, Aioffe flew down again to pick up the first scroll. Letting it drop on the table, she hovered, studying the Runish parts of the script.

"Why did my mother stop going?" She looked directly down at Uffer, who shrugged as he looked away.

"Perhaps she was too weak to make the journey?" Aioffe wondered aloud. "From the sadness?"

"But wouldn't the Lifeforce have revived her?" Uffer began to understand what she was talking about.

"Believers only go when they see the benefit in it... that's what Lord Spenser said. I think."

"Had the stones stopped working?"

"Or had my mother stopped working?" Aioffe countered. The payoff for Lifeforce was the blessings to the land. A fertility only a Queen could bestow. The scroll dropped from her hands and fell crumpled onto the floor.

Her next thought was unwelcome. The only person who would possibly give her the answers about that time was Lyrus. It meant asking either him or her mother, and she knew her mother would be obtuse. As the Leader of the Queen's guard, Lyrus would know her mother's movements. Why she had stopped attending the ceremonies. Very probably, he would know what happened afterwards.

Rolling her eyes, Aioffe resigned herself. Questioning Lyrus was a better option than trying to persuade her mother to open up. Even if she would have to restrain herself from killing him.

CHAPTER 22 - SIBLING RIVALRY

Aioffe, now emboldened by her realisation in the Scriptaerie, made haste to return the scrolls to their shelves. She submitted to the wing-clamp being fastened, before striding back down the corridor towards the High Hall. Uffer locked the door and fluttered up the hallway to catch up with her.

"I need to find Lyrus," she said as he alighted by her side. "Where will he be?"

Uffer gestured backwards, "In the Armoury, I suppose?"

"Then we should go there," Aioffe said, turning about.

"I don't think we ought to go now, your Highness." Uffer caught her arm. "The Queen will be wondering what has taken so long. I think we should return to Court, at least, for a little while."

Aioffe paused, her mind ticking over. "Maybe you are right," she said, heading once more towards the High Hall. She needed to consider more about what she wanted to say to her brother anyway. Being bored until he finds me in Court will give me a chance to reflect on what she had learned, she thought.

"Although Lyrus requested your presence," Uffer dropped his grip on her arm, and walked by her side. "I still have not received instruction as to when or where."

They rounded the corner into the vestibule of the High Hall, and Lyrus found them instead. On his way through the double doors he wheeled around, harsh blue eyes flaring with annoyance as he absorbed Aioffe's relative freedom. Although fractionally shorter than Aioffe, he was stockily built with a similar elfin cast to his face and the same long blond hair, tied in a plait hanging down his back. Only slightly larger than worker wings, his brown pair rose proudly outside his light, highly polished flying armour, inscribed with scrolls which detailed his achievements and responsibilities.

"Where are her chains?" He snarled at Uffer, already bowing his head to the floor. "She is supposed to be in Court, or in a cell! Why are you letting her wander around?"

Lyrus advanced on the pair, covering the distance from the doors in the blink of a wing and hovered above them menacingly. Whilst Uffer continued to look at the floor, Aioffe stared defiantly at her vine-sibling.

"I was given permission," she said simply. The feeling of wanting to rush at him, strangle him, made way for some kind of attempt at pulling rank instead. She was surprised at herself, but the urge to kill him was not as overwhelming as she feared it would be. His wings had reminded her that he was, after all, little more than an enslaved worker also. Even if he had grown from the same vine as she. He glared at her, his mouth twisting in surprise at her speaking.

"And I'm not sure what gives you the right to question my behaviour, brother. I am, after all, your superior."

"Superior what?" Lyrus mocked. "Outcasts have no status here, it's only for the sake of appearance you are even allowed in the Court."

"You are wrong. I am still the Princess."

"You are nothing more than a chained pet now, don't you see?" Lyrus said. Aioffe saw his point. She was essentially paraded out daily and made to sit at the Queen's feet.

"Then I'm not sure why you would want to meet with me?" Anger crept into her voice despite her attempts not to rise to his taunts. "Clearly I mean no more to you than a common Outcast."

"Our relationship is irrelevant. In fact, despite your return, I see *you* as largely irrelevant." He paused and peered closer until his head was barely a hand width away from hers. "Or at least, I did."

"Return? As if you gave me a choice!" Aioffe fought to quell her urge to lash out at him. Breathing in and out, before saying as calmly as she could, "I ask again: why did you want to see me?"

Lyrus sneered, "Because, dear sister, I have heard rumours."

"Rumours about what?"

His voice dropped slightly in volume, but the words were still spat out. "Rumours there is life in your cell."

"I'm not sure I follow?" Aioffe bluffed.

"So, I went to your cell this morning, to see for myself."

Uffer glanced at Aioffe, but she was focussing on Lyrus's face, waiting for him to elaborate. Between the siblings, the gaze turned intense, neither wanting to be the first to drop the standoff.

Uffer didn't quite know what to do with himself. Was he in even more trouble? He felt sure it was something he ought to have noticed and reported on, but he hadn't a clue what Lyrus was talking about. It could only have come from Elizae, if there was anything at all. He didn't know Lyrus well enough to gauge his intentions, couldn't read that haughty face to deduce what his superior was thinking. A worker fae interrupted his assessment of the situation, opening a nearby door and, eyes flaring as they saw the occupants of the hallway, hastily shutting it again.

Lyrus broke the glaring contest first. Landing lightly on his feet, he grabbed Aioffe by her arm and started marching her down the corridor.

"Get your hands off me!" Aioffe tried to wrench free, but his grip was tight and tightened further as she struggled. As if to show off his strength, Lyrus rose off the floor once more and used his wings to haul her down the passage towards the Armoury.

Uffer followed, but was stopped in his tracks by a snarl from Lyrus. "You will be sent for, when I'm done!" He could only watch with regret as his charge was pulled away, keeping her dignity intact by not screaming as they went.

Aioffe had been inside the Armoury many decades before, but her first impression of it now was that Lyrus had taken his senior status as Queen's guard to new, extravagant heights. Before she could say anything to bring him down a notch, Lyrus threw her down, sprawling, on what was clearly a foreign rug. He then abruptly spun on his heel in a military manner, and left.

Looking around with her head still on the floor, the large chamber screamed of his importance and power, with his name-crest intermingled with the Queen's inscribed in what appeared to be new decor on the walls. Aioffe was struck by the ornately carved panels around the room. Adorning this end of the long chamber, square vistas depicted battlegrounds. Paler than the wood which lined the sides; the etchings stood in stark relief against the darker tones of uncarved panels, bestowing the room with a curious chessboard effect. Inspiration for the wall decor must have been taken from the fashion for painted walls in the human world, although the carved panels serving as three-dimensional paintings could only have been created by Fae hands. The effect was thus a peculiar ornamentation, a blend of fae and human influence which jarred rather than complemented each other.

But who on earth did Lyrus think had been fighting? No Fae had been involved in wars, as far as she knew, for thousands of years. Fae had a policy of non-intervention with human battles, so which glorious wins were these supposed to depict? The skirmishes between the Norsemen and the humans had avoided fae-kind, she had thought until Uffer's recent comments, yet here was a picture of sinking boats with their curved prows, bird-like fae hovering over them. Other images proclaimed victorious Fae, including one which she presumed was meant to be Lyrus himself, presiding over battlegrounds. Hoards of winged warriors in each square panel depicted support for their conquering leader. The Fae had not even won the Sation wars, so why create such false illustrations? Motivation, she wondered?

On the far wall, in front of an empty space with a high ceiling, a display of weapons left no doubt as to the purpose of the room. Centuries ago, she had watched Lyrus practise and teach fighting to an array of worker-fighter fae. Deep grooves in the worn floor, dents in the walls, and a smell of sweat and old blood left a stark reminder of the damage their weapons could inflict. Aioffe sat up and rubbed her arm, questioning her brother's sanity. Who did he imagine he was? Or, perhaps more importantly, who did he want to be?

But no Fae army, no matter how well armoured, would be able to withstand the onslaught of a human rifleman battalion now, she realised. As she looked over at

293

the weapons on the wall, she knew not one of them could stop a speeding bullet from a matchlock pistol. Although she'd not seen many such pistols, this devastating invention was just the latest in a long line of ingenious firearm development she had witnessed or heard tell of over the last century. Arrows were still the main weapon for the common mortal man, but she could imagine them being replaced with guns as soon as availability improved and prices dropped.

Aioffe stood and straightened her dress, wondering whether Lyrus would be so confident then with his shiny, faelore inscribed armour. She wished she had a gun on her right now! How she would love to see her brother felled by a simple bullet. The image of him dying, bleeding out, and probably repenting for all the horror he had inflicted upon her, made her smile. Not that she was a cruel person, but she had heard the damage a pellet caused was infinitely more painful than an arrow wound.

"My Lady!" Aioffe turned at the familiar voice and saw Ambassador Spenser enter the room. "Are you alright?"

She hurried towards him, but Lyrus had followed Spenser in, frowning as he closed the door behind them.

Taking a deep breath and pushing the image of a dying Lyrus from her mind, she spat out, "Barely!" Shooting daggers with her eyes at her brother, she moved to a chair to sit. It surprised her to see the Ambassador here, but she was grateful for any ally. The two men looked awkwardly at each other, then stood before her. It was a peculiar sensation, Aioffe thought, as if they were waiting for her to regally acknowledge them. She watched them both steadily, lips pursed as she waited for one of them to speak.

Ambassador Spenser broke the now uncomfortable silence. "Your Highness, it was I who asked the Lord Guard Lyrus if you could be brought here."

Aioffe's eyes flicked to her brother, "It does not excuse the manner in which I was brought. To Naturae or this room."

"I know nothing about how or why you are returned, your Highness." Spenser continued in a gentler tone, his warm eyes encouraging her. "Only that I am very glad to see you home, as I have already said in front of your mother. There are matters, however, which..."

Ambassador Spenser glanced at Lyrus, "There is much we should discuss."

It was clear Lyrus had no intention of leaving them alone. Narrowing his eyes, he demanded, "How you are able to grow life in the dark?"

This was also news to Spenser, who blinked, then frowned at Aioffe as if she had deliberately withheld vital information from him. Aioffe said nothing, concentrating instead upon keeping a neutral expression.

Spenser tore his gaze from her, and began to pace about the room. Lyrus then moved into the gap, positioning himself in front of her. There was an implicit threat as he hovered slightly above her, although he kept darting his eyes between Aioffe and Spenser as if he was uncertain who was the bigger risk.

Aioffe studied Lyrus; although he was technically her brother, all that usually meant was that he was pupated at the same time as she was. He carried similar features, the blond hair and facial cast a result of his cocoon sharing her vine. But he was definitely worker fae - his brown wings betrayed him. She supposed he was only stronger than other worker fae because of their shared vine. All the fae

295

pupated during that moon cycle were officially siblings - she just didn't know who they were.

In that cycle, she had been told she was the only female, and was treated differently, kept apart. She wasn't sure quite why she had been marked as royal though, no-one had ever said precisely, although she had never seen other fae grow things the way she could. There were other female workers, albeit fewer than males, so it wasn't her gender. All vines designated a workers purpose, but no-one had ever told her what her vine had been, why it was different when clearly it could also produce a worker, a soldier, such as Lyrus.

There was also the slight matter of Joshua, his creation and rebirth as fae. He hadn't been grown on a vine at all, and his wings were black but large like hers. Aioffe pushed the thought away as soon as it entered her mind. She dare not think of him now. No-one could know about him, the risk was too great. She could not afford to crumble at this moment.

Watching Lyrus hover over her, though, she thought again how her wings were so different from his. More colourful, stronger, and akin in size to the Queen's. Of all things, her wings marked her out as peculiar. Perhaps Lyrus was jealous he hadn't been bestowed with such appendages. For whatever reason, the animosity which developed since she left meant he could not be trusted.

"I am hardly in a position to be able to grow anything in the sunlight when I can see so very little of it!" Aioffe tried to dodge out of Lyrus's way and meet Spenser's eyes.

"But you can grow?" Beginning to see the possibilities, Spenser returned to her side, although his eyes had become guarded.

Lyrus spat out, "It's what Royals do."

As if that were a fact which was commonly known, Aioffe wrestled to keep her shock hidden.

"I understand that, you impudent boy!" The Ambassador wheeled around to face Lyrus, who had remained in front of Aioffe, watching her every move.

The challenge to his authority rankled Lyrus. Spenser ignored him and knelt down next to her. "So you have the power? It's not dormant?"

The urgency in his voice reinforced to her that this innate gift was something to be treasured.

"I can nurture, yes" she said, still looking at Lyrus.

Spenser looked thoughtful. "There was some doubt, in European circles, about whether you would carry that same power. Usually it would come to fruition only when the previous Queen dies, but you...?" Inviting her to respond, the Ambassador smiled gently.

"I have always been able to breathe life into plants." Aioffe was careful in what she said. Her creation of Joshua was a secret she knew she could not share, a bastardisation of the usual manner of procreation in which fae were made. If anyone knew what she had done, it would raise serious questions about whether she should be the next Queen. Not that she wanted to be, at all.

"Then why have you not fixed all this?" Lyrus waved his arms around the air angrily.

"Because *you* forced me back here!" Aioffe snapped. There was no point in pretending this was civil after all. "At sword-point. You just swooped down, left chaos in your wake, then kept me holed up, away from everything!"

He was to blame for her capture, and her imprisonment. How dare he! She stood up, her wings straining against the clamps.

297

Ambassador Spencer put a restraining arm on hers. Diplomatically, he said, "If you were free to nurture, would you?" Aioffe turned to look at him. The fury within her dissipated as she realised that this was the question which had been gnawing at the back of her mind since the discoveries of last night.

"I'm not sure I can..... there's so much decay, and so little Lifeforce to give back. And I have nothing to nourish me here. I have no-one. I have lost everything." Her answer spilled from her lips before she could really consider reining it in. The compassion which Spenser had shown her, the friendship he offered, was her undoing. She dropped her head, fearing she would regret her confession. Restoring Naturae to its former glory seemed right now to be an impossible task. Her heart thumped painfully with sadness, loss. Overwhelmed with loneliness, she collapsed backwards, slumping against the hard back of the seat.

Ambassador Spenser knelt down beside her chair. Pushing the boundaries of propriety, he stroked a strand of hair which had fallen over her downcast face. "Princess, I do not know what happened while you were gone, but your Queendom needs you. Your mother - she is fading. It seems appropriate they have returned you to us at this time - however it occurred." He turned to glare at Lyrus.

Lyrus alighted close to the chair in which Aioffe sat, her head bowed. He watched the tears stream down her face. Leaning towards her, he whispered almost conspiratorially, "You will never be the Queen's equal."

Her eyes narrowed, and with what little strength she had, Aioffe railed against the cause of her unhappiness. "The last thing I want is to rule as she does. Failing to provide, failing to rule. How dare you! How dare you bring me here? Take me away from what I know, what I

298

loved?"

Spitting with anger and frustration, Aioffe shouted, "Did you really expect me to fall into line? To be like *she* is? Miserable! And I would be, for all I love was taken from me. By you!" Aioffe rose up swiftly and shoved Lyrus, hard.

Lyrus was forced backwards, doubled at his groin where she had hit him. His wings rallied to recover, and within moments he had drawn breath again. He snarled, "That boy? I should have known you'd take up with a foreign fae! A worker too, by the looks of him, not even from Naturae."

Lyrus looked maliciously at Ambassador Spenser, a twisted sneer spread over his face as he said, "How typical of your kind not to mention you had found our missing Princess! I should have you thrown out of Court for the centuries of misleading us!"

Spenser raised his eyebrows, "I had no idea!"

"He didn't last long though, did he?" Lyrus turned back to Aioffe, enjoying the distress on her face. "He dropped like a stone. Still, plenty of workers here to keep you occupied, *Princess*, if it's a bit of rough which you want to keep you warm at night."

Aioffe slapped him with all her might. Lyrus just kept on sneering whilst he held a hand up to his face where the red mark was slowly spreading across his cheek. Then, sarcastically, he mimicked her slap in the air as if it was a child's and hadn't hurt. He laughed cruelly. Then, his mocking abruptly stopped and he dived for his sister, both hands lifting her up by the throat. With barely a wing-flap, he slammed Aioffe against the wall.

Pinning her arms against the wood with his legs like a fly hovering over faeces, Lyrus brought his face in close to hers, whispering, "I should have just killed you too, *sister*, for all the good you have done coming back here. Just like that child you were with, I wonder, would you have tasted so sweet?"

Struggling to breathe, Aioffe was trapped by his bulk and the force of his wings pushing her against the panelling. Time seemed to slow down and she could feel her heartbeat throbbing against her skin, fighting for the air it needed to function. Suddenly, Lyrus released her as Spenser pulled his shoulder. She saw a fist striking a blow against the side of her aggressors' head. Lyrus dropped to the floor with a thud, the metal of his armour clanked against the wood as he landed.

Turning quickly to catch Aioffe as she fell, Spenser supported her with a long arm around her waist. She allowed her head to loll against his shoulder as she heaved air into her lungs. Keeping her eyes on Lyrus on the floor, after a few breaths, she recovered enough to pant out her thanks.

"We need to get you out of here," Spenser said as he flew them both across the room. Setting her down, he opened the door and peeked out. Aioffe leant against the panels and continued to watch Lyrus.

He hadn't moved.

"Do you think he's dead?" She whispered.

CHAPTER 23 - EYE SPY

William of Kircaldy sat nursing his sore head in his hands on a stone bench underneath the Cloisters. The wind had dropped, or at least its direction changed, and although cold, the rain had also abated.

Jeffries approached, calling out, "Why, your father would be proud. All grown up enough to have a hangover!"

The teenager looked up and his freckled face broke into a broad grin as he stood to greet his old friend. "Maister! Good to see you, I didn't know you were here? I thought you banished?" William had a surprisingly deep Scottish brogue that was unchanged by his five years in Northumbria except in timbre, his voice having broken since Jeffries had last seen him.

"I hope you are faring well in your studies?" Jeffries asked, with a definite twinkle in his eye for his former pupil.

"Alas," William laughed, shaking his gingery-blond hair with mock regret, "they continue to consider me a waste of time with bookish pursuits. But, you know, I have other reasons for being kept here."

"I do indeed, which is why I have come to ask for your help."

"Does it involve an escape from this place?" A boyish voice piped up from behind Jeffries, making him start slightly.

"It might be a timely exit if so," William said with a snort. "There was this girl last night..."

"That was no girl! More like a fishwife," laughed the newcomer.

Jeffries looked bemused. When he had last seen William, he was no more than ten, maybe eleven years old, and following girls was the last thing on his mind. How quickly they grew up, he marvelled to himself. Not five years later and he is chasing skirts!

"She told me she wasn't married," William said defensively.

"And you believed her - right up until her hulk of a stinking husband walked in on you, eh?" The lad jested, then laughed slightly manically. "I've never seen someone so desperate t'leave a mug of ale and run out into the cold as you! He was gunna 'propa dunch ya' if you stayed with his hinny!"

William looked down, his face reddened. Jeffries put a hand on his shoulder and ignored the boy still chortling behind him. "So perhaps this would be a good time to visit home for a while then, boy? Let things calm down a bit here?" Jeffries casually said, "I'd appreciate a trip there myself."

"I'll come! When do we leave?" The other lad said, sitting next to his friend and leaning forward conspiratorially.

"You appear to have assumed you are welcome?" Jeffries said cooly. "And I believe it is William who owns the ship, so it is for him to say."

William looked at his friends. His head throbbed, and he was not in the right frame of mind to make such a decision.

Sensing his friend's dilemma, the lanky boy put his arm around William in solidarity, reassuring the monk, "I'm a good sailor, the best! I'll get us to Kircaldy - I've made the trip many times." He slicked down his wispy brown mop in a practised manoeuvre designed to illustrate

302

his respectability and grinned confidently at Jeffries.

The monk examined his pinched face, noting the widely spaced bright green eyes sparkling with intelligence and wit, as well as daemonic energy.

William smiled and shook his head in defeat, "Fairfax, meet Maister Jeffries, honoured then dishonoured, the both of you. Fairfax is my father's ward, so, yes, he does know the way. He's not supposed to leave the Priory, but we could use the extra help to sail. I doubt anyone will miss him much."

Jeffries pulled himself upright and beamed at them both, hiding his reservations about Fairfax for now.

"I'm not dishonoured exactly..." Fairfax explained. "More - 'in need of an opportunity to show improvement in my behaviour' - as t'was suggested by the good Brother Aldwin."

"After you 'accidentally' set fire to his desks, you mean?" William rolled his eyes. Jeffries' lips tightened in their fixed smile. The daemon trait of leaving chaos in their wake increased Jeffries' concern about getting on a boat with the young man, but he didn't feel he could prevail upon William to leave his friend behind. Yet.

"I think we could all do with a little break from the festivities," William continued, rubbing his sore head again. "I'll send word down to ready the harbour, speak to the kitchens about some supplies. Shall we leave after New Year? I know Fairfax has his heart set on being the 'boy bishop' this year, and the crew will need some time to prepare the ship."

Fairfax gave a little whoop of excitement, and William rolled his eyes. "I'll be hanging back on the wine, I think," William said. He glanced up at Jeffries, then slid his eyes towards a jigging Fairfax. "As should you, the perpetual

Lord of Misrule!"

Fairfax's excited expression indicated he had absolutely no intention of following this advice.

Jeffries nodded and, smiling at the boys, clapped his hand on William's shoulder in thanks. "I have a travelling companion with me. He's a little run down at the moment, but I'm sure he will be much improved after a night of rest. He won't be a bother. But as we are progressing north anyway on his - I mean, Lord Hanley's, pilgrimage, I wanted to drop in on your father and pay my respects."

"He'll be glad to see you, I'm sure, Maister Jeffries." William's eyes stared deeply into the monk's, holding the gaze as if there was another question there yet to be answered. Jeffries spoke in a low voice, "Perhaps we could review the arrangements after Vespers? I will collect you and we can walk a while together." His nod towards Fairfax went unnoticed by the daemon, but William rolled his eyes then grinned.

*****

Jeffries entered his quarters to find Nemis lying down, quaking on the bed. Joshua stood awkwardly over her, panicked and dithering, clearly not knowing what to do. He looked up, relief flooding into his face when he saw the monk. "She just collapsed as she came in and then started shaking!"

Jeffries approached and smoothed the damp hair from her face. "I didn't know whether to leave her to find help, or stay with her in case she fell and hurt herself," Joshua blurted out. Part of him was concerned to be in the same room as someone clearly so unwell. The young woman's body was quaking all over as if she was shivering with the

304

darkest of cold. Her eyes rolled back into her head. Whole-body spasms then interrupted the violent tremors, her back arching and her arms waved out wildly. Joshua lent over and tried to trap the arms onto the bed so she wouldn't be flung off with the twisting wrenches.

Jeffries calmly observed the fit whilst his mind whirled with theories. He had seen tremors similar to this before. Usually they required a long-term supply of medicines which might help prevent the fitting, but did little to rid the patient of them permanently. The violence of this one though struck him as peculiar. He could see why she had been brought to the Priory for specialist attention. To a layperson, this would look like some kind of demonic possession. Indeed, frequently such fits were attributed to spiritual misbehaviour, especially in women. But he had never encountered it in a witch before, and that alone gave him a reason to pause.

He lent over the girl and after pausing a few moments to breathe in her panted, uneven breath, he double-checked over his shoulder for anyone else who could have entered the room. Joshua stood aside and watched as Jeffries placed his hands on her shoulders and breathed over her mouth, not touching but intimate nonetheless. Almost instantly the muscles clenched in spasm relaxed, and Nemis's whole being seemed to sink into the bed. Jeffries inhaled deeply while still hovering over her and, turning his head away from her, exhaled. His breath came out as a wispy yellow cloud, which smelt slightly of fear to Joshua's nose.

Nemis sat bolt upright on the bed. Facing Joshua with desperation in her eyes, she cried out, "We must leave! Now! She is in danger!"

"Who?" Joshua quickly came over to the bed, pushing

305

Jeffries away in his haste.

"The princess!"

Jeffries frowned as the realisation dawned on him that Nemis was a see'r witch. Why the visions should cause her seizures, he didn't know, but her presence at the Monastery was likely to mean they were investigating her for possible possession. Or, if she had had visions which were beneficial to the Church, they would be deemed miracles. Until they decided, no wonder she was hidden away here.

"We must leave, now!" Joshua begged Jeffries, "I must get to her!"

Calmer but with the same urgency, Nemis put her hand on Joshua's arm. "I can lead us, just get me closer, I have seen the way we must go. But I won't know until we are upon it," she apologised. "I couldn't describe it, but I would recognise it, I know."

"I have been making plans for a boat," Jeffries said, "but we didn't intend to sail for a good few days."

"It may be too late - we must get there as soon as we can!" The distress was obvious in Joshua's voice, "I will fly if I have to, she needs me!"

Jeffries looked at his young face, astounded by his naivety. "It is too far, you would not make it." However, if what Nemis said was true, about being able to lead Joshua to his destination, that would suit him well.

"Nor do you know where you are going, I think?" Nemis said pointedly to them both. Jeffries didn't meet her eyes.

Jeffries felt her pulse and checked her eyes as he considered their options. It might be possible to bring the journey forward, but it would take considerable effort to persuade William. "I will try to speak to our ride and see if we can move the timing forward a little."

Joshua's face sank. Part of him wanted to just break free of the smooth tongued monk and find his lover himself. Now he believed Nemis could also show him the way, and he was torn. In their weakened state, they both might still need Jeffries' ministrations.

Even if he could fly, which was undoubtedly faster, he couldn't carry Nemis. He doubted she would be able to describe in enough detail where they needed to be or draw a map. Somehow he would have to trust in them both for his journey north.

Resolved, Joshua said, "What do we need to do to prepare then?"

Sitting on the bed, Jeffries thought for a moment. "Nemis, as you seem 'recovered' now, we will need food supplies from the kitchen. Preferably some live animals. Can you find some? Bring them to the gatehouse and wait there for us. Pack lightly but warmly. I do not know how long we will be gone for. Tell no-one you are leaving, we cannot afford to raise the alarm."

Nemis smiled, "I'll try," and hurried from the room.

Turning to Joshua, Jeffries said earnestly, "I will speak to William, heir to Kircaldy. He will sail us northwards as far as his lands. I have already told him about you joining us as a passenger, but not Nemis. I will need you to concoct a reason for her being with us."

Joshua suggested, "She is perhaps coming into my employ, as Lord Hanley of course?"

Jeffries continued, "Kircaldy has a friend, a Master Fairfax, who I sense might be chaos incarnate. I need to try and avoid him being with us as we depart. Moving the schedule up will possibly enable us to slip out and leave him behind."

"I don't think we need any further upheaval, and the fewer people who see us leaving, the better," Joshua agreed. "Won't Nemis be missed, though? This Fairfax could cause us problems if he's left behind, and he knows of the plan to sail?"

Jeffries pondered. It was a risk, but everything about this journey was. He doubted they would come looking for a servant - even one who had visions - with the King's Commissioners present. Jeffries patted Joshua on the shoulder and shrugged. He stood up and retrieved his travel bag, checking inside for its contents. As he moved towards the door, he glanced back at Joshua. The boy was a ball of tension, furiously blinking. "Pack the rest of the belongings and pray," he said, hoping that a kindly tone and doing something practical would ease his mind. "Then rest. I will be back for you as soon as I can."

*****

As he walked around the cloister towards the gatehouse, Jeffries spotted two men in fine black robes. Sitting with their heads bowed together in a discussion on one of the benches, he had little doubt they were quite senior amongst Kings Commissioner's. They noted his approach, so he kept his pace even and steady, head down as if deep in contemplation. Intending to do no more than glide on by, he had almost made it past them when one spoke out in an accusatory voice. "I don't think we have met yet, Brother? Are you not due in Vespers shortly?"

As if this was simply a greeting and he had somewhere else to be, he carried on walking but tossed back, "Maister Jeffries, sirs. I'll be there, don't worry!"

"I was not aware we had visiting Brothers in residence

here," the older of the grey-haired Commissioners called out, his tone implying Jeffries should properly acknowledge them.

"I arrived late last night, sir, with my Patron. We will be leaving shortly." Jeffries turned to face their questions.

"We were not made aware of your presence, Maister Jeffries," the younger of the pair said, in a slightly friendlier voice.

"As I said, I arrived past Compline and, I'm afraid, without notifying the Prior of my intentions to visit. I used to be a resident here, so he has graciously extended his hospitality."

"And do you find the Priory much changed? Since your departure, when was that?"

"Why did you depart is more to the point," the elder man followed his colleague's question quickly. The tone of his voice belied his suspicion. "I recall seeing your name in the list of inhabitants of some years ago, no details of transfer, and yet, here you are, returned for an apparently fleeting visit."

The Commissioners fixed their beady eyes on Jeffries' half-hidden face and waited. Jeffries paused, realising he had a duty to fulfil his promise to the Prior and an opportunity to cover his own tracks. It occurred to him that the Commissioners might be sympathetic to his changing beliefs, having been appointed by Cromwell. And yet, his life depended on not fully revealing the extent of his commitment.

Unfortunately, at that moment, Fairfax bounded up to the group with a grin upon his face. "Packed already?" He called out gleefully to Jeffries.

Jeffries forced himself not to clutch at his satchel for fear the Commissioner's gaze might notice and enquire about its contents. Trying to contain the frustration in his voice, Jeffries attempted to move him on. "Master Fairfax, I am speaking with the King's Commissioners just now. So if you could excuse us...?"

The Commissioners looked startled at the boy's familiarity with the monk, highly improper behaviour for a student. Fairfax clapped his hand on Jeffries' arm and sang out, "A sailing' we will go, a-sailing' we will go..." before skipping off down the cloister path. The Commissioners turned back to Jeffries for an explanation.

"I was just on my way to speak with his friend, Master Kircaldy, about our arrangements for using his vessel. I believe Master Kircaldy intends that his friend, his father's ward, should join us in visiting his father before they resume their studies here in the New Year." Jeffries tried to smooth over the intrusion as much as convince himself.

"And when were you thinking of departing? We are mid Advent, a most holy time, and one should not be engaged in unnecessary travel." The elder man frowned upon his apparent flagrancy.

"My patron is on a pilgrimage and feels he urgently needs to progress northward to the sacred places he intends to visit. There is, I believe, some pressing matter he is desperate for the relics to bless him with. We haven't yet decided when we will be leaving, but Lord Hanley does not wish to tarry. I am, of course, trying to balance his desires with due reverence for the time of year."

"Lord Hanley?" The elder of the men said. "I wonder..." He looked lost for a moment, reaching for something in the recesses of his memory.

"I think we should perhaps meet with you more formally," the younger Commissioner said. "I have some questions we would ask about why you left. Perhaps, as you no longer are resident here, perhaps you could enlighten us as to any practises which may have contributed to your leaving."

Jeffries nodded, "I would be happy to meet you, my Lords, if it pleases you. I shall find you at the Priory House?" The Commissioners confirmed, but the older one still looked lost in thought. Jeffries raised a hand in farewell and continued up the path. Then he heard words to spur him onward faster.

"Be so kind as to bring Lord Hanley with you, Maister, for the last Lord Hanley I knew died some twenty years ago. Heirless."

CHAPTER 24 - CHOICES

"No, he's probably not dead." Spenser looked briefly at Lyrus's body on the floor and closed the door to the corridor. "The hallway seems empty at present, but doubtless someone will come soon."

"Are you sure?" Aioffe found she couldn't drag her eyes aside from Lyrus, prone and lifeless. How could they explain away an apparently healthy fae dying? And the Queen's Guard at that.

Spenser bent over, checking for a pulse on Lyrus's neck. Finding a strong beat despite his inertia, he stood back up and faced Aioffe. "We really don't have much time, your Highness. He could awaken at any moment, he's just unconscious."

She could not help but feel torn. Retribution would have been satisfying, but she realised now that she didn't want his death on her conscience, however well deserved it may be. Seizing the opportunity in front of her though, she said, "What was it you needed to see me about?"

Spenser approached and took her hands in his. Again, she felt the warmth of his touch and a curious intimacy reflected in his eyes. He smiled. "My Lady, I had quite forgotten, what with all I have learnt today."

"I thought perhaps you wanted me to confirm what I think you know about sources of Lifeforce?" She met his gaze then turned away, saying, "I looked at the records in Scriptaerie, of the old ways."

"Indeed, I wondered if whilst on your travels you had encountered the alternatives, which I believe could hold the key to bringing life back to Naturae?"

"I have found the joy in human nature, and the essence

of belief to be stimulating, yes. Is that what you are referring to?"

Spenser nodded, then flicking his eyes briefly to the Queen, he said, "In Europe, despite all the upheavals in worship, we have become able to draw Lifeforce from it as well as from humans themselves. But here, the very lack of human contact, of worship, and the declining nature around here means that Naturae is on a path to, well..." He rolled his eyes.

"On a path? It's almost dead! The Pupaetory is covered in dust and clearly hasn't been visited in centuries. The few workers still here, hate us. And there's something going on with them which I don't understand. People keep dropping down dead because they don't want to carry on eating awful dead fish! I don't see how there's any coming back from this. There is just too much..."

"But, you... you are the answer!"

"I cannot prevent what's going to happen. I cannot raise the dead."

"If you would only agree to take the throne once Queen Lana's rule ends, that would give hope, surely?"

Aioffe's eyes filled with tears as she considered his request. It was, after all, the reason she had been brought back by Lyrus. Paraded in front of the Court. But she had never wanted to rule.

"Are you working for my mother now?" She asked sadly, "Did she ask you to talk to me?"

"No, your Highness. But you must see that you are the only way in which Naturae can return to prosperity? With your gift for nurturing nature, in time this Queendom can be brought back."

"You don't understand - it takes Lifeforce to breathe back. I cannot do it alone, I need to be able to ingest

313

enough to give."

"Then we find you Lifeforce! The seas... or we could bring you animals, people even?"

"I am not a vampire! The kind of Lifeforce which enables Royals to create is the ethereal kind, from worship. I saw the plans and the logs. I know the stones, and I think I understand that they were used to channel the Lifeforce. But then it all changed, and I don't know why?"

Aioffe's frustration was evident to Spenser, and he saw her face crumple again. He realised it didn't matter how much he believed in her, something inside her was also broken. His attempt to heal the realm would never work if she didn't believe in herself.

Aioffe turned her head, breaking away from his uncomfortable gaze. Still not entirely convinced that this meeting wasn't an attempt by her mother to persuade her to stay of her own volition, prepare to rule whenever the time may come.

"Who was the fae Lyrus killed?" Spenser asked gently.

Aioffe paused before answering. How to explain? How much to explain? She took a breath and said in a small voice, "He was my lover, my partner. My husband."

"I'm sorry." Spenser placed a comforting hand on her shoulder. Aioffe shook it off and turned away. She'd cried enough today. Any sympathy now and she was liable to start again.

She walked over to Lyrus and looked over his body. She felt so empty at that moment. The room seemed to darken, and she heard nothing but Spenser's soft breathing as he approached behind her.

"You are not alone now, your Highness," he said quietly. "There are those here who would help. Would stand with you."

"Like him?" Aioffe replied sarcastically. "Could I ever rely on him to protect me when I am Queen? After what he has done?"

"You would have my support," Spenser said, laying his warm hand on her shoulder once more.

"Just me, and you. Against the workers, the Court...? Do you really think that would be enough?" Aioffe said, although she did not shrug him away this time. After a moment of heavy silence, she turned to face him. "I am not safe here. The workers are planning something. Something horrible, I fear. No-one is safe."

"You cannot just walk away from Naturae, your Highness. This is where you belong."

"I belonged with my husband, amongst people! Humans!" Aioffe's voice rose, "Not here!"

Lyrus started to stir. A low groan came from his lips. Spenser quickly brought a finger to his mouth and together they went to the door. With no time for protocol, he took her hand then propelled her into the corridor.

Aioffe and the Ambassador crept up the hallway, moving as swiftly and as quietly as they could. As they emerged into the atrium outside the High Hall, Uffer was waiting for them. "Are you alright, your Highness?" He ran his eyes over her, stopping at the redness on her neck from where Lyrus had held her. "Perhaps we should return to the Beneath?"

"I intend to speak to the Queen about that," Spenser said to Aioffe, as Uffer confirmed his suspicions about her living arrangements. "Maybe if you started to be treated like the Princess you are, you might have a change of heart?"

Aioffe nodded but kept looking down. The darkness of

315

the Beneath suited her mood. It felt almost comforting. However, now that he had suggested it, she wondered if the lightness of her old rooms might lift her spirits. Though she wasn't sure she was ready for that. Just talking about Joshua had brought the weight back to her heart, and after everything that had just happened, she longed to be alone. With her misery for company, and her memories. Perhaps there, she would find solace, inspiration even.

"Please, take me back to the Beneath, Lord Anaxis, I am tired."

"I will speak to the Queen, to see if she will consider moving your accommodation, your Highness," Spenser said. Without looking to see her reaction, he bowed neatly, then opened the double doors to the High Hall. Uffer and Aioffe walked slowly outside towards the landing area, leaving Spenser to his quest.

*****

Ever the diplomat, Ambassador Spenser took his time mingling with the courtiers as if his absence had been merely a break to eat. Having made his pleasantries, jovially chattering to the quieter Nobles about this and that and nothing of consequence, he made his way to the throne dais. Approaching with a confidence assumed from his rank, he cast his eyes over the Queen before she noticed him.

Her body was rake thin from a lack of nourishment, but he saw she had a core of strength which seemed at odds with her apparent frailty. Her pale face was lined with premature ageing. As a Noble fae himself, he knew she should still be in the prime of her life, yet she appeared close to the end of it. Bitterness and spite had worn away the youthful Queen he had visited for the half a millennium since she ascended to power. He had always understood that her mother's death, partly by the hands of his family, was the cause of her mistrust of him. But he had supported her, in his own way, since then. Although it was never spoken of openly here, the mistakes of her past had cost her. Every Noble and Royal in Europe knew it. This once great Queendom suffered as a result, failing to keep up with the evolving world around them. Never recovering from Lana's failure and sadness.

His grimace was barely concealed as he crossed the map on the floor, feeling the weight of his machinations with each footstep. All of Naturae's hopes and expectations should rest on Princess Aioffe. Although, she had little idea of the replacements for her that were lined up if she didn't take the throne. The European fae were waiting, expecting Lana to fall at any moment, and currently unaware of Aioffe's return. Time was short. Spenser cleared his mind and adjusted his face to its usual neutral expression.

He bowed, as was expected, as he reached the foot of the steps. The Queen looked down her nose, saying, "Lord Ambassador Spenser, I was not expecting you to still be here. Perhaps it is the charms of my daughter which keep you? I do hope they wear off quickly and you feel able to leave us. I am certain that your counterparts are eager to hear from you."

Meeting her eyes, he realised this was a thinly veiled warning. He blinked. The Queen's scathing attitude indicating she harboured scant love or parental protectiveness for Aioffe.

"Indeed, your Majesty, I did wish to speak to you about the Princess Aioffe, if I may be so bold?"

The Queen snorted, "I have never known you not to be bold, Ambassador. Get on with it, I have little time for pleasantries."

"Your Majesty," he began, "I wonder if I might make a suggestion? About her living quarters?"

"What of it? She is fine where she is."

"Indeed, your Majesty, she looks well enough when in Court." He raised an eyebrow and paused. "But looks are not all a Princess ought to have."

"These are *not* your concerns, Ambassador. I do not need your kind telling me where to keep my daughter!" Lana leant forwards, hissing, "Your kind should not be looking to a Princess at all."

"Your Majesty, I know my counterparts will all share your delight in having your heir returned to Naturae. It is indeed my dearest wish to be able to report back to them that she is happy to take her place by your side once again. Learning as she ought to, from your wisdom. Preparing to succeed when the time comes... but..." Spenser tailed off and looked away, raising his hand and shrugging. "It does not seem as though she is responding in that way just yet, your Majesty. I fear that others, like myself, might wonder at her reticence, her quiet demeanour. I noticed, whilst taking some exercise around the palace hallways, that her old rooms are still vacant? Perhaps, consider if she were to be treated more in accordance with her station, she might someday recover her sense of duty?"

His eyes slid back to the Queen once more to assess her reaction. Her narrowed gaze suggested she was considering his appeal. He held her eyes steadily, centuries of history passing unspoken between them. He straightened himself without breaking the stare. To remind her of the power he wielded with other fae, his wings began to fill his cape, just enough to hint, but the threat should still be taken seriously.

Lana's lips tightened. It wouldn't do to have European royalty thinking she couldn't control her daughter, now that she was home. Whilst she was angry at the man's blatant suggestion that he would carry his negative perceptions back to his masters, he raised an interesting question. But her mind would not quiet enough to consider it here. Her fingertips circled against each other, round and around, soothing her enough to say, "The Princess is free to do or live wherever she chooses."

Spenser saw how smoothly the lie slipped from her lips, and a part of him admired her for it.

Her voice then raised a fraction, so that those Nobles closest might hear. "Only just earlier, she was studying in Scriptaerie, to further her understanding of our history. So you see, Lord Ambassador, I do not see what point you are trying to make?"

Spenser flattened his wings, before bowing once again. "I merely wished to offer an observation, that is all, your Majesty."

"Very well. Safe travels for when you depart, Lord Ambassador. I do hope we won't be keeping you from your home Court for much longer."

With this dismissal - which he had no intention of abiding by - Spenser returned to the crowd of courtiers. Once more, he began to mingle, ignoring the tightness on Lana's face as she kept her eyes fastened to his back. Now that he had planted the seed that would hopefully mean he had greater access to the Princess, he intended to find out more about the situation with the workers. Surely someone there would know of their plans? How else had Aioffe found out, if not from overheard gossip?

*****

"Take me back to Thane, Uffer," Aioffe pleaded as they descended the passages. Their earthy darkness had already comforted her, and she began to revive just with the thought of being alone once more with her sadness.

"It is too dangerous." The finality in his voice suggested that her request to visit the worker homesteads again would not be heeded.

"I need to see more. I need to understand what they want."

"But why? It is inevitable. What they desire is understandable. When they will rise up to claim what they think is owed to them... it is probably better that we do not know. I cannot risk your safety, my Lady. It could be any day now."

A shiver, laden with doom, washed over Aioffe, and she sagged against the cool tunnel walls. Uffer returned to her side. Quietly, patiently, he took her hand and pulled her up.

Aioffe became lost in her memories as she put one foot in front of the other. Like Uffer had just done, Joshua would always pull her up when she fell. 'Clumsy on your feet, but a dancer in the air,' he'd say. He'd smooth her hair away from her face and tell her it was just one step in front of the other, careful as you go. This was Joshua's most human approach to life in general, she realised. Breaking things down into one step at a time, planning the next before he took it. One step was so small, so manageable, and yet took you towards the destination.

Her tentative smile at Uffer as he secured her in the Beneath betrayed nothing of her revelation, but he understood something had changed within her.

Leaving her with a candle to comfort her in the darkness, Uffer fluttered his way back up the passage. He had ignored her slim hand delicately picking his pockets of the key to her cell as he had turned to leave. He did not see the pale tendrils of hopeful plants flourishing in the dark shadows of the recess.

But, more importantly, he understood how much light one small candle could provide in the darkest corners of one's mind.

CHAPTER 25 - ESCAPE

Nemis waited, hugging a goat in the shadows by the side of the Gatehouse. The room above was occupied, she could hear the snores of the guard wafting through the open aperture. Thankfully, the wind had dropped and, although chilly, the late dusk air was refreshing. The animal nickered and shook its head as Joshua and Jeffries approached. At her feet sat a lumpy sack containing some loaves of bread and a wheel of cheese, which she had pinched from the kitchens. Not knowing how long they would be gone, she had opted to fill it with as much food and warm clothing as she could, and not worry about getting caught. She doubted she would be returning anyway, so the prospect of punishment didn't matter.

Across the way, the voices of monks chanting carried lightly in the stillness of the evening. In the distance across the interior courtyard, Nemis could see the glow of the candles lighting up the Chapel's rose window as the Vespers mass continued. They would miss the feast that evening, which she was quite glad of, for it had a tendency to get messy as the festivities carried on. Nemis knew leaving here was only the start of fulfilling her visions, but she wondered about whether they could make it out of the Monastery undiscovered.

"Were you able to speak to Master Kircaldy?" she said in a low voice, recognising the tall monk and well-built man next to him as they approached.

"Yes," Jeffries whispered. "He is already readying the ship." Although it had taken a little persuasion, the old monk had impressed the urgency to the young Lord, dropping in the impression that Fairfax had made a blunder which risked the Commissioners questions. William had understood the need for haste.

Jeffries muttered under his breath something about Fairfax hopefully not assisting with the boat preparations, as he tried to silently prise open the door to the Gatehouse interior. For a moment, they all froze when the creaking hinge announced their presence, but the snores from above continued their steady rhythm. Jeffries crept inside and returned with a small bunch of keys, which he slipped into his robe pockets before pulling the door to. He pointed to the wall beyond the Gatehouse, shaking his head when Nemis made to pick up one of the flaming torches in the archway to light their way.

Joshua picked up the sack by her feet and silently they filed past the doorway underneath the huge arch of the Gatehouse. Progress was slow. In single file, the escapees hugged the wall in the hope of evading the watchful gaze from the pair of guards patrolling the walled section at the land-facing side of the Priory. The narrow track round the base of the walls was still muddied and wet, requiring careful foot placement as they tried not to make squelching noises. The goat proved surprisingly biddable on its little rope lead held by Nemis; perhaps she had bewitched it somehow, thought Joshua. His experience of goats was that they were largely stubborn, stupid creatures, prone to nibbling, but she seemed to have this one trotting along behind her in a good fashion.

Reaching the hidden doorway through which they had entered the Priory only the night before, Jeffries fumbled out the keys from his robes and unlocked it. The passageway was completely dark once the monk had pulled the door closed behind them. A dank smell filled their nostrils as they felt along the wet slimy stones towards the other side of the enclosing walls. The goat panicked a little, digging its hooves in so Nemis had to half pull, half coax it, nickering all the way with its weedy bleat.

Jeffries fumbled for the lock once they reached the other doorway, nearly dropping the keys as he inserted them into the tiny hole. He left the bunch there to be retrieved, hoping they would be long gone before their absence was noticed.

"Mind the step," Joshua said, holding out a hand to steady Nemis as they exited the passage. She smiled at him and for a moment, her face brightened. Then, in the clear moonlight, her expression changed to one of awe. Joshua's skin had taken on the luminescence of the moon and he seemed to glow. He grinned at her and readjusted his bags, before gesturing for her to move ahead of him as they crept away. The goat noticed as well, and hugged Nemis's side in an attempt to avoid being close to Joshua.

The group made their way slowly around the exterior walls, following the rocky pathway they had taken the night before. This time, they had no guiding light other than the moon. Their trek down faltered, hampered by continually slipping in the mud. If any one of the group stumbled, they all paused and looked up towards the bobbing torchlights circling the high walls above, to see if they had been spotted.

Joshua murmured a low prayer as they continued in the darkness, pleading for deliverance. Free'd from the confines of the Monastery, and since he had lost his lover, his returning faith had rapidly become his last bastion of solace and companionship. In the chill of night, despite the presence of others, it felt as though that hope for divine guidance, deliverance even, was all his broken heart had left to lean on. He glanced up at the dark skies, wishing he could know whether Annabella too could see the same stars as he. Aware that despite repeated attempts, he still couldn't feel her with his mind. More than anything, that worried him. He remembered the last time they had flown together at night; it seemed like an age ago, that sensation of freedom, intimacy and trust. Despite the company here and now, they were no replacement for what he had lost; he had never felt so alone in his life.

Jeffries took a fork to the right before they reached the cliff pathway and led them over the windy headland a little way. They plodded towards the dim lights clustered by the riverside beneath, avoiding the built up streets to their right. Dusk had long since darkened, but navigation was faster and the group less noteworthy through the more open landscape. Panting as they picked up the pace with every yard further away from the Priory, Jeffries' route then steeply dropped away down a narrow track approaching the town. Before long, they were walking along a winding side street.

Approaching the quiet dockyard, Jeffries motioned for Joshua and Nemis to stay lurking in the alleyway so he could identify the right vessel without a group, including a nickering goat, attracting undue attention. He removed the cowl from his head and slipped into the darkness.

Joshua, his senses already heightened with adrenaline, took the moment to breathe in deeply, tasting the tang of the salty air mingled with the odour of the morning fish hauls. Ugh, fish, he thought, dreading having to sustain himself on a voyage of unknown length hunting from the sea when there was a perfectly good goat just... there.

Concerned he was feeling ill, Nemis gently touched Joshua's hand to enquire. "I'm fine," he said. "Just a little overwhelmed by how fast this is happening, though I'm worried it's not quick enough." She squeezed his arm as they stood in silence. He opted to focus on controlling his hunger pangs as they waited. Nemis's proximity and the scent of her anticipation made it tempting to pull Lifeforce from her, but he suspected she would know, or feel it somehow. It felt rude to taste someone who was aware of his needs without asking first.

Joshua smelled Jeffries return some seconds before they saw the familiar shape of his bald head and lanky frame. The monk gestured for them to follow. Heads covered, Joshua, Nemis and goat walked through the cobbled area, weaving past barrels and piles of nets until they reached one of the several long wooden jetties.

The harbour was crowded with a variety of different sized boats silently bobbing in the water - fishing vessels, flat and broad haulage wherries, and a few sleek trading ships. At the jetty, they approached one of the larger craft, hearing quiet activity aboard. Almost furtively, a few dark figures were preparing the boat fit to sail. In the half light from the moon and neighbouring dockside houses, the timbers creaked as they walked its forty-foot length, coiling ropes and making the sail ready.

Jeffries led the small group up a narrow slatted gangplank, stepping carefully onto the slightly slippery deck before holding his hand out to guide Nemis over the ledge. Joshua alighted, clambering over the benches and oars to the front of the ship. He dropped the bag from his back with relief and stretched to release the tension he'd been feeling with its weight against his sore ribs. Jeffries and Nemis passed him their baggage to stow in compartments in the prow, some already filled with baskets of food and ale stashed in amongst the various

326

pots, candle lamps, ropes and tools.

To Nemis, the ship looked almost alien, as it had both prow and stern curving steeply upwards, reminiscent of its Viking heritage. English boats favoured the flattened rear, yet this Scottish birlinn shouted its heritage and rough sea-worthiness proudly. In a further nod to its Norse ancestry, the prow heralded a wide-winged eagle, carved as if mid-swoop with an open beak, about to capture its prey. The boat was surprisingly spacious, especially in the midsection where the oak sides gracefully widened and dipped before rising towards the prows. Six benches straddled either side of the tall central mast, their oar handles neatly pulled in. Sturdy cups held the slim blades in place, ready to be pushed out quickly and used as necessary.

Fairfax and Kircaldy were standing by the rudder, talking in low voices with two unfamiliar older men. Discussion paused as Kircaldy beckoned for the new arrivals to gather together. Joshua glanced at Jeffries and caught slight pursing of his lips at the sight of the floppy-haired boys.

"We will need to row until we are around the headland before putting the sail up," Kircaldy said in a low voice, for the benefit of the new crew. "This is Jack and Ed." He nodded towards the two men in faded tan sea gowns and near-identical thrum caps placed on their heads next to him. "They'll take the front oars." Jeffries introduced Nemis and then Joshua as Lord Hanley, and they all nodded cautious greetings to each other.

Looking at the faces showing a mixture of fear, trepidation and unease, Fairfax piped up in his excited voice, "Good job I'm steering! Won't have to see your ugly mugs worrying away."

Rolling his eyes, Kircaldy said, "Fairfax will be at the helm as he knows these waters best. We won't light the rest of the lamps until we've got past the headland, all right? Then we can get sailing. Sorry about the small crew - I could only rouse this motley pair, so you'll all have to row until then. We should be fine though, I've made it home on fewer men, and it's calm waters since the storm blew out last night."

Joshua looked at the benches, clearly the ship was built to carry a far larger crew than the seven currently present. He inwardly winced at the prospect of manning oars with his battered chest, but quickly resigned himself to the inevitable. Nemis turned and sat down on the bench just behind the single, ten-foot high mast and began examining the oar. Joshua took the seat opposite and Jeffries arranged himself on the bench behind Jack, on the seaward side of the ship.

Fairfax dragged the gangplank on board, stowing it to the side. Kircaldy then leapt off the ship to untie the front stay rope from the wooden pole of the jetty. Leaning on the side of the boat to begin its turn, it floated away from the wharf easily. He then ran to the rear line to repeat the exercise.

The crew heard Fairfax whisper down, "Push man, push!" He bent out over the boat side, rudder held firmly to manage the drift with one hand. His other arm stretched to help catch Kircaldy jumping aboard. Joshua wondered how many times the pair had performed this slick manoeuvre, as the boys grinned at each other. He was also momentarily envious of their youthful strength, but he knew his would return greater than theirs would ever be, once he healed.

Digging his heels into the wooden struts on the keel,

Joshua followed Jack's lead, pulling their oars to turn the boat into the flow of the river. There was a bit of confusion then, as Nemis and Jeffries took a few strokes to get into the same rhythm as Ed and Jack.

Fairfax kept a firm hand on the tiller, and soon his whispered instructions became unnecessary. In the darkness, the crew focussed on with their rhythmic rowing, trusting him to steer the course. The shallow hull, with its clinker design, provided a smooth ride - far more stable than the wherry even, thought Joshua. This was a craft designed to navigate the seas, which thankfully were calm at the moment. The hull seemed to flex as it rose over the higher waves as they exited the harbour and moved away from the last land lights they would see for a good while. Joshua's chest began to ache with continued exertion of pulling the oars, his wings chafing against his bindings.

They navigated the headland without incident, and Fairfax told them to pull in their oars as the craft bobbed along in the tide. Kircaldy joined Fairfax, untying the ropes holding the sail neatly rolled up high. As it dropped with a whoosh, the light breeze filled it immediately and they all felt a measure of relief. Kircaldy and Ed secured the sail lines before pulling two small lanterns from the cubby holes near the rudder. Using the candle which was at Fairfax's feet, they lit the lamps for the front and mast. Dangling on tiny hooks, they barely cast out any light but their glow was at least comfort in the darkness.

*****

As the sun rose on the new day, Joshua's heavy eyelids flew open as his senses suddenly registered the rocking of the ship. Leaning against the side, still at his bench, he had only meant to rest his head for a moment. At the stern, Fairfax was wrestling with the rudder, Kircaldy stood next to him in camaraderie and they were both grinning as they steered the boat into the waves quite deliberately.

"'Tis a fine morning for sailing!" Kircaldy called out. He hid his smile as he watched Joshua attempting to stand gracefully, then lumbering over to the mast for support as the boat rose up a wave, then slid down over it on an angle. Joshua saw Nemis and Jeffries giggling, cosied up together against the other side of the boat, wrapped in jaunty red woollen blankets for warmth. Fairfax laughed with no attempt to conceal his amusement; Joshua scowled at him.

Sitting back down on a bench near the front, wisely, he thought, putting distance between himself and his new foe, but Joshua quickly realised his mistake. The problem with his new location was the goat. It was curled up underneath the ledge, contentedly snoozing, Joshua was acutely aware of its lazy heartbeat, pumping warm blood, Lifeforce, around its little body. In such close proximity, and tired and grumpy, Joshua was reminded of his need to feed. He would have succumbed but for the complete lack of privacy aboard. Closing his eyes, instead trying hard to just focus on the motion of the vessel on the waves, breathing in the sea air around him. Only minutes of wrestling his hunger later, the up and down lurching movement of the boat made him flick his eyes back open. He sat upright quickly, nauseated.

"It would be better if you looked at the horizon," Jeffries advised. Joshua knew he spoke the truth, but something stubborn in him made him turn his back, and keep his eyes shut to ignore him. The ship lurched once again, and he felt a painful kick to his calf. The goat had awoken and was scrabbling around trying to stand.

"How much further?" Joshua said as the desire to feed swept over him and he panicked a little. What if he couldn't restrain himself?

"We've barely begun," Kircaldy said. "Get yourself comfortable, my Lord, for we've a way to go yet."

"How long though?" Joshua pressed.

"We should make land by tomorrow morning, with this wind." Fairfax reassured him as he pulled the ropes to tack once more.

"You should rest," Jeffries said to Fairfax and Kircaldy. "You have held our course all night. Show me?" He asked, standing and walking towards the rudder with surprising sea legs for such an old man.

Kircaldy nodded and began explaining the complicated series of ropes and tacking manoeuvres to him. Before long, Ed and Jack were awake and assisting.

Joshua decided he had better just stay out of the way, no-one needed his lack of sea legs under-foot. He positioned himself on the bench as a lookout, leaning over the ship's sides, watching as they skirted the coastline. Desperately trying to focus on anything but the alluring smell of goat.

*****

They passed Lindisfarne around midday. The sun shone on its flat landscape, sea birds wheeling around the majestic towers of the monastery. Joshua felt his heart sink as watched. He again longed to be free - flying once more with his lover. Roaming wherever they chose, although he knew it was largely she who had determined their

331

destinations. He smiled to himself, Annabella could relish freedom like no-one else he knew, her thirst for discovery always inspired him. She would have readily embraced a quest, if only it were he that needed rescuing, she would be unstoppable.

Resolving not to get sucked into the abyss of reminiscing, he swallowed and bit back his tears. Instead, he tried to calculate how long the journey past Scotland and up towards the Orkneys might take. He didn't feel it was the right time to discuss plans with Jeffries or Nemis - preferring to maintain the cover they had for now. It seemed to pass muster, for Jack and Ed had barely spoken to him out of, he presumed, deference to his assumed station. Conversation had remained oddly lacking amongst the crew, as they just got about the business of sailing.

After a few hours, dusk had been and gone and darkness fell once more. The birlinn carried them swiftly on their course around the headland, past Berwick. The night sky was clear and bright, the nearly full moon casting an eerie glow upon the calm waters as they hugged the coastline closely.

At some point in the early dawn, Fairfax, aided by Ed, John and Kircaldy, began tacking more frequently to traverse the estuary and head north to the town of Kircaldy. Exhausted from his silent, hungry watch of the coast passing by, and lulled by the choppy waves for once, Joshua dozed fitfully. The creak of the sail and boom movement blended into soporific background noise.

Then Fairfax abruptly called out, "Oars! Drop the sail!" The resting crew awoke with a start. Scrabbling from their various states of sleep, they scrambled to get back to their benches and slide the poles back into the water. Ed pulled the halyard to bring the square luff-sail

332

down. Joshua could see a headland approaching at what seemed like an alarming rate, but once the sail dropped, their speed slowed. Again following the experienced sailor's lead, they hauled away with oars to guide the vessel into the small mouth of the harbour.

"Will your father be at Ravenscraig or Halyards?" Jeffries called out to Master Kircaldy as they entered the wide pool. As they rowed, the lights of his name-sake town could be seen pin-pricking through the night, and noises of harbour-side revelry reached their ears. It was a welcome sight to Joshua, and even more so to Jeffries.

"Probably Ravenscraig," Kircaldy replied, "He was preparing to go on a voyage with the King, so he'll be overseeing stocking the Wanderer."

Joshua saw Jeffries look relieved at this news. They all hauled away with renewed fervour, the thought of an imminent docking a welcome prospect. Kircaldy took the helm and Fairfax dragged out the ropes ready to secure the birlinn. Fairfax smoothed his wispy hair down as they drew in close to a large galleon docked at the far end of the harbour.

Pushing over the gangplank to the narrow jetty separating the two vessels, Joshua took a moment to wonder at the looming bulk of what he presumed was Lord Kircaldy's ship. The birlinn now felt like a low-slung dwarf compared to the splendid Wanderer.

Sitting high in the water, the enormous galleon was elaborately decorated with carvings around the windows running the length almost of the third deck level, and menacing-looking hatches on the second. Sporting three masts on the main deck and one more jutting from the front of the ship, he noticed a crow's nest on the top of the middle one, apparently unmanned at the moment. Hearing a crew inside the underbelly of the ship, moving around and an occasional burst of laughter, Joshua raised his finger to his lips in caution to the others disembarking.

The goat, however, let out an almighty bleat as Nemis and Jeffries struggled to lift it up onto the gangplank. Joshua's nostrils flared instinctively, and the goat continued to announce their arrival with skittery hooves as it tried to turn away from the hunter at the end of the plank.

"Who goes there?" A voice called from above. "Name yourselves and yer business!"

The crew of the birlinn froze. Looking up, his pale face glowing in the moonlight in a most unnatural way, Joshua could see the glint of a gun barrel pointing straight at him through the balustrades.

CHAPTER 26 –
FORTIFICATION

"Jones! It's me, William!" Kircaldy shouted up. "Put that thing away!" The gun barrel pointed at Joshua wavered, then lowered, much to his relief. Kircaldy and Fairfax dropped the gangplank down and appeared by his side. They took Joshua's candle from him and waved up at the man now peering over the balustrade, who grunted and doffed his misshapen wool hat at his superior.

"Yer daft bat!" Fairfax called up as he secured the smaller vessel tightly to the jetty, "That's Lord Hanley you nearly made holey!"

"Apologies," Jones said, looking decidedly abashed. "Anyone approaching at this hour is usually trouble, your Lordship. An'.... yer looked, well, pale?"

"Seasick is all," Joshua's smile didn't quite reach his eyes. "You were just doing your job, I'm sure."

"Aye, we're provisioning for France tomorrow," Jones said. "Can't be too careful with s'much hooch about right now."

Kircaldy asked up, "My father, is he at Ravenscraig or aboard?" He offered a hand to help Nemis off the gangplank.

"He's resting up after the feast at Ravenscraig, m'Lord, and probably praying' fer fittin' weather tomorrow with the tide!"

Gathering the bags, the crew of the birlinn trooped down the jetty and followed Kircaldy and an unusually subdued Fairfax to the harbourside. The sounds of carousing and feasting were louder now they were within spitting distance of civilisation. Jack and Ed looked longingly at the nearby public house and with a smirk, William nodded his assent. "Sleep it off on the ship though!"

The pair grinned and doffed their thrum caps at him, before sidling off. The harbour road led them away from the sea, in towards the main town of Kircaldy, but the remains of the group veered off to climb a cobbled street to the right, hugging the coastline a little further.

Up ahead of them loomed the huge round towers of the castle. High promontory walls jutted out along to the point of the cliff top, offered an unparalleled - as well as fortified - view of the waters below. As they approached the main arches of the doorway, there was no doubt they had been spotted approaching. The flickering flames of movement through the crenellations indicated they were being assessed. Kircaldy held the candle close to his head and raised his other arm in greeting. The dim light from the lantern, he hoped, would be enough to show his familiar face to those who would be watching from narrow slits in the walls.

"Show your colours!" A reedy voice called out. Kircaldy pulled his kerchief from his pouch and waved it in front of the candle.

A small hatch door, set inside hefty studded wooden fortifications, opened a crack. Enough to allow a menacing-looking pike staff to poke out, followed by a small, thin head bearing the Laird's uniform beret. A rat-like face glanced at the coloured linen square, then Fairfax and Kircaldy up and down before withdrawing with a quiet 'Milord.' The smaller door then flung open to them. The group stepped through one by one, each wrestling with misgivings and relief as they entered supposed safety.

Once inside the courtyard, William strode confidently towards the Hall building, pausing only to beckon them to follow. Flaming torches circled the yard, illuminating the strewn chests, sacks and equipment piled high on the cobblestones. Three servants in dark blue house-robes appeared from a side door to the largest building, carrying baskets of bread and cloth-wrapped parcels, followed by another pushing a small barrel. They stopped and bobbed deeply to acknowledge the son of the Laird approaching. In return, William tightly smiled a greeting and continued on his way.

Nemis wondered if she should be following or waiting to be shown the servant's entrance. In the absence of direction, she opted to stay with the group. She quickly tied the goat to a ring by the entrance door and hoped it wouldn't be taken as provisions for the Kircaldy voyage. She'd grown rather fond of it, but not too fond as she suspected its' destiny.

Out of habit and deference, the weary travellers wiped their feet on the large, coarse hemp rug inside the doorway. Traipsing after William like conspirators, and still carrying their burdens both physical and psychological, they followed him down a central hallway stretching into the heart of the Hall.

The sudden brightness of the well-candled room they entered made Joshua wince. All around hung huge tapestries depicting glorious battles, except for the far end where around a sea-facing, floor to ceiling window, a depiction of Eve, the tree in Eden and the Serpent adorned the wall. Accompanying Biblical passages painted in gilt warned of the dangers of succumbing to temptation and cautioned against misplaced trust in false prophets.

"William?" A booming voice acknowledged their

337

presence as soon as they entered. "What the devil are you doing here?"

A slim man sat at the far end of a long table, wearing robes of office with gravitas and dignity. The chain of Exchequer hung in a long loop over an elaborately embroidered cape, its weight seemingly of no consequence to the bearer. Joshua blinked, the timbre of his voice seemed more suited to someone with a far larger frame. But James of Kircaldy, close adviser and friend to King James of Scotland, was a man to be approached with trepidation and subservience.

"Father," Kircaldy removed his hat, swooping into a deep bow. He waited down there, head bowed, until his father rose and approached from behind the dark oak table.

Jeffries pushed himself forward and, standing next to William, dropped into a deep bow as well. "Get up man, get up!" James dismissed Jeffries' greeting. "Old friends need not curtsy like a woman." Kircaldy Senior then clapped his hands on his son's shoulder in greeting as William straightened, then he turned back to Jeffries with a piercing look. "I did not expect to see you, any of you, here?"

Jeffries said, "Your son was kind enough to bring us with all haste. Please forgive our lack of advance warning about our arrival. I am glad we have caught you before you sail, friend, I feared I would be too late."

James Kircaldy looked thoughtful, his hand moving up to stroke his trim beard as his eyes roamed over the rest of the group now assembled in the Dining Hall. His gaze stopped as he reached Fairfax's tousled head, remaining bowed to avoid meeting his protector's glare.

The Laird's face darkened, "Fairfax! I can see absolutely no reason for your presence either?" The boy squirmed. "I believe I was quite clear in my instructions that you were to remain studying at the Priory until such a time as I sent for you. Or have you done something stupid again, eh?" James advanced on the lad, but William stood up for his friend.

"Father, he came at my behest, I needed help to sail here. The usual crew-men were mostly all enjoying the season's festivities."

With a grunt, James then pursed his lips and whirled around, his quickly risen ire still in evidence. "I am about to depart for France at first light," he snapped, all business now, "so there had better be good reason for this intrusion, Maister. Perhaps you can enlighten me before I have to face this... diplomatic nightmare."

He turned to his papers still strewn across the dining table and began to shuffle them together. "Get the servants to show you to your rooms. William, I can entrust you to find those most appropriate for the rest of your... group. You may stay the night, but you will be returning to Tynemouth tomorrow. There is simply no excuse for your absence during this time."

James paused to glare at Fairfax again before continuing. "I will not, I cannot, have you causing undue attention to be paid to my movements because of your absenteeism. These are difficult times and I expect your obedience as my ward. Is that clear?"

Joshua half-expected witty retort from the usually confident Fairfax, but he took his patron's words seriously. The lad scurried out with his head bowed obediently. Without waiting for Jeffries to do his usual introduction, Joshua stepped forward, sweeping into a brief bow. "Lord Hanley, Sir. We have not been acquainted before, and I hope you can forgive our untimely intrusion on your preparations."

James Kircaldy returned the bow. Upon straightening, he cast his shrewd eyes over him, making the most of the opportunity to measure the surprisingly young man. He knew vaguely of the lands which the Hanley's held in England, but this fellow before him must have lost his father too soon. He was barely older than his William. And yet, something smelt off about him. Maybe he was ill, he looked very pale.

"You are welcome here, your Lordship. A friend of Maister Jeffries is a friend of mine." Lord Kircaldy couldn't resist, "Perhaps we should have met before though? I have travelled to the English Court before, but I was unaware of your late father's passing?" He bluffed, challenging the lad. He was only too aware of the ease with which clothes could suggest a position, having placed many spies himself.

"My Lord Hanley has charged me with a pilgrimage into your beloved country, m'Lord," Jeffries interrupted. "I was able to convince him that we should not pass up the opportunity to visit the most revered sites within your lands as we travelled."

Lord Kircaldy raised an eyebrow. "Seems a rather unusual time to be making a pilgrimage?" Joshua was tempted to try and offer some suitable reason to explain away his presence and the urgency of his journey, but his quick wits deserted him under the gaze of the superior peer.

"I also," Jeffries continued as if there were nothing at all surprising about the strange timing, "would be grateful for a reminder about the exact locations of these sites. Perhaps you might show me that book I saw last time I was here, in your library?"

The two men faced each other, unspoken messages carried between their eyes. Joshua felt the electricity between them and looked uneasily at Nemis to see if she too had witnessed it. Nemis however was more concerned with studying the fine tapestries. The look of horror on her pale face suggested they were not to her liking.

*****

William escorted them from the Dining Hall, depositing Nemis far away upstairs in an attic servant's quarters, and Joshua in a sparsely furnished chamber on the second floor. Jeffries briefly entered his allotted room, more out of propriety than necessity, then he returned downstairs to find Lord Kircaldy again. He kept his satchel slung over his shoulder, clutching it as his purpose neared.

Fairfax almost bumped into the monk as he exited his room, opposite Joshua's, and walked into the corridor. He was looking much more at ease away from his master's glare, his demonic energy restored in remarkably swift time. "Off to the kitchens too, Maister? There's a wench there who always has a sweet treat hidden about for me!" He giggled and pointed down the hallway, before setting off at a trot. "I'll see if she has some spare pies for you too!"

Jeffries just stood there, mouth agape. He suddenly felt old, too old to deal with the vibrancy of youth, especially one so destined to hurtle headlong into trouble. He was reminded of the last time he encountered a daemon, the swift mood transitions which had been of such torment to his friend, Lady Hanley. And of the passions, painted with violence, if the urges were suppressed. Turning the other way down the corridor,

341

Jeffries walked calmly down towards the library and tried to put his foreboding thoughts to the back of his mind. He had more important tasks to focus on.

Finding a comfortable chair placed in front of an enormous fireplace, he took out the precious wrapped package from his satchel and settled down. Almost reverently, he untied the thin laces binding the parcel, breathing in the slightly acidic smell of the newly bound leather book. With his shaking fingers, he traced the imprinted title, then he flexed the pages, found the passage he wanted and began to read.

He was interrupted a few minutes later by Joshua, uneasy and prowling around. Joshua acknowledged him briefly before heading to the window to look out into the darkness.

"I wish you could find somewhere else to lurk," Jeffries requested in as polite a tone as he could. "I need to speak to Lord Kircaldy alone if you don't mind."

"Is this to do with your mysterious book?" Joshua sensed the monk's unease, then noticed a leather volume in the monk's lap. Jeffries avoided Joshua's gaze, even when he commented, "I wouldn't have taken His Lordship for someone interested in your spell-making recipes?"

The monk appeared to freeze as Joshua approached, then glanced down at the page. His keen eyesight recognised that this was not the same book he had perused on the wherry. Printed in English, he read a few sentences in his head, knowing them as translations from a work he knew very well in Latin. Passages he had heard and mentally translated himself over decades of church services. And here it was, written. Printed. Forbidden.

Joshua's hands clenched; the monk had no intention of helping him reach Aioffe. As clarity struck, Joshua realised Jeffries only wanted the cover of travelling with a Lord to camouflage his own deceit. He replayed all the instances where Jeffries had spoken for him, smoothly lying about their intentions and placing the reason for their journey at Lord Hanley's feet to avoid questions about himself.

Joshua took a step backwards, realisation and anger flaring in his eyes. "You have led me a merry dance, to your own tune!"

"I beg your pardon?"

"I trusted you. But instead, you bought me along for legitimacy, serving your own needs, not mine!"

"Have you forgotten, in your haste to draw a conclusion, that it was I who arranged passage for us here?" Jeffries calmly responded. "Surely you would not have travelled this far north on your own, without my help?" The old monk was slow to rise to anger, so his words were not intended to inflame the situation. They had the opposite effect.

"You have deceived me! Led me into precarious places where this stupid disguise simply won't pass! And all for what? A book, a dangerous book? Why, the Lord of Kircaldy should throw you out, heretic!" Joshua railed, waving his arm around the sumptuous surroundings. "And him with the King's ear, you foolish old man!"

In truth, what Joshua felt most was betrayed. Angry. Hurt at the powerlessness of his situation. To avoid accepting the loss of Annabella, he had leaned back into his dormant Catholic faith in the last few days. Felt secure travelling with a monk, even one who was also a witch. Only to find out that all along, the monk and he did not share the same beliefs. This heretic was committing the ultimate act of betrayal to the church, subverting it whilst

343

pretending to preach its teachings. He had tried to overlook human prejudices about witches, but perhaps Jeffries had lain with the Devil? The more he knew of the man, the less he understood him.

Jeffries watched the conflict grow within Joshua but held his nerve. Grief had a way of outing itself once physical healing began; he was watching it before his eyes. But, with the loss of control which a temper brings, comes loose lips. The risk of exposure was too great, even if he was in a relatively safe haven now. "You forget yourself, young man. Have I not protected you? Healed you? Shielded you from harm?"

"You have used me as a cover for your own purposes. Cast some kind of spell to blind me to the truth!" Ruefully, Joshua almost laughed, "I should have known never to trust a witch."

"You have benefited from my help. Enlighten me about exactly what you think I have done to deceive you?"

"Perhaps you could enlighten us all then?" Lord Kircaldy and his son stood in the open doorway to the library. "About who you are and what you are really here for. Both of you."

*****

Nemis had found her way to the kitchens and tarried long enough to hear the gossip about which of the servants would be going with the Lord on his voyage. Paying little heed to the jokes that were being made about a 'flame-haired' maid who was lighting fires with his Lordship, she enquired politely about where she might find some carrots to feed her goat.

Directed to the outhouses around the courtyard edges,

she checked the goat was still securely tied, then unbolted the second doorway along. As she poked her head in with a stub of a candle before her, she was greeted with a squeal and a giggle.

Lying on the sacks, spread-eagled underneath blue and brown petticoats, was Fairfax. He sat up and grinned at Nemis through his companion's arms. "Ah, come to join us?" he said, with hope in his nonchalant voice.

"Not. Bloody. Likely!" Nemis shot back, grabbing a carrot from the sack just inside the door. Slamming the door shut on Fairfax and the red-head, almost immediately, she opened it up again, and shouted in, "And you'd best not tarry long with his Lordships' favourite!"

Fairfax sat back up and peered at the maid astride him. "Emma? Tell me it's not true?"

The girl giggled and nodded. "But I could never resist you either, me hinny. So much more energy than the Master!"

Fairfax looked horrified and pushed her off. He pulled up his breeches and buttoned them before hurriedly running out of the door. He hoped to catch up with Nemis, but the courtyard was quiet and empty. The goat stared at him, bleated and carried on nibbling the carrot. Fairfax dashed into the hall, frantically tucking in his shirt.

*****

The Library fell silent. Joshua glowered at Jeffries. Jeffries looked beseechingly at Lord Kircaldy. William looked at Joshua's gaunt frame and realised the man was barely keeping himself held together. His clothes were ill fitting, decidedly as if they were made for another man. Was he, as his father suggested just moments earlier, another man?

"My Lord..." Jeffries began. "You have known me for many a year. I am your true and humble servant."

"I begin to wonder," James's steely voice said. "Talk of spells and witchcraft, as if our country doesn't have enough to contend with. I have no intention of taking proof of witch-craft to King James of Scotland, he has more pressing marital and religious matters to wrestle with."

"It is with these very matters I wish to help, My Lord." Jeffries stood, approaching James with his little leather-bound book at arm's length. To Joshua's surprise, Lord Kircaldy's eyes widened, and he grasped the Monk by the arm, taking the book with his other hand.

"My friend, you have risked much to bring me this!"

Jeffries acknowledged the compliment and backed away deferentially. William leaned in to examine the spine in his father's hands.

Reverently, William said, "I have never seen a copy. How did you come by it?"

Jeffries opened his mouth as if he was going to respond, but then thought the better of it. Some things were best left unsaid.

Joshua strode out of the room. For once, he was grateful for the distraction the profane book had provided. In that instant, when Kircaldy accepted the translation, he knew. His mind resolved. He needed to part ways with the duplicitous monk and make haste away from here. If the monk's purpose had been to spread the Protestant word, he wanted no more of it. He had his own battles to fight, his own identity to protect. And a wife to find.

James flicked his fingers at William, directing him to follow. He then led the monk to the fireplace and together they began examining the Tyndale Bible. Jeffries felt the weight of responsibility fall from his shoulders - the contraband book would have meant certain imprisonment, death even, had he been caught with it these past few weeks.

Only a few copies had made their way into the country and Jeffries had worked tirelessly to secure one to be put into the hands of the only man who was sympathetic to the cause and had access to the King of Scotland. He hoped it would be enough to dissuade him from further persecuting Protestants here.

He also now harboured the hopes that James would be so taken with the opportunity to persuade his King of the true Protestant cause whilst away, that he would forget entirely to ask about any other contraband which he knew King James of Scotland would have even more to say about.

*****

William caught up with Joshua as he was ascending the stairs. Catching his arm, he had to check himself as the look of fury on Joshua's face took him off guard. "Leave me alone!" Joshua spat out, shaking himself free of William's grasp. "I do not have to answer to anyone, certainly not a pup like you!"

Joshua carried on storming up the stairs, leaving William looking bewildered. Lord Hanley had been a relatively quiet passenger, but now something had tipped him into a temper. Had he not known the company he kept? He felt mildly affronted at the man who appeared only a few years older than himself calling him a pup!

Fairfax came running up behind William, nearly bowling him over. "What's got into you?" William said to

Fairfax's receding back.

"It's not what, but *who* I got into!" Fairfax shouted back before the door to his room slammed.

William grinned in spite of himself. What a strange evening this was turning into! Deciding to ignore his father's wishes, sensing the sickly Lord Hanley needed to calm down before he would get any answers from him, he turned to go back down the stairs. Besides, William justified, he was unlikely to leave the fortified buildings having only just arrived, and with Jeffries currently occupied with his father. He didn't think Lord Hanley was that foolish.

At the bottom of the stairs, Nemis appeared. Her pale face framed by long wisps of hair which had fallen loose from her cap. Blue teary eyes met his, and he watched her sway, eyeballs rolling up into her head. With long strides, he bounded down to attempt to catch her before she hit the ground with a thud.

"Maister!" William called out as he reached her, crumpled on the floor. Her slim frame began to shake and her head lolled back as he picked up her torso and gathered her in his arms. "Maister! Come quickly!"

Hearing the noise, both Fairfax and Joshua opened their doors simultaneously. Their eyes met, both harboring mild panic. As one, they looked down the corridor towards where William was shouting, before looking back at each other. Each was wearing their overcoat and carrying a pack, ready to leave. Fairfax recovered first. Raising an eyebrow, he cocked his head the other way down the hall. Joshua nodded in understanding and they closed their respective doors behind them quietly.

"Maister!" William cried out again, his voice reverberating down the wooden clad corridor. "Anyone? I need help here!" As Joshua and Fairfax crept towards the servants' stairs at the far end, they heard footsteps.

"She just collapsed," William said. Joshua's eyes flared - who had collapsed?

"Let us take her to the library, it's closer," Maister Jeffries said, his voice low. "I have a tonic for when this has passed."

Pausing at the top of the stairwell, Joshua's heart sank. His plan to sneak out, find Nemis and beg her to run with him would need altering, and fast. Joshua listened carefully, worried if she was hurting herself with the tremors. If she was having another fit, he also hoped Jeffries would work his magic on her before she blurted out something others ought not to hear. He heard instead the grunts of a body being lifted, shuffling footsteps then faded deep into the house.

Joshua glanced again at Fairfax and remembered how confident the boy had been aboard the boat. Another idea sprang into his mind, and he reached to his belt for the bag of money. "Can you make ready the birlinn?" he whispered.

"Aye," he replied, "but don't tarry long. I need to leave right now. I was going to take a horse, but the boat would be faster if you'll crew with me?"

"Set off, we'll meet you at the beachhead." He opened the pouch and dropped a few coins into Fairfax's hand.

Fairfax looked confused for a moment but shrugged it off. Ed and Jack might still be aboard. He was sure he could convince them with a little of the gold to accompany him on a moonlight flit. As for Hanley, well, if he appeared, then it was another pair of hands. But, now he needed to get away from his protector - before he discovered where he'd dipped his wick most recently!

349

*****

Joshua went into Jeffries' room and grabbed the monk's travel bag, which he knew contained various herbs and medications he would doubtless need. Stuffing it into his own sack, he then removed his coat, jacket and shirt and unwound the bandages about his chest. He shook his wings free. Flexing them to be sure they would work, before robing himself again. They were a little stiff, but in better shape than he thought they might have been. He fixed his bags low on his back, wincing as the straps pulled tight around his waist. Slinging his cape over his shoulder, he muttered a quick prayer and opened the window.

The courtyard directly beneath him was mercifully clear. The entire space lay silent. Empty of barrels, boxes and people, although the torches remained lit. Joshua clambered onto the ledge and, with fingers barely clinging on to the leaded frame of the middle window, he eased his unwieldy body through the aperture. Crouched on the stone ledge, he opened his wings out and jumped backwards, trusting in his appendages. One quick painful flap and he descended to the cobbles and his quarry below. The goat nickered, unaware it was about to bleat its last bleat.

*****

Jeffries and William had carried Nemis through to the library. James pulled back the chairs in front of the fireplace and they placed her shaking body on the rug before the flaming logs. The Kircaldy's wore matching

350

expressions of concern as, from the relative safety of a few feet away, they watched the pretty young girl convulsing before them.

Jeffries reassured them it would pass, and after a few minutes where he held her head steady in his lap, the tremors subsided. Jeffries was relieved; this fit had been less violent than the one he witnessed in Tynemouth, but he was still concerned she would shout out something inappropriate.

"Warm water," he commanded as her body went limp. Eager to be away from the frightening sight, William scurried off to the kitchens.

"Is she possessed?" James asked nervously, as he recalled rumours in Court of such matters, especially in women. His faith in his old friend was shaken. What had the monk brought into his house? He suppressed the question about whether this was an ill-omen about his impending voyage. Although not a superstitious man by nature, he was practical about the known realities of sea travel and nervous. "I want her out of here, immediately!"

"She is not possessed, my Lord. Merely afflicted with an aegue I have yet to find a cure for."

"Well how do I know she hasn't passed it onto me?" Lord Kircaldy shrank from the woman, frightened. Possession, or witchery, wasn't contagious, but illnesses were. He drew further back, almost stumbling into the chair in his haste to get away. "Or my son!" The horror in his face showed the depths of his fear.

"I have felt no ill-effects after being in her presence," Jeffries reasoned, "and I need that warm water, and my bags, if you could be so kind as to fetch them, Sir?"

Keen to leave the room as quickly as was practical, James didn't bother to question that his insubordinate had effectively issued him an order. "William! Make haste with that water," he called out as he left the room.

Jeffries bent low over Nemis's face and smelt her uneven and shallow breaths. Tinged with acidity, he paused, unsure if his magic would be needed this time. Gently shaking her shoulders, "Nemis," he whispered. "Nemis, are you with me?" A little louder. A soft groan came from her lips and her head lolled once more. Jeffries thought her pallor was improving, but he carried on jigging her shoulders in his lap to rouse her. The doorway behind him opened once more.

"Just put it there," he gestured to the rug beside him.

"I will look after her now."

Joshua's voice startled Jeffries. As he stepped into sight, Jeffries saw that Joshua was fully restored, flushed even. Jeffries eased Nemis's torso up from his lap, as if to make her sit, and Joshua's strong arms scooped under her. With ease, he lifted her slim form and stood up. Jeffries realised Joshua was carrying both Nemis and his travel bags.

"You leave now? She is unwell and should rest..."

"We must," Joshua said firmly.

"Then, let me give you some tonic, for when she comes around?"

"I have your bag, old man. I will find what she requires in there, no doubt. There is no need of your magic now."

Jeffries looked at this Fae-man, rejuvenated by Lifeforce, now standing strong and healed in front of him. He was amazed and not a little awed. But, the medic in him knew he was not completely restored. Nor was he yet the man he needed to be. The new forcefulness in him was a step in the right direction though. But was it enough?

"You will need more than tonic for what awaits you, I fear." Jeffries cautioned. "I would come with you, if you let me get my things?"

Nemis stirred in Joshua's arms. "Just cover for us, that is all I ask of you now Maister," Joshua replied, finding his earlier anger at the monk had subsided. Perhaps it had gone in the moment he determined to take grip of his own destiny. "For my silence, you owe me that much."

Nodding his head with regret for a relationship soured, Jeffries led them to the doorway. Joshua pushed past into the hallway, then glanced back. There was a peculiar yet kindly look about the monk.

"Faith is faith," Jeffries muttered, "it doesn't matter how you practise that belief, as long as you believe in something." His witch's eyes glowed as he pronounced darkly, "Everything hath a time."

Joshua blinked, frowning. Was that some kind of apology? An excuse? An omen?

"Go! We will meet again," Jeffries urged. Joshua heard the footsteps racing up the stone stairs from the kitchen. Turning, his cape flared out behind him as he ran for the exit, clutching Nemis to his chest. He pulled up at the bolted oak door, and slung Nemis like a sack over his shoulder to free his hands. With swift fingers, he slammed the bolts back and flung open the door. Jeffries just caught a glimpse of his boot heels as Joshua took off and disappeared into the darkness.

Exhaling, Jeffries closed the front door and shut the locks home. The time for explanations was doubtless upon him now. But he smiled as he crossed himself and sent a silent prayer up. Now was the time to focus on hope.

*****

Fairfax looked up at the dark cliffs edging the shoreline; he had weighed anchor as instructed, but Jack and Ed were restless to be moving. The birlinn bobbed gracefully in the choppy waves. Fairfax thought he'd be looking out for some kind of light, a candle at the front of a small rowing boat paddling through to join them.

As it happened, Joshua landed quite heavily, stumbling for his feet as he crashed down at the prow of the boat. Jolted by the noise, Jack and Ed stared at his huge wings - still wafting as they tried to help Joshua find his sea legs.

Nemis was still inert in his arms as he carefully bent down to nestle her against the sides of the ship, protected as much as possible by the swooping curves of the high prow-line. Joshua turned and panted out, "Go! What are you waiting for now?"

Ed was the first to close his gaping mouth and hurriedly began to haul up the anchor, head down to avoid Joshua's eyes.

"I wasn't looking to the skies," Fairfax said, his shocked tone failing to hide his curiosity. "If you can do that, then why are we bothering with a boat?"

"Because we need Nemis. She knows the way," Joshua replied as if it were obvious. He bent down to check on her again. She was unconscious, breathing shallowly, but had stopped fitting at least. "Head north, she will come around soon and tell us directions when she does."

The daemon nodded. He wasn't entirely sure why Nemis was important, but he hadn't exactly anticipated this evenings' events. Pushing Jack on his shoulder to break his trance, he called over to Ed, "Come on man, you will see stranger things in your life, I'm sure!"

"Did...do you have...?" Jack was still staring at Joshua's wings.

"Yes I do, praise the Lord above, and no, you probably shouldn't tell anyone what you just saw. They will think you mad, seeing angels! And you know what gossips priests are - so no confessing it either, or they will drag you off to Bedlam with all the other lunatics!"

This was the line which he and Annabella had always agreed was the best response to deflect questions. It preyed nicely on the greater fear of being considered an idiot and sent away to be purged. Being confused for an angel made it easier for them to think there was some divine purpose for the wings, that the observer was blessed to be seeing them. Joshua lowered his extra appendages and wrapped them under his cape as if it were a perfectly ordinary thing to do. Fairfax snorted and began to hoist the sail, shaking his head.

The crew continued to shoot nervous glances at Joshua as they worked to get the sail in position and secure it. The sheet billowed as it picked up the rising winds and before long, Fairfax began tacking to sail them zig-zagging up the coastline.

Joshua placed a candle on the bench next to the prow and rummaged through Jeffries' sack of medicines. He was no expert, but he found the little brown bottle he had seen the monk treat Nemis with before and set it to one side. He smelt the contents of a small square wooden box lurking at the bottom of the bag without even opening it. The intrusive stink reminded Joshua of a healer many years ago, who wafted the strongly scented crystals about, rousing a man knocked out cold by the blow of a fallen branch. He kept the box out, just in case.

Tenderly, he pulled Nemis onto his lap and tried to rouse her again. He trickled some water from his flagon on to her face, then shook her shoulders gently. After a few moments, she was still unresponsive, so he reached for the box. Prying the lid slightly, he wafted it under her nose, hoping its contents would work their magic. Almost immediately, Nemis coughed, eyes opening to look up at him in shock.

"I've got you, don't worry," Joshua said. Firmly shutting the box, he leaned over and picked up the curative tincture bottle. "Do you need some of Jeffries' concoction or are you alright?"

Nemis turned away, taking stock of where she was. Her eyes cleared and she inhaled deeply. The salty air seemed to revive her and, after a mouthful of water, she sat up and moved from Joshua's lap. They rested companionably against the side of the ship for a few minutes. He then turned and looked Nemis full in the face. "I have to know, Nemis, and I don't suppose I have a right to ask given I brought you here when you were unconscious..."

She frowned, "Know why I am supposed to be here?"

"If you are happy to be here? On this journey with me?"

Nemis gazed over the calm seas and sighed. "I saw you in my visions, and I know deep within me that we are destined to travel together, to reach her."

"But did, sorry, do, you *want* to come? I should have asked. Jeffries should have asked. This could be a dangerous voyage. Just because you saw us, doesn't mean you had to come with us. And you have left a place of sanctuary to be here. I don't even know if you could go back?"

When she smiled, radiance lit up her eyes, and Joshua glimpsed the same magic as within his lover - they shared the same brilliance when they were happy.

"I couldn't be anywhere else," she said. "For the first time, I am embracing my destiny, following the path I have seen before me." She took his hand and smoothed the skin on the top. "I leave behind nothing of value, and you bring me the opportunity to taste the world. Why wouldn't I choose to travel with you?" She giggled. "After all, you don't know where to go. And I do."

"We head north already," Joshua said, the corners of his mouth creasing into a smile of relief. "Have you seen if we succeed in finding her? Please, tell me?"

She squeezed his hand, shaking her head. "That much I cannot see. Our destinies hang. Diverge. I cannot tell the future - only a destination I am drawn to. And you are there, and I hope, somewhere, so is she." She watched Joshua's shoulders slump, his gaze fixated on his boot in front of him.

His lips tightened, then he gathered himself. "You should rest until you can tell us where to go, when it's time."

Nemis nodded, "The seas here look all the same, just an endless dark horizon. But, I hope I will know, when the right time is upon us."

"We all do," Fairfax said, joining them. "Where are we trying to get to anyway?"

Nemis smiled mysteriously.

"A place called Naturae," Joshua said.

"And it's north you say?" Fairfax grinned, his little teeth white in the gathering night.

"I have never been," Joshua said, "but Nemis will guide us." Faith is faith, he thought, hoping that was true.

"Then how do you know it's north?" Fairfax asked reasonably. "I've never seen such a place on a map."

"It is shrouded by a mist," answered Nemis, her eyes taking on a faraway cast. She stood to look over the prow of the boat.

"And it's north because I am from the Islands of Orkney," Joshua said, "and it must be close to there."

Jack and Ed looked over, then at each other. "Strange things happen in places like Orkney," Jack said to Ed under his breath, but Joshua still caught it. He wondered what strangeness he was leading them towards also. But he had no choice. His heart beat steadily, as if marching them towards an inevitable battle. He had to find her, and if it came to it, fight for her. He crossed himself, hoping they would be in time and praying for a fast wind.

CHAPTER 27 - RIGHT TO RULE

The tunnels were becoming so familiar to Aioffe now that she could guide herself by smell alone. She scurried down the twists and turns until she reached the sea-salty fork which would take her above. With a smile on her face, she remembered the last time she walked these dark enclosures with Uffer. This time, the anticipation of stepping into the daylight filled her with hope, rather than the fear she once held.

Although the sunlight was fading to a tawny pink, enough remained for Aioffe to see that pathway through the trees as she emerged. She had not bothered with applying a costume on this occasion, not least because she didn't have the time to. Moreover, she hoped that her visible and clamped wings would serve as a reminder that she, also, was trapped here.

The mist was colder this time and, now she knew what scent to follow, her nose quickly picked up the stink of the fish oil burners which the workers used. The wind was picking up as she traced her way along the dusty pathways. The gusts carried the promise of a storm with a vague burning smell upon them. This day, she revelled in the breeze blowing her hair around her face. It didn't matter how polished she looked, she intended to be seen as a person, not an object to be admired or just another worker enslaved like them. This time, Aioffe was herself.

"Thane?" Aioffe called out as she entered the empty camp. "I would speak with Thane."

She strode to the central fireplace in the clearing. She

couldn't recall which of the tree-dens she had been in before with Uffer, so the still-smoking remains seemed like a good place to stand instead.

"Thane?" Her voice sounded thin and reedy, but she hoped, just confident enough that they would not assume she came in a regal capacity. She had no intention to threaten or begin a conflict, but to reconcile for her own peace of mind.

Fae began to emerge from through the thick trunks and approached, their curiosity evident on their faces. Some held wooden plates with half-eaten fish on them, quickly pointing a small knife towards her but advanced only as far as the logs around the camp fire. Aioffe supposed she should feel threatened, but, standing there alone, her desperation apparent, she felt no fear. If they overwhelmed her, then she had at least tried.

"What do you want with Thane?" It was the older woman with whom she had tangled before.

"I wish to speak to Thane. Is he here?" Aioffe made an effort to not look down her nose as the Queen would, but faced her fully, arms by her sides and hands open.

"Why should he want to talk to the likes of you? You should go back to where you belong and leave well enough alone."

Aioffe was taken aback at the venom in the woman's voice.

"Oh yes, we know who you are, dearie." The fae approached, her face almost twisted as she pushed through the gathering crowd.

"And that is why she has no place here!" A louder, angry voice called out, followed by grunts of approval from others who were creeping closer. Aioffe's heart sped up, thinking she recognised the tone - was it the one who challenged Uffer before?

"That is also why you should leave, your Highness." Thane appeared before her, hovering a foot above the ground. He held his hand back to stay the other fae. Aioffe bowed her head and considered if she should curtsy to acknowledge his leadership.

Thinking the better of it, she raised her head and spoke in a modulated tone of deference instead. "I have come to speak with you, to ask for your help."

"My help?" Thane laughed, the sound was deep and authoritative. "Princess, it is true you need 'our help' but we have no inclination to give it to you. What. So. Ever."

The assembled fae roared their approval, and began chanting, "Our time will come!"

Through the noise, Thane appraised Aioffe, circling her as her mother often flew above the Court. Asserting dominance, he had learned the trick but she had learned much herself in how to counter it over the last century. This did not need to be a confrontation, she reminded herself. Aioffe kept her nerve, holding her back straight and her eyes on him. The chants grew louder and the fae clustered closer to the fireplace. Some began to rise from the ground, the flutter of their stubby brown wings as they advanced drifting her loose hair about her head.

"Please!" Aioffe tried to raise her voice over the crowd, but it was drowned out. "I came to talk..."

Thane held out his arm again, spinning mid-air to still his coworkers. The chanting faltered. Aioffe couldn't help but admire his control over them. A few still hovered in a vaguely menacing way but most returned to the ground. Waiting.

Thane turned to face her, still hovering a foot from the earth but close enough that he could read her expression by the low firelight. His brown eyes were cold with steely resolve as he waited for the chants to subside completely.

"Talk." His civil tone disarmed her and, for a moment, Aioffe felt flustered. She looked at his mouth, hardened and tight-lipped. Focusing on the crowd rather than meeting his gaze, she began in a clear voice, which all could hear.

"I have been away. For a long time. I have seen much in my travels, many wars, many hard times. I have lived like you do, in subservience. A worker. A servant. But I knew, at that time, all of the time, I was free. Free to make my own decisions, my own choices. I want that for you too."

She glanced around, wanting to see if they were listening. Gratifyingly, all eyes were now upon her. Thane nodded at her, encouraging her to say her piece.

"I come now, amongst you, not as your Princess, but as one who would understand."

She fluttered her wing joints and looked beseechingly at the crowd. "I am in bondage, a prisoner. Not free, and in servitude too, as you are, to one whom I would not wish to be." She turned expectantly, hopeful as she pleaded with the crowd. Would they be able to see beyond their preconceived notions of who she was?

Thane's stern mouth turned into a sneer. "A prisoner who has her every need met? Pupaeted into a life in court, right next to the Queen. *Safe* in the knowledge that you will always be above us?" He looked across to the workers, and his face cleared as he dismissed her talk. Nodding, encouraging them. "Never one of us!"

Aioffe watched in horror as the fae again began beating their wings and shouting, "Our time will come!" The rallying call washed over her and, underneath her gown, she felt her knees weaken slightly.

"You see?" Thane called over to her. "Did you really think you could come here and try to persuade us you like us? As one of us?"

"I didn't come here for that," Aioffe pleaded as she watched his mouth lift as if about to laugh. "I just wanted to understand."

"Understand?" Thane frowned. As his face was turned aside, she couldn't quite see whether it was from incredulity or confusion, so she ploughed on.

"I know what is happening to Naturae. And I wanted - needed - to be sure of *why* you are doing what you plan to. Because, you are free." Aioffe swung her arm around at the crowd, turning as she looked around at them before raising her eyes again to his. "Free to leave. Free to leave us to our fate and choose your own. So, I need to understand why you stay?"

Aioffe had raised her voice so that he could hear over the rabble, who were moving to the point in the chant where they were carried away with enjoyment of solidarity. Her fingertips tingled and she flexed them, involuntarily breathing in as Thane flew closer to her. When his chest was just a hands-width from her face, Aioffe tipped her head back to hold him in her stare. Knowing this was a last-ditch effort, she sought with her clear eyes to convince the man that she should be heard.

His voice was surprisingly soft, absent of the venom she half expected, as he said, "All you need to understand, Princess, is that the end is coming to all of us."

"I know. And I know you plan to enjoy your last years of it." A note of sorrow had crept into her statement, which she hadn't intended to reveal, but she kept her gaze steady.

"Living like you do? Oh yes, we shall live like Queens, and free too! Why should we leave our lands, when we can take them?" Thane's eyes glittered with the possibility, but she read a hesitation in their depths as well.

Aioffe dropped her voice so that only he could hear. "Then what is stopping you moving forward with your plan - now?"

Thane glanced away, scanning the other fae, thankfully now more preoccupied with back slapping and chattering between themselves. Their attention had been successfully diverted away from her intrusion by the prospect of better days to come. He turned back and bowed his head to her ear. "I need to be sure."

"Sure of what?" Aioffe frowned. From where she stood, it looked like the entire camp was ready to claim what they wanted.

"Ah, Princess..." Thane smiled. "You never start a war unless you know you can win it. So you carry on living your long, long life Princess, and one day, one day soon, it will all be over."

Aioffe's eyes flared, "Since my return, I haven't been living. I've been waiting to die."

Thane looked deep into her blue eyes and was actually saddened to see it was the truth. Whilst he had no misgivings about what his planned course of action would entail, he had expected more resistance from a royal.

"However," she continued, "I came to see for myself if death was what you really all wanted as well. Because I think I can change our race's future - if you will just listen to me."

Bending down, she plucked a dead flower from the woodland floor. Bringing it to her lips, she thought about the hope it represented, and breathed on it. Thane's eyes widened, watching as the flower's petals opened and its limp leaves stiffened. Aioffe's confidence grew, and she raised an eyebrow at Thane. He froze, as she offered him the now blooming flora.

The scent of it barely registered with her nose before Thane grabbed her arm and yanked her towards his tree. The crowds parted to let them through, thinking he was taking her to her doom. The cheers of "Our time is now!" started as he dragged her along the ground. As he flew, his brain whirled with possibilities.

Aioffe's feet scrabbled as she tried to follow him with dignity, but that was not his intention, it seemed. Her ears began to hum as the volume of the chanting increased, accompanied by claps and whistles of victory.

Pushing aside the opening to his den, Thane pulled her inside and released her wrist. Aioffe stumbled on the dusty floor and collapsed. As the thick curtain covering the doorway dropped, the noises from just beyond it seemed to diminish.

For a moment, unsure momentarily if his exclusion of the other fae was a good or bad omen, the closing of the aperture reminded her of Joshua. Of that moment of silence between them as he paused to consider his words when it was something which mattered. How he would always try to make a plan, prepare, before they undertook any big changes. She groaned inwardly, watching Thane fasten the curtains together. This was one of those times when she wished she had thought to pause and evaluate beforehand. At least acknowledge likely scenarios, as Joshua would have. She realised with regret that she hadn't even considered an escape route, to be used if they wouldn't listen to her. Aioffe closed her eyes. She hadn't thought that far ahead.

"What did you do?" Thane demanded as he advanced on her again. "What kind of magic do you wield? It's not possible to bring back the dead!"

Aioffe pushed herself up from the dirt before answering. Taking a breath in and out, she said calmly, "I have always done it. I don't know how or why I can, but I can."

"Is it a royal thing? Why doesn't the Queen do it?"

"I don't have the answers, I'm sorry." Aioffe picked herself up from the floor and dusted off her skirts. He looked dismayed. She went to him and touched his arm, as no royal would ever normally do.

"I only wanted to understand what is driving you. I know the fear, the hunger which impels people to rebel, but I also know that the only cure is hope." Raising the flower to him once more, she tried to catch his gaze. "So I thought I'd show you there is hope."

Thane took a step back from her. Outside, the chants had subsided, as if the crowd was straining to hear their conversation, or her screams.

"Why?" He whispered.

Aioffe thought for a moment she had misheard him, but then she understood the conundrum she had placed him in.

"I don't expect you to spare me, just because I can revive nature," she said. "I don't know if it can work on more than just a few flowers. But, it's cause for hope for Naturae, surely?"

Thane glanced at the entrance, thinking for a moment. "Your problem, Princess, is that even if you could bring life back to Naturae, you cannot wield control over the workers. Or without something solid and impressive, change the fate of your mother and the court."

Aioffe looked at his weather-beaten face. The vigour of Lifeforce didn't cause the same glow it gave her, yet she sensed the strength of the man, the resolve. The intelligence behind his brown eyes struck her, and she realised deep within that she had misjudged many like him before. A century of living amongst the common folk, as one of them, had made her understand that leadership was not a matter of bloodlines. Before her was a fae who would make a better leader than she ever could.

And yet, those eyes told her he was as reluctant to be in that position as she was. Both of them were drawn to help their people, though neither wanted the solitary, highly visible and precarious power which was required to achieve it. There was a way, she realised, to share that burden.

"I believe we can help each other," she said, as a smile widened across her face. Thane took her hand and led her towards some log stools near the tree trunk. Although he was no Joshua, Aioffe appreciated the gallantry. "I think," she said, taking a seat, "we need a way for everyone's voice to be heard if there is to be a future for us all."

Thane nodded, then sat on a neighbouring log. "I will listen to suggestions." Perhaps, as she claimed, there was some hope. He would be negligent if he didn't at least discuss it with her. Diplomacy also won wars.

CHAPTER 28 – NORTHWARD BOUND

Through the night, the crew worked with the strong winds to make their way swiftly up the edge of Scotland. The nimble birlinn flexed and creaked as she tackled the waves like a cat easing over long grass. Joshua was better able to cope with the rise and fall of the seas this time, his stomach settled and mind alert.

As night deepened, they all took turns to rest except for Nemis, who remained resolute in her position. Acting as their scout, she withstood the battering of the spray at the front of the ship, shouting out when she could see the glow of a beacon on the shores cautioning them. She seemed in her element, invigorated by the winds and crisp night air. Her hair, damp from the splatters thrown up as they tossed about on the waves, streamed about her head in long ropes in the wind. Fairfax started calling her Medusa when she turned around and screamed a warning to tack away from potentially hazardous shores.

Ed and Jack hid their increasing nerves by scurrying across the boat, stuck between watching the wild banshee to the front and avoiding eye contact with the strange angel-man-beast they had formerly thought a Lord. Conversation was impossible over the rising winds, so their unanswered curiosity was only briefly tempered by the frequent crossing of themselves every time they moved within Joshua's proximity.

As dawn broke, the grey light allowed them all a brief respite from the near-blind sailing they had endured. Although the clouds still loomed overhead, some relief was felt by all from being able to see a wider expanse of sea ahead. Nemis finally sat down on the front bench and nibbled on a stale hunk of bread she found in one of the sacks Fairfax brought on board. The filched pie was long gone, and the water supply was rationed.

Circling the northern tip of Scotland, the winds dipped and progress slowed. Nemis kept pointing north, and Fairfax began to check with the chip log how fast they were progressing. Dipping the knotted line into the wash, he would count up to fourteen as he watched how quickly the float pulled away, before screwing up his face as he mentally calculated their speed.

Joshua observed with interest, mostly because this seemingly ordered measurement showed a more intellectual side to the chaotic young daemon. It made little difference to the rest of the crew how fast they were going of course. Joshua accepted that they were almost totally dependent upon how quickly the winds could take them to their destination. The sooner the better, as far as Joshua was concerned.

Having continued beyond the top of Scotland, they headed roughly for the islands Joshua had once called home. Positioning himself closer to Nemis, he watched keenly for familiar sights as the craggy outlines became visible from a distance. Idly Joshua wondered if Nemis's course would take them past his home isle of Wrye. Since he had left, Joshua didn't expect much had changed on these sleepy, low-lying mounds. He shivered as he remembered the wind which would howl over the treeless isle, and the isolation he felt as it drove the few inhabitants into their homesteads for shelter when a tempest rose.

Early in his childhood, the family had realised the importance of staying close to a dwelling during the winter months, such was the speed a storm could approach. His sister had been too near a cliff when a gusty wind arose, and tragedy had struck. Even now, he avoided coastal cliffs and disliked flying in high winds.

Through the day, the crew followed Nemis's guidance as she meditated on the course. The birlinn skirted the edges of Stronsay and continued up, the winds from the east buffeting them ever closer to the shorelines. Looking ahead of them towards the sun as they rounded the island, Nemis turned to Fairfax. "We can go through the islands here, or around," she said, her arms pointed to highlight the choice. "Either way, we need to be more north-west," she concluded. Fairfax consulted his compass, shrugged but offered no opinion.

"Which is fastest?" Joshua said. Being so close to the lands they needed to travel beyond was making him itchy with anticipation.

Fairfax held his nose up into the air, Jack and Ed quickly did the same as if this was some kind of group consultation. "The wind will push us faster through the islands," Fairfax said, "but it is shallower, more dangerous and we are like to be working harder to maintain our course."

Ed spoke up next, "If the winds picked up much more, we could have some problems skirting the shoreline? We've not seen any other boats out, not even fishing. Maybes we can stop for some ale on the islands though?"

"Moor up and rest a while? Tis the season, the fisher-folk are probably all at feast by now," Jack followed hopefully. "There must be safe harbour somewhere hereabouts?"

"We have no time for rest!" Joshua exploded. "We must push on!"

Only Nemis failed to look shocked by this sudden retort - she understood the pressure Joshua was under. She also rather suspected that Ed and Jack were looking for any way to escape being on the boat with Joshua.

"We are not far..." she tried to say, although the tremor in her voice belied her uncertainty in her own senses.

"Alright then," Fairfax recovered first, "dangerous and quickly it is! My kind of adventure!"

Joshua reminded himself that Fairfax was the sort of person who needed extremes, needed the chaos of a challenge into the unknown. However, the fact that he was nominally in charge of the ship and therefore their lives upon it sent shivers down Joshua's spine.

CHAPTER 29 – UNRAVELLING

The smell of the fish oil candle Thane had given her to guide her back to the Beneath still lingered in the tunnels late the next afternoon. Reminding herself of the positive plans now underway, she smiled as she walked alongside Uffer towards the palace. She was tired but hopeful that the day would bring new light to the darkness which was lying so heavily upon Naturae.

"You seem in better spirits today, my Lady," Uffer noted as they emerged into the dim clearing. He appeared distracted, not meeting her glance.

"I am," she answered, quite glad that she didn't have to guard her giveaway eyes. They began the climb to the landing platform. The winds last night had blown the dead leaves into the corners of the balconies, scattering twigs around the open spaces of the forest. Yet, there was a lingering mugginess in the air and Aioffe breathed it in deeply before she entered the atrium. A storm was rolling in - clouds were low and hastened across the sky, and, glancing back, the veil of mist was closer to the treetops. She swallowed back the nervous taste in her mouth, hoping the storm wasn't as portentous as she suspected it would be.

Looking over at Uffer as he followed, his eyes downcast, she felt a tinge of affection for him. Faster ageing in worker fae lent the appearance of maturity, although he had inferred he was not much older than she. His wrinkled face and greying hair made him look fatherly, grandfatherly even by human standards. She supposed a mortal parent would have offered support as the kindly keeper had. Wondered about how different life might have been if two parents had reared her.

Her subconscious intruded, and unwelcome, uncomfortable thoughts snuck into her mind. What kind of family would she and Joshua have raised? It wasn't an option, of course, and hadn't been discussed since she had warned him that fae were not created like that, but still... to love a child was an experience she would never know. She sighed and pushed her sorrow aside - the absence of a family was a grief which she would have to face alongside accepting Joshua's death at another time. As swiftly as the notion entered her head, she resolved only to focus on the next small step. Just a step.

Outside the double doors, after a brief touch to her arm, Uffer turned and walked briskly away; his comfort then felt almost apologetic. Upon entering the High Hall, Aioffe sensed a difference, an ambiance which hinted at something off kilter. The courtiers, despite the gaudy colours of their clothing, appeared fatigued beyond their usual lacklustre selves. As she approached the throne, she heard barely stifled sobs as she passed, and realised that many were not standing, but leaning against the ornate walls or chairs. Even her mother looked more haggard, her white skin stretched thinly over the dark moons of her glare. Her expression didn't flicker as Aioffe took her place on the stool. Lyrus, statue-like at the back of the dais, disregarded her completely, and she refused to acknowledge him either.

"Your Highness," she said respectfully, as she arranged her skirts and looked up from her low vantage point. She waited for a reply but the Queen continued dully staring at the courtiers. Aioffe turned to watch also, looking for Lord Spenser and trying to appear casual. The atmosphere started to weave its curse on her and she felt lethargic, wavering in her resolve.

After a few moments of wondering what was going on, the absence of movement in the room struck her. There were no workers! Usually, there would be stubby brown wings flitting between people, bringing drinks, or fish chunks, running errands. Was their absence, and the lack of energy, causing the fug? Was it Their Time?

She frowned. Her discussion last night with Thane had led her to believe that she had some leeway on the timing of the uprising. Time she desperately needed to make her case to the Queen.

"Your Highness?" Aioffe said. No response. "Mother?"

"What?" Even the monosyllabic reply lacked its usual enmity.

"Where are the workers?"

The Queen stiffened, then rose up from her throne in a smooth motion and took to the air. Had she really not noticed, Aioffe thought? The Queen's huge wings beat strongly as she circled the room, searching. Her shoulders sagged, and she returned to the dais and stood tight-lipped before Aioffe.

"We have no need of them." Dismissing their significance with a wave of her hand, she said, "They can do what they will."

"But," Aioffe said, "the courtiers clearly do?"

"It matters not what they think, most are refusing to eat now anyway."

"Then, shouldn't you make them?"

"Why bother?"

Aioffe was shocked into silence, although not entirely

surprised by her mother's callousness. The Queen's movement towards the throne slowed before she sat down, her mouth pursed even tighter. She checked with a wavering hand that her crown was on straight and smoothed her skirts once more. From under her eyelashes, Aioffe watched as the Queen's jaw clenched and then wobbled. She reached out a hand and gently touched Lana's knee.

"I cannot even look at you," the Queen said through her teeth. "This is your doing."

"How is that, Mother?" Although Aioffe felt little emotion towards Lana, she would not pull away from her without this last chance to try and reach her.

"Your obstinacy has brought us to this. I know you have something to do with the workers. Do not presume that I don't know."

Uffer, Aioffe thought, or was it Elizae? Maybe one of the fae from last night? Surely not Thane? Either way, clearly her mother knew more about her explorations than she realised.

"And to think I was considering moving you back to your old rooms. That you were taking an interest in acknowledging your place here. I was misled. You will never change. Wilful, disobedient, and untrustworthy."

"Mother, I am here now. Whether or not I wished for it, I am a part of it, of us."

The Queen hissed, "But you will not stay. If you survive. You will not fulfil your destiny to rule, I see that now."

Aioffe looked at the floor, wondering if she had misjudged the situation? Did the Queen know what was about to happen with the workers? Accept it even? She was lost for a moment before remembering her plan. One step.

Aioffe's voice was quiet but carried with conviction. "Mother, I cannot deny I want to leave. I think you know that. Your rule has led us to the demise of all that was good about Naturae. I don't understand why, but I can see now - we all can - that this is not sustainable. I will not be party to this ongoing disaster of a Queendom. It is not where I want to be. There is nothing left here for me to stay for." She glanced at the Queen, "But out of duty and to show my obedience, I will do what I can. But then, you *must* release me. Accept I will never be like you. Naturae will no longer be ruled by a Queen once you have passed."

She paused and held her breath. Had this been a human land, such talk would be treasonous, but Aioffe had already accepted the risk of death. The Queen had turned her hard stare onto her.

"So there is nothing here for you, child? Is that what you suggest? You should ignore your destiny, your given duty, because I have failed as a ruler? As a parent?"

A warning shiver ran through Aioffe as the Queen drew herself up, the challenge lying between them like a gauntlet. Her step forward was turning out to be a step backward, and off a cliff. Quickly, she tried to bring it around.

"No, your Highness! That isn't the issue."

Well, it was, but now was not the time.

"As one who has never ruled, and clearly has no desire to, you have no concept of what it is to preside." The Queen's ire rose alongside her indignation.

From the corner of her eye, Aioffe registered Lyrus approaching from behind the throne.

The Queen began to screech. "You have consistently failed to live up to your destiny, when you should accept it, embrace it even. After all I sacrificed for you... it has been in vain. The final hours approach, and yet you still refuse to do what needs to be done. What is the point in you, child?"

Lyrus now pulled his silver sword from its scabbard, the sneer in his eyes showed he was more than willing to follow through on what he felt sure the Queen would next order. Aioffe stood, the rising adrenaline from imminent threat coursing through her. She rose onto her toes as if her wings could have followed through and also risen.

Stretching both her arms, palms up in submission, Aioffe pleaded for her life.

"This is not the way for us to end, Mother!" Lyrus's blade hovered closer to her chest. He looked at the Queen, his eyes begging for her command. Aioffe glanced at the blade then back at her mother, "Nor is it the way to lead! I will stay! I will stay and work with you to mend this! So you can continue to rule peacefully."

Lana's eyes hardened, glittering with spite as they met hers. "There is no mending what is broken, stupid child."

But then, she gestured for Lyrus to lower his sword.

Aioffe drew in a jagged breath; her heart felt like it would pound out of her chest as she narrowed her eyes at Lyrus, daring him to disobey his Queen.

The Queen pushed Lyrus's still hovering blade down with two fingers on its flat. "No blood of yours will be spilt today," she commanded, and moved closer to Aioffe, blocking the swords path. "But there is no 'fixing' either, without blood being spilt. What is done, what is to come, cannot be changed."

Aioffe lent over and took her mother's hand into hers. "I believe it can be changed," she said softly, pleading. "The future has not yet been fully written, Mother, and perhaps, it can be altered? Improved even?"

The Queen gazed at their hands, as if they held the answer. Her voice sounded sad as she said, "But it has been written. And you are required to play your part in it."

Lyrus spat, "And, you already said, you wouldn't be a part of it. Why don't you just leave now?"

"I didn't say you needed me," Aioffe retorted, glaring at Lyrus. She turned back to the Queen in desperation, "I think I can help at least."

Aioffe sensed the change in the High Hall, and looked over to find that all eyes were studying her. She wavered, unready to make a public statement about her stance. Her mind flicking between the options - to further provoke her mother's antipathy towards her or to announce an untested theory?

It was an impossible choice.

She turned to her mother. Aioffe's heart thumped through fear. Afraid to put herself and her fragile plans in jeopardy, but needing to know if Lana would allow her the freedom to try.

Taking a deep breath, the Queen once more gestured for Lyrus to stand down. Like a well-trained guard dog, he took a step back but the silent, threatening snarl remained on his face.

From the corner of her eye, Aioffe saw Ambassador Spenser pushing his way through the gathering crowds. Beyond him, Uffer stood by the doors, gazing straight towards the dais with horror in his eyes. Next to him was Elizae, frowning.

Aioffe's heart skipped a beat and the world seemed to slow. In Uffer's hands, the earth dripping from its shallow roots, he lifted the pale-leaved but defiantly living plant which had been sprouting in her cell.

CHAPTER 30 - A GATHERING STORM

Nemis returned to the ship's prow as dusk began to fall. The winds picked up once more, whirling around the vessel as it howled over hidden headlands. Joshua and Jack seated themselves with oars, correcting their course when the wind pulled the boat in the wrong direction. As darkness approached and the gusts showed little sign of abating, Fairfax called for them to drop the sail entirely. Ignoring cries from Jack and Ed to put into safe harbour, Nemis and Fairfax seemed to team up and view the larger, still gathering, storm in the distance as a battle they could fight.

Joshua's arms and chest ached as he tried to pull in time with Jack. Even with Ed and Nemis pitching in, his fear of capsizing grew. By now, the vessel was barely making headway through the islands and he had lost all sense of direction. Nemis began to mutter under her breath - Joshua wasn't sure if the words were some kind of curse or enchantment, but she seemed focused on leading them with pulling the oars in a rhythm, towards her choice of destination. Despite not being at all in control of matters, he became aware of the hum of energy as the crew worked together to ride the waves, hauling in synchronisation with each other.

Their faces grim with exertion, Jack and Ed emitted a faint but concentrated Lifeforce without even realising it. It might have been fear, possibly of himself, but Joshua stopped resisting. He breathed in gulps of it under the guise of being out of breath, to give himself strength.

Almost immediately, his arms ached less and he hauled away with renewed vigour. Ruddy, streaming with water, together the crew stoically ignored the constant spray and lashing winds and focused on the task. Unspoken optimism grew in their shared battle with the waves.

Glancing backwards to the stern, Joshua's heart sank at the sight of Fairfax. The lad's expressions alternated between a slightly manic grin when they crested a particularly large wave, and a glare whenever the crew lost the rhythm of the stroke. Jeffries' warning echoed in Joshua's mind, and inwardly he cursed their situation. His own desperation had led him to put all their lives at risk, but it was too late now to turn back and make for land. Angry winds slapped around his face with increasing force until the skin became numb.

Constant spray had long ago extinguished the candles, although they had only provided little more light than a tiny glow. "How much further?" Joshua called out to Nemis. He wasn't sure if she heard him because at that moment, a huge dark wave crested. The boat pitched backwards, lurching on a steep angle. With a splash, the birlinn fell down the other side of the wall of water, completely drenching the already sodden crew. Foamy sea-water sloshed around the floor of the ship, battering their ankles and calves. Their wet torsos then felt the brunt of a cold wind assaulting them afresh.

Joshua thought he heard Nemis cry out, "Rock!" He couldn't be sure until the boat tipped even further to the side with a terrible crunch.

*****

In the High Hall, a nervous silence fell as the Court

absorbed the arrival of the plant, held outstretched in Uffer's hands. Transfixed by the pale green leaves, Queen Lana paled and swayed slightly as she stood. Outside, the wind whistled around, audible in the quietness. Aioffe's glance darted around - searching for a sign that someone understood its significance, aside from Uffer, motionless and anxious, and Spenser, who carried on walking towards the throne. He stopped when the Queen noticed him and looked at Aioffe, raising his eyebrow.

The Queen recovered herself, turning, and arranging herself back on the throne as if this was absolutely nothing of concern or out of the ordinary! She shifted and, looking down her nose at Aioffe, pointed at the stool. The court seemed to breathe a sigh of relief, then whispers started amongst the courtiers. The chances of public fratricide dropped measurably.

Taking a deep breath herself, Aioffe lent in to her mother and whispered, "Perhaps we might talk somewhere more private?"

Lyrus was still hovering beside the Queen's shoulder. Lana, flicked her eyes between the two siblings, assessing the threat level. That Lyrus was ready to find any excuse to remove Aioffe from the line of succession was now obvious to all. She turned to her guards, saying in a tight, light voice, "Lyrus, remain to ensure the Court continues. Aioffe, you will present yourself to my chambers."

Aioffe breathed a sigh of relief as her mother issued her orders. Her stony-faced brother straightened and looked as if he were about to object, but the Queen ignored him.

As Lana spread her wings, one of the guards appeared from behind the throne. He whispered something in his Captain's ear, and Lyrus's expression hardened further.

"There is a matter I have to deal with," Lyrus said, shooting Aioffe a spiteful glance. He turned his back deliberately on his monarch and sister before walking stiffly away.

The Queen's eyes narrowed but, this time, she allowed it to pass. His role encompassed the security of the Queendom; better she release him to focus on that. Especially now. Turning to the assembled crowd, Lana rose up and imperiously waved dismissively at the crowd. "You may all retire, there will be no further business today." Confusion and relief rippled through the room, and the exhausted courtiers dropped into deep bows. Uffer and Elizae were trapped amongst their backs.

Her mother flew up into the heights of the Hall then over the Court, leaving Aioffe alone on the dias. She rushed down to push through the crowd, rising out of their posturing as soon as the Queen had passed above. Reaching Uffer and Elizae, Aioffe gathered the plant up from Uffer's cupped hands. Before he could say anything, Aioffe tried to smile reassuringly, saying, "I'll find you later."

The shaken pair looked at each other briefly, then warily nodded. They stood aside to let her pass, watching Aioffe holding herself straight and dignified as she continued towards the exit.

Spenser appeared by her side and walked alongside as the crowd parted to let her through. She was glad of his unspoken support. The stares of the courtiers followed her; all whispering had ceased but she sensed their confusion. Their nerves. Their hunger.

As they reached the doors, Spenser turned to her. With some formality, he bowed and asked, "My Lady, do you wish me to accompany you further? Is there anything I can do to help?"

Aioffe grimaced. "I fear you may be even less in favour than myself, Ambassador. I thank you, but this step I must undertake on my own." She glanced out to the empty Atrium, then back to check there was a space between them and any courtiers. In a low voice, she requested that he find out what was happening with Lyrus instead. "I trust you to act in the best interests of Naturae, but I do not trust him to make that same judgement," she added. The sceptical expression on the Ambassador's face indicated he was of the same mind.

CHAPTER 31 – WRECKAGE

Jolted headfirst into wood with the force of the impact, the sea-water in the bottom of the ship engulfed Joshua as he was rolled. He tried to push against something, anything in a desperate quest for air whilst not knowing which way was up for a moment. As he managed to get his head up and out from the wash, he realised he was still holding his oar. The hull began to crack, as the waves continued to drive the stricken vessel against its stony anchor. Joshua looked frantically around in the darkness, his predator night-sight picking out dark shapes in the water.

"Here!" Joshua turned towards the sound of the shout, although it was carried by the wind and deceptive. He managed to wedge the oar underneath and against the bench sufficiently to give him purchase. Pushing himself up as the current wave receded slightly, he saw Fairfax.

The boy was dangling, hanging from the tiller, his legs submerged. With every wave, his torso and face disappeared, leaving only white hands clenched around the wooden pole.

The back of the boat was almost entirely above the water but completely twisted. Leaning on its side and pinned by the force of the tide, the vessel now resembled a bucket; repeatedly filled but only half-emptied with each powerful wave. Such was the pressure of the wash, the long lithe hull beam was being forced to break against the jagged rocks. A rock, only visible when the waves receded, held the front of the birlinn fast. The rowlock in the middle of the vessel where Joshua had been sitting was just a gaping, splintered hole.

Joshua looked back at the lowered half of the boat,

desperately hoping to see Nemis. The swooping prow where he had last seen her was twisted down, submerged. "Nemis!" he screamed, but the sound disappeared back into his throat with the wind. He levered himself against the oar and tried to push against the wave and over, to where the wood began submerging. His hand found the mast, although it was now completely underwater. A piece of loose rigging snagged on his foot and he reached down to try to catch it. Another wave slammed into his chest and the oar wrenched out of his hand. For a moment he was pinned against the mast, his breath torn from him. But his free hand snagged the rope!

Allowing the receding water to pull him away, with one hand clutching at the line, he kicked towards the front of the boat. "Nemis!" His shout strained against the wind but at least he hoped it was audible. He drove his legs harder, head submerging briefly through the next wave. He waved the other arm around the water, blindly searching.

Surfacing, then blinking the wet from his eyes, he thought he saw a broad dark shape lying ahead, rising on a crest just beyond the outline of the prow. He was too far away to be sure of anything.

Another dreadful cracking sound accompanied the wave as it receded, the cry of ancient trees furiously resisting the pounding of the stormy tide. In the back of his mind, some part of Joshua registered the creaking as the vessel breaking into two.

The rope and his cape were pulling him down while he dragged a lungful of air in. Grabbing the side of the boat that was still above water, he hauled himself higher above the waves. Hanging onto the edge of the birlinn, he paused for a moment, his mind frantically trying to consider the options.

The choice now before him was impossible: Fairfax was at least alive, but Nemis, whom he felt more allegiance to, was possibly dead. At best, out of reach. Regrettably, there was no sign at all of Jack and Ed. Joshua looked briefly to the skies, praying and hoping they had been pushed onto a shore somewhere. The impression he had left them with - of him as an angel - flashed into his mind. Refusing to concede, to prioritise one life ahead of another, Joshua knew he alone had to try to save both Nemis and Fairfax. A plan crystallised.

Using the next wave for extra height, Joshua dropped the rope and with both hands on the side of the boat not yet under water, hauled himself up. He managed to grab his cape before it could pull him back in as the wave receded. Chest prone against the outer side of the vessel, his legs scrabbled upwards to join the rest of his body as he gripped the slippery wood with numb hands. The ship was unsteady as he took another deep, salty breath, then pushed up to a kneeling position.

He drew his sodden cape across his neck so it would hang down, then looked back to check Fairfax was still hanging in there. The boat groaned and creaked once more. From his new vantage point, Joshua could see it was barely holding together, with only rigging to resist the relentless sea. Another few waves and the hull would completely fracture. The back of the craft would be free to dash against the rocks behind with the full force of the tide.

Joshua raised his wings, shook them free of spray, then jumped up into the air. Beating furiously against the winds, in seconds he reached the stern. Fairfax turned his face towards the movement he sensed in the black of the night.

"Grab my cape!" Joshua shouted, hovering in the air like a dark angel. Fairfax gazed up at him. Although his hands were frozen onto the tiller and his body near-paralyzed with cold, the boy had the presence of mind to look down to watch the wave recede. With a leap of faith in this strange man-angel, Fairfax flung his right hand out to the dangling cloak and tried to grasp it. His fingers were too numb to flex, unable to form a grip. His right arm sagged in failure and the daemon glanced at his other arm, stretching as it bore his own full weight.

Joshua shouted, "Try again!" The next wave gathered underneath Fairfax, lifting him slightly. Fairfax flexed his fingers, wincing with pain, and pushed his arm out anew. Dipping, Joshua angled himself down and grasped Fairfax's hand, closing it on the folds of the cape. Then, using his legs on the rudder for extra steadiness, he pulled Fairfax's other hand from the shaft and similarly placed it, curling his fingers around the fabric.

Joshua had no time to ensure Fairfax's grip was firm enough. The next wave buffeted the boat with a force strong enough to sever the vessel in half completely. Joshua lost his footing and pitched forwards, his wings frantically pulsing to compensate. Fairfax briefly submerged but somehow kept his hold. Feeling the pull of the increased weight and the drag of the wave, agony soared through Joshua's neck. A fleeting question about whether the clasp on the cape would hold flashed into Joshua's mind, yet he pulled up.

As his wings flapped against the driving wind, Joshua reached down and grabbed the back of the lad's coat. Bearing Fairfax's weight thus steadied them and reduced the pull on his neck, although his bicep screamed in protest. Flying low over the sea but high enough he could avoid the swell, Joshua searched. The winds kept pushing them towards the headland, but Joshua didn't dare waste time dropping Fairfax on land.

In the waters below, smashed boxes and cups bobbed, merely awaiting their final doom as they gradually edged closer to the rocks. Joshua glanced back at the birlinn. The stern had now dashed against the boulders beyond, and broken up into jagged shafts palely poking up like deadly fingers.

His eyes picked out the wide shape across the water: a cloak fanned out across the wave? Swooping down, Joshua panicked. If Nemis was still in her coat, then surely it would have sunk by now? As he approached, he saw with relief that the object was not quite flat. Hovering then dipping, Fairfax squealed with horror as he was half dunked yet again. Joshua reached out. Not close enough...

He didn't want to completely submerge Fairfax if this was going to be a false lead, so Joshua hooked his foot underneath the bulge in the water and kicked to flip it over. The bundle turned sufficiently for him to see. As if trying to prevent him from claiming the prize, a gust of wind rose out of nowhere and buffeted Joshua away. Fairfax however, screamed at the storm, mimicking the wild banshee he had accused Nemis of being.

Joshua was able to approach again, his wings beating furiously against the assault. He reached down into the sea once more with his spare hand and grabbed the bundle. With all his might, he focused on pulling up. As soon as Fairfax was free of the water, Joshua let go of his coat-back and wrapped his arms around the small body, clutching the bulk to his chest.

Cradling his precious cargo, he turned towards land at

last. The effort of hauling a load around his neck and the witch in his arms was immense. Never before had Joshua felt such pain, but, he concentrated, praying he could make just one more flap, just one more beat to bring them all closer to land.

As the unwieldy threesome crept along towards the coastline, Fairfax opened his eyes long enough to notice they were flying through dense mist. He couldn't feel his fingers or his arms at all. But, when his feet seemed to catch and drag on something, he instinctively tried to pull his legs up. Fairfax looked down to see what he had touched. "Land!" He shouted.

Fairfax wriggled in the air, his feet reaching for solid ground once more. Joshua, preoccupied with battling through each beat of his own wings and blindly flying through the mist, had not realised they were beyond the sea. Fairfax grinned as Joshua now slowed, dipping until Fairfax's feet touched sand. He let go of the cape and collapsed onto the beach.

The sudden lightness around his neck caused Joshua to briefly rise again, wings still beating hard. But he dropped down, alighting beside Fairfax. Using his wings for support as he bent over, Joshua placed the inert body in his arms on the sand as well. Unwrapping the cape which had cocooned his bundle, he gasped in horror. Nemis's too-pale face lolled back towards the sand. Blue lips opened slightly and a trickle of sea-water dripped onto the wet beach. Clasped in her arms was the wooden figurehead which had adorned the front of the birlinn - the eagle's wingspread formed a life-saving cross, which she had clutched to her chest. Her torso aligned to the bird, as if she were hitching a ride on its back.

Joshua didn't know what to do; Nemis lay entirely

still, showing no signs of life. Fairfax, however, leaned over and began to pull the eagle away from her. "No!" cried Joshua, reluctant to remove the last vestiges of comfort the wood had clearly provided. A lump rose in his throat as Joshua felt a wave of defeat wash over him. He stroked her face with his hand. But Fairfax continued to pull at the figurehead with determination. Joshua could only watch as the lad wrenched the eagle away from her frozen fingers and shoved Nemis onto her side.

With the change in position, more sea-water poured out of Nemis's lips, more than Joshua thought was possible to hold in the cavity. Fairfax started shaking her, rocking her back and forth. More water spewed from her mouth, then Fairfax laid her back on the sand, her face twisted over towards the sand. His face looked serious, utterly focussed for once.

Curiously, the daemon then put his hands in the middle of her chest. As he knelt over her, he stretched his arms and pushed down with a sharp jolt. Even more water spat out from Nemis's mouth. He did it again, then once more.

Joshua was about to haul him off Nemis when she coughed, a horrible splutter. Fairfax quickly turned her onto her side again. She continued to cough, drawing in great ragged breaths which collapsed into coughs as more water evacuated. A wave of relief swept over Joshua as he sank into the sand and touched her arm. Grinning, Fairfax kept slapping her back until she lifted a limp arm and pushed him away.

"Take them Beneath!" A strange voice ordered. Joshua felt a new presence set down on the beach. I know that voice, thought Joshua.

Lyrus alighted next to the trio. Looking up in

bewilderment, Joshua recognised his snarling face. His attacker and Annabella's kidnapper! From behind, his arms were seized, yanked up together, trapping his wings. Shadowy figures hauled Fairfax up, circling his wrists with a rope which glinted in the moonlight. Instinctively, they both wrestled against the bondage, but the hands gripping them were too strong. Too exhausted to resist for long, within moments Joshua and Fairfax were pushed back down to their knees, into submission.

Nemis was last to be dragged to her feet, but, through the darkness shrouding them, Joshua thought he saw her smiling. "We are here. Naturae." There was an unmistakable sense of accomplishment in her voice. Almost as if she were deliberately ignoring the fact that they were surrounded and chained.

One step closer, Joshua felt the sides of his mouth twitch up as well, as she confirmed his hopes. He had survived worse than this, all things considered. But then, he didn't know what this Beneath place was?

CHAPTER 32 - ROYAL RECONCILIATION

The dusky smell of the Queen's gown was all that occupied the corridor outside the High Hall. Aioffe set off at a pace not befitting a princess towards the Queen's Chambers. In her hands, the plant seemed to perk up, its roots drinking in her energy.

As she trotted along, away from the tongues which had started wagging as soon as she left the Hall, Aioffe's senses bounced into full alert. The surrounding palace was virtually silent. An absence of workers all the more obvious as she dashed past empty service corridors branching off towards other treetop staterooms. Only the winds provided an almost musical whisper as they whirled around the branches and leaves, jarring with the ragged sound of her breath.

The Queen's Chambers at the end of the long corridor were heralded by a once rich-red doorway. The aperture, whilst large and similar in grandeur to the High Hall entrance, was decorated with simpler carvings, denoting an ancient lineage of occupants. The wood had a sheen to it developed from years of buffing, wax polish darkening the cracks in the carpentry. One of the double doors had been left ajar. Aioffe paused before entering into view and gathered herself, smoothing down her hair and moistening her lips. Preparing for the battle as best she could.

The Queen sat on a high-backed chair behind a desk, where bright candlelight highlighted the faded decor. Pale moonlight streamed in through the tall oval windows. Lana made no acknowledgement of her appearance, continuing to scribble away. Her head dipped in concentration, her crown tilted to the point of slipping from her black hair. Aioffe approached and silently proffered the plant to her mother.

The Queen paused scratching, her quill hovered motionless over the pages with a bead of dark ink still formed on the nib. Looking down at the sheets on the desk, Aioffe read the freshly scribbled Faelore. Lines and lines, repeating the same stanza, covered the cream parchment with increasingly erratic writing.

Out of the darkness, she shall bring light,
To kill for the reign and scourge out the
blight.

Aioffe glanced across the room. Scattered on the floor, trailed around the edges of a room and bed, lay countless scraps with the phrase scrawled across them. Evidence of a shredded mind on little strips of parchment. Footprints in the dusty wooden floorboards told of repetitive pacing, of barely clinging onto rationality through routine. Aioffe thought of the Queen's constant smoothing her hands down her dress, checking her crown to be sure it was straight.

Aioffe's heart sank. Had she always been like this? The wording which seemed to be consuming her, what was it? The obsession her mother had with Aioffe's destiny to reign, to perform her duty - was it from some sort of prophecy? Or had her mother simply lost her wits and created these words to justify her actions? Aioffe crouched beside the desk, "Mother, what is this?"

Lana looked down at the papers. Her eyes glazed over, trance-like.

"Mother?" Aioffe prompted.

"It is time," the Queen said sadly, glancing at the plant.

"Time for what?"

"Time for you to accept your destiny. There can be no more excuses, child."

The Queen slowly tilted her head and studied her daughter. Behind the tears forming in her eyes, Aioffe thought she saw a depth of emotion she hadn't believed her mother capable of. The sight rendered her speechless, and she took a step back. A bony hand shot out and grabbed her wrist, jolting Aioffe into clasping the plant to ensure it didn't fall to the ground.

With surprising strength, Lana pulled Aioffe towards her once more, gesturing for her to look at the pages. "It was written. It *is* written," she muttered.

The Queen was making no sense. "What is this?" Aioffe said.

"Your destiny!" The Queen stood, anger starting to rise with frustration about Aioffe's inability to see what, to her, was obvious.

"Mother," Aioffe said, forcing a placatory tone as if she were the parent, "these are just words. Why have you written them?"

"I....don't know," Lana admitted. "They just flow out of me! I can't stop them!"

"Why do you think they relate to me?" Aioffe asked.

"Because I am the blight!"

Years of neglect, abuse and distance fell into place in Aioffe's mind. The conflict which must have raged inside her mother - to have a daughter destined to take the reins once her tenure as Queen finished was one thing, but to have your offspring kill you was quite another. Maybe this was why she kept Lyrus so close - did she really trust him to protect her? Why could he not perform this function?

Because he was a male, she knew. 'She shall bring light.' And Aioffe was female. With the powers of a Royal. Lyrus could never ascend, no matter how much he wanted to. Aioffe thought she now understood - how could you love someone, love her, knowing they would be your downfall?

"Then why try so hard to find me, bring me home, if you expected that I would be the one to end your reign?"

The Queen's eyes filled with hopelessness. The child still refused to see what was in front of her. What was so obvious. "Because it is written - you must end the blight. I cannot do it. It is near impossible for a Fae to take their own life. Especially a royal."

"I cannot!" Aioffe cried, "I will not kill you. Not when there is hope we can survive this."

She thrust the plant once more at her mother. It had become more than a simple symbol of hope. The green shoots seemed to perk up with the emotion running through her hands, funnelling through the roots and adding lustre to the tiny leaves.

Aioffe knelt beside her. Placing the plant on the polished wooden floor, she took her mother's hand.

"Mother, even if this is some form of prophecy, there is no timeline for it? You might have many more years to reign."

"Except there is. The blight that causes the decay has spread too far, child. You have come into your powers already. But you shouldn't have. It's too soon!" Lana's eyes pleaded with Aioffe to understand, but before she could respond, the Queen continued, "Don't think I don't know about the rebellion the workers are about to enact. But, they mustn't be the one to take me down. They risk taking you with them."

The conflict within Aioffe reached new heights. After her discussions with Thane, she had been led to believe there was time to try and work with them. To make them see that there was hope for another way out of the problem facing all Naturae fae.

"I'm not afraid of the workers, or of death." Aioffe's defiance had started out honestly, but as she said the word 'death,' she realised that it was no longer true. Holding the plant earlier - a symbol of the fight for survival itself and a token of hope - had subtly altered her mindset. She no longer wished to die as she once had. And through embracing the hope that her powers offered Naturae, she - in fact - wanted to live. Very much.

Emboldened by the prospect of changing the future, she began to see that possibly she could embrace her destiny to rule as well, at some point... but she wasn't there yet. Nor could Aioffe reconcile ruling as a result of killing her own mother.

"You must step into your light, my child." Lana's voice was dangerously firm. "The only way to do that is to crush out my feeble flame. Deal with the consequences. And rule as you were born to do. You must find the violence within you to take my life and claim your destiny."

In a gesture of submission, the Queen joined her daughter on the floor. Mother and child, Queen and Princess, faced each other on their knees. Lana tilted her head back to one side, baring her neck. Her eyes rolled towards Aioffe and blazed, challenging her to take up the offer. Put her out of her misery and end this rotten rule.

"Mother, why?" Aioffe choked, her throat tightened as she tried to push away the emotion.

"Why?" The Queen straightened her head and glared at Aioffe.

"Why must I take your life? It doesn't say that in these words, nor why it has to be now?"

"Because you have come into your full growth power child, and because we do not have the luxury of time. The plant shows you can regenerate these lands, even without the human Lifeforce. And so you must rid our world of the blight, of me, before it is too late to use your abilities."

"I cannot." Aioffe shook her head. She barely knew her mother. She certainly didn't like her very much, but to take her life? "I cannot," she said firmly. "Not like this, not when I can help without violent endings."

The Queen's mood flipped again. With a smooth movement, her wings pushed her airborne and she hovered over her daughter, fury shooting from her eyes. "Your father would have taken this opportunity! There is so much of him in you, yet you still refuse to give in to it!"

"My father?" Aioffe felt the blood drain from her face.

"He knew that for change to happen, sometimes we have to take extreme action! Kill me!" Lana taunted, "Or must I bring Lyrus in to show you how to do it?"

"I don't understand what you mean? What has a father to do with this?"

"You stupid child," the Queen spat. "His blood runs through you. Why else would you have this 'wanderlust'? His blood and mine, our Lifeforces, our tears. And my sacrifice... Do you think we did it all just to have you turn your back on me? Face me and do what I have asked! Do what must be done!"

Aioffe's head reeled. Despite kneeling on the ground, she thought she might fall over. Grasping at the arms of the chair, she focused on the floor to centre herself.

Against her back though, she felt the brush of beating wings. Then, a well-aimed kick to her side brought her sharply back to the situation. Her mother laughed cruelly. Aioffe could hear where Lyrus got his tone from. "Get up child! Face me!"

Aioffe turned, frowning at her mother. Disbelief that she would so obviously goad her like this spread across her face. She knew exactly how this game went - often during her growth years had her mother flipped from one mood to another in an effort to get her to 'show some backbone.' Even then, Aioffe hadn't understood why the Queen should want her to become angry, lash out.

What almost always happened if she had failed to dodge the confrontation, then and as she wanted to now, was that Aioffe would run. Run away rather than let out the violence rising within her. Joshua had found a way to calm her down like no-one else had; he gently held her close instead, whilst she brought the anger under control. Before he was in her life, she had run, flown, channelled the energy out of herself without resorting to violence. Without becoming like her. Like Lana.

This time, here, Aioffe was trapped. Her mother would goad and push her, dance around the air, winding her up and keeping her in this room, until she would have no choice but to resort to physical means to defend herself. Without wings, she was further hemmed down. Her own anger would be faster to rise out of that frustration.

Aioffe looked around, anything to avoid meeting the challenge in her mother's eyes. Forcing herself to draw in a breath with her mouth, and exhale through her nose, she tried to dampen the rising ire. She could not allow herself to fail now, there was too much at stake. Her eyes fell on the plant, and almost instantly she started to feel calmer, more focused. This was why she was here, to fight for hope.

Standing, she reached her hand out to grasp for her mother's. With tears in her eyes, she mourned, grateful for the reminder of the lessons her lover had left her with. Aioffe tugged at the spidery fingers on her mother's hand.

Lana frowned. "What are you doing? Don't touch me!" She jerked the hand away, revulsion spreading across her face.

Gently, insistently, Aioffe again reached for her mother's hand, pulling it firmly towards her. The Queen was taken aback but saw the resolve in Aioffe's face. Cautiously, Lana allowed herself to be pulled into her daughter's arms. Aioffe then tightened her grip on Lana's thin frame, gentle yet firm, as Joshua had been with her. After a few shared breaths, the Queen relaxed her wings and the weight of the comfort released her. As her head sank onto Aioffe's shoulders, in this first-ever embrace, the narrow silver crown loosened. Aioffe caught it before it could fall to the ground, and placed it on the desk.

They stayed pressed together, each mourning their lost loves, for many minutes. Lana was so unused to physical contact, that for some time she railed against the self-preservation instinct which rose unbidden in her, clenching her muscles and trying to push back from the embrace. But Aioffe kept a light hold on her throughout, softly breathing into the old woman's hair and sometimes stroking her shoulders. Brushing off the weight of responsibility the Queen had carried alone for so long. Gradually the fight drained out of Lana.

*****

Aioffe was the first to pull back and look clear-eyed at her mother's face. It seemed remarkable to her now, having been close to human family behaviour and a part of a loving couple, that she had never thought before to be physically familiar with her own mother. But it was not the Fae way, not the royal way. The Queen had never shown any sign of affection for her in the past. Looking into her eyes now, Aioffe wondered if they should have had this reconciliation decades before. Perhaps it could have saved some heartache.

"Mother, I need to know..."

"I know you have questions, my child," Lana interrupted softly.

"How could you ask me to kill you, without knowing all I need to?" Aioffe chastised her.

"You are right, but we have no time for this. All you need to learn is in the Scriptaerie."

"There is too much there, I could spend all my hours at study and still not understand."

"What happened in the past is irrelevant to our present situation. You are the future and you must forge your own path."

"It is important, Mother! How can I make good decisions without understanding what went before? How Naturae came to be in this state?"

Lana's eyes filled with tears, "That is simple. I am the blight. My sadness cast a pall over us all. And now it must be scourged." She took her daughter's hand and squeezed it tightly. "You must do this, there is no other choice."

Aioffe fell silent, then reached up and stroked the tears from Lana's cheek away. She said, "Mother, tell me of the sadness? Of my father."

Lana looked briefly over her shoulder at the crown,

dimly glinting on the desk in the dusty sunlight. "It was so long ago. It does not matter." She had never spoken of him over the centuries, despite his presence always in her thoughts.

Aioffe sighed, "Please tell me. I deserve to know about him. Until now, I didn't even know I had a father. I... do not want to make mistakes." Aioffe did not add the 'like you did' which ran through her mind.

The Queen considered this for a moment, turning the question in her mind. It seemed to her that Aioffe might be coming to a point of acceptance after all. That this request heralded her intent to take up her destiny at last. Lana also began to understand that her daughter's stubbornness would prevail; Aioffe would not kill her without getting the answers first. She would have to open the box of pain within and hope it satisfied her daughter sufficiently. She must be persuaded to complete the task.

Lana stood and led Aioffe to the chairs on the far side of the room. They both sat and gazed out over the treetops waving in the moonlight in companionable silence. Aioffe waited calmly for her mother to begin as she imagined a child might wait for a bedtime story. Except, her mother had never sat with her like this before, even when she had been a pupae. As they watched the clouds draw past the moon, Aioffe noticed the pain on her mother's face deepen as she began to talk of her lover, Aioffe's father.

"I had never met someone like him before, never interacted with humans at all," Lana started. "His people arrived on ships and laid waste to the islands to the south of Naturae. We didn't know what had happened at first, only that there were fewer villagers at the Circles of Faeth, for the ceremonies. So I sent spies to the homesteads, to find out where the humans had gone. Without their energy, their crops would fail to thrive, and we would all suffer. The men from the North, they knew nothing of our ways. They had their own rituals, their own beliefs. They killed the Orkneans and moved in with their own ways.

I had my spies watch and report back. I blamed their leader, Sigurd, at first, for the chaos. They had kept a few of the Orkneans, made them their slaves. I thought they might go once they had what they wanted, but I didn't know what that was. But the islanders' blood continued to be spilt.

They reached an island closer to us. It was too much, so I told my soldiers to take him. Bring Sigurd here so I could make him understand what he was doing. Find out what the invaders wanted so they would go away again."

Lana sniffed, then smudged away a tear from her cheek. Talking of what happened in the broadest sense was easier than she thought it would be. The harder part would be when it became personal. Glancing at Aioffe's open face, which some might see as trusting, Lana considered that perhaps it was time to share of herself, in order that her offspring might understand the risks of getting involved with human concerns.

"I kept him in the Beneath, watched him, learned from him. He was fascinated by me, every time he saw me, his own faith in what he knew before diminished. He thought for a while I was a god - a 'gud' he called it. No-one had shown such curiosity about fae for so many years. The people here had blindly followed their traditions of worship at the stones and life thrived without them needing to know any more. Yet, he took an interest and I saw our life, our ways, from a different perspective.

Then, without their leader, the men from the North stopped killing and settled. I couldn't release him back to them in case they started again."

Lana swallowed; the lump which had been growing in her throat threatened to rise and prevent her talking further. She had been alone for so long, unable to speak of him, but now, she allowed herself to remember.

"Over time, Sigurd ceased to be a prisoner. I became equally intrigued by him. I suppose we fell in love. But it was more than that. I grew to need him, to need his presence. It was addictive. We shared Lifeforce between us, but it was more. The differences between us, him a daemon, and me, a fae - it was a dangerous combination. I craved his approval as well as his essence, and he began to need mine. It became all-consuming. His thirst for life, for knowledge ignited a passion in me.

I shared more than I should have about our kind. We even wrote together in the Scriptaerie, marking his entry into my life to give some indication of the permanence of our joining. Of course, no-one could know. Although I am Queen, it is surprisingly hard to keep things private. If the Council, other Nobles, knew who was on Naturae, I would have been replaced by a European Queen for breaking agreed upon covenants. What started as illicit quickly became chains which bound us. So tightly, at times it was suffocating - I could think of nothing else. Of no-one else."

Lana stood and from a drawer in the desk, drew out two small objects, barely fitting her palm. Smiling crookedly as she looked at them, she passed the larger to her daughter, but clenched the other. "This is his likeness," she said simply. It was too painful for her to look at, even now that she had begun talking about her lover and seven or more centuries had passed. She could no longer focus on it anyhow, the memory of how he looked was fixed in her mind instead.

Aioffe studied the oval miniature; looking back were her own vivid blue eyes, blond hair and a slightly larger up-tilted nose.

A wry smile played on Lana's face as she continued. "Even when events forced us into parting, we were drawn to one another. We tried so hard to live our lives in tandem. We communicated in secret, wanting to be together but unable to leave our duties behind."

Lana's skin began to crawl with the memory of her craving, and she started to pace around the room. Aioffe, not knowing what to do or say, stared at the miniature, absorbed in imagining what he was like, and what other traits she shared with this virtual stranger.

After a few laps of the chamber, Lana continued. "We were trapped by our responsibilities. Unable to publically choose each other, yet unable to stay apart."

"Go on," Aioffe whispered, barely audible through the lump in her throat. "Was this why you were so sad? Because you couldn't be together?"

"Oh child, that was just the start of it." Lana shook her head, "We could possibly have survived with only our stolen moments of happiness. But," she sighed deeply, "you must know by now, that is not the way of the human world. Their lives are so short, guided by the thought of what happens after their life ends. This affects their judgement, believing they must grab what they can in this world to secure their place afterwards. Glory, reputation! That is what drove the men from the North. For us, they are alien concepts, as we have no afterlife."

Lana sighed, then her lips pressed together. Aioffe touched her hand, "What happened to my father?"

Lana's voice trembled as she spoke. "During a

ceremony, others from the North attacked. Slaughtering their own people. Sigurd was defending my humans when he fell. He died. Defending me."

Aioffe stood up and turned away, her face pale in the moonlight as her heart thumped in her chest. At once, the loss of Joshua washed over her again, and she blinked furiously. She knew the agony, the helplessness which Lana must have felt at that moment.

Lana sobbed openly, her shoulders shaking with the release of confession.

"So what did you do?" Aioffe croaked out, wondering why her mother hadn't made her father immortal, as she had done for Joshua when he had nearly died. Already, Aioffe mourned the loss of a father she had never met.

"We made you." Although choked out, Lana's statement shocked Aioffe. All her life, she had assumed that her vine had been nurtured, blessed like the others. Was this why she was Royal? Because of the life-giving tears of her mother? She struggled to comprehend what part her so-called 'Father' could have played in her pupaetion if he was dead? Fae did not create the same way humans did, by lying together.

"But you could have given him your blood, your Lifeforce, and made him immortal?"

"As I said, he was dead. One cannot bring someone back to life if the body is unable to ingest the blood. Too much of his had been spilt back in their dwellings. He died in my arms." Lana drew a ragged breath in, then said, "I had brought him back to the Vine Room, I knew not what else to do. I remembered my mother saying it took pain to make a child, and my pain was so great. A vine takes more than blood or blessings, it pulls essence. Lifeforce. A vine is always greedy to drink. To live. My need to have him was so strong and it was the only way to keep him with me. His essence, and his blood, decayed onto your roots."

An image of her mother crying over the corpse of her lover at the foot of her vine, as he bled into the earth, overcame Aioffe. She reached over and hugged Lana again, and they softly cried together.

"But you are too much like him for me to bear to be with you..." Lana wailed, barely forming the words. Her fist clenched the only possession of his she retained, Sigurd's hammer on its leather thong. Her fingers moulded around its knobbly shape so tightly, as if the metal would lend its strength to her very bones. Sorrow for all that was lost overwhelmed her.

CHAPTER 33 - BENEATH

Spenser had followed Lyrus as he led his guards to the edge of the land. He watched, hidden high above, as they approached a group of people on the beachhead. Silently, and leaving a suitable gap between them and himself, he flew behind them carrying their chained captives. The arrivals put up little resistance, probably worn out from their journey through the storm, Spenser reasoned. He could see the wreckage all around and marvelled at the luck these humans had in finding Naturae, landing on it when their ship had broken up on the jagged rocks surrounding it. Most certainly, they had been surprised by Lyrus's arrival, and lack of assistance.

During the flight back to the city, the fae soldiers struggled to carry one of the figures. It kept wriggling in the air, seemingly unafraid to be dropped in his desperation to break free of the soldier's grasp. Spenser thought he saw a glimpse of wings through the blackness of the night.

The troops and their prisoners headed towards the clearing before the entrance to the Beneath. Spenser landed near the sacred trees and sprinted up the path towards them. He arrived in time to see the first captive to arrive falling to the ground in a heap. Then immediately he sprang up, legs balanced and holding his fists ready for a fight. This one had managed to wrangle his arms free during the flight, preparing to resist. Spenser waited, hidden from view behind a supporting trunk, observing and assessing. The youngest-looking, whose clothing was adorned with ornate decorations and frills, kicked out at the soldiers with square-toed feet. Lyrus laughed at him as his men circled, drawing out their swords.

Meanwhile, the second figure they brought was a woman, with long rat tails of hair and a pale face. Spenser recognised her blue robe as that of a monastic servant, which seemed even more incongruous and unlikely than the frilly lad. Her reaction to their arrival in the citadel was stranger, as she looked around the torch-lit clearing with an expression of curious wonder upon her face.

Finally, other man-boy, the wriggly one, was unceremoniously dumped on the ground. The four guards did not release his arms though, held by silver chains as he sprawled on the dirt. Lyrus strode over to poke him. A sodden cape slipped from the prisoner's shoulder. Spenser hid his gasp as he saw a long black wing, it's wet translucence reflecting the yellow glow of the flaming torch attached at the entrance to the Beneath. This man with wings was the person of most interest to Spenser.

As his men brought out their swords and took control of the situation with the fisticuff-ready boy, Lyrus dragged the winged one upright. The pair locked eyes.

"I thought I had already dealt with you," Lyrus hissed.

"You didn't finish the job," the man spat back. Spenser liked the deep timbre of his voice, and the deliberate absence of an accent. It told him of a life of concealment, familiar to all fae living amongst humans. He wondered again about the strange size and colour of the man's wings.

"Why did you come here, spy?"

The man chose not to answer, despite Lyrus shaking him before shoving him down to the dirt. The winged one scrabbled to his knees. Lyrus advanced again and kicked the winged man in the stomach.

"No!" The woman cried out. Her guard quickly pushed her head to the ground, grunting "Beneath?"

408

Lyrus nodded briskly. Grabbing his hair as the injured man doubled over, Lyrus then hauled him towards the gaping hole through the roots. Hearing the gasping attempts to draw breath as he tried to resist, Spenser almost broke cover to assist. But the rest of the soldiers were closing in on the young lad, poking him with their drawn swords but not drawing blood. Stabbing at him just hard enough to make him re-think his pointless fisticuff attempt, the boy capitulated and started to follow his friend. There were too many guards and only inadequate explanations for his presence. Spenser pulled back into the shadows.

The woman, whom the soldiers seemed to have temporarily forgotten, turned her head and looked directly at the tree where Spenser was standing. He caught her eyes and held their gaze. Although he was largely hidden by the trunk and some distance away, the look bored through the darkness with a desperation he could feel in his core.

Then, one of the soldiers broke away from the circle still surrounding the boy and grabbed her arm. She kept the contact with Spenser, allowing herself to be dragged up to standing. Thankfully, the soldier gave no thought to look at where this captive was staring. She stumbled whilst being pushed around to face the roots, but continued looking back all the while, searching for their broken connection.

Her gaze was an eerie sensation for Spenser. The hope and curiosity he saw in her eyes, along with something else. Attraction? Was it kinship? He was intrigued. There was no doubt in his mind now that the young woman was a witch. There was no other explanation for how they had found the shrouded isle.

*****

Joshua felt the cold earth rush up to meet him as his captor
threw him through a doorway. They had walked down an
endless tunnel in almost complete darkness. Even his
night-tuned eyesight had failed to provide much detail.
Only the changing pressure of descent and lack of fresh air
told him they were deep underground. Pulling against his
chains, he had stumbled a few times - on purpose - to try
and get a better feel for where he was heading, but the
twists and turns played with his mental map. By the time
he had been shoved into the absolute obscurity of where
he was now, he was totally disorientated.

Nemis screamed - she was nearby, Joshua thought. He
heard a kerfuffle, feet grinding into dust, close by. Then
Fairfax shouted, "Gerroff!" A thud of a door slamming. At
least, Joshua thought, it sounded as if his friends were in
neighbouring dungeons. Nemis screamed again, but it was
cut short and muffled. His heart sank.

Joshua sat up and tried to look around him. His
movement disturbed the dirt floor, reminding him of the
peatlands of home, ancient and dank-smelling. The dark
was absolute. Not even a chink of light gave any clues to
the size of where he was. On hands and knees, crawling
about, he tentatively touched the earth, trying to estimate
the dimensions of the room with his fingertips. Feeling up
the walls, he realised the ceiling was low as he struggled
to raise his wings. Dust scattered down, dislodged by the
disturbance. With his fingertip, Joshua clawed at the edges
of the ceiling, touching tiny roots poking into the cramped
hole. He pinched one - it felt dry and lifeless. Whatever
tree was above him was dying. These roots would not
sustain it and drew no moisture from the earth surrounding

410

him.

Still standing, he stretched his arms up and wings out. All his extremities touched the same soil. He could barely stand upright, but he circled, trying to find the doorway. There! He touched a wooden frame edge, then a rough-hewn panel with no internal lock. His delicate fingers ran over the hinges, deciphering whether he could pull out a pin to free himself.

All the while, he listened. Outside, in the tunnels, it had fallen quiet. Having determined the hinge was un-pickable, he began to work at the chains with his teeth, recognising pliant silver when he felt it.

CHAPTER 34 – BURIED

Aioffe and Lana were still sitting with their heads together in sorrow as the dawn broke. Aioffe had been considering how to tell Lana about her lost love. How she knew her mother's pain and grief. How she wanted to not fall into the trap of bitterness and loneliness as she had.

From over the seas, the echo of a horn interrupted their reverie. "A call to arms!" Lana whispered. "That sound, I have heard it before. The men from the North used it before battle." Her fingers stroked the outline of the hammer necklace.

"I must leave," Aioffe said as she stood and strode to the window. The horn was the signal which she agreed upon with Thane. How could he have moved so fast? She was bewildered, she didn't even know where he was! The mists had thickened, and she could not see the seas through them anymore, despite their height.

"And go where? They will be here before long. You must kill me now daughter!"

"I will not," Aioffe said. "Not while there is a chance to prevent this happening."

"There is no chance, my child. You should not delude yourself that a plant will stop a war."

"It may not. But if I do not try, then I am as weak as the workers think I am, and that is not the truth of it."

"What do you think you can do about it, child? They want us dead!"

"No, Mother, I believe they want to be heard. To have hope that things can change." Aioffe turned and presented her wings to her mother, "Release me?"

Lana looked at her daughter. Standing tall, there by

412

the window, so emotional only a few moments earlier. Now she seemed to glow with the luminescence of purpose.

The Queen in her still resisted freeing her, but from the determined expression on Aioffe's face, Lana knew she would leave regardless. Keeping her clamped had served its purpose now. She gave the hammer one last squeeze before standing also. Sigurd would have wanted freedom above all else, she knew. Perhaps it was time to allow his blood to guide Aioffe. Although hesitant about her decision, Lana extracted a small silver key from the desk drawer. She placed the hammer in its place before unlocking her daughter's wing clasp. "But what has that to do with the plant?" Lana said.

Aioffe flexed her shoulders and freed appendages, before turning to face the Queen. Relieved that the opportunity had come for her to share what she had originally come here to talk to her mother about, she said, "I have seen how desperate people get when they think there is no future. The plant shows there can be a future. We - Naturae - can re-grow. But that won't be enough if the workers think they won't have a part in it. A voice."

The Queen's eyes narrowed, "What do you propose to do about that? They are just common workers. They have their own place in how our society works, don't they?"

"That is no longer enough. They, no, *we*, need to show them how important they are to us. Look what happens when they are not appreciated! They know they are stronger now than most of the court. We depend on them. And yet, we give them no reward for this service, no payment."

"Payment systems are for humans, they have no place here. The workers serve us. That is how it has always been. They are different from us. Weaker. Powerless. Born to serve!"

Aioffe felt a rising frustration with the re-emergence of Queen Lana once again. Her narrow mindedness had caused the situation to fester like a boil, and she refused to acknowledge the consequences of it bursting.

"The workers, and the soldiers, have seen the human world. When you sent them out to search for me, they saw how ordinary people, mortals, who have been given a voice are flourishing. They saw the passion of belief - in something higher than themselves. How humans take a stance for what they believe in. You cannot ignore what the future holds, Mother. They know we need them more than they need us. It is time to start listening to what they want."

The Queen stepped back, shocked by this suggestion. For all of her lengthy lifetime, for all of fae history, the rulers had depended on the workers to provide for them, their superiors. She barely acknowledged that they had a voice, opinions even, to consider listening to.

"You imply that the humans are better than us?"

"No!" Aioffe sighed, "but they have evolved, and continue to. They accommodate the challenges meeting them by facing them." Aioffe gazed out to the mists, admitting to herself as much as Lana, "It is sometimes messy, or violent. Undoubtedly complex, but when groups of people collaborate, they find a way through the fear and uncertainty."

The Queen sniffed, affronted by Aioffe's insinuation that faekind was stuck in time, therefore not meeting the changes which were ahead. Then, Lana realised there was a truth in that, and looked down at her hands. By bearing the burden of leadership on her own, neither Naturae nor herself had been able to evolve. Because of fear. Her fear.

And now here they were. With change being forced upon her. Knowing that her own lifetime was soon to close made her think again about what Aioffe was proposing.

Lana touched Aioffe's shoulder, saying, "You think, if you give them a voice, it will change their minds?"

Aioffe turned to face her, and Lana saw the fear in her eyes as well. "I have to believe I can try at least," she said, shrugging her shoulders.

Finally, her daughter was accepting her role and leading. "Then go," Lana said, drawing back her shoulders, briefly reverting to the domineering Queen of old. "But, come back and finish what you must here, child. Take your future into the light."

"I cannot promise that." Aioffe took her mother's fingers in hers. "I am not yet reconciled to losing you, especially by my own hand. Not when I have just found you."

"I will come with you then." Lana's voice wobbled, and she felt as if someone else were speaking for her as she said, "To show them that we are united now?"

"I think I need to do this on my own."

Lana sighed with relief, "I understand." Her heart sped up, as she realised the danger Aioffe was putting herself into. The resulting dilemma this placed her rule in. "You must be the one to end me though, child, not some rabble," she beseeched, clutching her hands to hide their tremor.

Aioffe started to walk across the chamber towards the door, "Let me do this step, talk to them about the idea. Then we will discuss what to do next." Glancing at a scrap of parchment on the floor, she picked up the plant from the floor, allowing some of the soil to fall onto it, before packing the root ball carefully in a small leather pouch.

The Queen nodded, but her lips tightened. She heard the splatter of earth, even if she could not clearly see it. Picking up the crown, she said tightly, "Wear this?"

"I cannot. Not yet," Aioffe said, although she knew in her heart it was a burden she would soon have to bear.

*****

"You have new guests," Lyrus said with a sneer as he rushed past Uffer in the corridors towards the Armoury. "But leave them for me!" He called back as he disappeared into his office.

Uffer tried not to be affronted but, his curiosity was piqued. The cells had been empty, bar Aioffe, for so long now, he wondered who could Lyrus have detained there? He carried on down the hall towards the Queen's chambers. It had been many hours since Aioffe had left the Court. Hours he had spent pacing around the Palace since he received the message from Thane. Alone, walking the corridors through the night until he heard the horn.

His heart sank. It was time. Yet Aioffe still hadn't emerged.

Lyrus dashed past Uffer again, heading back out of the Palace. In his hands was the case which Uffer knew contained his torture instruments. The horn's warning clearly deemed irrelevant compared to what was in the Beneath. Uffer paused, worrying. He had to find his Princess, but who, or what, was in the cells? Curiosity almost swayed him, but he continued up the dark hallways, determined instead to interrupt and find his Princess.

The doors to the Queen's chambers opened just as he

approached, and Aioffe stepped out. Her eyes flared as she pulled the doors shut behind her.

"Your Highness..."

"Lord Anaxis!"

They both spoke over each other, then smiled. Her heart warmed at the sight of her friend, and Uffer felt eased to find her alive.

"Your Highness," Uffer began, "I am heartened to see you, but we must make haste."

"Did I hear the horn? Is it time?"

"Yes, I heard they are gathering. I must get you to safety."

Aioffe looked at him, so kind and protective. She had no doubt he would assist her. The childish part of her wanted to run from the confrontation. Yet she couldn't. Not this time.

"Where are they now?" Aioffe asked.

Uffer had decided earlier whilst pacing the hallways that the more sensible course of action was to facilitate Aioffe's escape. The Princess's presence could only inflame matters, he thought. Better to let the mob do what they must and protect his charge by fleeing the island. "They gather at the standing stones, my Lady. Thane wants to make sure all workers are united and prepared before they come here, to the Palace. We should go anywhere but there."

"The circles of faeth are where we must go," Aioffe smiled. Thane had moved the timetable up, but he was gathering the workers from across the lands as she'd requested! Uffer took a step back, the horror evident in his deep brown eyes.

"That would be unwise, your Highness! They mean to kill all Royals and courtiers!"

Aioffe took his hand and squeezed it gently, "Have faith in me, dear Uffer. It is sooner than I thought, but I believe in Thane."

"He is their leader! You need to be as far away from him as possible!"

"No," Aioffe said, "I need to be there, standing alongside him." She turned and started down the corridor, pulling him with her. "I must talk to them before they arrive here. Talk to everyone. And listen to them."

"Listen?"

"Yes," Aioffe said firmly, "Listen to them. As equals."

Uffer blinked in confusion. "Your Highness, I beg you. They will not talk to you. They... we... are not equal."

As they reached the landing platform, Uffer realised Aioffe's wings had been freed. She said nothing more, but flexed her glorious appendages and turned to him. "Are you coming with me?" Uffer dithered. However, before they could rise, Ambassador Spenser's head appeared over the balustrade.

Hovering mid air, he called over, "Your Highness! I was just coming to find you!"

Aioffe felt caught. "Sorry - I can't stop now, I will find you later!" She raised her wings and quickly took to the sky.

Uffer looked back at Spenser as he too rose up. "Where are you going?" Spenser dashed closer to him, before they could disappear into the mists.

"Stenness Stones," Uffer called back as he flew off after Aioffe.

"Wait!" Spenser called out, taking off after them. "I need your keys!"

Uffer paused, hovering. Looking him full in the eye, Uffer said, "Why?"

"I think Lyrus has one of my fae in the Beneath," Spenser improvised. "I need to check for myself before he can hurt them. You know he won't tell me anything himself."

To hand over the keys was tantamount to treason, but, knowing what was coming, did it really matter? Aioffe was already almost out of sight. With reluctance, Uffer handed his bunch of keys over to the Ambassador. After all, he thought as he flew after her, he would probably need safe refuge with Aioffe, and a well-connected Ambassador could help. If he could only persuade her to come away with him, that was.

*****

When Spenser returned to the cleared entrance of the Beneath, he searched the ground for the outline of the shoe sole of the feisty one. A squared-off toe would leave a distinctive mark; he hoped the imprint would make his path easier to follow through the twists of the unfamiliar tunnels. As he descended, the temperature dropped and the gloom quickly darkened as he left the misty dawn light behind. Spenser tracked the footprints, faintly visible in the dried mud floor until he heard echoes of a deep scream ahead.

Taking to the air, Spenser knew he was on the right path to where the prisoners were housed in the notorious dungeon. Feeling wretched inside, the next shout of pain suggested to him that the owner was putting up more resistance to the torture than perhaps Lyrus expected. He was certain that Lyrus would take the first opportunity to practise his hobby on the winged man.

Ahead, a guard stood silently outside a door. Not clear

419

which way the soldier was facing, Spenser quietly stepped forwards. As he drew closer, he realised the fae had his back turned, intently looking through a crack in the doorway. A gurgled cry came from the cell. Raising his arm, Spenser brought the edge of his hand down swiftly on the fae's neck. The soldier dropped in a heap of wings and armour to the floor before the noise petered out.

Without any guilt, Spenser pushed the guard aside with his foot and peered through the slight opening himself. Inside the dark cell, Lyrus bent over a figure bound in a chair, holding a slim instrument to its throat. In his other hand, a needle-like pick, delicately curved and dripping. Spenser could smell the tang from the droplet of fresh blood, heightened with Lifeforce.

"Unless you want to lose another tooth, tell me who you are!" Lyrus hissed. Spenser realised Lyrus's tenuous control was already pushed to its limit. The man mumbled something incoherently, then seemed to laugh. As the laugh descended into a cough, the man's bloody spittle landed on Lyrus's chest plate. Lyrus lost patience and leaned closer, looming over his captive. As he had his back to the door, Spenser could only picture the snarl on Lyrus's face.

The needle-pick dropped to the floor, and Lyrus gripped the man's face. His other hand holding the curved knife retracted from the man's neck and hovered over an eye. Instead of looking at the weapon, the puffy eye looked beyond Lyrus's shoulder and made contact with Spenser.

Spenser inched the door open a little further. The man in the chair suddenly kicked upwards, his knee contacting with Lyrus's groin. Caught off guard, Lyrus grunted in pain as he doubled up, lashing down with the knife. His victim gasped, dodging his head to one side. The curved instrument missed his neck by a whisper.

Sensing his moment, Spenser dashed into the cell and without any hesitation, chopped Lyrus on the back of his exposed neck with his hand. He couldn't resist a smile as he watched the tormentor of so many drop to the ground.

"Are you alright?" Spenser approached the man on the chair with concern. Joshua looked up and Spenser was relieved to see the broadest grin spread across his face.

"He ha' 'at comin'," Joshua thickly mumbled out, then swallowed the blood gathering at the back of his throat. "'Hank you."

"Who are you?"

"Does i'matter?" Joshua replied. "Can you 'elp me ge' out of 'ere, or do you jus' wan' a'sers too?"

Spenser put a finger to his mouth, and Joshua nodded his understanding. Moving around to the back of the chair Joshua was sitting on, he untied the ropes pinning him down.

"Where did he hurt you?" Spenser asked.

Joshua leaned over and spat on the floor. "Toof, eye," Joshua grunted out, not willing to grumble about the other bruises he had sustained.

"It will heal soon enough. I've heard he can do far worse," Spenser reassured the man. Indeed, it was lucky Lyrus hadn't moved onto his wings just yet. The ropes fell free and Joshua shook his hands to restore feeling.

Checking the doorway and Lyrus, Spenser turned to look at the captive he had freed. "It is not a good time to be a prisoner," Spenser whispered. "I suggest you go back to where you came from." He paused as Joshua tried to stand. "Where is that exactly?"

Joshua smiled and, using his cuff, wiped yet more

blood which had seeped from his lips. He swallowed again, then in a clearer voice stated, "I am not leaving until I find Annabella."

"Annabella?"

"Do you know her? She has pretty remarkable wings, about so high?" Joshua held his hand to his shoulder. "I've been told she was brought here, to Naturae?"

Spenser tightened his lips, then glanced over the clothing Joshua wore. Distinctly English with his breeches, fine (if soiled) jacket, and expensive-looking but slightly tatty shoes. He looked like a nobleman who had been through hell and back. He was certain that this was the man his Princess mourned for. "Do you mean Princess Aioffe?" Spenser said.

Joshua cursed to himself - of course they wouldn't call her Annabella! That blow to the head must have knocked the sense out of him. "I know her by many names, but yes, Aioffe," he said, unable to keep the excitement from his voice as he watched the gentleman's mouth twitch up slightly. "Where is she?"

Spenser glanced back at the door, frowning a warning. Joshua's urgent desperation was obvious as he grabbed Spenser's arm. "Is she here? Is she alright? Safe?"

"Are you... her husband?" Spenser studied the man's face through the gloom of the cell, although he already half knew. Aside from the blood and swollen eye, he was a handsome young man. Strong too. Immediately, he approved.

"Yes," Joshua said. His rescuer hadn't answered the question. "Am I too late?"

"She thinks you are dead!"

Joshua attempted a lopsided grin, "Seems to happen a lot these days." Joshua flexed his wings as much as he

422

could in the small space.

"How did you find Naturae?" Spenser whispered.

"I had some help to get here." Joshua's one good eye flared as he remembered, "Nemis! You must find her. She came down here with us. And Fairfax."

Spenser put his hand on the man's arm, "I fear you should hurry elsewhere now, Aioffe is not here."

"Then where is she?" The anguish in Joshua's voice evidenced his pain. To have come so close, only to find her gone again.

"Not far, but there is something happening. I'm not sure exactly what, but Naturae is not a safe place right now."

Joshua pursed his lips together. "I'm not sure it ever could be with the likes of him here." They both glanced down at Lyrus, still out cold on the earth.

Spenser said wryly, "You have met Lyrus before, I gather?"

"Yes. I barely survived. But, I need to find Aioffe and my friends!"

Spenser corrected him, "Princess Aioffe." He poked his head around the door before quickly pulling it back in. "There are guards further down, your friends must be in other holes nearby." Drawing out Uffer's keys from his pocket, Spenser faced Joshua with a smile. "I can see to their release, but, unless they can fly, they won't be able to come with us to find Aioffe."

Joshua thought for a moment. Even though Aioffe was foremost in his mind, there seemed little sense in dashing off to find her when he knew Nemis and Fairfax were close by, and also in imminent danger. This well dressed, well intentioned, gentleman had the means to release them. He grasped the opportunity. "Free them, then we go to Aioffe."

"As you wish," Spenser said. This escapade was stretching the boundaries of what he had intended to achieve. But then, he reasoned to himself, he wasn't sure how much longer he would be staying in Naturae anyway. Or if he ever wanted to return. "Wait here." Spenser gestured towards Lyrus, "I suggest you restrain him whilst I free your friends. Especially that young witch!" Spenser winked before disappearing into the tunnel.

"My pleasure." Joshua made no attempt to keep the relish from his voice.

Straightening his jacket, Spenser headed along the passage to approach the guards there. "I have authority to see these prisoners," he said imperiously. "Your Captain orders you to report to the training room. Immediately."

"Where is he now then?" piped up the soldier standing outside the further cell.

"Still seeing to the prisoner, back there I believe." Spenser dismissed the question and carried on towards the doorways, keys in hand as if this was official business. "I have no doubt he will join you in his own time. Get to it, soldier!" Too nervous to query why an Ambassador would be the Beneath, but also in possession of keys, the guards flew off through the darkness of the tunnels.

The attractive witch was in the first cell Spenser unlocked. She swivelled around, her fingers leaving tracks in the dirt as soon as she heard the click of the lock. Fear turned to relief as she recognised his profile through the dim aperture.

"You!" She breathed. "I hoped it would be."

"I am Ambassador Spenser." He flashed a smile through the darkness at her. "I hope you are not hurt?"

"Nemis," she replied, "and thanks, I am unharmed.

424

Just... what is this place?"

Spenser reached out his arm and helped her up. As she dusted off her skirts, he realised she was really very young, yet the speed of her recovery and courage impressed him further.

Holding open the door, he said, "This is the Beneath. One as beautiful as yourself should not spend any more time here. I am about to go and find your feisty friend, and the winged one is just taking care of something in his cell," Spenser told her. He beamed, then bowed slightly, with his arm pointing towards the gloom outside. "My Lady?"

Nemis hoped he couldn't see her blushing as she walked past him, into the tunnel. Just past her cell door, a small lamp nestled in the earth wall, casting just enough flickering light for Nemis to see Joshua. Bloodied, but largely in one piece. Nemis sighed deeply as he approached and silently hugged her. His wings filled the tunnel-space as he pulled back to search her face. Despite the swollen eye, she could read his determined look. Nemis reached her hand to his shoulder, and Joshua winced. Nemis's eyes told him there was still much to be frightened of.

Fairfax had heard voices, and the earlier screams. As Spenser unlocked his door, he rushed out as if he had been leaning next to it, furious energy leeching from his every pore. Barging past Spenser with barely a second glance, he stood poised for a fight on tiptoes, jumping around with clenched fists. As he sprang about, no-one appeared to hurt or restrain him. Jutting his head forward, Fairfax stopped bouncing, peering instead through the dim light at the figure who released him. As he wasn't wearing a suit of armour - instead, a rather fine dark red cape which he immediately coveted - Fairfax lowered his arms and grinned.

An eyebrow already raised as he tasted the lad's Lifeforce, Spenser couldn't help but grin as well. The young pup's energy was infectious. And very alluring.

Joshua and Nemis rushed up towards them, but before they could say anything, a great creak from above echoed through the passages. Dust poured down onto their heads. Joshua barked, "Aioffe! We need to find her. Now!"

They felt a tremor in the earth beneath them, and the tiny lamp fell from its niche. As it broke into pieces, the oil within ignited. A brief flare of light temporarily blinded the fae, but Nemis and Fairfax could see clouds of dirt thrown into the air by the upheaval.

Ahead of them, the tunnel was beginning to collapse! Fairfax pushed Nemis, spun her around and shouted, "Run!"

Spenser recovered first and, grabbing another lamp from its hole as he ran, held it up high and set off back through the tunnels. His feet barely touched the ground as he started to fly. The draft from his wings urging the others to follow as fast as they could before they lost him. Joshua grabbed Nemis's hand and together they ran as the earth beneath them vibrated, Fairfax close on their heels. The tunnels turned, twisted and blurred but the newcomers had no choice but to trust Spenser.

Joshua realised that they must be nearing the outside as he inhaled gulps of increasingly fresher-smelling air. Nemis stumbled on her skirts, unused to the pace they were running at. With Joshua yanking on her hand, she somehow kept up with his longer legs. Clumps of soil sporadically dropped on or close to them as they rushed on, dislodged by more creaks they could hear from deep within the earth itself.

Spenser flew on ahead of them, then paused at a junction, uncertain as to which turning to take. He raised his lamp so they could see him as they caught up, whilst he inhaled deeply to identify which route was the closest to the outside.

Then suddenly, they turned a corner and the dawn light flooded into the gaping hole of the exit. As they tumbled out, Joshua let go of Nemis's hand. He looked back at where they had emerged. From within the depths, a loud thud of earth heralded the closing of the tunnels.

Circling the clearing, a breeze whisked shreds of leaves and twigs on the dusty ground. Spenser looked up at the trunks and his heart sank. One of the trees, although not a supporting one, was swaying more than the others - even in such a relatively light wind. He knew, where one was falling, uprooting, the rest could follow. "You must find Aioffe on your own," he said, turning to Joshua. "I have to warn the courtiers their homes are no longer a sanctuary." He glanced up at the staterooms leading off from the main palace anxiously. "Today, nowhere is."

Nemis looked at the trees surrounding them, the expression of wonder from the last occasion she stood here now replaced with fear. "It is nearly time," she said quietly to Joshua. "You must go to the stone circle."

Spenser frowned in confusion. How did she know about the stones? But Joshua knew, and without hesitation he launched himself upward.

CHAPTER 35 - THE STANDING STONES

In the distance across the lochs, faintly glowing in the dawn light, was the larger Circle of Faeth at Brodgar. South of the slim landmass dividing the two lakes was the older, more spiritually significant Stones of Stenness. The jagged points of the monoliths stood proudly visible from all directions in the flat landscape. What was less visible, except from a higher vantage point, was the deep ditch which surrounded the stones - the henge. Approaching the great stones, embedded securely so they reached always for the sky, Aioffe felt her heart soar. Flying low over the loch with Uffer frantically flapping behind her, she dipped her fingers, trailing them in the cool, clear waters.

Soaring higher to wonder and appreciate the aerial view, enjoyed by only fae and birds, she noticed the henge depths were filled with worker fae. A feeling of apprehension swept over her, which Uffer seemed to sense. He stretched out his fingers towards her, pointing down with the other hand, and smiled. Following his lead, she saw a figure standing next to one of the stones. Thane.

As they drew closer, they parted and Uffer headed towards the middle of the circle. Flying around the outer ditch, whispers of dissent, cackles of anticipation floated up and over the edges. Aioffe realised Thane had not been completely honest about the agreed purpose of the gathering. Amongst the throng, it chilled her to see branches and shells fashioned into rudimentary weapons of clubs and spears. Simultaneously, the energy of the crowd hit her like a wave; she felt if she reached out with her fingertips, the Lifeforce might become tangible, visible.

Uffer alighted on the ground by the old hearth at the centre of the circle and Thane approached him. "Do you have it?" Thane asked. Uffer handed over a small heavy pouch which Aioffe had passed to him on the journey there. They turned to watch her, still circling the twelve monoliths. People started to notice - the maroon fabric of her gown flapping in the wind, bright against the grey sarcen stones.

"Workers of Naturae, I am Princess Aioffe," she called out, swooping up towards the centre of the circle so she could be heard all around. "Your Princess of this realm. In line to be your Queen." It was a bold claim, she knew, but she had learned from many mortal Kings the power of declaring oneself in charge. She continued, a little louder. "My name means The Beginning. It also means to breathe, to live." She paused again to allow the voices to quieten a little. "I have known many lives during my time away from you all, and today, I choose to begin again. Standing by you. *With* you.

The murmurings fell silent, and Aioffe could see heads turning towards her, tilting up so they could get a better view. This was fresh territory for a Royal, addressing the masses, but Aioffe knew she would have no other chance but now. Thane had gathered them as requested, only she could now unite them.

"But I cannot lead alone. I am but one. You are the backbone of Naturae if I am its head. We must work together to build a new path for us all."

As she flew closer to the henge edge, Aioffe tried to meet as many eyes as she could before continuing.

"I ask you - as your guardian, soon-to-be creator, and

the embodiment of your hopes for a better life - join me. Honouring our past and looking to our future. Together, we can build a fairer Fae. So please, lay down your weapons and work with me. Let us look to a tomorrow where there is life, not decay. Where we can all choose who we are destined to be. As I have."

The faces staring up at her looked sceptical still, although they were at least listening. Without delay, Aioffe carried on.

"I am not asking that you give up your dreams of living as royalty. We should all be able to live well, not just a select few. That is the way in which realms and Fae-kind can prosper. But think on this before you decide..."

Aioffe sought Thane and beckoned. As he flew up to hover by her side, he unwrapped the pouch, and passed it to her reverently. Spinning slowly so all could see her, Aioffe blew gently on the plant. A pale tendril which had grown during the emotional meeting with her mother stretched visibly taller, stretching towards the hazy sunlight which peeked through the mists. From the corner of her eye, she could see Thane watching her closely, urging her and the plant on.

"Is it better to be living in hope of prosperity," Thane said as the crowd watched expectantly. "Live in hope that there is continuity? There is a way. A way we can co-exist together. Choose our future, together."

Aioffe held the plant aloft and continued her show of unity. "Many countries, many other cultures and realms have achieved this. I know some of you have seen them. They have begun to give a voice to their people. I promise I will give voice to all of you, when it is my time to rule."

The tendril swelled and a bud formed. She began to hope that her plan was working when she noticed some workers could not take their eyes off the plant growing in their midst. Aioffe breathed once more on the leaves, drawing in the energy the fae were unwittingly emanating. She alighted on the top of the tallest stone, calling out with renewed vigour:

"My question to you now is this - would you rather squander the short amount of time you have left here living a life you know is restricted? Limited. To only have the strength to venture within these shores? Or, would you prefer to bring forth new life to Naturae, to nurture and live amongst in peace? Create a society which shares its burdens. Shares its leadership so that all are represented. This much I can offer. This is your choice today."

Aioffe turned slowly with the plant in her hands, trying to show it to as many people as possible from her high vantage point. However, for those deep in the ditches, she worried that the small green shoots weren't visible enough.

"I want you all to see that I bring hope. Only a royal wields the gift of creation. Of growth. But, if you threaten our line of Queens, indeed, threaten my mother the Queen, that choice of a future for us all will not be yours to make." She was shouting now, in the hope that her words would convince those who could not see the growing plant, or did not want to. Aioffe half expected people to start calling back, challenging her. Telling her to go even, that she wasn't wanted. A part of her almost wanted them to, just so that she could see what sort of adversity she was facing. But, as they didn't, she threw down her conditions and hoped.

"I cannot rule where I am unwanted. The choice I made, and agreed with the Queen today, was that if *you*, my brothers and sisters, daughters and sons of the vines, wanted the fae of Naturae to continue their long tradition.... then I would make that possible. And I can."

Once more, she breathed in their energy. The crowd's attention seemed fully on her, curiosity at least was helping. As she exhaled, the bud opened and red petals unfurled. The workers nearest to her, who could see the miracle clearly, were unable to contain their joy. Before their own eyes, magic had been delivered and their smiles were reflected in a smattering of claps.

But, Aioffe knew there were many more behind them who could only hear her voice, could not see the plant which had convinced those closer. The murmurings began, the frustration of inactivity when action had been promised started to sweep through from the rear. They had not arrived here for a demonstration or to hear promises from a distant and unknown royal. They had come prepared for a fight.

Thane flew to the edges of the henge, and motioned them to settle down. "Let her continue, she has not yet finished," he ordered, glancing back at her. Aioffe could see his face was drawn, his dilemma as the mood of the masses wavered.

The voices fell silent. His authority was held out of respect, his leadership proven. Aioffe nodded to him and rose slightly higher so all could see her again. That the plant had responded to her was enough to spur her onto the final stage of her request. Her heart raced as she pleaded.

"Now, will you join me and live in peace until that time comes? It will not be long, for I know the Queen tires. But let us give her a natural end. Not at the tip of a sword or a knife, but a quiet end to a sad lifetime.

In the meantime, she will agree, I know now, that we

can start to grow this new life. The realm which we all dream of, can come together.

This is my promise to you: allow this Queendom to pass naturally into my hands and I will listen to you. Nurture you. Show you how we can survive. We will live in freedom. If you choose to continue to work with us - as a collective, a community - we will survive. If you choose to believe in Naturae - in us - believe in a shared responsibility for each other's happiness, we will do more than thrive. We can create our own magic, our own Lifeforce."

Aioffe fell silent. Thane paused also, hovering over the ditches as he assessed the mood of the crowd. From the far side of the circle, a lone voice cried out, "Our time will come!" More voices joined. She heard, "That plant was probably gonna flower anyway, I don't even recognise it." Another voice grumbled, "Why are we wasting time here?"

Before long, as Aioffe and Thane circled desperately trying to make eye contact with the fae below them, the chant rippled through the crowd. With a speed which shocked Aioffe, the voices morphed together into one call. "Our time is now!"

From deep within the ditches, a thumping of feet and wings began. Aioffe looked at Thane in panic. The chanting took on an ugly tone, words spat from angry faces tired of mistreatment. Mistrustful of everything. And maybe everyone?

Shooting her an unreadable dark look, Thane rose into the air. His stubby brown wings blending into the darkness of his clothing as he rose higher, silhouetted against the sun. She could tell he was wavering, pulled between loyalty to his own and hope. He hovered above the tallest monolith, the watch stone, towering at three times his height. Would he abandon her and return to his kind? His gaze seemed to pour through her as she landed.

Then, he turned away.

Aioffe fell to her knees. She hadn't done enough. She bowed her head as tears ran down her face. So strange - she had felt so empowered by their energy just a few moments earlier. The flower had been so easy to grow. She knew in her heart that she - they - could have accomplished so much more, if they had only believed her, and been patient.

She sensed a flurry of wings next to her, then a fingers touched her shoulder. Dear Uffer, she thought, what a comfort he had been these last few days. And Thane, she had failed him as well. She closed her eyes and felt a sob rise in her throat.

A gentle hand cupped her lowered chin. Rough fingers smoothed the tears from her cheek in a familiar, comforting gesture. She opened her eyes.

"Joshua!" she gasped. Here, in front of her! Alive!

CHAPTER 36 - SWARM

Lana stopped flitting around her chambers. She had begun almost as soon as Aioffe had left - a frantic effort to ward off the anxiety, regain control of herself. Pacing had failed to calm her mind though, so she had started to fly, hoping to tire herself into oblivion as she was used to doing. The act of unburdening herself she called into question with every step, each flap of her wings.

She regretted it. The memories of that pain rippled through her, disrupting her tenuous balance. If anything, the yearning for Sigurd, for his Lifeforce, was stronger than it had ever been. She needed his strength now. Change was imminent, and she couldn't bear it.

Picking up one of the shreds of parchment still lying on the floor, Lana looked at the mangled half of the phrase again. 'Out the blight' she read, the letters blurring in front of her. She grabbed another piece, 'to kill' written upon it. Another - 'the darkness.' That was all she could see, Lana thought. Her eyes were playing tricks on her. All she saw since unburdening herself to Aioffe was light and dark. The room was now just shades of shadows, and her head hurt. Whatever she tried, this darkness kept threatening to consume her. And she was terrified of it.

The urge to re-write the familiar stanza, as if to drain her overflowing mind of the terrible words, nearly overcame her. Whirling around, she started to beat her wings angrily. The down-draft lifted the pieces up, tossing them into the air about her. Her feet left the floor and she rose up, spinning around and around. The light parchment shreds fluttered as snow, twirling and dancing before sashaying to the ground. Taunting her with their presence.

As she descended to the floor, the Queen looked around her confettied chamber and sank to her knees. She'd made no promises to Aioffe to get rid of the wretched curses. Hours later, despite tearing and scrunching, the words lay all around to torment her.

And yet, could there be any hope? A twist to the prophecy? Aioffe seemed so sure, so confident that she would make a difference. Convinced with the conviction of youth that just by trying, she could bring the workers around, and curb their rebellion. She had even indicated a willingness to rule. If her terms were met.

But that meant the curse must be broken. Aioffe must be made to see that the prophecy - her prophecy - must be fulfilled. There was no other option. She would have to trust Aioffe to do the right thing when she returned. Only then would she be free. Only in death would she find Valhalla, and Sigurd.

Lana stood, and walked unsteadily to the door. She needed to be ready to accept her death in more formal surroundings. She would go to the High Hall and wait. Wait for the light.

*****

Fairfax took Nemis's hand and together they walked around the clearing. Spenser had abruptly flown off through the trees, abruptly leaving them alone, saying nothing further to explain or tell them what to do now. "I thought it would be greener," observed Nemis, "less... dead."

Chandeliers of cobwebs dripping with beads of mist in the lower branches lent the forest around them a certain elegance. Palatial columns, the trunks of the trees surrounding them and supporting - becoming - the buildings above. Yet even in the dawn light they were dull. As she looked up at the branches looming ominously high above them, Nemis shivered. Tall as the trees grew, and completely at odds with the barren, treeless landscape of the other islands, their deep roots were withering. Foundations crumbling. Her heart filled with pity for the ancient woods.

Fairfax pointed to a tree close to the tunnel entrance, leaning at an angle, almost nudging against the overhanging balcony above them. "That could topple the whole citadel," he said, as he led them towards steps on the far side of the clearing. After their claustrophobic escape, the thought of more falling trees made him even more on edge, jumpy. At least the ground had stopped shaking, for now.

Finding a staircase, they ascended with care - the treads looked worn and neither wanted to lean on the rickety guide rail gracefully curving around the currently straight tree. Once on the balcony, Nemis touched the carvings adorning the edges of the wooden platform. Her sensitive fingers traced the rotting swirls, touching the faded ancient magic within.

Fairfax approached the huge double doors and paused to examine them himself. Reaching twice his height and firmly closed, his curiosity urged him to push against them. "We shouldn't," Nemis said, although she too was curious. "I feel like this is the sort of place you have to be invited into?"

"No-one here to invite us in," Fairfax said, somewhat nervously. Shrugging, Nemis joined him in heaving the great doors open. They entered into a high vaulted but dim atrium, the dawn light peeking through the ceiling.

Glancing up, Nemis saw that the roof was crumbling inside, exposing the chamber to the elements. Unclean pools of water stained the once polished white wooden floor as their boots slapped through. At the far side, another set of double doors - slightly smaller than the exterior ones - glinted with faded silver inlay. The silence was eerie. Even Fairfax seemed to sense the desolation threatening, his skin pale and pinched.

Taking one door each, they slowly pulled open the inner doors to reveal a large circular atrium, corridors like branches leading off from a central trunk. Rounding the smooth tree, Nemis and Fairfax paused as they reached another set of doors, ornately carved with silver symbols again. Laying her hands on the wood, she felt its power, an ancient call inviting her to investigate.

They entered the cavernous High Hall, gazing down the long and narrow walls, to a raised platform at the end in near darkness. Fairfax followed her down the cathedral-like chamber, marvelling as their eyes adjusted in the quiet space. Both were awestruck by the naturally soaring arches formed from enormous branches, now greying with cobwebs obscuring the carvings. They were both still looking up when a flash of green and black hurtled silently towards them from the back of the room.

Instinctively, Fairfax waved his arms wildly, as if to swat an enormous fly away. His right arm made contact. Such was the force of his swipe, the creature was driven off course. It wheeled around with frightening speed, acrobatically spinning until its legs landed a glancing blow on his shoulders. Fairfax dropped to the ground and Nemis stood there with her mouth agape, staring at him.

Before she could say anything, the thing had circled around to her, grabbing her arm, yanking it back. Nemis was forced into bending forwards. Wrestling to get away, she managed only a step, but the grip remained iron-strong.

"Who are you?" The voice hissed close to her ear. The creature smelt stale - Nemis couldn't quite place it for a moment, then realised it was the stench of decay, of dried blood and acidic sweat. "Who is he?" Its screech somehow echoed with longing and of fear. Nemis shook her head, trying to push away a vision which threatened to overwhelm her just as she was weakened.

Nemis cried out in pain as the winged creature pushed her to her knees. From the corner of her eye, Nemis glimpsed Fairfax pushing himself off the floor. Straining her head around, Nemis saw only a cloud of black hair in her periphery, but she heard the pounding footsteps - running, then jumping to reach up to her assailant.

A scream pierced the air, full of anguish as well as pain, and Nemis felt her arm wrench as she was whirled around. They fell, awkwardly, into a pile of limbs and clothing, wings and boots. The creature let out another short scream, high pitched and shrill. Nemis, miraculously atop the bundle of people, made to roll off, but a white-knuckled hand still gripped her arm.

She looked down quickly. Fairfax's boot was poking out from under her dress. On the floor to the side of it, an enormous translucent green wing was torn, ripped and barely hanging on by its thicker edge. She felt a head move underneath her ribs, near her shoulder. Nemis realised she was on top of the writhing creature, who was on top of Fairfax.

A sharp pain pierced her skin. Was it teeth? Biting into her! Yelping, Nemis rolled the other way off the bundle, rotating her arm at the same time. This forced the grip to release, and she tumbled away, onto the wooden floor, landing on all fours. She glanced under her arms, catching a glimpse of the two remaining bodies locked together, wrestling for control.

The creature emitted another scream, of frustration, but Fairfax managed to untangle himself from beneath her. He shuffled, scooting on his bottom, away from the thing. Through the snarl twisting its face, Nemis now saw that the creature was a fae, hair floating around its head; the thin frame of it's body shaking. A broken wing hung forlornly from its back. Rather than darting around, its eyes looked vacant, glazed with a cloud.

Nemis's face fell, the pain it must be in. She must be in, Nemis corrected herself, as the fae wore an ornate, long shift. The vision threatened to overwhelm her again. Nemis was no longer able to resist the icy edges trickling up her arms, reaching through her neck and into her eyes. As she fell backwards, eyelids closing, Fairfax seemed to grow. Was he coming closer to her? Or had he become something else... It confused her.

Nemis felt herself shift and the sight she now held was darker, blurred. The vision was narrower too. Then the sensation of yearning overtook her completely. A man, tall and blond, stood in front of her, over her. He smelled divine, delicious. Of fresh air and freedom. Her mouth became moist, filled with anticipation. As though she were leaning in towards him, he grew and Nemis felt the pull of her heart, tugging them together.

"Sigurd..." A wispy voice reached her ears, the unfamiliar name breathed out as a caress. But then, thin hands reached forwards and began to encircle his neck. Nemis knew this was not entirely a tender gesture, but one driven by longing, a desire to be as one.

But the man did not yield willingly. With every heartbeat, the vision dimmed a little more. The man was fighting, pulling away. Resisting. Nemis felt the anger, the pain that this was causing, but she was unable to break free. The man let out a bellow of rage - loud and somehow familiar to Nemis. Slightly manic.

Then there was nothing, a dreadful darkness.

Nemis felt herself released.

The thud close by made her eyes fly open. Turning her head, with her own, clear sight she saw the crumpled form on the floor not ten paces from her. Standing over it was Fairfax, his face utterly bewildered. His arm still hung in the air with fist clenched.

"Sigurd..." Pale lips whispered out again, blank eyes rolled towards Fairfax. Then, with a long exhale, the broken neck no longer able to support its weight. The tousled hair dropped as it's head twisted to the floor.

Nemis's eyes widened as the body then began to break off, flying up into the air in shards of green glittering snowflakes. By the time Nemis had drawn her breath in, the essence of the creature had collapsed in on itself, disintegrated and drawn up into the heights of the chamber. Only a silver crown endured, rolling as it circled rapidly on the smooth wooden floor. Fairfax let out a cry, "Oh!" as its sonorous announcement ceased.

*****

Aioffe flung herself into Joshua's arms and they clung to each other as he propelled them upwards, away from the thuds and chants arising from the ditches. Without looking back, Aioffe fell limp, succumbing to his embrace. Allowing herself to be carried - just for a moment - by her

441

lover's strong arms. Feeling the wind in her skirts with the speed of his flight, she raised her head from where it was buried in his shoulder and looked up at him. She could barely believe that the curve of his chin, his tousled hair and gentle hands were here, with her, carrying her.

He slowed in the middle of the lake and hovered. Flapping her wings now, she supported herself as they drew apart to face each other. Aioffe had never seen a grin form on his face as large as the one he now wore and knew her own matched it. Still drinking in the sight of her, he lowered his head and they kissed.

Joshua could have stayed like that, in the bright sunlight high above the lands, forever. He felt his whole being once again melt into hers, perfectly fitting as it always had. She sighed. Pulling away from the embrace before she got too lost, she exclaimed, "I thought you were dead!"

"I nearly was." The smile on his face now so wide she saw the wrinkles straining painfully around his eyes and a hole where he had lost a tooth. He said, "I thought you might be too, but I never lost faith!"

As they hovered, her eyes and fingers running over his head, hair, neck - still not quite certain he had been returned to her, she saw him wince. "You are hurt?"

"Not enough to stop me finding you, Princess. You don't need worry yourself about me. I am here, that is all that matters. With you. For always. The rest we can work out."

Aioffe glimpsed from the corner of her eye a cloud of darkness rising towards them. A mass of tiny brown dots swarming upwards, hazy with wing beats. She grabbed his hand. "Not here! Hurry!" She said, pulling him higher again. Her wings beat furiously, but he kept up with her as they flew, hand in hand, across the skies.

"Where are we going, my love?" Joshua called out.

Aioffe flew on, her mind churning with indecision. With Joshua by her side, she knew they could outrun the worker swarm, and start again. The temptation to return to their old life was suddenly overwhelming. She looked at him, and he squeezed her hand as he gazed at her, grinning madly still. Why was she not smiling as brightly also? He had come so far, found her. And yet...

"Who shall we be today, my love?" He said again. Aioffe smiled then, reminded of their familiar banter. She took a deep breath and decided. "I like the name Prince. Do you?"

Joshua laughed, "I've never tried it. Do you think it will suit me?"

"I think, as long as we are together, we can make it suit each other! The title does come with a ready-made home..."

Joshua said, "I'm afraid the lovely dark tunnels are somewhat closed off now. I had hoped you meant somewhere a little brighter!"

Aioffe looked shocked, "No, the Palace above! In the trees?"

"You will have to show me around, I didn't have time to properly visit," Joshua said. "I wasn't offered that as a rooming option when I arrived. Unfortunately, I don't think Lyrus made it out of the tunnels."

"Lyrus? You were in the Beneath?" Slowing mid-air, Aioffe was desperate to find out more, but looking beyond Joshua's shoulder, she knew they had to press on.

"The tunnels caved in behind us, the earth was shaking. He was... indisposed at the time. I hope you weren't close?"

Aioffe felt little sorrow for her brother's demise - after all, she had almost killed him herself at one time. Better her cruel brother should die in the place where he seemed happiest. "What did he do to you?"

"Don't fret. We escaped. He didn't. But, I fear it won't take many more earthquakes to uproot the whole island," Joshua said with a grim face.

"It's far worse than I thought," she said worriedly.

"You are sure you want to go back?" Joshua looked over his shoulder - in the distance, the brown cloud was closing in.

"My attempt to reason with the masses failed. Mother is in danger."

"Your mother, the Queen?"

Aioffe flew ahead of him before turning to hover in front of him. She took his other hand, saying, "I owe you so many explanations, I am sorry."

He reached over and smoothed a lock of hair back behind her ear. "Let's make time for all that." He dropped a kiss on her cheek. "Definitely want to go back to Naturae though?"

"This time," Aioffe decided, "I choose to."

He squeezed her hand in acceptance. Where she went, he would be by her side from now until ever.

*****

Fairfax's panic rose. His eyes darted around the room, at Nemis, then stopped at the door. Spenser stood there, his mouth open in horror. "It wasn't my fault!" Fairfax blurted out.

"It was an accident!" Nemis concurred.

Spenser appraised the pair. He had detected no malice

in the boy or the woman, but you could never be sure with other creatures. No, he decided, they were telling the truth. That only left the question of what to do now. He straightened his shoulders and adjusted his cape whilst he played for time. "You must leave. Now."

"But what about her?" Nemis said, "Who was she?"

"The Queen," Spenser replied darkly. "I fear you have merely hastened what was an inevitable demise." He was not sad she had passed, he admitted to himself. Rather, his concern was for Aioffe and whether she was still alive to restore Naturae.

Fairfax gasped, "The Queen?" In his next breath, he wondered at his own chaos. "I am going to Hell for sure now."

"That rather depends on your definition of Hell, young man." Spenser arched his eyebrow. "If I am correct, then all manner of Hell is headed this way shortly, anyway." He beckoned the pair, saying, "We need to get you out of Naturae. You can worry about what happens in your afterlife later."

Nemis couldn't stand, gazing instead at the silver circlet on the floor. There had been no warning of this calamity in her visions of Naturae. Although she was sad for the loss of a life, some part of her felt this shift in fortune was positive. Already the room around her was less oppressive, brighter.

She looked at the daemon then, his youthful face morose beneath his unkempt hair. The energy which usually exuded from him seemed spent, along with his confidence and bluster. He appeared as a frightened child might, terrified of a now uncertain future. Her heart swelled with gratitude. This boy had saved her life, again. He also had been lucky to survive the Queen's crazed attack, and in fighting for it, accidental tragedy had struck. Although, having been inside the Queen's mind, she felt the touch of inevitability about her death. There had been curiously no fear about it, no regard for what might happen to her soul.

Closing her eyes, she reached into Fairfax's mind, touching his hand for comfort. There, she felt the wretched turning. Multiple strands of possibility for his future, twisting and knotted. She could no more untangle the mass than he could. How could anyone understand the implications of what had been done when a simple thread could not be pulled from the bundle? No wonder he felt the constant urge to pull a strand of fate and see what happens. Curiosity and chaos were bedfellows in a daemon. The best she could do for him was ease the frantic motion of the twists, slow it down in the hopes he might calm.

Fairfax gripped her hand so hard, Nemis knew she had reached him. She stood, pulling him with her, and they walked in silence towards Spenser. Neither looked back as they made their way out towards the sunlight.

*****

Aioffe swooped down to the balcony platform with Joshua in tow, both landing lightly. Turning to him, she said, "I must find my mother." She placed a hand on his chest and warned, "The workers will be here very shortly. We must stand with the Queen and try once more to reason with them. Perhaps with her by my side, they will see we are united in what I proposed for the future."

"You cannot reason with a rabble!" Joshua was shocked she should even think of it. They both knew too well the fear of being chased by angry or vengeful crowds. He looked beyond the rooftops of camouflaged buildings, to where he could make out the cloud of the swarm, approaching them through the skies.

"We don't have time to find your mother anyway," he said, pointing.

Aioffe saw, and her face took on that determined set which he knew so well. Just as she turned towards the doors at the end of the wooden expanse, someone emerged. Joshua recognised the man who had freed them, as he rushed towards them calling out, "Princess Aioffe! You are safe!"

Aioffe smiled at him warmly, and Joshua felt a flash of jealousy. Before he could ask who the man was to her, Spenser shot him a grateful look, then turned to Aioffe and blurted out his problem. "There's been an accident, your Highness. More than one actually."

"I know about Lyrus and the tunnels, Ambassador. Where is my mother?" Aioffe asked. Something in his tone warned her there was more.

Spenser avoided answering her question. "We need to get these people off Naturae, your Highness." He glanced beyond her and saw the brown cloud advancing. His lips tightened.

Joshua ran over to Nemis and Fairfax, who emerged from the doors behind Spenser. "These are my friends," he told Aioffe, barely hiding his relief at seeing them again. Aioffe frowned, recognising a guilty look on the boy's downcast face.

"What was the accident you were going to tell me of?" Aioffe turned to face Spenser again, but her eyes remained on the boy. Spenser flicked his eyes at Fairfax, then carefully spoke. "Your mother, I'm afraid to say, is dead."

Aioffe's face fell and she reached for Joshua. Wrenching her eyes from the boy who was slicking down his hair, she pleaded with Spenser, "Tell me, are you sure?"

"You are Queen now," Spenser said. "She is definitely no longer with us. I saw her dissipate." He paused, then said formally, "I am so sorry, your Highness, to be the bearer of this news. And for your loss."

Gasping as the implications started to sink in, suddenly Aioffe whirled and flew at Fairfax. Frightened of repeating his past mistakes, this time, Fairfax brought his hands up to protect his face and ducked down.

"It was you! You did this!" Having pulled herself up just before making contact with the young daemon, Aioffe railed at him. Her wings stood proud of her slim torso, her arms wide and fingers ready to grasp. Her glare, so like Lana's, was enough to whither.

"It was an accident!" Fairfax said, muffled by his own jacket.

Nemis stepped forwards, "Your Highness, I believe it was an accident also. She, the Queen, flew at us! Out of nowhere! We meant no harm but she just... attacked." Aioffe's head swivelled around, acknowledging Nemis for the first time. There was a bloody patch just above her breasts, the red soaked and still damp on her grubby blue robe. Aioffe's body, remained in its attack stance, poised to defend her accusation.

"My love," Joshua said, "I owe my life to Nemis and Fairfax here. I do not think them capable of deliberately causing harm."

Recalling the times her mother had rushed at her, how fast she had appeared, dancing away after landing a blow, Aioffe knew the woman was telling the truth. She studied the boy for a moment, taking in his long, unkempt hair, his stature and the smell of something emanating from him. There was an attractive tinge to the scent; the more she breathed it in, the more alluring she felt it become. She wondered whether the youth realised he was so enticing to their kind. She also smelt the fear radiating from him. Lana's death may have been his fault, but accidental nonetheless.

Breathing deeply to calm herself, Aioffe felt the weight of one responsibility - her mother's last request - slip from her, and another burden replace it. Joshua's hand then rested on her shoulder. This time she would not have to face the hordes alone.

"We should get them out of Naturae," Spenser urged. "It is not safe here, perhaps for any of us."

Aioffe looked at the assembled group, her lover, friends and supporters. From above the treeline, the hum and chants of the angry swarm drifted on the wind towards them as they drew closer.

CHAPTER 37 -
METAMORPHOSIS

"Join hands! Everyone. It is time to listen to their voices!" Aioffe cried, moving to the balustrade at the edge of the landing platform. Warily, the group assembled in a line. The fae amongst them lifted their wings in readiness for a fight, or flight, forming a shimmering wall behind them. Nemis stood between Joshua and Spenser; Fairfax, his face still downcast and reluctant, moved himself to stand apologetically next to Aioffe. Joshua and Aioffe braced so closely to each other in the middle of the line, their wings beat as one.

The cloud of brown workers streamed over the treetops and approached, their stubby wings humming. At the front, leading their charge, was Thane. As he saw the group of people along the balcony, he held up his arms and slowed. Behind him, the throng paused, hovering with weapons still in their hands. The worker's faces were grim with determination and expectation of carnage.

"The Queen is dead!" Aioffe called out. "Our time - yours and mine - has come!"

Taken by surprise, and expecting a battle, the crowds' energy dipped momentarily as this announcement disarmed them. Aioffe watched as disappointment spread over some faces, frustration appearing on others. They looked around at each other, unsure of the impact of this revelation.

"Let me hear your voices!" she continued. "Our time has come! Tell me how you want to work as one?"

At first, no-one said anything. Then Uffer called from

within the throng, loud in his deep clear voice: "I stand with you Princess! I know you will listen, as you have to me before."

A few fae hovering next to him turned and glared. Without taking his eyes from Aioffe, he ignored their mutters of 'traitor', and pushed his way forward. Uffer alighted on the balcony and walked to stand shoulder to shoulder with Spenser.

Aioffe smiled at him and he smiled nervously back. He had made his brave decision whilst in the midst of the swarm, listening himself to their chatter. Uffer knew that other fae needed to see they also could stand with Aioffe, talk to her as he had.

But he left behind confusion. Those who had been closer to Aioffe at the circle, and had been persuaded by her offer of hope, turned to other workers close to them, seeking encouragement to follow Uffer's lead. Swept up in solidarity, then flying - which was very tiring - this was the first chance many older worker fae had to discuss what had been said at the Circle of Faeth. Objections raised, like a flock of birds bickering for morsels of food, and arguments broke out. Before long, an array of shouting, and the odd chant, washed over the balustrade. The swarm rippled with divisive voices and discord.

Almost ignored by the disenchanted workers, Aioffe, who was desperate to hear what they were saying, lent so far over the balcony she started floating up without realising, tethered only by Joshua's hand. Joshua dropped his wings so that he could better plant his weight in his feet to steady her. Everyone on the platform tried to lean into the wall of sound, consternation on their anxious faces. Having invited the fae to voice themselves, it was impossible to pick out individual concerns and objections.

The volume grew as the fae got more and more frustrated, repeating themselves to each other and occasionally turning to shout at the group on the platform, but not being heard.

Before it could turn to anger, Thane flew forwards, between the swarm and Palace, turning so he could address both sides. He shot a look of frustration to Aioffe, then glared at the workers assembled in the clearing, so tightly packed buzzing with discussion, they appeared as one rippling sheet of mottled browns and grey. Thane drew out the horn he had used before to call them to attention once more.

The low vibration and piercing noise of the relic broke the spell, insistently pulling their focus to him. Voices gradually fell and, once he felt most eyes upon him, he addressed the hoard. "I will speak for us."

The fae turned and whispered amongst themselves, nodding their respect and gratitude to their leader for offering a solution to what had become a divisive matter. Thane hovered around small groups who whispered their concerns and opinions with urgency, disbelief.

As he fluttered between the crowd gathering an array of their thoughts, on the platform Joshua gripped his princess's hand while they waited. Despite calm faces, everyone on the balcony understood their vulnerability. One rush from the swarm and they would be overcome completely. Joshua hoped that their leader was worth their trust. He glanced at Aioffe, staring intently at Thane's progress around the fae. Did she trust him, he wondered?

After a few minutes, Thane flew up to the balcony. Clearly and loudly so they could all hear his report, he said, "Some are afraid. They do not know you. Many fear this could just mean more of the same!" Then, he laid down their biggest challenge. "You can grow a plant, but how do we know you can resurrect an entire, dead city?"

In his eyes, Aioffe saw the opportunity he was giving her. Her mouth lifted into a small affirmation and acceptance.

Thane turned directly to the crowd, hoping she could deliver. "There is little point in having a voice if we have nowhere to live!" He pumped his fist for emphasis, and faced the balcony once more. "For it to be our time, we need proof of resurrection."

Aioffe turned her head to look at Joshua, seeking his permission to reveal what they both knew. He nodded and smiled at her. "Tell them."

Her eyes twinkled back with hope and love, then she faced the fae again. "This man - this human - is my husband." Thane looked confused, and a murmur of shock spread through the crowds. Aioffe continued, her voice confident and clear, "A century ago, he was dying. As close to death as a human can be without actually being dead. Something in me at that moment poured my love and powers into resurrecting him. I believed he was supposed to live more of a life. To live with me. So I breathed, and bled. Crying tears of desperation, I wanted him to live so much! I believed so much that we had a shared future, it flowed out of me and into him."

Aioffe paused to glance at Joshua, miraculously by her side again, as he had been revived from the dead before. His eyes met hers, steady and loving. She beamed at him, her heart full of gratitude for all that he was to her and returned to her whole. Turning back to the crowd, she said, "I expected him to just recover. To just heal, as I have healed many animals and plants before. But he changed. I changed him."

Joshua slowly raised, then flapped his huge black wings to the crowd. Glittering as the sunlight bounced off their translucent panes, their height framed both himself and Aioffe in a shimmering tableau. Audible gasps spread through the swarm. Everyone knew - fae were pupated! Nourished by a Queen but grown on vines! This hybrid confused some, including most of the occupants of the balcony. Spenser's mind immediately began to whirl with the possibilities which this manner of procreation presented.

Joshua, turning to face the crowds again, called out: "I am the living embodiment of your Queen's abilities, to create life from the dead. I am as much Fae as you or any other Fae-kind. I am over 119 years old, and yet," he laughed, "I look as young as the human boy you see over there!"

Fairfax tried to look a little affronted, but in truth he was stunned at the raw power which had created such a being. And envious.

"What is more," Aioffe continued, "I believe I have found a sustainable way to channel that Lifeforce we all so desperately need."

Thane approached, and the crowd followed, flocking closer still to the balcony. Their interest signified a mood shift - from aggression to opportunity, hope even. Humming - from the many wings beating as one - intensified.

"Earlier today, at Stenness, I drew on all of *your* energy." She swept her arm to include them all. "I believe, because you were all focused on one aim... with ONE purpose for gathering, the ethereal Lifeforce I need to bless was generated. By that single focus you held, Fae Lifeforce was allowed to be set free. From you - Fae-kind

- not humans!"

The eyes of the crowd seemed to widen as she demystified her powers, what made her Royal, to them. Through their reaction, Aioffe herself began to believe that this time, she would be able to convince them.

"Growing that flower for you all to see earlier has never been easier for me. Your collective drive was as powerful as any humankind's belief. But only a Royal can channel it. You need me, as much as I need you! If you want to have a future, and a free one, we must work together."

Aioffe rose slowly up from the platform, Joshua with her. They flew hand in hand through the swarm of workers, which parted to let them pass. Aioffe led them down a short pathway to a pair of huge trees which were set slightly back from the clearing. Aioffe knew the spiritual significance of Ash and Elm to her people, the origin trees they were fondly known as. Enormous bare branches now haunting the gloomy woodland, withered and lifeless.

Thane swooped down and flew behind them. As they neared the wide trunks, Aioffe turned, imploring, "Believe in me!" Hoping more would follow and join - for more would be needed if she were to succeed. But how many? Aioffe addressed the small group who had alighted close by, "I need you to think about the life we could have now. The joy of the green forest, our future, celebrating the cycles, of life..."

Standing at the base of the tree next to her, Joshua saw that most people were watching her. Some had closed their eyes whilst hovering but remained a distance away. Although the mass was largely paying attention, in their various expressions he noticed a worrying similarity. A confusion. As he considered what Aioffe was asking them to do - believe - it struck him that he had seen this same scepticism before. A congregation in Church - despite what they were being told to believe in - could still be hesitant and questioning. He knew he had also worn that expression, especially in private.

Joshua's faith in Aioffe did not waver, but rather, as he considered it, his own had grown during their absence. He believed in her, and he believed in his God, even though the path to Him was, for Joshua himself, through the comfort of his prayers and familiarity of Catholic ritual. His recent experiences flashed through his mind, and he remembered that peculiar conversation with Maister Jeffries. *"Faith is faith,"* Jeffries had muttered, *"it doesn't matter how you practise that belief, as long as you believe in something."*

Joshua glanced over the workers, so similar to look at, and he wondered if what they needed here and now, was to remind them of how much they had in common? To have a collective purpose for Aioffe to feed from? Each individual must find their own reasons to believe. Joshua thought about what he wanted out of life. What made him happiest. Maybe the workers wished for the same?

"Imagine more palaces in the sky," he called out. Even though he had no standing here, he poured into his voice the power of his conviction. "Here, on Earth, in Naturae. Palaces where you can each live freely. Small or large, they will be your home. Bountiful lands where you are your own people. Free to live as you will, love who you will." He glanced at Aioffe, "You can make your own choice. Trust yourselves to know what is right for each of you! Believe what you see before you. Believe in hope... "

Aioffe saw in Thane's eyes a light of encouragement

and approval. She reached out her hand to Thane. Together they descended to the earth below. The mood of the crowd seemed to change as they watched their representative Thane, then a few others approached to stand in solidarity with their new Queen and her unexpected consort.

Walking to the trunk of the nearest tree, Aioffe breathed in the waves of hope and expectancy. She placed her hands on the roots and exhaled. Instinctively visualising the energy as ribbons of light being pulled from all about her, then pouring out through her fingertips. The magic felt tangible, stronger than anything she had ever received in a church. All of her senses tingled and her eyes narrowed in on the dusty wood before her. She breathed out again, emptying her lungs. The air seemed to shimmer as it pulsed over the plant. Her ears picked out slight creaks in the trunk and branches, almost like a sigh of relief. She dared not look up, focussing instead on the base. She trusted the light around her to float upwards, fulfilling its promise on the green which would appear above.

Joshua landed and stood close to her, protective in case this failed. He was still wary that despite all of their efforts, the crowd would descend and ravage their Queen. One man, one Fae, could not stop them if they turned, but he was prepared to die trying to save Aioffe if it came to it. He gently touched her wings with his, knowing the sensation would keep her grounded. Through the thin edges which linked them, there was a vibration running through her, reaching him.

As he looked around at the workers surrounding them, he thought he saw a hazy vapour emanating from them. Joshua blinked, and stared above their heads at the ribbons. Focussing just on Thane, he was sure he saw a definite swirl of a shimmering something flow from his shoulders and over to Aioffe. He blinked again, and it was gone.

Rising up from the balcony, Uffer began to flit between the gathered workers, encouraging them to fly in a circular direction. He spoke with individuals he knew and could see were supporting their Princess with their intense focus. With a gentle guiding hand he encouraged, and set them flying around and around. Before long, many had joined the forming vortex which rose up from ground to above the treetops.

Down in the eye of the funnel, Joshua saw the strands of belief glow, pulsing with energy, streaming down to Aioffe.

Nemis was the first to spot the life returning to the ancient tree, causing tingles to run through her arms. Turning to Spenser, she pointed, "Look! At the tips!"

Smiling broadly, Spenser leaned over the balustrade. "She's right! Green tips!" He wrapped his arms around the witch and flew up and over the railing in a smooth move.

More fae, not flying in the vortex, joined them on the ground, circling the tree on foot as Aioffe continued to breathe life into the roots. The branches began to sprout new leaves, and those dead leaves still remaining on the tree filled and uncurled, green once more. The trunk, formerly a dull brown, took on a sheen as if re-hydrated, plump with life. Beneath their feet, the earth seemed to ripple as roots reached out and anchored themselves again.

The swarming workers slowed and clustered around the tree, enveloping it - and their queen - in a haze of brown wings. A few joined hands and smiled as the blight was replaced by fresh, green hope.

Standing up as she tilted her eyes up the trunk to see the effects of her labours, Aioffe's pale face radiated joy. Turning to Thane, Aioffe's eyes sought encouragement, and his approval. Relief swept through her as Thane grinned, lowering himself into a kneel before Aioffe. His head remained tilted up, maintaining their eye contact. This was not the gesture of a submissive. Aioffe reached out her hand, happy and grateful for what they had achieved. Her huge wings splayed behind her, glittering in the sunlight as she then drew him up to stand beside her.

Together they watched as their people examined the tree, testing it, flexing the branches to see if it would break. Satisfied there was no trickery, the workers alighted on the ground and stood in clusters, filling the forest with voices ringing with amazement and wonder.

Aioffe, Joshua and Thane began to move between the groups, stepping over discarded weapons on the floor. They shook hands with the workers, thanking them for their efforts and listened as people introduced themselves. Some put forward ideas for which areas should be prioritised for re-greening, others suggested plans for extending the city to encompass the worker camps into the palace grounds.

All were welcomed, heard and acknowledged as the sun rose overhead.

Fairfax had watched the events unfold alone on the balcony. Awed as the swarm formed a wall of wings, spiralling concentrically, he reached out his hand to feel its power for himself. One of his own tangled ribbons unfurled from his mind as he was absorbed in observing the phenomenon. With a gentle tug, it pulled free, and he felt its vibrant energy join the whirl. He smiled. Well, nature is a little chaotic, he reasoned. It felt right to have a part of himself merge with this strange land. As the fae descended, he walked over to the stairs and joined the throng on the ground.

Uffer had disappeared whilst the workers were examining the fruits of their belief. Now, as the discussions with the worker fae continued, he found Spenser on the ground, talking quietly with Nemis. Silently, he held out the delicate silver circle he had collected from the High Hall. Spenser put a hand on Uffer's shoulder and nodded. Together they approached Joshua and Aioffe.

Thane saw them as they walked past, then stuck out his arm to stop them. "Uffer," he said, how did you know about the circling?" Looking at the crown in Uffer's hand, he dropped his block and began to walk with them.

Holding the shining band in front of him, Uffer replied, "She shared the knowledge about rituals at the Circles of Faeth with me. Encouraged me to think for myself about what we can learn from our history. Until I saw it at the stones, I didn't understand."

"A circle revolves," Spenser said thoughtfully. "There is no beginning so there can be no end."

"Exactly," Uffer nodded, "to start it rolling though, sometimes you have to give it a push."

Thane looked at Uffer with new respect. Now that he'd said it, the concept seemed obvious. "Well, I thank you for the push," the leader said. "Aioffe will need all of us to support her into the future. We must keep up the momentum."

The purposeful movement of the trio as they navigated clumps of people started to be noticed. Fairfax and Nemis tailed after them, motioning 'get up' to any eyes that they met - to stand, walk with them. Before they had crossed the clearing in its entirety, most of the crowd had taken flight around them, filling the air with a throb of beating wings.

Disturbed by the increasing noise, Aioffe broke off her conversation about which areas of the forest to assign to dwellings. The old worker, who had been advising Aioffe on aspects of the sunrise she should consider, saw the rising brown haze darken a wall between the trees and ground. Understanding what was happening as she saw Uffer and Thane appear behind Aioffe, she said, "We have more immediate matters though." The fae smiled, nodding her head sagely as she pointed behind Aioffe. "You do what is right, your Highness. I believe you will."

Aioffe wheeled around, her gaze widening as she saw the swaying wall, and for a moment her heart skipped. But on the ground, in Uffer's hands, a silver circlet glinted in the sunlight. Aioffe closed her eyes as memories of her mother flooded through her and shook her head. This was not what she wanted.

Joshua lent over and whispered in her ear, "They believe in you. I believe in you. Now it is time for you to have faith in yourself - as they do." She looked up at him, her eyes pools of blue. He traced the outline of her chin, then ran his fingertips over her shoulder, down to her shaking hand. She felt calmer as he asked, "Who shall you be today, my love?"

Uffer and Thane stood in front of her, holding the thin silver circle between them.

Aioffe dropped Joshua's hand after a slight squeeze and stepped forwards. Her heart didn't seem as heavy as she thought it might have. The humming grew louder. She looked around, and saw the expectation on their faces. No acrimony, just bright eyed hope and acceptance.

She knelt down and bowed her head to receive the crown.

CHAPTER 38 – NEW BEGINNINGS

Stretching as she awoke, Aioffe blinked against the stream of sunlight pouring through her window. She turned over and snuggled back into Joshua's warm chest, tracing where the scars should have been on his torso from his centuries-old, near-mortal wound. Now that the injury from his more recent battle had returned to its usual pallor, she knew the weight of her head on his ribs wouldn't hurt. He stirred and gathered her into his arms.

They lay a while together in companionable sleepy silence, studying the high vaulted ceiling with flowering vines criss-crossing the beams. Their bed was set under a window to the skies which Joshua had fashioned when they moved into Aioffe's old chambers. The aperture was large enough for them to fit through should they fancy a flight before sleep. At night, both enjoyed watching the stars align, marking out the seasons over a longer time-span than even they could comprehend.

"We had better arise, your Highness," Joshua said. She burrowed under the covers, hiding from the day. "Your people await, come on!" He insisted, but then he decided to tickle her a little. They then delayed some way past what was deemed a proper arising time.

Emerging from their chambers, Aioffe wished good morning to Elizae who was diligently polishing the hallway carvings to a sheen. Smiling graciously, Elizae expressed her pride and enjoyment in the restoration of the dark wood, and Aioffe took care to thank her and duly admire its new lustre. A lifetime ago, Aioffe had to acknowledge that cleaning to that degree was beyond her. Even now, Aioffe was baffled by how to shine wood so it showed off the layers of life within the timber. But, she also knew how much someone noting the effort itself meant. "It makes such a difference, you can see the history of the Palace right there in the glow."

Joshua also noticed, complimenting her as he closed their chamber doors behind him. Elizae warmed with the praise. She had a soft spot for their handsome new Prince.

It seemed the entire palace had been lifted into brightness over the last few weeks. The green foliage bathed a bright hue through the enormous windows as they entered the High Hall. Keen to build themselves the idyll promised by Aioffe when she ascended to the throne, the community had thrown itself into an ambitious building and repair programme.

Now, transformed from a claustrophobic court to a gathering area for all, the High Hall had been expanded four-fold, large enough to encompass the courtiers, workers and guests from afar. The original ceiling was still central to the room, but canopies and platforms had been erected at various levels expanding it, forming smaller discussion areas whilst still remaining part of the huge chamber.

The walls around the room had been removed, opening up the Hall to the elements in part. Trunk pillars which held up the ceiling now featured comfortable seating spaces as they met the floor, where families or smaller groups could congregate. There was always warmth to be found here, even in the colder weather.

A new hub within Naturae itself, no longer an elitist and secretive place, High Hall formed the basis of the equal nation now emerging. Much discussion had occurred about renaming the area, but as yet, they had reached no consensus. Determined to rule as democratically as possible, Aioffe had questioned Spenser relentlessly about how such systems worked in Europe in an effort to understand how it could work in Naturae. Aware of how much she needed the support of Ambassadors, and the Nobles which returned to offer their counsel, she was reluctant to take major decisions on her own, preferring to rule after considered debate which included worker representation.

Aioffe and Joshua wandered amongst their people, dipping in and out of conversations about housing and building projects, artistic performances, and even a demonstration of crafting techniques observed on the mainland. Travel, in suitable disguise of course, was now encouraged in order to develop skills necessary to bring Naturae into its new golden age.

Reaching where the dais and throne had originally been, a massive oval table which Joshua had helped to carve was being constructed in situ. They examined the piece with Thane and another carpenter, and before long they were engaged in an energetic discussion about chair design. The plan was for the table to be a leadership area, where representatives could discuss matters pertaining to the community.

Nemis, with Spenser in tow, found them while they were talking. Joshua hugged his friend tightly in greeting. He would never forget the debt he owed her in bringing him here. She fiercely hugged him back, for he had saved her and she loved him as a sister would. "Is it that time already?" Aioffe interrupted, the dismay on her face matching the mournful note to her voice.

"It is, my Queen," Spenser confirmed. "Will you be

joining us at the jetty?"

"I believe it is customary in some parts for a Queen to christen a vessel, is it not?" She replied with a curtsy and dancing eyes. "I am at your service." The group made their way to one of the newly built platforms outside. With Spenser carrying Nemis, they flew into the air.

As they skirted the treetops, the extent of the re-greening and building works was still astonishing to them all. The palace now reached further into the forest, even into the mists, with new accommodation for the fae. No longer relegated to the outskirts, from the walkways to the huts constructed from fresh wood, workers laughed as they built homes for all.

They flew past the Pupaetory, where Aioffe had spent much of her time these last few days. Strong, healthy creepers, adorned with colourful flowers, now reached around the building. Inside, Aioffe had blessed the roots of the vines, nurturing them as only a Royal could. Pupaetion was underway as vines bowed under the weight of their precious cocoons. Everyone looked forward to the day, which would come soon, when a new generation of fae would emerge. Families would soon be created, their houses already under construction. She planned to call all the females born in this first growing a derivative of Alice, in honour and remembrance of the sweet girl from Beesworth.

The group continued through the mists until they reached the edge of Naturae. Landing on the beach, Joshua took Aioffe's hand as they walked across the sand to the newly built jetty. Waiting for them, practically jumping around in anticipation, was Fairfax. He wore a strange combination of fae worker clothing, onto which Nemis had stitched parts of his old, tattered cape and breeches.

466

The effect was part patchwork, part fashion statement, completely chaotic like its owner, yet actually quite practical for sailing. Entirely his design, Aioffe and Joshua couldn't help but laugh under their breaths as they considered that he might not pass too easily back into society dressed thus.

From the treeline where the end of the jetty reached, Uffer approached, dragging sacks of provisions for the journey behind him. "The young 'un wanted wine." He grumbled as he reached them. His face ruddy from exertion, but his eyes twinkled still - proud to be a part of their intimate ceremony. "I've said, he'll have to make do with mead or water. And I'm not making pie, whatever that is. Sounds revolting, meat and flour paste. Where does he think I'm going to get that from?"

Spenser chuckled, "He can indulge in that fare soon enough."

"I am grateful for your efforts in finding something for us to eat, Lord Anaxis," Nemis comforted him. "We appreciate how much you have put yourself out to feed us mortals appropriately." She shot Fairfax a look.

"Yes, thank you very much," the boy said, heartily tired of the diet of fish and longing for red meat. At least he wasn't hungry. Nemis had even taught some of the fae how to cook the fish until it was partially palatable.

"Are you ready then?" Joshua said, walking up to the vessel. The boat had been the focus of Fairfax's efforts since the realisation that no fae could fly and carry both himself and Nemis far enough to return them to 'civilisation'. Joshua, on the grounds that he was still recovering, had ruled himself out of accompanying them, and Aioffe was too busy replenishing Naturae to go. Everyone suspected Joshua's reluctance to leave was because he was still hesitant to let the Queen out of his sight for long, but they all understood and tactfully said nothing.

With support from Thane, who sensed the removal of the enticing daemon from their shores was a matter of urgency, Fairfax had overseen construction of the craft. A small crew of trusted, well-fed workers had assisted under strict instructions not to get too close to him. The result was only vaguely reminiscent of the shattered birlinn, in that its sail had been salvaged. Torn but patched, it was gathered on the mast, along with oars to help propel the occupants to human shores if necessary.

Joshua stepped over the side of the ship and walked towards the prow. Newly fashioned from fresh wood, the elegant lines of the birlinn were reconfigured into a somewhat triangular-shaped vessel - more a small rowing boat with a low sail than a sea-worthy vessel suitable for long voyages. Instead of a large crew, this invention would hold just two human passengers. However, the prow still rose up proudly, and at the tip a narrow hole had been carefully carved.

Joshua reached into his pocket and pulled out a miniature eagle, no larger than his palm. Using precious silver taken from the inlay of the High Hall doors, Joshua had fashioned a token for luck on their voyage. The tiny replica of the life-saving eagle fitted snugly into the gap, secured by tiny nails he had forged from bits of washed-up iron. Nemis would be able to remove it when they arrived on safe land. What she did with it after that, well, Joshua hoped it would at least guide her back here someday.

At the front of the ship, tied and tucked neatly behind the prow, lay the alternative to the tatty sail or oars. Designed to fit around a chest, leaving room for wings, the straps had been fashioned from rigging salvaged also from the shipwreck. Joshua pulled on them to make sure they were firmly fastened, then he carefully checked all the knots on the harnesses themselves. It never hurt to be cautious, especially where Fairfax's designs were concerned.

Gathering on the jetty, Spenser and Fairfax loaded the sacks into the boat. Aioffe and Nemis warmly embraced, and with a few tears at parting, the young woman settled herself in the vessel. Joshua lent over and hugged her goodbye, suddenly at a loss for the right words to say. He settled instead for clasping her hands, and together they whispered a short prayer for guidance and protection.

Aioffe was sad to see Nemis leave. Over the last few weeks, the young witch and she had grown close. Together, they had spent a number of hours in the Scriptaerie trying to find out more about Nemis's magic. Nemis had assisted Aioffe by preparing restorative potions to help build up her energy after long days focusing on re-greening and nurturing the vines. With her gentle manner, Nemis provided much needed support whilst the island was being restored and Aioffe would miss the easy, girlish chatter they shared. She also had no hesitation in encouraging the growing desire between Nemis and Spenser, keen for her new friends to share the joy and encouragement of a relationship, now that there was no need for secrecy.

Aioffe's primary source of comfort was her husband, ever ready to encourage her. He had slipped into the role of consort easily. His friendly manner constantly reminded her to be approachable to her people; not to show the stand-offishness that she might otherwise have retreated into from sheer exhaustion. By her side, he could tell when

469

she was at the point of overexertion and liaised with the crowd in support of her efforts. He also appreciated how frightened she was of parallels being drawn between her and the old Queen, her mother. He knew that she still struggled to control her temper when tired, or frustrated, and she needed his gentleness the most during those moments, to fly with her and calm her once more.

She smiled as she watched Joshua, head bowed in prayer with Nemis. He seemed truly content even though Aioffe knew he would miss Nemis and - perhaps to a lesser degree - Fairfax as well. It still felt miraculous they were here with her now, although she ignored Joshua's claims that it was prayers which kept his resolve to find her. It seemed to her that Nemis and her magic were really their salvation, not God. Yet she recognised the power of belief.

Joshua completed his checks and clambered back on the jetty. He loosened the tether rope as Spenser strapped himself into one of the harnesses. "Sure I can't tempt you on a trip?" Spenser said, knowing full well that Joshua would decline.

Shaking his head, smiling although he rolled his eyes at the Ambassador, Joshua turned to Aioffe. "Whenever you are ready, my love?" She took a flagon of mead from Uffer and flew from the edge of the jetty. The sky was a clear, bright blue, and the sunshine glowed through her rainbow wings as she hovered feet ahead of the prow.

Joshua clapped Fairfax on his shoulder before stepping back with the rope. Shooting his young friend a warning glance to remove the glee from his face. "Be good," he said, "and more importantly, be careful. Choose the safer route over the exciting one - at least whilst you have passengers!" Fairfax grinned and sat down next to

470

Nemis, twitchy excitement prompting her to lay a calming hand on his knee within seconds.

Uffer and Joshua kicked the boat away from the jetty and threw the rope into the boat. Spenser rose up and joined Aioffe, pulling the vessel around with him.

"I've never done this before," Aioffe said, laughing. "So I'm not entirely sure what to say other than sail safely!"

"Bon voyage!" Spenser shouted. "We could reach Europe by the end of the week!"

Fairfax's face fell, until he saw Spenser wink at him and realised he was being teased. A moment later he thought, maybe after fortifying himself on the mainland, he could be tempted? He would try to discover more of England first though. Fairfax fancied he could fit in with the chaos of London quite well.

"Bon voyage!" called Joshua. "Come back soon!"

Nemis smiled mysteriously, "Of course we will. Build us a large guest room," she added, "You're going to be an honorary uncle!"

Aioffe smashed the flagon onto the side of the ship as it passed. Spenser raised his eyebrow, then he laughed as he turned into the headwind. "It seems we are to be busy when we land once more!" Then he turned in his harness to fly backwards, shouting, "If it has wings, we'll need to return often! Just for the rest!"

As Spenser pulled through the air, the boat picked up speed. Joshua joined Aioffe in the sky, waving until their friends dipped towards the horizon.

"Uncle, eh?" Aioffe said.

"Anything's possible," he grinned back.

Dear Reader

If you have enjoyed this book, why not visit **www.escapeintoatale.com** to find out more about Jan Foster and the Naturae Book series?

A Polite Request:
I am an independently published author and as such, reviews are critical to successfully getting my stories seen by readers. It would mean the world to me if you could leave a review on Amazon or Goodreads about this book so that others can find it!

A Prequel to the Naturae Series - **Risking Destiny** is available to purchase at
https://www.books2read.com/riskingdestiny
The prequel is also available as a free gift to you if you would like to stay in touch via my newsletter, sign up at
www.escapeintoatale.com

Book 2 of the Naturae Series, **Anarchic Destiny**

Dying young prevented Henry Fitzroy from achieving his human destiny to succeed Henry VIII. Now vampire, he is forced to decide which path to follow when his half-brother also dies. The thrones of England and Naturae are in jeopardy once more and chaos will reign.

Available Autumn 2021

ACHNOWLEDGEMENTS

This book would be sorely lacking without the illuminating studies and inspiring stories from the following people:

Although I am but an armchair historian, I have referred to and enjoyed Ruth Goodman's - How to be a Tudor (Penguin) - an invaluable reference exploring daily life in the Tudor times amongst others. Other noteworthy reference books which have coloured my research include: Houses of Power (Simon Thurley, Penguin); The Time Travellers Guide to Elizabethan England (Ian Mortimer, Vintage Books) and other historical authors, fiction and non fiction.

A fascinating database of medieval shipping routes which I used to plot Joshua's voyage can be found at http://www.medievalandtudorships.org/search_map/

I also owe a debt of gratitude to various experts who have checked my nautical explanations for authenticity and friends from the North East who have helped ensure dialect is appropriate and accessible! Thanks also to the staff at Tynemouth Priory (English Heritage) for answering my many questions about life in the Monastery.

The historian and author Deborah Harkness – the 'All Souls' series, provided my first introduction to alternative history mixed with fantasy. To lose myself in her world where creatures walk amongst us was a revelation and I cannot thank her enough for planting the seed of how such a world could exist, although Naturae is substantially different!

Finally, I could not have written this and other books without the support of my loving family and friends. Thank you all – especially ADH, JR, AM, and CF, this book wouldn't have been possible without your belief and encouragement.

Printed in Great Britain
by Amazon

61314242R00281